Zeno Was Here

Jan Mark was born in Welwyn, Hertfordshire, in 1943 and
attended art school before becoming a teacher. She is
a distinguished children's author – she was twice winner of the
Carnegie Medal – and has won other awards including
the Angel Award for Fiction for her adult short stories.

Jan Mark

ZENO WAS HERE

Pan Books
in association with Jonathan Cape

First published 1987 by Jonathan Cape Ltd
This edition published 1989 by Pan Books Ltd,
Cavaye Place, London SW10 9PG
in association with Jonathan Cape
9 8 7 6 5 4 3 2 1
© Jan Mark 1987
ISBN 0 330 30195 0
Printed and bound in Great Britain by
Cox & Wyman Ltd, Reading

For Cedric

1

McEvoy pauses, in mid-turn the lapels of his jacket fly apart and for a stalled instant of inappropriate whimsy he sees himself spatchcocked, pinned like a specimen to the black-board. Charlie Brewer's question which has transfixed him is one that he often asks himself; it is almost reassuring to hear it asked by someone else, and discomfiting because he is no more able to answer Brewer's question than he is able to answer his own.

'Sir: how do we know this is a poem?'

Well, Charles, it is in a poetry book, is it not? Poetry books are easily identified; the words *poem* or *poet* will appear somewhere on the jacket; inside, the print will not reach to the edge of the page. He is less sure of himself with those lines that appear arbitrarily corralled amid the textual prairies of, say, the *Times Literary Supplement*. They seem to be poems because clearly they are not advertisements, but too often he finds himself wondering: why is this *here*? Why was it considered good enough to go in when possibly hundreds of others more immediately accessible were not? Is it a *good* poem? How do I know it is a good poem?

Or, as Brewer has just asked: how do I know that it is a poem at all?

Charles, how the hell should I know?

Because you are the teacher, Sir.

He resorts to the time-honoured teacher's method of dodging the issue; he throws it open to the floor.

'Well, how do we know that this is a poem?' At this point he realizes that the others are laughing; laughing, presumably, at Brewer's naivety. When they see that Mr McEvoy is taking the question seriously the laughter dies; they employ their own method of dodging the issue by looking at the book. Brewer darts glances left and right, gratified because he asked in seriousness, innocent of his unwilling ally up at the front. New to the school, to the class, to Mr McEvoy, he exposed himself to ridicule and contempt; now he finds that he has come out of it a declared sophisticate, also perilous because it will raise people's expectations unreasonably. All his other teachers will lie in wait for provocative questions, he will encounter their encouraging smiles and shrivel. He looks at his book as hard as anyone, but nobody risks an answer.

In the silence the electric clock over the door swallows nervously.

'Look,' says McEvoy, 'we've been reading poetry together for five months. That is to say, we have been looking at pages of print each arranged in a particular way that is, we are assured, the form of a poem and these ways are heterogeneous . . . Heterogeneous? Philip?'

'All different, Sir.'

'Exactly; they aren't all in iambic pentameters, they are not all in stanzas; some rhyme, some do not, some have no discernible structure at all on first sight, and yet we have accepted them as poems. We may not have liked them all – some of you haven't liked *any* – but we have never doubted their claim to be poetry. Now, as Charles points out, we have to ask ourselves, how do we know? How do we know that this is a poem?'

An arm at the centre of the room rises ponderously as if on a counterweight. It is Dermot Crane, the lateral thinker.

'Dermot?'

'Sir? It says Ted Hughes at the bottom.'

Back in his office he looks again at the book, not the poetry book, the *other* book. How do we know this is a book?

How do we know that this is an office? It does not look like an office, it looks like a shed. That is what the boys call it, not derisively but because, with its clinker-built clapboards and prefabricated window frames it can be nothing else. In summer it smells of creosote. It is acknowledged to be the office of the English Department because it houses the Head of the English Department, himself. English lessons take place in dark classrooms with Gothic windows, like Nonconformist Sunday Schools but this is the heart of the operation; it is The Shed.

The book is definitely a book. Between its covers of glossy

8

card it has pages, British Library Cataloguing Data and copyright; a dedication; it has an ISBN. What is it doing on his desk?

When he took it out of its envelope this morning he assumed that it was an inspection copy. He recognized the publisher, Clockhouse Press, as a bona fide publisher, but he was fairly sure that he had not requested any books from it. The colophon is just what you would expect it to be, a wee cottage with a clock face on it, the hands standing at ten to two. He presses his thumb against the oval cartouche. The book has a title, *Acid Test*, and an author, Caroline Hill, who sounds familiar, but then one would expect an author to sound familiar. An author would expect to sound familiar – what else has she written? Nothing is listed and, this being a paperback, the biographical note is truncated, amalgamated with the blurb. *This is a book that may shock and sadden but still ultimately warm the reader with the author's courage.* It will not, he is relieved to discover, change his life. *Caroline Hill was born in 1944 and at the age of eighteen, after a school career that promised a brilliant future, began to study design at a provincial art school, at the same time leaving home after a history of family tension. It was here that she first began to experience the hallucinations that led to her becoming a patient in a psychiatric hospital. There, as her condition worsened, she was treated with what was then regarded as a new miracle drug – LSD. This is her story; a searing indictment of attitudes to and treatment of the mentally ill, and an agonized appraisal of the effect of mental illness on friends and relationships. It is also a compelling testament to the strength and determination of a courageous woman.*

He swore, long ago, to have nothing more to do with the insane, neglecting to take into account the fact that this would assume some form of co-operation on the part of the insane. He does not want to read about them; what lunatic has sent him this? Unwillingly he looks at the first paragraph of the first chapter: *I woke shuddering and drenched in sweat. The street lamp opposite flung heaving shadows on to the wall above my bed as it shone through the wind-tossed branches of the lime tree. Amid the confused babble of threatening voices in my head I felt the Smile again.* He looks at the last paragraph of the last chapter: *It would be easy to dismiss me as a latter-day Joan of Arc, hearing*

9

voices and believing that they came from God, but somehow it seems to me that it was through the Smile and the voices that Jesus showed Himself to me and in Him I trust.

McEvoy entertains an irrational hatred of people who refer to the second person of the Trinity as Jesus. It is unbearably matey, as if the Word made Flesh lived in the next street and might be encountered over a jar in the Red Lion. Jesus, he feels sure, prefers to be known as Christ, public school fashion; Jehovah Two. Only God and Mary are permitted the familiar handle in private, behind drawn clouds, when the other chaps are out of earshot. What does he call *them*, McEvoy wonders: Mater and Pater? Muv and Farve?

So what is he supposed to do with this thing, order a set? hand them out to Brewer and Crane?

Now then, Charlie, how do we know this is a book?

It could be passed on to the RE Department, but as the school's arbiter of literary taste, with a reputation to maintain, he feels inclined to suppress it: Oxfam, perhaps? Intending to drop it into his briefcase and take it home he replaces it in the envelope, but something blocks its entrance, something not entirely yielding. As he prods the book at the mouth of the envelope, attempting unsuccessful penetration, he begins to understand that he is about to discover the answers to his questions, and tweezering out the folded letter between crossed fingers, suspects that perhaps he does not wish for answers after all. As soon as the book were in his briefcase he would, in effect, have closed the file on it, but it is too late. He is withdrawing the letter and opens it.

It is a proper letter; typewritten, but not a publisher's Xerox nor a circular. It has all the accoutrements of a letter.

How do we know this is a letter, Dermot?

Sir, it's got an address and a date and it says Dear John . . .

Indeed it does; not Dear Sir, not Dear Mr McEvoy: Dear John.

The address is in Chester, to match the postmark on the envelope which he had not previously examined. He once went to a conference in Chester, seven years ago; has someone dredged him up? He notices that he is doing what most annoys him in his wife when she receives a letter, or is scrutinizing one of his, postponing the opening in order to extract as much Lumpkinesque enjoyment as possible from the envelope.

'Who on *earth*?' Sarah says, quizzing stamp, frank and handwriting. 'Bradford on Avon . . . ? Who . . . ?' *Particularly* if it is one of his.

Chester. Who . . . ?

Dear John, you won't remember me I'm sure,

Well, that's a rational hypothesis. The name at the foot of the letter is Margaret. He has known several Margarets; how was this one to guess that she would forfeit the bulk of his sympathy with that single opening line? He has seen such a line several times, recently.

but perhaps you will remember the enclosed.

The book? No – there is a second sheet, attached by a paper clip, of very old ruled narrow feint foolscap, many times folded and furred along the creases. It carries a poem (Hold back. How do we know this is a poem?) what appears to be a poem, in small faded handwriting rather resembling his own. Which should be read first, the text he ought to remember or the text that will remind him? He wishes to read neither. This free period was to be spent marking Sixth Form essays; he resents the unexpected and the time spent in negotiating it. Perhaps if he reads the letter he will decide that he need not read the poem.

To tell you the truth, I had almost forgotten you, until I saw the television debate the other night.

Today is Thursday. The television debate, in which he figured for possibly five minutes, was transmitted on Tuesday of last week. In the intervening eight days he has received four letters and five telephone calls from people who recognized him or, as several have explained, who would not have recognized him had he not been introduced by name.

I was on the edge of my seat wondering where I'd seen you before, until I heard your name mentioned, and then it all came back, and of course, I couldn't really ever forget that weekend in Bath. Does it come back to you, now?

No, Margaret. It does not come back to me.

You wrote a poem for me in the restaurant. I thought it was sweet at the time. At any rate, I kept it.

The very poem that nestles between the sheet and his hand?

No wonder the writing looks like his; he denies himself a second glance.

It really did seem then that there might be something between us, until you met me that day and said, 'I shan't be seeing you again, but it's been a lot of fun, hasn't it?' I was so hurt at the time, but John, it's a long while ago. It's strange how things turn out, isn't it?

You can say that again. McEvoy finds his eyes straying toward the book. Is it possible that Caroline Hill is the pen name of his correspondent? He has heard of demented women who send letters to strange men, but if they are not the same person where does the mad Caroline fit into all this? She and Margaret may not be the same but possibly one knows the other, hence the book. He now wishes less than ever to read the book, or the poem; back to the letter.

Someone you must remember though is Caroline Hill and what an effect she had on us all at the time. I don't think any of us realized how frightfully she was suffering, or what tremendous inner strength she must have had – I'm sure you didn't, at any rate. Well, anyway, now she has written a book. Clockhouse brought it out in January so I'm sending you a copy. Do read it. I'm sure you'll find what she says a revelation in more ways than one, and do feel free to get in touch if you need anything explained.

I'm posting this to your school as I don't know your home address. With warmest regards, Margaret Anderson (née Hardwicke)

Now he begins to consider; Margaret Anderson he does not know, but Margaret Hardwicke he did know once, briefly, although long enough for the name to take root. Caroline Hill he does not recall but recalling Margaret Hardwicke implies a tenuous connection with his vow to eschew the mentally unstable, in future. He must have known her at about the time he shared the flat with Andrew, but the connection continues to elude him: Margaret, arch and threatening; Caroline, courageous and insane, and still he cannot remember the weekend in Bath. He unfastens the paper clip and reads the poem, and he cannot remember that, either. He has no recollection of writing it and no wish to recollect a time when he was capable of producing such lubricious drivel (although it rhymes impeccably. Look, Charlie, Dermot, it does *rhyme*), a time when he was conceited enough to write it down and sufficiently arrogant to present it to a young woman by way of a compliment. Nor can he imagine himself at a period when he associated with young women who were stupid enough to cherish this tripe; or did he, in those unidentified days, take it for granted that *all* young women were so stupid as to be flattered by his attentions and his poetry? If so, he was right about this one. It is an idolatrous hymn to John Thomas and she, poor innocent, had taken it as an ode to Lady Jane. At the bottom his overweening signature, which has certainly detumesced over the years, partially obliterates a final line of writing, long ago smudged either by her mourning lips or his own sweaty hand: *Bath, 5 July 1964.*

One thing of which he is certain, as he sits blushing at his desk, he wants nothing more to do with any of this. The blush and an incipient headache combine to make physical his unease, for did he not, when he first glanced at the jacket design, fancy that the name of Caroline Hill was familiar? Now he is told that it is familiar not because of her reputation as a writer, but because he knew her once; once she knew him.

As a teacher of English, cribbed between curriculum and syllabus, he is in thrall to set books, mostly by authors safely underground in deference to the unwritten rule of literary criticism that the only good writer is a dead one, in fact he seriously doubts if he has in the last twenty years read anything published since 1960, aside from the complete works of G. L. Stevens, but now he must go out into the rough. He will have to read the book.

But he does not start to read it at once; instead he stalls with some mental arithmetic. According to the date on the poem he knew Margaret in 1964, when he was twenty-two and Caroline, according to her publisher, was twenty; the time of his postgraduate year, and yes, if he ever knew Caroline Hill, it would have been then, without doubt, but whenever he knew her, he could not have known her well, which makes Margaret's eagerness for him to read the book all the more unsettling. He is accustomed to people urging him to read books under the misapprehension that, being an English teacher, this is what he wants to do in his spare time.

Others, still further misled, solicit his opinion of their own unpublished work, on the grounds that he has an expert eye. He thinks sympathetically of Disraeli on such occasions (Thank you for sending me your book. I shall waste no time in reading it). The person who most significantly does not ask him to read her work is Geneva who, being a professional writer, supposes reasonably that if people really want to read her books they will buy them, and although she always gives him a copy of her latest, in friendship, she never asks him what he thinks of it. He does not know whether this is a manifestation of Geneva's tact or if she simply does not mind what he thinks. She has a very measured and accurate notion of her own worth which renders her immune equally to flattery and insult. McEvoy admires her confidence, only he wishes sometimes that he had known her before she became quite so distinguished, that he might have enjoyed her rise to eminence. He met her when, newly married, he and Sarah rented a flat in the same house as her own, and although this was eleven years ago, she was already confirmed in her distinction. To this day he is sometimes revisited by the astonishment of that first visit to her flat, when he realized that G. L. Stevens, whose name appeared on the spines of a row of books in the public library – two of which were at that moment in his living-room – was the same amiable Mrs Stevens who had invited the new tenants in for coffee. Geneva now has a much larger flat in a much larger house, while Sarah and John have long owned a house of their own, but he still sees her often. Sarah never took to her, perhaps because their acquaintance was made in the days when, to Sarah, any woman presented a threat of rivalry, even a woman like Geneva, heavily and happily married. Geneva is now widowed, renewing that obscure, unresolved threat. John visits, Sarah does not, and Sarah would prefer that John did not, either, but he likes Geneva. Talking to her is a pleasure that he will not forgo.

Packing away his problems in a series of telescopic movements – letter clapped into book, book rammed into envelope, envelope thrust into briefcase – he has already decided that he will show the book to Geneva, when he has read it, and maybe the letter too, and the poem. Sarah had better see none of them, for Sarah still imagines herself besieged among rivals; any woman, all women, even the mad and possibly the dead.

In the event it is more than a week before he reads *Acid Test*. He wishes to be alone when he opens it, does not want Sarah to ask what he is reading, does not want the children to distract him, hopes to get through it in a single sitting. At least once a day he takes it out of the briefcase, having by now consigned the letter to his filing cabinet, and snatches a furtive look inside. What he sees is not reassuring; this searing indictment is written less in scalding tears than in tepid spit. Her prose is generally unexceptionable, but every page he scans impugns the failure of one, the treachery of another, the myopic ignorance of a third. On all sides she is betrayed, the betrayals related in a tone not of acute outrage but of chronic disgruntlement; she comes on like Eeyore rather than Margaret of Anjou. Then he berates himself for judging the whole by the sum of a very few parts read with a jaundiced eye, closes the book and drops it back into the briefcase. What can there be in it for him, who scarcely knew the woman? The most he can hope to discover, by the end of it, is who she was and why he should care. He consoles himself with the certainty that he never trifled with her affections, his girls were many but none was barmy. Then he panics; did he perhaps know her *before* she ran mad, cast her aside as Hamlet spurned Ophelia, with like result? This awful book; is he the only begetter? It is dedicated to Nimrod; the mighty hunter; was he a mighty hunter once? Never mind what is in it for *him* – is he in *it*? He must read it at once – how? The Ministry of Transport intervenes.

On the second Friday following its arrival, he is at last left in peace. Sarah takes the children to visit Granny in Sevenoaks, for the weekend, her mother not his. He should have gone too, only the car is discovered to be due for its MOT test. After school he drives his family to the station, delivers the car to Tim at the garage for attention tomorrow morning, returns home to wash up the tea things, lights the living-room fire – inevitably the moment draws closer – and at last sits down with the book.

The first chapter allays his last fear; whatever drove her to distraction was not himself. *I woke shuddering and drenched in sweat. The street lamp opposite flung heaving shadows on to the wall above my bed as it shone through the wind-tossed branches of the lime tree . . . Across the room Elizabeth lay sleeping unaware of the turmoil happening only a few feet from her unconscious head.*

He quarrels primarily with the idea of a turmoil happening. The verb seems objectionably limp, but by the time he reaches the foot of the page he understands that he has witnessed the first betrayal, by the hapless Elizabeth, heartlessly sleeping through her flatmate's attack.

Compulsively, I began to beat my head against the bedpost . . .

He reads on and for a long while makes no discernible progress except that the wad of pages under his left hand grows thicker. He is among art students and they are a numbingly dull bunch. When they are not painting and sculpting, which seems to be most of the time, they gather together damply like snails on a rainy night and *talk*. Their conversations are rehearsed with the minute detail that indicates an exhaustive memory, for these exchanges took place at least twenty years ago. It is the historical factor that most disturbs him about the mind which recorded them. These sententious windbags are in their late teens and, as he knows only too well, people in their late teens are honestly convinced that their inmost thoughts are worth logging for posterity, but the writer is no longer in her late teens; she must be approaching forty. Most adults looking back on that final period of painful convulsions before the bones of the skull knit with a conclusive click, would sum it up succinctly, thus: *we used to talk about ourselves obsessively for half the night. No one listened to anyone else because no one was interested in anyone else*; but not Caroline. She cannot sum up anything succinctly. She has got the lot stored away on a spool and unreels it relentlessly. For an entire chapter they *talk*. Then at last something happens. One night as they sit round chatting of global annihilation (which he can forgive them: Cuba was not far behind) Caroline becomes aware of a smile in the darkness, not a benign smile but a menacing rictus, meant for her. It is evidently a kind of cosmic smile, since it is not attached to anyone; there is no face behind it, no teeth in it, no lips round it, no lickerish tongue waiting to spring out.

Caroline is suffocating with nameless terror as Chapter One ends. It is a cliff-hanger.

At least, by now, he has assembled a cast list. There is Elizabeth, the sleeping friend who, awake, alas, is no less garrulous than the others, Corrinne, bitch goddess, Gilda with three abortions to her credit, randy Bob and his straight man Cliff. Walk-on parts are allotted to Richard, an intellectual layabout, and Terry who lives nearby and from time to time is helplessly engulfed by the mob as they swarm out of the Padova coffee bar. They call it Padders.

He has also tumbled to the fact that she must have changed all the names except her own, led on by the certainty that there is no such town as Saintshill and the suspicion that few publishers would risk releasing the data on Gilda's backstreet encounters and Bob's pox, if Bob and Gilda were identifiable and likely to walk in waving a writ.

But he is not among them. He never fraternized with art students; there was no art school in the town where he lived in 1964. He admits to a nauseous apprehension when he encounters Richard, loath though he is to confess to the possibility that he might ever have been described as an intellectual layabout, and Terry gives him momentary qualms, but by the end of the chapter he has learned that Richard is about to die of leukaemia and that Terry is a divorced alcoholic who earns a precarious living by posing for the sculpture classes. This is none of I.

He makes some coffee, feeds the cat and returns to Chapter Two. Caroline's Smile becomes omnipresent. At night it wakes her and mocks her while Elizabeth slumbers unaware, by day it interposes between Caroline and her work. Voices mutter and gibe, not to her alone; by stealth they poison the minds of her friends who conspire to destroy her. To drive away the Smile and drown the voices she rocks back and forth over her folded arms, slamming her forehead against walls, doorframes, radiators, bedposts. She wears a permanent bloody caste mark between her brows and gradually people begin to notice, forced to look up from the contemplation of their own fascinating navels. At home for the vacation, persuaded by her parents, she enters the local mental hospital.

But isn't this textbook schizophrenia? McEvoy wonders, now hurt and distressed by what he is reading. The same wakeful memory that hoarded the banal pronouncements of her circle has likewise stored every miserable detail of her accelerating insanity; the worse she gets, the faster she gets worse. He shares the frustration of her inability to paint the Smile, appreciates her terror of it but more, he thinks, because of his own powers of imagination than her talent for description, and his sympathy is eroded by the adolescent exhibitionism that informs the narrative; the posing, the performance. Like a child *then*, she could not see that the enormity of her disorder was sufficient to speak for itself, and she cannot see it *now*.

With Chapter Three there comes a change of cast. In this latest act new players strut and fret; Bob and Gilda, Cliff, Corrinne and Elizabeth are written out; Richard and Terry die or decline offstage. Egoistic and amoral they may have been; they were unarguably sane. Caroline's new friends are drawn from among her fellow inmates and at weekends they all board the hospital bus, descending on the town like vengeful ghosts returned to visit retribution on those still at liberty. Well aware of their embarrassment potential they disseminate their sufferings with the feckless promiscuity of Typhoid Mary.

Here is David who overdosed, Brian who slashed his wrists, James pronounced cured and sent home only to brain his brother the same evening, Gerald who haunts the bus station to spy on the woman he loves. Brian slashes his wrists again. Caroline falls in love with David. Remorselessly they all begin to talk.

And still there is no hidden McEvoy among them. He feels his eyelids dropping, he has forgotten how insufferably repetitious the mentally ill can be. He remembers now the weary resignation with which he would open the bathroom door after Andrew's first suicide attempt, wondering with glum irony if he were going to find another body sloshing about in a tub full of pink water, remembers the feeling of intense relief when Andrew finally went to hospital and the grim impulsions of friendship that made him renew the acquaintance by going to visit the silly poor sod who had by that time begun to make some very bizarre friends of his own, one of whom . . . some of whom . . .

Some of whom at least became known to him, one of whom, Tony Meredith, was celebrated throughout the hospital for confounding the doctors who pronounced him cured by going home and on the same day half killing his brother by beating him over the head with a knitting machine.

McEvoy gets up, fetches a pad and pen and begins to make comparative lists. Let James = Tony, then Brian = Andrew, David = Robert and of course, now that it all comes back, Caroline = Caroline. Gerald he cannot place but never mind Gerald, how will he himself appear when he does appear? for now, he sees, he is bound to appear. One day, as visiting time begins, the door of Wren Ward flies open and Brian's handsome, charming, debonair friend from university strides in. *Brian introduced us. 'This is Michael. If it weren't for him I wouldn't be here.'*

So taken is McEvoy with the double-edged comment, surely relayed verbatim since Caroline does not operate at this level, that it dawns on him only very slowly that Michael = John. John/Michael finds that his hand is shaking. How he blushes now, how his head aches. He reaches for the pot of pens, cut from the bottom of a hock bottle, plucks out the Stabiloboss and without bothering to read further scrambles through the remainder of the book slashing a yellow streak across his name, *Michael*, wherever it occurs.

Midnight has passed before he has marked his final appearance in *Acid Test* and then he returns to the place where he left off reading, the doorway of Wren Ward. She has changed the name of the hospital but not the names of the wards. They were all called after birds, Wren, Swallow, Bullfinch, Lark, Linnet; violent cases being confined to Dove. Wren was an ambulant ward; most of the inmates were ubiquitously ambulant but those in Wren Ward were voluntary patients and not, as a rule, undergoing treatment that required bedrest. It was in a single-storey wing set apart from the louring red brick ramparts of the main blocks, and with an effort he can retrace the walk from the car park along a path beside a walled garden, across a lawn and up a flight of shallow steps. Inside was a reception hall and a short corridor before one reached the common room where visitors were received. The door of the common room was not locked, one simply depressed a handle and went in. He remembers the handle because it was plastic and often sticky, he grasped it only once. After that he would knock it down with the heel of his hand so that the door swung inward heralding an unintentionally theatrical entrance.

He has not remembered any of this for a long while, for the excellent reason that he has not wished to remember it. The entire period has receded into a haze of exasperation; he made no effort to forget, for had he done so he would certainly have remembered, he simply turned his attention swiftly to other things, things that would respond to a rational approach. He never knew what became of Andrew finally, although he now has a premonition that he is about to find out. Arrested on the threshold of Wren Ward he begins to recall what he will discover on the other side of it: Andrew, Robert, Tony, Caroline, all of whom he left supposedly locked for ever in their dreary cycles of dementia. Well, at least one of them survived to tell the tale.

So, he opens the door, with one blow, and enters although he is, in a sense, inside already, watching himself come in.

Most visitors, even the hardened regulars, entered cautiously, first putting a head round the door to see if it was safe. Aware that they were entering a loony bin they expected to find loonies, rolling on the carpet, frothing at the mouth or standing with their hands inside their jackets thinking that they were Napoleon. Brian's friend threw open the door and paused, as if expecting his adoring public to rise up and applaud. He smiled round at us and swept aside a lock of long brown hair, looking for Brian, but sharing the smile with everyone.

'He must have been practising that for days,' David said to me.

Michael was wearing a green corduroy suit and elastic sided boots. 'Who does he think he is?' David muttered. 'One of the Rolling Stones?'

Brian introduced us. 'This is Michael. If it weren't for him I wouldn't be here.' We all knew what he meant, of course, but Michael took it as a compliment . . .

And so it goes on, the envious sniping. His every remark, which even now looks harmless and mundane in the extreme, is glossed with derisive asides. Easy, twenty years on, to laugh at a young man with long hair, a green suit – he remembers that green suit, oh yes, he remembers *that* – and Chelsea boots; then he would have passed unnoticed in a crowd. If only she would admit that, coming in unhindered as he did from the outside world and free to return to it when he wished, he must have represented everything that they most resented, but no; it seems they loathed him for his own sweet self alone. He is easy, charming, funny, generous; oh, detestable Michael. How precious is his charm, how calculated his ease, how false his fun, how *acquisitive* his generosity. McEvoy foresees that whatever it was he ultimately did, it will not be what he remembers doing. He reads on fearfully, unforgiven.

2

Geneva's flat is on the first floor but her front door is at street level, and it is opened by her younger daughter. Geneva has revenged herself on floridly-minded parents by naming her children Jane and Mary. In their middle teens, they have been trained to respond amiably to adults, to be gracious on the telephone and to smile *vis-à-vis*, for which McEvoy, who spends his days among shy and sullen adolescents, is properly grateful. Mary beams at him and beckons him upstairs.

'Geneva's not working, is she?'

'No, she's having a week off. There's a friend staying but she's in the kitchen,' Mary says, preceding him along the hall. They are passing the kitchen where McEvoy catches a glimpse of a woman crouched over a portable typewriter at the edge of the table; who, as he looks in, jerks forward and pecks at a key. The carriage lurches and she strikes again as she passes out of sight. He rarely encounters Geneva's other friends, who are variously successful novelists like herself or spectacularly unsuccessful poets; successful at writing poetry, that is; failures at making any money out of it. This one looks like neither kind; already he retains the image of a beaky spinster of Christian leanings, tapping out little verses on Geneva's portable while cooing vindictively over dear Geneva's success. McEvoy is glad, for the sake of his own self-image, that he has no ambitions in that direction.

Geneva and the daughters spend their leisure hours in needlework. He seems to have disturbed them in the middle of a quilting bee, for an amorphous medley covers the red carpet, its outlines absorbed into the kaleidoscope of textures that figure on everything else. As Geneva, in small-print floral needlecord, rises to greet him, Mary and Jane withdraw tactfully, taking the quilt with them and leaving on the carpet a bland vacancy in the macramé, plush, crochet, appliqué and batik, like an uncompleted patch in a painting by numbers. McEvoy advances into it, locating Geneva by her outspread hands.

'John, how nice. Coffee?'

'Yes, please.'

'Coffee!' A daughter reappears, in tied and dyed calico, and heads for the kitchen, whence comes a short querulous burst from the typewriter.

'I'm not breaking up your Sunday sewing session?'

'You make us sound as if we're stitching flannel shirts for the deserving poor while Marmee reads to us from *Pilgrim's Progress*.'

'Isn't it for the deserving poor?'

'Good God, what would the deserving poor do with it, cut it up for dusters? It's for us, we like to watch it grow. I'll either hang it on the wall or buy a bigger bed to fit it.'

'How are the proofs?'

'Hairy; Shrdlu ran amuk. Reptile delivered them last Monday and practically demanded them back by return of post. I'm waiting a week before I start, on principle.' Geneva's publishers are not known in the trade as Reptile Books. 'Eighty thousand words! I hate reading proofs anyway, it's like an exhumation. You were very persuasive on telly, the other week. What was it all about?'

'Haven't I seen you since then? I couldn't have made much impression if you didn't know what it was about.'

'I missed most of it. Jane switched on and suddenly yelled, "Mum! John's on the box." I only saw the bit where you restrained yourself from seizing Councillor Mrs Nitpick by the wattles and asked her what she thought children read out of school. She seemed to be campaigning for the return of the asterisk.'

'Her name's Pitney. She rose to prominence on the family values ticket which is why she was there. Questions have been asked in the House, would you believe, about the inclusion of dirty books on Public Examination syllabi, and as our Honourable Member, who asked the question, was sensibly out of the country on a fact-finding mission, they dredged up Mrs P as the nearest thing to a local substitute. Being a power-crazed mother of four she accepted eagerly. I didn't realize I'd be the only one speaking for the defence.'

'How did you come to be involved?'

'I was a local substitute, too. It should have been the County Adviser but he's in hospital and kindly suggested me because he remembered my bearing up well in a radio interview in '77. I agreed because I thought it might be fun.'

'You contained yourself wonderfully. Possibly only I noticed your hands quivering towards the end. Have you had any response?'

'Yes, I have.' He hesitates and feels the copy of *Acid Test* leaning against his thigh. In the brief silence the typewriter clucks distantly. 'Geneva, who's that woman in the kitchen who looks like a chicken?'

'What a horrible thing to say – I suppose she does, a bit. It's Ruth. She's a poet.'

'Oh,' he says, significantly, 'fifty rejection slips and a triolet in *This England*?'

'You condescending sod. Triolets are bloody difficult, try one, why don't you? No, she's real, Ruth Prochak – don't tell me you haven't heard of her?'

'Of course I have.' He is not at all certain of it, although Prochak is a name not easily forgotten.

'I suppose she's not on your syllabus, well, she wouldn't be, would she? Still alive.'

Jane comes in with a tray of coffee cups. 'You were brilliant on telly. Are you doing sex education, now?'

'No, just corrupting the young through the medium of English literature. Have you read *The Catcher in the Rye*?'

'That wasn't the book, was it?' Geneva says.

'One of them. We had the same trouble fifteen years ago.'

'Is it a dirty book?' Jane goes out again with the evident intention of re-reading it to see what she has missed the first time.

'Salinger's still alive,' McEvoy remarks, defiantly.

'You said you'd had a response. Hate mail?'

'You could call it that. Three letters implying that moral degenerates should be locked up safely away from innocent children – have you seen our Fifth Formers? – and one referring me to Exodus Chapter 20 verse 7, on the matter of taking the Lord's name in vain. No, the oddest thing is people I knew years ago, who've been getting in touch. They write and ring up. "I often wondered what happened to you," they say. "I don't suppose you remember me." Mostly they're right. Actually, that's why I came to see you.'

'To be kissed better? Isn't Sarah answering the door to the tripe hounds and telling them she intends to stand by her husband?'

'Oh, Geneva, it isn't that. No one gives a damn what I think about anything. It's not as if I'd *written* a filthy book.'

'One of your voices from the past, then?'

He draws the envelope from his pocket and unpacks it. 'Read this.'

'They're sending you poems? Proposals of marriage, too?'

'It's not what you think. Read it.'

Geneva puts on her spectacles and bends over the aged foolscap. McEvoy leans back in his chair and feels himself receding into the restless furnishings. If he sits there long enough he might become one of the cushions. Through the wall he hears Prochak pecking at her poetry; Geneva looks up.

'How you've got the nerve to sneer at triolets in *This England* – '

'I should have cut the signature off.'

'But you didn't want to diminish the value?'

'I don't think the University of Texas is queuing up for it.'

'I'm not being fair,' Geneva says. '1964 . . . you were nobbut a lad when you wrote this. Did you ever write any more?'

'No I didn't. I gave it up when I left full-time education, in the national interest. I decided it was actively injurious for people to read my poetry. That was probably the last poem I ever wrote. We were all poets at university.'

'My crowd were writing novels, that is, we were all writing the same novel. It was eight years before I started on the real thing. Did someone treasure this, then?'

'I don't know about treasuring, but she kept it. It turned up in a letter last week.'

'Do I get to see the letter?'

He hands it over. She reads it, her eyebrows two circumflex accents over the 'o's of her glasses. 'A book? You mean there's more to come? I say, *weren't* you a lout at twenty-two? "I shan't be seeing you again but it's been a lot of fun, hasn't it?"'

He takes *Acid Test* out of the envelope. 'I'm sure I never said anything of the sort. It's not like me at all.'

'It's not like you now. I don't know,' Geneva says, thoughtfully, 'young men can be very nasty without much provocation – or without any provocation at all, come to that. I wonder why she waited so long to get back at you.'

'She's only just got the wherewithal. This is the book.' Geneva is still conning the letter.

'Caroline Hill . . . I don't know the name. Clockhouse specialize in uplifting biographies, don't they?'

'This is an uplifting autobiography.'

'A kind of expanded version of the penitent's bench? Where do you come into all this?'

'That's the trouble – I *am* in it.'

'In the book? She – ' Geneva rattles the letter, ' – doesn't say so.'

'I worked it out. It wasn't difficult.'

'Who are you?'

'Michael, university friend of a friend. Handsome, charming, trendy dresser – '

'How did you recognize yourself apart from that?' Geneva asks, waspishly.

'It was the circumstances. I thought I recognized the author's name, and after a bit I placed her. Then I placed myself, too.'

'This is a voice from the past with knobs on,' Geneva says. 'Had you done her wrong? Has she spilled the beans?'

'I never did anything to her; I hardly knew her. She doesn't pretend that I did, but it's a hateful portrait.'

Geneva removes her glasses and studies him keenly.

'And Margaret Whatsername thought it would be a pity if you didn't see it? I think I begin to understand. This is revenge in the Kipling mode, brought slowly to the boil. Remember the maniac in *Dayspring Mishandled* who waits ten years to nail the man who gave his sweetheart syphilis? Your Margaret's never forgiven you for casting her off like an old shoe and now this book's turned up to deliver her vengeance for her.

26

You used her, Hill's used you, Margaret's used Hill, is that it? What's the book like?'

'Hard to judge. I thought it was bad to begin with but after a while I couldn't tell any more. I was too busy looking for clues.'

'Is there a dedication? *To Nimrod . . . he knows why*. Who's Nimrod?'

'God knows. Does it matter?'

'Might be another clue. You can sometimes learn a lot from a dedication. Writing's a very solitary profession, there's always an urge to involve someone else, even as an accessory after the fact. You may have noticed a growing tendency for dedications to carry a cast of thousands, all up there being thanked for their love and support, like an Academy Award ceremony, but that's all nonsense. You're on your own.'

'When you look at some dedications', McEvoy says, 'you wonder what the dedicatee did to deserve it. Sometimes in a really erotic book – I don't mean necessarily pornographic – it says, for so-and-so, and you can't help wondering if so-and-so is meant to think that it was done especially for him. Everybody else must think so.'

'Quite. Be very thankful', Geneva says, tapping *Acid Test*, 'that she didn't dedicate it to you.'

'Why should she? She seems to have loathed all of us, not me above anyone else. I mean, we all committed our acts of betrayal – the thing's practically a list of let-downs – mine didn't involve her at all, though I did forget her birthday, I see. I'm certain I couldn't have known it was her birthday. I don't forget things like that.'

'This has upset you badly, hasn't it?' Geneva says. 'Has it been on your conscience for so long?'

'It hasn't been on my conscience at all. I tell you, I didn't do anything – that is, what I did was nothing. There were results, but I never knew about them.'

'You know now, though.'

'Yes, look, Geneva, I don't want to explain. Just read the book.'

'Poor John.' Geneva leaves her seat among the Paisley shawls at the end of the sofa, perches on the chair's arm and fondles his back hair. 'I'll read it at once. I'll read it tonight. Shall I ring you?'

'No, I'll call in during the week.'

'Huh; Sarah doesn't know about it, then?'

'Of course Sarah doesn't know about it. There are five women in that book, she'd think I'd laid them all, end to end. What do you suppose she'd make of that letter?'

Geneva stands and stumps across the room to place the book among pots of bulbs on a shelf below the bay window. 'John, why do you want me to read it?'

'I need a second opinion. I can't believe that I was quite such an unctuous bastard. I don't really want anyone to read it, but I keep going back to it, over and over.'

'At least it will be out of the house, for a while.'

'No, that's not the copy she sent. I marked that.'

'Marked it? Spit? Bile? Blood?'

'A Stabiloboss. I didn't read it straight away, I just went through and marked my name wherever I saw it, once I'd realized who I was.'

Geneva comes back to his chair, leans down and kisses him. 'Dear John, I do love you; you're so honest. But I wish you hadn't told me who you were, it would have been fun trying to guess. Would you have known – if you hadn't had a hint?'

'I'd never have read it if I hadn't had a hint. It's not the kind of thing I want to be seen with, let alone seen buying. I kept looking over my shoulder to make sure no one I knew was about, while I was getting that copy. I had to go to the SPCK for it.'

'Oh, I see. Can the Head of English at Thomas Paine afford to be seen coming out of the SPCK bookshop? I know it was founded by humanists, but they won't chuck you out for that, surely? That's one thing about the public sector; apart from paedophilia there's not much they can do you for. It's like the Church of England.'

The door to the hall opens and the chicken looks disconcertingly round it, gesturing strangely. Geneva hurries over to the door and there is a muted conference. The chicken retreats.

'Reciting her latest poem?' McEvoy says. The woman looks even more avian in three-quarter profile, being very nearly chinless with a swooping nose cursorily tweaked into a hook. He can imagine her in flat brown shoes and a camel-hair coat, craning a scrawny neck after the Holy wafer of a weekday morning, in a cold urban church; the sole communicant and in love with the vicar.

'Don't be such a bitch,' Geneva chides him. 'She's going down to the post and wanted to know if I had anything ready.'

'Why the whispering?'

'Probably because she didn't want to disturb us. You *have* taken against her.'

'Is she deranged?'

'Ruth? She looks it, poor love,' Geneva says, comfortably. 'No, not at all; just solipsistic, I think. She never tries to account for anyone's actions but her own. It gives her rather a curious outlook. *She* wouldn't have any trouble with your book.'

'It's not my book. Don't for Christ's sake show it to her.'

'Without your consent – never. I wonder if this Margaret had Hill's consent to send it to you. It's an odd set-up, you know. Do you think *she'd* want you to read it?'

'I don't suppose she thought that I'd ever know about it – or discover that I was in it. No one was expecting that television debate, were they?'

'Funny, so many people recognizing you.'

'Only by name, most of them said.'

'Have you changed so much?'

'In appearance, certainly. And in a lot of ways, I hope, judging by the book.'

'Don't let's talk about it any more. I'll read it.'

'You don't know what she's said – '

'I'll know when I've read it. You said you didn't want to explain; more coffee?'

'Better not. I have to meet Sarah and the boys at seven. I must get back and clear up.'

On his way past the kitchen he glances in at the poet hen. She is humped over the typewriter again, head resting on hand, hair raked up into a comb by her fingers, staring vacantly at the sink.

'I thought she was going down to the post,' McEvoy says, at the front door. 'Are you sure she's not cataleptic?'

'I dare say she's been and come back. It's only on the corner,' Geneva says. 'In fact, you're parked by it, as you very well know. You could have offered to take her letters.'

'She might have thought I was making a pass.'

'Get out, you arrogant swine,' Geneva says, fondly. 'No one makes a pass at Ruth.'

'That's more or less what I meant. It might have lightened her day.'

'That's not what *I* meant. She's a killer.'

'She'd fight like a tiger for her honour?'

'Get out.'

Sarah's train is late. Sarah believes devoutly in the antipathy of inanimate objects; her trains are always late, solely because she is in them. Cars sidle together and filch available parking spaces, shops close as she approaches, electrical appliances fuse, drains become blocked, books go out of print. Having abdicated all responsibility for her own misfortunes she is very nearly in a position to enjoy the accuracy of her forecasts when they come to pass.

'Did you have a good weekend?' she asks. McEvoy knows that she hopes he did not have a good weekend, without her, but that she would prefer to think that her weekend was worse, and he derives some sulky enjoyment from observing the way she engineers this. Sarah sits beside him in the front passenger seat, celebrating the dereliction of British Rail's signalling system, which she might have avoided by taking the Metropolitan Line. Behind them his two sons chant and gibber, after the fashion of children in rear seats.

'Was it all right apart from the trains?'

'As all right as it ever is. It rained, of course.'

'It rained here.'

'All the time?'

'No.'

Appeased, she sits back. 'What have you been doing?'

'Working. And I dropped by to see Geneva.' He makes a point of never concealing from her these visits, even when there is no need to mention them for if he should chance to refer to them later, she would wonder why he had omitted to mention them in the first place. He does not tell her of the female poet, however. It is never sensible to mention women; even the presence of that ageing virgin would alarm his wife.

'And how is Geneva?'

'It's the usual madhouse. Patchwork quilts all over the living-room, knitting in the coal scuttle. I swear the cushions are multiplying.'

Offended by his own disloyalty he makes it a point also, to mock sporadically that serene household. Since it consoles Sarah to suppose that the late Mr Stevens perished of neglect while his wife pursued her career at the expense of his well-being, and that her glorious daughters are unprincipled trollops for the same reason, he allows her to believe that Geneva's *modus vivendi* causes him scornful amusement. It hurts him abominably every time he does it and he cannot even assuage the pain by explaining to Geneva. He knows that probably Geneva would understand and sympathize, but this is one area where he does not want her sympathy. He cannot imagine that she would fail to think less of him, not for the misrepresentation – Geneva knows too well that necessity is the mother of invention, but for the necessity itself. She sympathizes already with what he allows her to believe; for the truth she would pity him.

On Sunday evenings Geneva's daughters dress with care and take to the streets, trawling the neighbouring pavements for admirers. They robe themselves as for a ritual, Jane stark in pale maquillage, black and white stripes and chequers, fish-net tights and high heels; Mary blonde and blooming rosily in flounces. Ruth Prochak stands by the window in the kitchen, where she and Geneva are drinking before dinner, and watches the sisters promenade slowly down Avenue Road, arm in arm.

'Don't they ever get picked up for soliciting?'

'Good God, no. They're well known around here.'

'So I should imagine.'

'It's entirely innocent, they just start conversations with likely-looking lads. I don't think they've ever been rebuffed.'

Geneva joins Ruth at the window and stares lovingly down at the receding figures. 'Who'd dare rebuff *them*?'

'Do the likely lads ever turn up here?'

'No, but they sometimes phone, coyly, the following Saturday. There's nothing hit or miss about this, you know. It's all done strictly according to the rules.'

'You make it sound uncommonly sanitary and asexual.'

'And eminently sensible.' Geneva is affronted for her darlings. 'They've got examinations to worry about. This kind of social intercourse calls for extreme delicacy. You should have gone with them – you'd have learned a lot about rites of passage.'

'I don't need to, thank you very much,' Ruth says, turning away. 'I see enough of that at work. Unlike you, I don't regard everyone I see as possible copy.'

'Yes,' Geneva says, with heavy stress, 'we have something to discuss, haven't we?'

'Have we?' Ruth's enormous eyes widen farther. 'Oh yes, you wanted to talk about the stories.'

'No,' says Geneva, 'I do not want to talk about the stories, but what I have to say won't improve with keeping. Sit down.'

She goes to her bureau in the living-room and fetches a folder of typed sheets. Ruth, who has obediently sat down at once, is erect at the table, hands clasped before her on the scrubbed boards, straight backed like the good child in class who longs to be chosen to hand out the atlases. Her eyes add often irrelevant or downright misleading emphasis to her remarks, and more so to her silences. It is something to do with the surface area, Geneva thinks. Probably no more than nervous now, she looks terrified.

Geneva places the typescript on the table between them as she sits. Ruth puts out a tentative hand, sees Geneva's face and thinks better of it. Geneva reaches for the bottle of Scotch and pours them each a heavy slug.

'You don't like them?'

'They're appalling.'

'All of them?' Ruth retracts her inconsiderable chin and ducks her head. Just like a chicken, thinks Geneva, who never noticed the resemblance until John pointed it out.

'All of them, right through – no, that's not quite fair. They open splendidly, but you can't keep it up for more than about two sentences.'

'Like Francis Bacon?' Ruth says, squinting slightly, an alarming skew. 'Brilliant at first lines? Everyone's heard of jesting Pilate but who knows that Truth may perhaps come to the price of a pearl?'

'Who said that?'

'Duncan Hamilton. Why, did he say it to you, too?'

'No, I said it to him.' Geneva is irritated. 'I don't like being quoted in my own lifetime. Anyway, I originally said it about John Donne.'

'There's no copyright on oral *mots*. OK, I'll give you a byline next time I quote you. I don't agree, mind you.'

'I always feel there's a kind of falling-off with Donne,' Geneva says, 'a loss of impetus. Shouldn't a poem grow toward a predetermined conclusion, like a short story?'

'Is that how short stories grow?'

'Yes it is.' Geneva opens a script and glares into it. 'I rather thought you'd missed that elementary point. You have to know how the thing is going to end before you begin it – it's not like a novel. Why don't you stick to writing poems?' She scans a paragraph. 'This is embarrassing. You don't talk like this . . . you don't write poems like this.'

Ruth leans across to see what is wrong. 'I was playing with words.'

'The way a cat plays with mice. You've killed them stone dead.'

'Oh, stop delivering aphorisms, you're not on telly now,' Ruth says, repossessing her scripts.

'You'd rather hear it from me than from an editor, wouldn't you? Where's your professional pride?'

'They'd never have got as far as an editor. That's why I showed them to you, all I'd have got from an editor is rejection slips.'

'Which editor? Duncan? If he'd seen them he'd have started wondering how anyone who produced *Midland City* – which he admires enormously – could have had a hand in those. He'd have wondered out loud,' Geneva says, meaningly. 'He's got a tongue like a stair carpet.'

'You think I should stop trying?'

'Definitely; you can't possibly enjoy it. And look, Ruth, you simply aren't equipped for fiction writing, you've got no curiosity. You love to record the quirks of human behaviour but you aren't at all interested in investigating the mysteries of the organism. Don't look so hurt,' says Geneva, 'you'd be just as rude to me if I showed you my poetry.'

'I don't think I would,' Ruth says. 'I didn't know you wrote poetry.'

'I don't, really, but I try, just for the exercise. I suppress them in the national interest.' Geneva hesitates, mindful of the absence of copyright on oral *mots*. 'As John says,' she adds, scrupulously.

'John?'

'John McEvoy, the chap who was here this afternoon, he showed me a poem he wrote in his early twenties. If you'd seen it you'd have advised him to stop. Fortunately he stopped himself.'

'Can I see it?'

'Without his consent? No.'

'I should like to see a really bad poem,' Ruth murmurs. 'It would cheer me up no end.' She hoods her eyes as best she can and looks slyly at Geneva across the table. 'Show me one of yours.'

'They're not meant to be read. I told you, I do it for the exercise.'

'Everything should be written with an audience in mind,' Ruth says. '*You* said that. You're the one who goes round drawing up rules for the rest of us. Go on, show me.'

'I think I've destroyed most of them.'

Ruth folds her long arms and leans back, tilting her chair. She grins.

'All right. But only one.' Geneva returns to the bureau, sorely tempted to show John's poem to Ruth and pass it off as her own. She doubts, however that Ruth would be fooled. What woman would have written *that* crud-and-water claptrap?

The poems are in an old Eastlight file in the bottom drawer. On top are the few that she can look at unblushingly and think: Not bad; underneath are the fifty or so that make her grow warm just by coming to mind. Although she knows that Ruth is dreadfully hurt by her criticism she cannot quite bring herself to console her with one of those. She takes the topmost and returns to the kitchen.

'Try this.'

Ruth takes the top sheet, pushes back her chair and clears her throat.

'Oh no, for God's sake!' Geneva cries. 'Not out loud.'

Ruth smiles sleepily, not very pleasantly, and reads in silence. Geneva looks over her shoulder.

> He who denies, belies denying,
> Circumspection alerts suspicion.
> To the practised and the prying
> Effacement becomes an exhibition.

> Nothing wakens the dormant ear
> Sooner than clandestine creeping.
> Camouflage makes the occluded clear,
> Muted whispers rouse the sleeping.

'I wouldn't argue with the premise,' says Ruth.

> A stranger striding through crowds and light
> Proceeds unnoticed, his safety certain.
> The interloper who sneaks by night,
> Is betrayed by his feet beneath the curtain.

Geneva can bear Ruth's downturned smile no longer and swipes the paper away.

'Oh my,' Ruth says, 'what untapped reserves of naughtiness this hints at.'

'Whaddya mean, naughtiness? It's a metaphor.'

'What, this guy behind the curtains? Only a metaphor? I thought you were writing from experience.'

'That's your province,' Geneva says. 'I need something factual to go on but the rest is surmise – what might have been. That's what scuppered your story about the man who drove to Matlock.'

'It happened to a friend of mine. He was driving north

when he stopped to ask directions outside Derby and this other guy – the one who gave him the directions – actually said, "You know, a couple of years ago a chap stopped here and asked me for directions and we stood around chatting, just like we're doing now, and then he drove off and went slap into the side of an oil tanker – just there, at the T-junction. Killed instantly. If he hadn't stopped to talk he'd have missed that tanker. Still be alive, very likely."

'"Might have been killed by someone else instead," my friend said, and then he realized he was being delayed in exactly the same way. He abandoned the journey and came straight home again.'

'I know,' Geneva says. 'That's more or less what you wrote.'

'I thought it would make a good story.'

'It's a good anecdote. You've spun it out to three thousand words – now it's a long dull anecdote. To turn it into a story you've got to speculate about what might have happened if he'd gone on to Matlock.'

'He might just as well have been killed coming home again,' Ruth says.

'Indeed. There *is* a story in that, but you're not the one to write it. You've no bent for speculation.'

3

Dermot Crane, the lateral thinker, and Rhodri Davies, a Second Year, assist Mr McEvoy to his car with a box of books.

'Hold it underneath,' McEvoy says, 'the bottom will drop out.'

Crane peers in at the top.

'*The Catcher in the Rye*? Isn't that the one you were talking about on telly, Sir?'

'You saw it too, did you?'

'Why are you taking it home, Sir? Is it banned?' Davies inquires, hopefully.

'No it is not banned. I want to make some notes – there are about fifty others in there, Rhodri – under*neath*. Have you read it?'

'Oh yes, Sir, years ago.' Davies must be pushing thirteen.

'Do you think it should be banned?'

'I am opposed to all forms of censorship,' Davies remarks primly. 'Except perhaps video nasties.'

'Have you ever seen a video nasty?'

Davies wears black-rimmed spectacles. He looks shocked. Crane smiles, tolerantly.

'What did you think of *Catcher in the Rye*, Dermot?'

'I didn't think it was very realistic.'

'Perhaps the world has moved on since 1951. It is generally regarded as highly realistic.'

'1951? My mother was born in 1951. I thought it was meant to be modern,' Davies complains. McEvoy regards his earnest little mug in its swot's glasses. He will still look like that at forty.

'It is, relatively. What, particularly, did you find unrealistic?'

Dermot considers. 'Well, the hero, you know, Sir. Caldwell.'

'Caulfield.'

'Yes, him Sir. Well, Sir, he doesn't wank.'

'Maybe he just didn't feel like talking about it,' McEvoy suggests.

'He talks about everything else,' Crane replies, accurately. 'He's on his own all the time, isn't he, and he keeps saying he feels – horny, but he doesn't do anything about it, does he, Sir?'

'He does talk about *bull* sessions a bit,' Davies suggests, helpfully, his mouth quirked into a prudish moue to indicate that he is quoting. 'Could that be . . . ?'

'No, Rhodri. That's just conversation.' They reach the car.

Crane salutes, man to man, and heads for the bicycle sheds, no wanker he. Rhodri Davies stows the carton of books in the boot and says goodbye. McEvoy does not linger to watch him bustle away toward the side gate, his sports bag bouncing against his solid Welsh bottom. He gets into the car and starts the engine before pausing to decide where he will go.

Sarah will not expect him at home until after eight. A departmental meeting was scheduled for this evening and such meetings normally end in the Cross Keys, but with his second-in-command off sick and two teachers due at their own children's open evenings, he has cancelled it. He might as well call on Geneva. Traffic is building up in the town centre; school coaches, mothers in cars full of home-bound children; he takes the back streets to Avenue Road, through Thomas Paine's catchment area where many maroon blazers are dawdling and loitering. Going comprehensive has made no appreciable difference to Thomas Paine's social standing; it is still, to all intents and purposes, a grammar school.

Avenue Road is diametrically opposed to his own street; they could not be further apart in any respect. Geneva's neighbours work mostly in London and few of them have returned home when he draws up outside the double-fronted brick villa where she has her flat. Usually he has to park halfway down the road, or even in the next street. Not until he stands on the doorstep and has rung the bell does he notice that Geneva's red Datsun is nowhere in sight, but already he can hear footsteps on the stairs. The door is opened by Geneva's friend who looks like a chicken. She does not recognize him.

In the first instant he does not recognize her. Seen full face

38

there is no suggestion of beak or comb; all he notices are her eyes and he wonders that he did not notice them before. They are enormously, painfully prominent; when she blinks the lids scarcely meet over them; he thinks of ping pong balls, gobstoppers, hardboiled eggs; the irises light grey: *oysters*.

'Hello,' she says, 'are you wanting Geneva?'

'Yes,' he says, 'but I've just noticed her car's not here.'

'She was meeting Jane and Mary from school. They've all gone to the hairdresser's.' She grins mischievously as she retails this information, as if there were something impossibly risible about going to the hairdresser *en famille*, all girls together. 'Still,' she is saying, 'I don't suppose they'll be long. Why don't you come in?'

He follows her indoors and up the stairs, regretting his unkind conjecture about the camel-hair coat at Holy Communion. Today she is wearing jeans and a woollen shirt, and the brief glimpse of her peculiar profile on Sunday, that suggested the forlorn and scrawny spinster, has misled him badly. She is obviously much younger than he thought, probably not much above thirty.

'Coffee?' she asks, after the fashion of the house, when they reach the kitchen. 'It's Geneva's coffee but she won't mind.'

'Please. Aren't you Ruth Prochak? I saw you here on Sunday.'

'I thought you looked familiar. Geneva mentioned your name — I can't remember it.'

'McEvoy. John McEvoy.'

Prochak bends over the sink to fill the kettle, a paperback book thrust under her arm, but too soon she plugs it in and turns to face him. McEvoy stares and tries not to. The eyes worry him. He is sure they must hurt her, they turn her most cursory glance into a mesmeric gaze. Unless one of them speaks they will be standing here in paralysed silence until the kettle boils and he knows this kettle. It is old and slow.

'Have you known Geneva long?' he asks.

'About three years.'

'I'm surprised we haven't met before.'

'This is the first time I've come here. We usually see each other in London.'

'Do you live in London?'

'I live mainly on railway trains,' says Prochak, without a vestige of a smile. He notices that the paperback, which she is still carrying, is not a volume of poetry nor, though its bulk suggests as much, a best-selling novel of dynastic mayhem, but the British Rail Passenger Timetable.

'You must get off them sometimes.'

'I have a flat in London, on Primrose Hill. Are you a neighbour?'

'I live on the other side of town but when I first came here we lived in the same house.'

'Together?'

She is not joking.

'No.' Boil, kettle, boil.

The telephone rings instead and Prochak, as overtly relieved as he is, darts out of the room to answer it. Before she comes back the kettle does boil. In her absence he makes the coffee, places mugs on a tray with milk jug and sugar bowl and takes it all through to the living-room, where Prochak is just replacing the receiver. Her back is turned to him but he cannot rid himself of the fancy that, like a hare, she can see behind her without turning her head.

'Oh,' she says, looking at the tray, 'you know your way about.'

'It seemed silly to wait.'

'I'm sorry I took so long.' The eyes bulge. 'That was Geneva's editor.'

'Duncan Hamilton?'

'You know about him? He does rabbit.'

'You know him too?'

'He's bringing out my next collection – well, not him directly; his poetry editor.'

McEvoy sits down on the sofa among the Paisley shawls, Prochak lounges on the floor.

'I didn't realize you were with Reptile Books as well.'

'*I* don't call them Reptile Books,' Prochak says, severely.

'Judging from what Geneva says it sounds like a very apposite name.'

'Geneva is a contentious old bat', Prochak says, 'when it comes to publishers. Why else do you think she's on her third? Not that I blame her.' She swoops over her coffee mug, a chicken once more. 'Novelists have muscle, it behoves them to use it. If I went for Duncan the way she does I'd be back on the small presses again.'

'Have you published much?'

'This is the third collection.'

'All poetry?'

'So far. I've done one or two short stories, but I haven't tried to publish.' She changes the subject abruptly. 'Do you write?'

'No, I'm an English teacher.'

'I suppose that means you don't read, either.'

'I thought you said Geneva was contentious.'

'Teaching is the *worst*-read profession. I visit schools quite often. There's always some smug tit in the staffroom who says, "I'm afraid I haven't read anything of yours. I don't have time for reading."'

McEvoy knows the tone exactly. 'Don't take it personally. You won't be the only one they haven't read.'

'Of course not – they won't have read anyone, but why do they think I want to know, anyway? They make a virtue out of being illiterate. Have you noticed how many people think it's clever in some way, *not* to be able to do things. As if they've made a conscious decision to be inept. "If I can't do it it's not worth doing."' She suddenly smiles up at him over the rim of the coffee mug. 'Are you looking for something?'

McEvoy has been glancing round the room to see if *Acid Test* is lying anywhere about.

'It doesn't seem as if Geneva's coming back.'

'She might be turning the corner at this very moment, how can you know? Was it urgent?'

'No. I came to pick up a book. It can wait.'

'I could probably find it . . .'

'Don't worry. Really, it's not important.' She has begun to rise, bonelessly, from the carpet. '*Please* don't trouble. I ought to be going anyway, my wife will be expecting me.'

'I'll tell Geneva you called.'

'Will she be in tomorrow afternoon, do you know?'

'I don't know – but I'll tell her you'll come by, if you're going to come by, that is.'

'Thanks. She can ring if it's not convenient.'

'She seems to be home most evenings,' Prochak observes, 'tatting typewriter cosies.'

'She's amazingly gifted.'

'And prolific. Don't you think,' says Prochak, waving a long hand, 'that this is a very *full* room?'

'She's worked hard on it.'

'It's rather a lot for the eye to take in at once, though.'

You shouldn't have much trouble, McEvoy thinks, unkindly, as she sees him out.

His return home is badly timed; too late for a sprint start from school, too early for the departmental meeting, *far* too early to blame on the commuter traffic.

'What happened to the meeting?'

'Cancelled.'

'Was the traffic bad, then?' Sarah says.

'I stopped off at Geneva's to pick up a book.'

'Which one?' (i.e. Where is it?)

'*At Swim-Two-Birds.*' He knows she has it, he lent it to her at Christmas. 'But there was no one at home. I expect she was collecting the girls from school. They may have gone shopping.'

Sarah looks at the clock.

'I didn't get away till four thirty. One of the boys stopped to talk about some books.'

'Which boy was that?'

'Rhodri Davies – in the Second Year. He's worth taking trouble over.' This accounts for the missing twenty minutes.

'*At Swim-Two-Birds?*' Sarah inquires, suddenly, as if she suspected him of having invented it. 'That's a strange name for a book.'

'It's a strange book.'

'What's it about?' By Christ, she *does* think he's invented it.

'It's a book about a book that's being written about a man who's writing a book. His characters conspire to get him before he gets them.'

Sarah, who doesn't have time for reading, is lost. 'And do they?'

'Oh no,' says McEvoy. 'The author of the first book allows

the author of the second book to allow the author of the third book to win – after a fashion. Authors must stick together,' he says.

'Your friend John came round this afternoon,' Ruth says, recalling the fact only after dinner while they are washing up.

'And I missed him,' Geneva says, with regret. 'By how long?'

'Dunno. He came about half four,' Ruth says. 'By quite a lot, I suppose. He said he'd come back tomorrow. He wanted a book, he said.'

'Yes.' Geneva smiles downward, privately.

'I offered to find it for him but he seemed very anxious that I shouldn't. In fact,' says Ruth, 'he went.'

'You let him in, then?'

'Of course I let him in. I gave him coffee. Wasn't that right?'

'Very trusting of you. He might have been a rapist burglar.'

'Get away. I thought he looked familiar – then he said it was him here on Sunday.'

'Did he tell you about the book?'

'I didn't ask, which seems to have been a good thing. I don't think he wanted me to see it.'

Geneva, hanging up a tea-towel, looks thoughtfully at her friend. She does not know her well, although she has always liked her. After five days in the same flat she likes her no less, but she is beginning to ask herself if there is anything more to know. 'Didn't you wonder about that?'

'What?'

'That he didn't want you to see it?'

'No, is it important?'

'I'll tell you. It's rather odd, funny in a way . . . and sad.'

'Do you think you should tell me – if he wouldn't want me to know?'

'It doesn't matter. It's not as though you know each other.' Ruth looks doubtful but Geneva does not notice. She has given up trying to read any meaning into Ruth's expression, her eyes distort it so. 'Some woman that he knew years ago has written a book and he's in it.'

'That must happen rather often.'

'Not to John.'

'Aren't all your characters based on people you know? Where else would you get them from?'

'Yes they are – but out of context. They're never recognizable, least of all to themselves. It's placing a character – or characters – out of context that makes the reader appreciate the sharpness of your observation. That's the true sense of humour; an eye for incongruity. The things one notices about people are never the things that they notice about themselves. That doesn't just apply to writers.'

'How did John recognize himself, then?'

'He was as good as told, and there's no attempt at disguise, either, as far as I can tell, apart from names being changed. Mind you, *I* wouldn't have recognized him, but he must have changed a lot in twenty years. One does. I haven't discussed it with him but it looks to me like straight reporting; biased, naturally, but straight.'

'It's true, then – not fiction, I mean; he's not a character in a novel? Is that why he doesn't like it?'

'Not quite. I can't tell how accurate it is, but there's no way of knowing how much his memory is at variance with the author's. Now I', says Geneva, 'would have taken him out of context and I doubt very much if I'd have used him even as I'd remembered him. I tend to assemble characters the way Frankenstein did; I have to do their thinking for them, in the first place – no one ever takes that into consideration – but I might use John's charm, which would be difficult to convey because it's almost entirely in his facial expression; say this character stammered; where would I go for a stammer? Eddy – my husband – had a corker. And of course, the whole process is transsexual. This character's a man, so far, but he might have your eyes – '

Geneva stops. She has felt for some time that Ruth's unnerving eyeballs might be useful and indeed, she does fully intend to use them one day, but she never meant to tell Ruth. She would have gone on to explain that nine-tenths of a fictional character are submerged; the part observed by the reader being only a proportion of the author's view, who must know so much more than he or she ever sets down; but to say it now would seem like the mere making of excuses.

She turns regretfully and would apologize, but Ruth shrugs slightly and smiles.

'The point is', Geneva explains, gabbling a little, 'it wouldn't be *you* and it wouldn't be *him*; what this character does might be something that neither of you would ever do and yet *what* he does will nevertheless be influenced by the personae involved. But there's no fun for a fiction writer in using a real person, unadulterated, the whole action of the novel would have to be subverted to accommodate his behavioural patterns. I favour allowing the characters to develop the plot, and the plot to influence the characters. They have to grow together – a sort of symbiosis.'

Ruth is hanging cups on the dresser, carefully fitting each handle over each hook. She would not wish to break any of Geneva's crockery.

'Still,' says Geneva, 'in this particular case, the reverse is true.'

'Which case?'

'John's book, well, no, not *his* book. The author is Caroline Hill.'

'What's she write?'

'Nothing, apart from this. She's not an author, she's a graphic designer, and she's evidently one of those people who believe that there is at least one book in everybody.'

'There's not even a paragraph in most people.'

'Anyway, what she's written down purports to be a true story and I suppose in a way it is. It's a record of events and I wouldn't presume to suggest that they never took place, but they're all warped by *her* assumptions of people's motives for making them happen.'

'Is that what you mean by saying it's not fiction?'

'It isn't. If it were fiction she'd be trying to fabricate something out of those events, making them grow not pinning them out on a board stark dead, for inspection. A novelist has got to understand everyone's *modus operandi*, not just his own. He's examining motives, trying to discover the thinking that shapes events, he has to *know*, but only by finding out. This woman doesn't know, and she's not up to guessing, which is what upset John, I imagine. It's such an unintelligent reading.'

'It can't really damage him, though, can it? Whatever he did can't have changed civilization as we know it – or can it? Is he something I wot not of?'

'He's Head of English at Thomas Paine.'

'He said he was a teacher. Not exactly a cosmic force.'

'It's damaged his self-esteem. Strange, really, because everything she writes about happened twenty years ago.'

'Time he forgot about it, then.'

'He had forgotten about it, until this book turned up.' Geneva really does have no wish to break John's confidence but Ruth's unsympathetic reaction stirs her to rehearse and defend her opinions of *Acid Test* before she articulates them to him. If Ruth will not discuss perhaps she can be persuaded to listen; nothing, however, can disguise the fact that Ruth is not interested; this is the peculiar outlook of which Geneva complained to John. Most of Geneva's associates are in the same line of business; they write fiction and their lives are dedicated to conjecture. Ruth is so *incurious*.

'What actually happened', Geneva says, bashing on regardless, 'is that this girl, Hill, was a patient in a psychiatric hospital and John – she calls him Michael – was a friend of one of her fellow patients. He used to visit, under the impression that he was doing good, I imagine, and they all hated him.'

'Because he *wasn't* a patient, presumably.'

'Why – yes. That's the trouble, I think. She doesn't try to describe him as he must have been, only as he seemed to her then, and she hasn't the wit to realize that her impression of him had to be filtered through her mental state. She behaves *now* as if she'd been entirely normal *then*. In that sense, the whole thing's quite valueless, but he's too close to see it.'

'She's revenged herself. If he's offended by it then presumably that's all that matters – to her.'

'Funny you should say that. The revenge element is quite extraneous to the book, there's a *tertium quid*.'

'She had no idea he was still around, then; or that he'd read it and recognize himself.'

'I don't think that was the idea at all, to be frank.' Geneva warms up. Having finally hooked Ruth's interest she is not prepared to throw it back because it is too small to keep. 'I don't think any of them had any notion of what had become of the others, or interest in them, come to that, until John appeared in a television debate a few weeks back. Someone saw the book as a glorious chance to settle an old score.'

'The *tertium quid?*'

'Whose involvement was quite as peripheral as John's was. Will you be in tomorrow night?'

'I shan't be here at all tomorrow night. I'm going in the morning, had you forgotten?'

'Of course – you've been packing. It hadn't sunk in; I've got so used to your being here.'

'It's only a week,' Ruth says. 'Perhaps it felt like longer.'

'Not at all. I've really enjoyed having you – we all have. So nice to have the chance to really get to know you at last,' says Geneva. 'You will come again?'

'Surely,' Ruth says. 'Why did you want to know if I'd be here? I could stay.'

'Well, if John's coming round to talk about his book . . . '

'Oh, I see. You were hoping I *wouldn't* be here,' Ruth says, without rancour. '*Does* he want to talk about it?'

'I can't tell him it's all lies, obviously,' Geneva muses, 'because I'm not at all sure that it is, but if I can persuade him to see how faulty the thinking behind it must be he may at least understand that it can't be true.'

'But it's not lies and it's not fiction . . . '

'They aren't synonymous. If it were fiction there might be some truth in it, but it's done from memory,' Geneva says. 'That's the biggest liar of all.'

'The diary that we all carry about with us.'

'Come again?'

'Oscar Wilde – "Memory is the diary that we all carry with us".'

'How honest is a diary?'

'Like this book, I should think. Nothing but the truth, but not the whole truth.'

'You're better, then?' McEvoy says as Simon Headley, his second-in-command staggers whey-faced into The Shed.

'"Nay, I'm killed, Sire." I shall now fall dead, smiling, my chief beside.'

'You could have had a couple more days.'

'I don't like missing the end of term,' Simon says. 'Whatever I don't do now will look ten times worse if I leave it till next week.'

'We shan't be here next week,' McEvoy reminds him. 'NATE. Durham.'

'No.' Simon coughs, pitiably. 'I can't face it. Sorry, John, you'll have to go alone. Leave me here.' He sinks into the easy chair and clutches McEvoy's sleeve. 'I'll only hold you back. Old man, it's been wonderful knowing you . . . '

'Ah shit,' says McEvoy. 'Can you really not make it? What if I do all the driving?'

'No, sorry. I'm not going to throw this off over the weekend.'

'Go home and throw it off now.'

'It's a chest infection. I'm full of antibiotics, mustn't drink. Christ, John, NATE without the booze?'

'I can see that,' McEvoy says. 'I wonder if any of the others could come instead?'

'I thought they declined fairly persuasively when you first suggested it,' Simon says. 'I'm really sorry about this, John. That's partly why I came in. I didn't want you to think I was making lame excuses over the phone.'

'You wanted me to *see* you being ill. You look bloody awful, actually. I wish you'd go home, anyway.'

'Nah . . . I want a last look at the A level mob.'

'Have a coffee, then.'

McEvoy plugs in the kettle that stands on the floor by his desk and has been blasting steam at the Warwick Shakespeares for so long that they have bled on to the shelf. 'Mind if I finish these reports?'

'Go ahead. I'll die quietly.'

'Simon?'

'Uh?'

'What's another word for bug-eyed?'

'Whose report are you writing, for Christ's sake?'

'Nothing to do with reports. I've been wondering.'

'Bug-eyed? *Is* there another word for it?'

'I'm sure there's a medical term. Something to do with the thyroid gland.'

'This isn't the *Grauniad* crossword, is it?'

'I was only wondering.'

McEvoy turns back to the reports. The kettle boils, Simon resignedly drags himself down to floor level and makes coffee for both of them.

'Exophthalmic.'

'What?'

'Bug-eyes – exophthalmus. I think it has got something to do with the thyroid.'

'It certainly sounds better.'

'What does?'

'Exophthalmic sounds better than bug-eyed. That is, if you had to describe somebody, it would sound better.'

'Are you writing a novel?' Simon says.

'Mum's in the bath!' cries Mary, in a crystalline soprano, opening the door to him wearing a dress that seems to have been adapted from a Nottingham lace bedspread.

'Is she going out?'

'No, she's expecting you, but she's been proof-reading all day. She likes a bath after a bout with Shrdlu only we're going to a disco so she had to wait for us to finish.' The whole flat is filled with the oddly watery scent of cologne and bath oils with chemical overtones of hair spray. McEvoy thinks that Geneva does well to stay out of the way while her daughters flit about half dressed. She would look like the Madam.

'Gin and tonic?' Jane asks him, creaking a little in black leather trousers.

'It's a bit early, isn't it? I'd rather have coffee; if I may.'

'Coffee? Don't spoil the image, man!'

'I'd have thought coffee was exactly my image. I don't mind making it myself.'

'You slay me. Mary, make the guy a coffee.'

Mary waltzes in again, frou-frou-frou. 'Hi, chaps! Coffee? Coo-ool.'

'So make it, slag.'

'Don't hassle me, man; I can't take this *hassle*.'

'Breathe on my fingernails, peasant. Lay me back.'

'Breathe? I can't *breathe*. I'm hyperventilating.'

Eddy Stevens timed his exit admirably, when Mary and Jane were still in the infants. He was a mild man; his daughters would do for him now, if cancer had not claimed him first.

'I've got PMT!'

'I've got PND!'

Jane leans over the back of the sofa, slides her arms round his neck and across his chest while whispering in his ear, 'I've got AIDS.'

Mary slithers up from below and massages his shoulders. 'I've got NACODS.'

'Ruthie's got ASLEF.'

'Is it catching, white trash?'

'Only from lavatory seats at St Pancras.'

'Travel the Bedpan line! This is the age of the train!'

'Put him down,' Geneva says, passing the door in a house-coat on her way from bathroom to bedroom. 'And one of you make the coffee.'

Jane tittups to the kitchen on spike heels. 'Goodnight, goodnight, farting is such sweet sorrow . . . '

'Is this the new small talk?' McEvoy asks.

'What's small talk?' says Mary.

'Is Ruth Prochak still with you?'

'No, she went home this morning.'

'Sweet lass of Primrose Hill . . . ' from the kitchen.

'I didn't know you'd met her,' Mary says.

'I came round yesterday while you were at the hair-dresser's,' McEvoy says. 'We had coffee.'

'Did she talk?'

'Yes.'

'What about?'

McEvoy tries to remember. 'Publishers, I think.'

'Oh Jeez, these writers. They slay me.'

'Why, doesn't she talk to you?'

'Yes . . . in a way.' Mary looks perplexed. 'But she doesn't seem to be with you half the time. You tell her something really crazy, she just smiles, like it was dead normal. She never asks questions.'

'Just smiles?'

'And rolls her eyes a bit,' Jane says, re-entering with the coffee.

'Did you notice the eyes?' Mary says. 'They worry me. They look like they might fly open while she's asleep.'

'Shut up and get out,' Geneva says, fully dressed now and brushing her damp hair. 'Don't rubbish my friends, I never say a word about yours.'

'You wouldn't dare.' They drape themselves affectionately about their mother then barge through the door, taking the hairbrush with them.

'Is this something new?'

'The double act? They don't usually carry on at this pitch. I think they're getting ready for the disco, winding themselves up for an entrance, to carry all before them. They'll be a hard act to follow.'

'Aren't they going to dance?'

'They may indulge in a little light bopping before midnight,' says Geneva, 'but that's not the purpose of going. The whole point is *being there*; or not – depending on the statement you wish to make. Half the evening is taken up with *getting there*, anyway. They're dining out *en route* – Sakki's fast-food barrow in the precinct.'

'What did Ruth Prochak make of them?'

'Hard to tell, with Ruth. She takes the line of least resistance. What did you make of her?'

'She was very pleasant; I'm sorry I called her a chicken. She doesn't look at all like a chicken.'

'Not really; more like one of those small primates that come out at night in the rain forests.'

'What's wrong with her?'

'Nothing; she's a very good poet.'

'I meant the eyes; thyroid gland?'

'It could be, I suppose, but doesn't that make you terribly sluggish or frightfully twitchy? Ruth rides a very even keel. I could box her ears sometimes, just for the pleasure of seeing her off-balance. Have you read her poetry?'

'No. I ought to.'

'She wouldn't expect it, but you might enjoy it. I find it great fun.'

'What does she think of your novels?'

'I doubt if she reads novels,' Geneva says. 'She reads time-tables.'

4

In the living-room the boys are watching television. Sarah registers multi-coloured flickers reflected on the sill of the serving hatch, and hears the occasional shriek. It is a quiz programme of some kind hosted by those people, seemingly peculiar to show business, who believe that children are fully conscious only when screaming, but Sarah's eyes are on the kitchen clock; she is listening for the car.

John promised to be home by seven, saying that he must go to the Hatfield Teachers' Centre and then, no necessity involved here, to Geneva's, to collect his book. He said he would leave school as soon as lessons ended, so as to reach the Centre by four thirty; an hour and a half there – he is giving a talk – say half an hour to drive back, leaving him thirty minutes to stop off at Avenue Road for the book. This could be done in as many seconds, surely, if he really wanted to get home. There is no need at all to spend half an hour at Geneva's flat, but he must be allowed a little leeway. After all, under Sarah's guidance, his extra-curricular activities are now confined solely to family outings and visits to Geneva which are carefully monitored. She has to make an exception for his conference next week, but never mind, he will be going under supervision, with Simon Headley.

It is ten to seven. How she would like to ring Geneva's flat to check that he has left, but she can think of no excuse that would not expose her to Geneva's ridicule. Geneva can have no idea how vital it is to have a sense of timing.

Geneva pontificates.

'Fiction is a speculative process – why do you think novelists write such boring autobiographies?'

'Do they?'

'I wish you'd read more; of course they do. By and large we've lost interest in what's happened – we've already used it all, and we aren't so much interested in what has taken place as in what might have taken place; not interested in the incident, only in what may develop from it. If this Hill woman were writing fiction she'd have taken one particular incident, or an amalgam of several, and inquired into the possible outcomes. But she isn't. She's got no idea how to set about such an undertaking, she's just written down what happened as far as she understood it. There's no law against that; she can write what she likes.'

'But she didn't understand.'

'That's neither here nor there. If she'd understood she'd never have revealed herself in print the way she has. She's made far more of a spectacle of herself than she has of you; everyone who reads the book will know who she is; how many people could identify Michael? At least three of those involved are dead; she says as much herself.'

'But *I* know,' says McEvoy.

'Only because you were told. You'd never have read the thing, otherwise – you said that. I wouldn't have recognized you. If I'd been in her position, which God forbid, and I'd found you an interesting subject, I'd have changed one factor. I'd have supposed that you – Michael – knew the result of the meeting with Gerald, and traced the effect that it had on him afterwards. That's what I mean by plotting.'

'I don't care how you write your bloody books,' McEvoy snarls, 'this isn't a character, it's *me*.'

'Don't hone your tongue on me, young man,' Geneva says, tartly. 'You should have stuck to coffee.' She tops up his gin and tonic, with gin.

'I'm sorry.'

'I know it's you – well, it isn't, but it's meant to be. If I'd written it, it wouldn't have been you. Something – someone – else entirely would have evolved. I mean', Geneva massages his fingers placatingly, 'ever since you told me about this book I've been wondering what I could make of the situation. It would be a fascinating point of departure, wouldn't it? A man discovers that he's been used in a book – perhaps I *would* make it a work of fiction – how does this affect him subsequently?'

McEvoy looks at her incredulously. 'Don't tell me you'd actually write it?'

'No no, of course not. It's an intellectual exercise and

53

anyway, I can't help doing it. That's how I operate and as I said, it wouldn't be about you. This would be a fictional character.'

'And where would *he* come from?'

'The same place that Frankenstein found his components. One man's voice, another's mannerisms, here an eye, there an ear; I might give him your job or your children. I can never see the point of using a whole real person, everything you write is distorted by your knowledge of how that person would behave. That's fatal to speculation. He might influence your plot, but the plot could never influence him.'

'And what about his mind, this character?'

'That's mine, every time, however disguised. But already the ideas I've had diverge very widely from the way you actually have reacted. There are so many possibilities; only the original event remains constant. I work through four drafts, always, but they develop from the known constant.'

'What known constant.'

'The one certain fact from which all else proceeds. In my hypothetical version of *Acid Test* it would be the last meeting you had with Gerald; sorry, the last meeting that Michael had with Gerald. In fact the concept is irrelevant to *Acid Test* because it isn't fiction, but if it were, and I were writing it, that's what it would be. If I did write a book about a man who had a book written about him, the known constant would be the day you walked in here with the book and told me you were in it – or perhaps it would be the paired facts of your appearing on telly and Margaret seeing you. I don't think so, though. That's coincidence.'

'But it happened. People who appear on telly do get seen, that's what they appear on telly for. Is that coincidence?'

'Literally, yes. What convinces in real life doesn't necessarily convince in print; coincidence can be the death of convincing fiction. Mind you, by the time I've got to the end of the third draft the known constant may have changed.'

'As a result of your speculations?'

'Yes.'

'Then it isn't constant. It can't be called certain fact.'

'In fiction it can be. We're talking now about the finished article; what is read. In the making it is as fluid as real life.

54

The place where I begin isn't necessarily the place the story begins.'

'Ah,' McEvoy says, feeling very profound. 'Retrospective fact.'

'If you like,' Geneva says, mentally filing the notion for future consideration in case it should turn out to mean something.

'There *are* no known constants in real life. That is, none of us shares the same perception of anything. You leave the reader out of your calculations, you all do. Do you think readers don't speculate? We even do it to poems. Look at what we do to poetry in schools. There's this artefact, finished, enclosed, the author's seal stamped on it. What do we do? Poke it open. There is no authority in print.'

'Then,' says Geneva, 'you can take heart from the thought that perhaps many of the people who read *Acid Test* may like Michael very much.'

'No one could like that condescending sod. I wasn't like that, Geneva. Truly, I was never like that. *It isn't true.*'

'You are distinctly over the limit,' Geneva says, looking at him hard. 'My fault. How on earth am I to get you home?'

'Drive me?'

'Sarah will love that, won't she? And you'll need your car in the morning.'

'Take my car.'

'And how do I get back.'

'I know, I'll drive yours and you drive mine.'

She sees that he means it. 'Stay here. I'll ring her. She does know you're here, doesn't she?'

'Yes, and she's expecting me back by seven. I've got minus nine minutes. Are you going to tell her a story?'

'Shut up.' Geneva dials and speaks. Her voice changes subtly. 'Sarah? Oh Sarah, this is Geneva . . . no, he's not here at the moment. Look, I'm sorry, I've got into a bit of a mess and your love of a husband's helping me out. I had a visit from an admirer – a *fan*, Sarah, not a lover – ' That is *echt* Geneva, McEvoy thinks, dozily, ' – and he turned out to be a wild man. Drank all my gin and wouldn't go away. In the end John offered to drive him home – yes. St Albans. I know, a hell of a way. Well, no, he can't. He didn't have enough petrol, so he took my Datsun. He'll have to come back here . . . do you mind if I give him supper? It's the least I can do. I feel dreadful about it – he was worn out when he arrived – at twenty-five past six, Sarah – but I dared not trust myself to that lunatic. Sweet of you. Lovely.'

'You lying old trout,' McEvoy says, admiringly. 'Come here, Ginny. Let me kiss you properly.'

'Certainly not,' Geneva snaps. 'I strongly disapprove of this kind of thing. Why do you think you're driving this maniac back to St Albans?'

'You mean he tried to – '

'Yes. You arrived just as things were getting desperate. His name's Keith Allard, by the way, graduate student, 27 Reaumur Close. He's writing a thesis on me.'

'He exists?'

'After a fashion. He's married with three children and drinks sparingly. How come you got into this state in half an hour?'

'There was wine and cheese at the meeting. I didn't have any cheese. I didn't have any lunch, either.' The pathos of his condition threatens to overwhelm him. He rubs his eyes.

'Well, thank God for Keith Allard. If Sarah wants to check on the details she can look in the phone book. She wouldn't go so far as to ring him up, would she?'

McEvoy, stricken with misery at Geneva's acumen, turns his head to hide his face in the stump-work cushion. He cannot bring himself to explain that her predictions are probably dead accurate. Matching her lightness of tone with great effort he says, 'She might.'

'They're all in Canada visiting his brother-in-law for three weeks. Don't worry, John, I really will give you supper. You needn't tell too many tarradiddles.'

'Why do you bother with four drafts?' McEvoy asks the cushion. 'You can do it *ex tempore*.'

'I've used that one before – anyway it was a lie, not fiction.'

'What's the difference?'

He is sulking, not requesting an exposition, but being Geneva, she expounds. 'Oh, come now, what about the suspension of disbelief? When you read fiction you want to believe it, even if you know it's codswallop. The writer expects your connivance – it's part of the agreement. The lie excludes your participation. You're the victim, the fall guy, not the accomplice.'

'Sarah's the victim.'

'Serves her right,' Geneva says. 'She always thinks you're lying; this time she'll be right.' McEvoy presses his forehead against her crocheted sweater, overlaying with impressions of pineapple stitch the indentations made by the stump work on his skin. Geneva, believing along with Francis Bacon that a mixture of a lie doth ever add pleasure, has no idea of what she has let him in for. There will be no pleasure in it for him when he reaches home and finds her frivolous soufflé collapsed and solidified into scum.

'Oh Ginny, I wish I were in love with you,' he says later, holding her hand across the table and eating spaghetti Bolognese with a fork only. It is after nine. The spaghetti slithers with reptilian persistence through the tines and back on to the plate.

'You'd better sober up,' Geneva says. 'I'll have to send you home, soon.'

'I am sober. This is just post-prandial tristesse.'

'You've hardly eaten anything. The pasta was supposed to soak up the booze. I'll make coffee. Let go, John.'

There are squawks and footsteps in the street below. Geneva pulls the curtain aside. 'The girls are back.'

'Oh fuck,' McEvoy says, but under his breath, prudently. Sober or not, he has a fearful headache and fond though he is of Jane and Mary he hopes that Geneva is mistaken, but no. The front door slams and footsteps come walloping up the carpeted stairs.

'What ho, chaps!' The kitchen door crashes open.

'You're back early,' Geneva says. 'Coffee? Was it a wash-out?'

'A washout? It was a white-out, oh, Dragsville, man. Oh Momma, the wimps and the flids. Peel me a grape.'

'Belt up, serf,' Jane rebukes her sister, sternly. 'John's still here.'

Jane, he reflects, is as sharp in her way as her mother,

having deduced instantly that were all well he would have gone home long ago.

'I've got a bit of a headache,' he says, gratefully.

'You look rough. Go in the living-room, you two. We'll do the coffee.'

Jane takes charge, shoos them out. Mary is dancing again but McEvoy suspects that once the door is closed she will drop the soubrette act and ask questions to which Jane will have no answers, he hopes. He sits on one end of the sofa, Geneva at the other.

'You shouldn't have done it,' he says. 'I've always told Sarah everything – '

'*Everything*?'

'That is, I've always taken care to do only things I could tell her about.'

'Sure, but you haven't cracked up tonight because I spun her a yarn? I know you'll have to back it up, but really, such a small thing?'

'It's one small thing after another. I can't tell her the truth about why I stayed here because I didn't tell her about the book – or the letter.'

'I know you said you hadn't – '

'I still haven't. Tonight's nothing, you made up a tale, it's quite funny, but the book; that's different.'

'I see, *suggestio falsi* is all right but not *suppressio veri*?'

'Oh Ginny, not now. Not Latin.'

'Is it worse to suppress the truth than to actively tell a falsehood? You can deceive far more effectively by allowing people to deceive themselves, simply by withholding facts. If you aren't even asked for the facts you can hardly be said to be lying at all.'

'False sophist. What the eye doesn't see, you mean?'

'*Suppressio veri* is more elegant.'

'Why didn't you just tell her I was drunk?'

'Sarah doesn't really believe that you lie to her, does she, she merely assumes that you would if you had to. The real truth is that you don't have to, but she won't believe it. I don't know . . . why didn't I just tell her you were drunk?'

'Association of ideas; drunken and licentious.' Whether or

not this is a joke depends on Geneva's reception of it. She laughs: it is a joke.

Right on cue in comes Jane with the coffee. Lightminded Mary is confined to the kitchen by her sober sister until the all-clear sounds.

'May we join you?'

'Not if you're going to talk Jive.'

'We're tame now, Mam. Try us.'

'I see you've put four cups on the tray.'

'There's a limit even to my tact,' says Jane and retires to fetch Mary.

'She's going to be just like you,' McEvoy says. 'She's lovely.'

'I'm not so sure. I wasn't like her when I was sixteen.'

'A different path to the same goal?'

They sit formally round the coffee table, passing milk, sugar, spoons.

'Have you broken up, yet?' Mary asks. (This is small talk, Mary.)

'Friday. The same as you, surely.'

'You've got your NATE conference next week, haven't you?' Geneva asks.

'What's NATE?'

'National Association of Teachers of English. We have an annual conference, at Easter. It's in Durham this year.'

'Don't you see enough of each other during termtime?' Jane says.

'We scarcely see each other at all; all we see is kids. I was going to go up with Simon Headley, share the driving and the petrol. Now he's gone sick.'

'Go by train. Ruth would,' Jane says.

'I hadn't thought of that.' He cannot remember when he was last on a train, discounting the Metropolitan Line.

'It's a pity Ruth isn't here,' Mary says. 'She'd have worked out your timetable for you. You haven't seen Ruth doing a timetable, have you? It's like a guru chanting a mantra. Her eyes go all glazed and inward-looking.'

'As opposed to being all glazed and outward-looking,' Jane says. 'You know what the trouble is – she hasn't got any cheekbones. She doesn't look like a Russian, does she, Mum?'

'Is she Russian?' McEvoy says. She does not look like a Russian, he thinks, although those features suggest a definitive representative of some particular racial type or, more accurately, a species.

'I think her grandfather was Polish or Czech, which is why she pronounces it Pro*ch*ak,' Geneva says, gargling the aspirate exotically.

'I thought she was just being awkward,' Mary grumbles, 'like Cholmondely or Marjoribanks.'

'Can you pronounce this?' Jane writes *Woolfardisworthy* on the back of her hand with a ballpoint pen.

'Woolsery, peasant, nyah nyah!'

'I'd better be going,' McEvoy says.

'You know that story about the night nurse?' Mary says. 'The sister comes up to her and says, "By the way, nurse, I think I ought to warn you, the patient in bed eleven has got the word ludo tattooed on his willie," and the nurse says, "Oh no, sister. That says Llandudno."'

Mary can scarcely pronounce the last word before she is rolling on the floor, screaming with laughter.

'She has no sense of occasion,' says grave Jane and falls on top of her sister, as Geneva shows McEvoy to the door.

'You know what I long for?' she says. 'The day when they can keep a conversation going for more than fifteen seconds.'

McEvoy puts his arms round her. 'Push me down the steps and slam the door,' he whispers. 'I can't bear to go.'

'What's the last thing that goes through a bee's mind when it hits the windscreen? ITS BUM!'

'You're that enchanted by two dirty-minded schoolgirls?'

'You're all so happy together.'

She kisses him dismissively on the mouth, which is more chaste than not kissing him at all, and pushes him gently.

'Go home to your sons.'

'Well, she made a mistake, that's all. The girls went out at twenty-five past – I got there at ten past. The meeting finished early.'

If only she would nag he could defend himself, he could snarl, he could shout *Mind your own bloody business!* but she has perfected her method of questioning; it is not Third

Degree it is nth Degree. It is sublime. By couching every query in a friendly, conversational tone she leaves him defenceless, and she has a seventh honest serving man; Which.

'What was his name again?'

'Allard. Keith Allard.'

'And you had to drive him all the way back?'

'To St Albans, yes.'

'Which street did he live in?'

'Reaumur Close.'

'I don't think I know it.' (Why should you know it? When were you last in St Albans?) 'What was it like?'

'Reaumur Close?'

'His house.'

'I didn't see his house. He asked me to drop him off.' (This is what Geneva failed to take into account; that her lie was only the beginning, the known constant. He is on his own, now.)

'Before you got there? Where?'

'A pub – as if he wasn't pissed enough already.'

'Which?'

'I didn't notice.'

'Didn't it have a sign up?' Her face is beside him on the pillow, her mouth against his hair, her tongue busy in his ear.

'Yes, a sign . . . but no picture. I think it was a brewer's sign – you know, a temporary job.'

'Which brewer?'

Oh sweet Jesus, oh Sarah, Sarah, oh Sarah . . . 'I dunno. It was red. Watney's?'

All the while she is rhythmically squeezing his penis as if she would pump the answers out. The other hand draws trembling parentheses round his nipples, his navel. He grinds his teeth.

'I don't think Geneva should have made you do it. Couldn't the girls help? I wouldn't want to be the man who tried anything with those two looking on.'

Eh? Oh, a flash-back. 'They'd gone to a disco.'

'But you said they went out at twenty-five past six.'

'Yes, well, they were getting ready. They weren't *around*.'

'But you said they were there when you came home.'

'They got back early. I think they found it a bit dull.'

'Where did they go?'

'To a disco, I said.'

'Which one?'

'I don't know which one.'

'A disco at half past six?'

'They were eating out, first.'

Now her palm cradles his balls like a cook weighing eggs by hand; before cracking them. 'I think Geneva takes you for granted.' She is *forgiving* him. 'Where was he studying?'

'*Who?*'

'This Allard person. You said he was a student. Where at?'

It was never this bad before. You've won, Sarah, you've won. I swear, I'll never lie to you again. You'll have to go back to deceiving yourself.

'Did you get your book?'

'What?' Book . . . how can she know?

'*At Swim-Two-Birds.*'

'Oh yes. Yes, I did. It's on the sideboard.' It is, too.

Christopher McEvoy. C. McEvoy. C. W. McEvoy. Chris McEvoy. He is at the stage of writing his name on everything (round the masthead of the *Guardian* this morning) as if to convince himself of his own reality. Attempting to develop a signature he has devised a loopy colophon that looks as if it would unravel if you tugged the final pot hook. He is chiefly charmed by the capital letter in the middle of his surname, a singularity that sets him apart from his friends who if not mere Smiths and Joneses are nevertheless confined to the lower case throughout. McEvoy, watching his bent head, longs to fondle the tender curls on the nape of his neck, but stays his hand. Christopher would be affronted by such an *outré* advance over the breakfast table. He still loves to be cuddled, but only at bedtime. Julian has not yet learned to fear fortune and men's eyes, he sits on his father's lap and pushes his head against McEvoy's chin, like an ingratiating cat, paddling his chest with sticky paws.

I can never leave them, McEvoy thinks.

'Go and get washed,' he says. 'Chris, stop writing on your plate.'

'It's a felt-tip pen,' Chris explains, patiently. 'It's solvent.'

'Soluble. You'll be late for school. Go on, put it in the sink – no, not the pen.'

Sarah is making a shopping list, characteristically stuttered with question marks. It is Friday, and John promised Sarah that she should have the car so that she could visit Waitrose and do the holiday shopping early, forgetting that it would be the last day of term and he will have a load of work and books to bring home from school. They will all have to go tomorrow, instead. Routine has been further disrupted by John's imminent departure for Durham on Monday.

'How can anyone *plan*?' Sarah demands, hand to forehead, in despair.

'Well, take the car,' McEvoy says. 'It's not that inconvenient. I'll get home by myself.'

'You'll have too much to carry. If I have to I can shop with the boys next week.'

'Take the car. I'll drive back tomorrow and pick up my stuff.'

Having wound herself up to suffer, Sarah now has to unwind. The children simply look relieved, they hate going round Waitrose; in fact, there is not the slightest reason why they should all have to go shopping because the day has been changed. It is no one's idea of a recreational way to spend Saturday morning, simply an unrepealed custom from the time when Sarah and John went everywhere together for the pleasure of it, or the novelty, and would not allow even a little baby to keep them apart; the time when they rented the top floor of 114 Bedford Road, with Geneva and Eddy Stevens and their two little girls in the garden flat. Could not Sarah trust him alone on a Saturday morning even then, he wonders now; alone, that is, with Geneva whose husband worked on Saturdays and any permutation of the four nurses from the middle flat who might or might not have been sleeping off their night duty.

Llandudno!

So Geneva puts her characters together as Frankenstein did? She says she would not use him whole, but how much of him has she used already? When he first knew her she was writing her celebrated novel *Harold in Islington*. How much did newly married John McEvoy contribute to newly married Harold Clandon? But no, the book was two-thirds finished when they met. Harold was already married, thirty-two and self-destructively honest long before the McEvoys moved into 114 Bedford Road. But yes! What was Harold's known constant, his marital status? his age? his honesty? In fiction the known constant can be changed. The Harold that Geneva began with may not be the Harold of the finished novel. McEvoy would like a look at the first draft of *Harold in Islington*; what has she had of him? However many additions there may be, someone has to furnish the basic armature, the essential form that withstands all the subsequent cutting and moulding. Or do one's personal experiences only inform the author's understanding of the fictional character's responses? Is it better to be part of Harold or the whole of Michael? Is Harold the whole truth and Michael nothing but the truth?

'You know,' Sarah says, looking up, 'there's plenty of petrol in the car.'

'There wouldn't have been,' he says cleverly, 'if I'd driven it to St Albans.'

Jane reads:

It was my twentieth birthday. A glowing summer morning that threw dancing shadows of young leaves on the wall of my room over the clean patch of distemper where the bloodstains had been washed away. I looked into my diary. It was now exactly two months since I had last seen the Smile. Outside a bird was singing somewhere. It seemed that nothing could go wrong on this day of all days. How could I know, at that stage, that this euphoria would come regularly to presage disaster? I took my shower in the bathroom, as carefree as the bird in the branches of the cherry tree outside my window. At breakfast Brian and David sat beside me and gave me their gifts, small cheap things, but how could they be anything else? Even these little presents, toilet water from David, twenty of my favourite Gauloises from Brian, must have represented weeks of careful saving.

Jane, planning an academic career, makes a marginal note: *Sob sob.*

Michael had arranged to pick us up at ten thirty. Once we used to wait for him on the steps of the main block but one day Brian pointed out how we must look to him, gathered together like a group of anxious orphans, afraid that no one would remember us.

'Michael can't do anyone a favour,' Brian explained to me, 'unless he feels that people will suffer if he doesn't do it. He's so tremendously insecure, and we all have to overreact to compensate for his inadequacy. Haven't you noticed how he waits to be thanked if he gives you something?'

Who wouldn't? writes Jane.

I had no idea whether he would give me a birthday present but I knew that if he did I must make an effort to seem extra grateful, even if it meant running the risk of making David jealous. David, in spite of his illness, was generous enough to understand. Michael, ostensibly sane, had to be humoured.

We saw his smart little car roaring up the drive, from the window of the common room. 'He's slowing down,' said David, as it passed the main entrance. 'I bet he's wondering why we're not all out there jumping up and down with excitement.'

Deliberately we sat down again with our backs to the door. It was several minutes before we heard footsteps in the corridor and by that time we could hardly keep from laughing out loud. When the door opened we had to screen Brian, who was almost choking with mirth. Michael made his usual entrance, and we all applauded to let him know how we appreciated his effort. Then we saw that he had someone with him, a girl with long pale hair and dark eyes strikingly outlined in mascara. She wore a short black dress, outrageously short it seemed to us — the mini skirt had not yet made its appearance — but it seemed perfect on her slender, long-legged figure.

'This is Katherine,' said Michael. 'I'm afraid it'll be a bit of a squash in the back but she did want to come and meet you all. We're going to Bath.'

'All of us,' asked David.

'No, just us,' said Michael and gave the girl a possessive squeeze. He looked unbelievably pleased with himself. In the satisfaction of this latest conquest he had forgotten my birthday.

At that moment I hated Katherine. I couldn't guess what an important part she was to play in my slow journey back to the real world.

'What have you got there?' Geneva asks, stepping round her daughter to reach the sink.

'I found it on the sideboard,' Jane says. 'What are you doing with it?'

'I was sent it for reviewing,' Geneva ad libs, as she sees what it is. 'Who said you could write on it?'

'Well, it won't lower its market value, will it?' Jane says. 'Oh Mum, it just asks to be written on.'

'What do you make of it?'

'It's got fifty villains and one heroine,' Jane says, 'so far. Every man's hand is against her but I think the good fairy's just turned up.'

'Margaret?'

'No. Who's Margaret? She's called Katherine.'

'That's right, Katherine. What do you think of her?'

'She's only just walked into the room. Michael is drooling over her.'

'Ah. And what do you think of Michael?'

'Sorry for him, mainly,' Jane says. 'He's just off to Bath with his girl friend and they expect him to take them all along too. He keeps bringing them ciggies and buying them drinks and taking them out and you can see he's feeling guilty as hell because he can't really *do* anything, and they all behave like he'd had them committed in the first place. You'd think she'd see that, I mean, she's supposed to be cured now.'

'My sentiments entirely,' Geneva says. 'Does he remind you of anyone?'

'Michael? Yes, there's this kid at school, his little sister's a mong – she's got Down's Syndrome and she's at a special school. He feels guilty about her and there's no reason to. It's nothing to do with him – I mean, it's not his fault.'

'I'm glad you make that distinction,' Geneva says. 'Little Miss Hill's very good at apportioning blame, don't you think?'

'Do you know her?'

'Good God, no.'

'I just wondered why it had been sent to you. It's not the sort of thing you usually write up. Are you going to review it?'

'No need. The Christian press will warmly recommend it as an ennobling example of something or other – it's all in the blurb. It's not going to win the Booker.'

'I didn't mean that. I thought you might say it was a load of old rope.'

'With my limited column inches I usually leave out the real rubbish, unless it's by someone with an undeserved reputation.'

'I like what you said about that one on last year's short list,' Jane says. 'Noble rot.'

'I only managed to get that in because it was about a wine grower,' Geneva admits, 'and I knew if I didn't the sub would.'

McEvoy reads:

Harold Clandon, a little over six feet tall, walked in crowds with his head up and his eyes cast down. Everything worth looking at seemed to be at least six inches shorter than he was but he had discovered that if he proceeded thus many of the sleek bobbing heads on a level with his shoulder tilted slyly as if to investigate the direction of his glance. It was in the cause of soliciting a reciprocal oeillade *from a tawny blonde that he walked into a traffic light.*

Certainly they are the same height. McEvoy closes the paperback copy of *Harold in Islington* and replaces it on the shelf. Unable to find his own signed copy at home he has dropped into the bookshop on the way back from school, to sneak a look at one of theirs. It is always in print. His fears unallayed he turns from the fiction to the poetry collection. It is all displayed on one shelf but the volumes are slim except for the occasional collected works in hardback. There is really quite a lot on offer, in a limited kind of way.

He is struck by the obliquity of many of the titles, alienating epigrams, conveying a sense of apartness, of some other where, places not acknowledged to exist, or acknowledged not to exist: *Time's Oriel, From the House Opposite, The Room Outside, Secret Narratives, From an Unexposed Film.*

This last is by Ruth Prochak, the only volume of hers in stock, he discovers, when he inquires at the cash desk.

'*Midland City*'ll be out in a couple of weeks,' says the proprietor. 'We could reserve it for you.'

'I'll read this one first,' McEvoy says, suddenly parsimonious. He rarely purchases poetry books and he has just noticed that for the price of Prochak's slender collection he could have

the entire output of Edgar Allen Poe, in the Penguin edition.
   Then he leaves, round shouldered, head down, eyes peering furtively; not at all like Harold Clandon.

5

After Easter Julian will go to the infant school and Sarah will look for work. Already she has placed advertisements in the newsagent's window, the glass case outside the Post Office and in the local paper, offering secretarial assistance. These two weeks of the Easter holiday will mark the end of her identity as a full-time mother and almost gloomily she steers the Hoover into John's study, followed by Julian, embarking on his last fortnight as a full-time baby, who carries the spray polish and a duster.

'You help Mummy by polishing the door,' Sarah suggests cannily, choosing the one item that he cannot damage. Julian removes the plastic cap, depresses the button and zaps a spider. A Bren gun rattles in his soft pink throat.

The study is also the spare bedroom. When Sarah begins earning they will build an extension, John will move into it and Julian will take over this room. At present Julian shares with Chris and gentle bookish Christopher, not surprisingly, wants him out. To confirm its status as a study the room is furnished not only with a bed, but also a desk and a filing cabinet. Sarah flicks the desk with a feather duster before Julian can make depredations with his aerosol, flirting it round the plinths of books and the paper tray where the cat is sleeping. The filing cabinet she wipes with a damp cloth. Sarah presses her palm against the uppermost drawer. Behind her Julian, who is savage but not sadistic, has put the spider out of its misery – he had thought it would die at once like a mown-down soldier – and is strenuously scrubbing at the painted panel with his duster.

Sarah slips her fingers under the handle of the drawer and tugs discreetly. By half an inch the drawer slides out and then back again as she relaxes; he has not locked it. If John locked the cabinet she would know that he had something to hide, but he leaves it unlocked. Because he trusts her by leaving it unlocked she must not open it. If she trusted him she would not even try to see if it were locked, but if he had something to conceal he would still leave the cabinet unlocked because, if it were locked, she would know that he had something to conceal. He knows she will not look inside because she trusts him, does she not? And she would never seek to find whether he has locked it or not because, after all, does not he trust her?

Oh. Oh. The cruel hooks of the paradox tear her so sharp she cries out and smites the grey face of the cabinet with the flat of her hand.

Julian looks round.

'Mummy slipped.'

When Julian enters the reception class and discovers that Miss Cleeve does not refer to herself in the third person he will begin to wonder, as Chris did before him, if his mother, grandmothers, aunties, are quite right in the head, but meanwhile only Daddy, boastfully declaring I, Me, Mine, is out of step. He does wonder, though, why she lied, for he saw her smack the filing cabinet quite distinctly. It is just the substitute he himself would choose if he wanted to hit his father.

It is three weeks now since Mrs Anderson, née Hardwicke, posted her little letter bomb. By now, McEvoy thinks, looking at the telephone extension where it hangs on the wall above his desk, she will be expecting him to ring her, the more so because he did not reply to the letter. Or *does* she expect him to ring? *Did* she anticipate a thank-you note? Is it not possible that, secure in the certainty of the damage she has inflicted, she is simply basking in that certainty. But then, again, if he really is as deplorable as they all seemed to think, will not his impregnable self-regard have protected him? For all née Hardwicke knows he chucked the whole boiling into the waste-paper basket, letter, poem, book, chucked them in unread. Perhaps the thing was not delivered; went astray in the post.

Quite so; he never received it. Only himself and Geneva know of the harm done to the foundations; the superstructure is intact. But up in Chester sits Katherine, née Margaret, at the centre of her web, with mad Caroline and God knows how many others who have been caught in the toils. If he does not make contact with her she may attempt to get in touch with him, she may write again, she may ring.

She does not know his number; she does not even know his address; but she could find out: couldn't she? And she could ring here, while he is at school, and Sarah will answer.

In front of him, on the desk, twin dials, clock and barometer, set in a block of Vesuvian pumice and brought home from holiday by his mother, fix him with a bulbous gaze. The horrible thing is up here because it accords poorly with the living-room decor. He is reminded of Ruth Prochak's lugubrious eyeballs and reaches for his timetable; trouble again, here.

Simon Headley would have made an acceptable chaperon and his illness has afflicted Sarah out of all proportion to the ailment. McEvoy saw bright panic in her eyes when he announced that he would be travelling north alone, in a train. She has not mentioned this since, has not, that is, mentioned it directly, but in all her conversations he has detected a leitmotiv of concern for his impending solitude. He will be alone (unsupervised) in Durham (whoredom of the northeast) without Simon's company (steadying influence). Sarah's opinion of Simon's steadiness derives mainly from the fact that she has met him only in school or at a function. Simon out of bounds is unknown to her.

Personally, McEvoy likes Simon very much, he is a good colleague, but having seen him in action he can understand why people are afraid of spiders. Simon is slight, crisp, brittle and unpredictable; he scuttles laterally toward women twice his size and usually half his age; at courses and conferences he selects instantly the juiciest, freshest virgin, crunch crunch, a suspicion of mandibles. If the course is residential he wraps her up and takes her away and next morning she presents a bewildered and slightly dehydrated appearance. Oh Sarah, Big John will be *much* safer without Little Simon to inveigle him into Simony. But Sarah will never believe this for Simon is small and initially unprepossessing. McEvoy is neither; he knows it, as Caroline Hill did not fail to point out. On the other hand he knows, as it were, passively; he does nothing about it. With his looks and Simon's minimal scruples he could be really prolific, and he has more than once entertained the unworthy thought that Simon uses him as bait. He suddenly envisions Simon leaping upon Ruth Prochak and biting her eyeballs, and having seen this cannot dismiss the image. He intends to read her poems on the train.

Last night he looked at *Acid Test* again, regretting the yellow insistence of the Stabiloboss. He is all over it, he can see himself coming, smug, confident, unprincipled, picking up girls and putting them down again as casually as, casually as, casually as Simon. Geneva said to him, comfortingly, that because the portrait purported to be a facsimile there could be no likeness in it, but if he were sure of that, would he mind so much? And now, thanks to Geneva, he sees himself coming with his head back and his eyes cast down, soliciting *oeillades* and colliding with traffic lights. But he still cannot remember much about Katherine, née Margaret in her black dress and mascara, giving herself to him in Bath. He cannot even remember what she looked like. Long hair, long legs, black and white . . . *everyone* looked like that. He ought at least to remember her legs. And he cannot believe that he ever said, 'It's been a lot of fun, hasn't it?' He doesn't say that kind of thing, never has done. Even Harold Clandon doesn't say things like that.

Sarah, beside him in the driving seat, would believe it, wouldn't you, Sarah? Sarah is only too ready to believe that she, like all the rest, was as casually picked up and differed from them only in the fact that she had refused to be put down. Ah no, he thinks, the difference is that the others were too proud to refuse.

'Why me, John?' she had asked, in the beginning, mentally comparing herself with the other hypothetical lovelies that he had putatively discarded in her favour, unable to credit her good fortune. He had seen only the astonishment, then, and in his kindly efforts to convince her that the astonishment was unjustified he busily digged a pit and fell into the midst of it himself. Then he saw the fear.

The fear is very evident today. She can just about drag herself down to Sevenoaks without him but the prospect of his leaving *her*, to go north, alone, without Simon, has revived her terrors, as if his every departure were a rehearsal for the final, inevitable defection, the day when he does not come back. She dislikes going anywhere without him but the discovery last weekend that the car was due for its MOT test and needed prior attention was no more than an act of God, none of his engineering, (unless she imagines him underneath it one night, sawing at the brake cables) he won't escape another time. Now, to convey him to King's Cross she faces the A5 in rush hour on a Monday morning, brushing aside his original plan to take the Metropolitan Line to Baker Street and complete the journey on the Underground. Instead all four of them crawl miserably down the Euston Road toward the surrogate spires of St Pancras. Chris sulks, Julian grizzles. She has promised them museums. They do not want museums.

'You'll be half an hour early,' Sarah frets, as they reach King's Cross. Oh, Jesus Christ, what does she expect him to get up to in half an hour?

'I've got to get my ticket – and there's bound to be a queue.'

'Where can I park?'

'Don't bother about that. Just pull in and I'll get out.'

'But we want to see you off.'

'That'll mean platform tickets.' (You want to see if I'm sitting near a woman.) 'No, really, don't bother.' Outside, the pavements are teeming with purposeful travellers; in a second he can be lost among them. He kisses Sarah, kisses his sons, leaps out of the door, opens the hatch to collect his bag and briefcase and sprints round to the driver's window where she sits aghast, stunned.

'You can't wait here.'

'I can find a parking place.'

'Don't try. I'll ring this evening. I'll see you Thursday – sometime after six.' He stoops to kiss her again.

'If I can find a place we'll come on to the platform.'

'Don't bother. Please. Look, you *must* move on –'

He does not stop to see if she takes his advice, he hefts his luggage and hurries toward the automatic doors of the entrance without looking back.

He is not used to railway stations. Now that he is among them the passengers seem less purposeful, they meander and eddy in mindless surges, encumbered with suitcases and backpacks. The commuters, impeded by tourists and provincials, butt and shoulder their way through the standing battalions fixating on the louvred destination boards that click and riffle overhead. McEvoy makes for the ticket office and joins a queue of foreigners unfamiliar not only with the layout, as he is, but with the currency, language and procedure; also with timetables. It is twenty past nine before he gains his platform; if there ever was a queue here it is now on the train. Out of the tail of his eye he glimpses Sarah and the boys, across the concourse, staring about them in confusion. They see him. He does not see them; he runs.

It did not occur to him to reserve a seat. He travels the length of the train before he finds a vacant place and falls into it as they begin to move, so he can disguise his heaving efforts to breathe as the result of almost missing the bugger, ha-ha, but he has to hide behind the *Guardian* to screen the tears of rage and frustration. He always leaves Sarah with a sense of relief, never before with such a sense of escape. He could have cursed aloud to see her drag her suffering into the maelstrom of the concourse. How restful it would be now to lay his head again on Geneva's *belle poitrine*, and whisper his despair always remembering, though, that Geneva still sees the funny side of it. He has only himself to thank for that, having conscientiously omitted to show her the other side, out of loyalty to Sarah, who in return trusts neither of them.

Geneva is not here. He must make do with the Second Class upholstery, apparently cobbled up out of old tablecloths; still, thinking of Geneva is restful; she is his friend, and he imagines that what he feels for her is love, in which case she is the only woman he does love; what a threadbare consolation that seems to be.

'I took your name in vain, last week,' Geneva confides to Keith Allard, behind the reredos in St Albans Abbey. 'Should you ever meet a Mrs Sarah McEvoy I had better warn you that she believes you to be a licentious lush.'

'Which you told her, I suppose,' murmurs the besotted Allard, into Geneva's hair.

'Only to get her husband out of a hole. She'd have wanted to know where he was so I told her he was driving an importunate and incapable postgraduate thesis writer back to St Albans. Yours was the first name that came to mind. It was a desperate case; he needed an alibi.'

'What was he really doing?'

'Dining at my flat being too stewed to drive himself home. Don't do that here, Keith. I had to convince her that you had made such demonstrative overtures that John's intervention was nothing more than straight-from-the-shoulder gallantry.'

'He wasn't making demonstrative overtures of his own, was he?'

'Not at all, we've been friends for years. He's a most upright man; you should be happy to have yourself defamed on his behalf.'

'I'm delirious, Ginny. Why was he stewed?'

'He was miserable. Talking of being defamed, that was why, come to think of it. He'd just discovered that someone he knew years ago has used him in a book.'

'Actionable?'

'Not for someone on John's income. In any case, he'd never admit to being the character he's supposed to be, even if he were.'

'I thought you said he was.'

'Supposed to be. It isn't fiction.'

'Is it meant to be fiction?'

'How very acute,' Geneva says, approvingly. 'It's untruthful, but not intentionally so, and it isn't a lie. Poor John can't tell the difference.'

'Nothing but the truth, but not the whole truth? I'll let you be in my lie if I can be in yours.'

'I thought it was the same lie,' Geneva sighs. 'What did you tell Brenda, this morning?'

'British Library. I said I'd walk to the station through the Abbey grounds. Our meeting is just a coincidence.'

'Lies thrive on coincidence – unlike fiction. I never touch it.'

'Sweetheart, do stop talking shop,' Keith begs. Fingers entwined they saunter down the nave, Geneva leaning warmly against her much taller, much younger lover. Jane and Mary would not approve and nor, very probably, would John, who has quaint conceptions of fidelity.

'Tell me about Quebec.'

Britain may be a small country, McEvoy decides, but it is a bloody big island. This fast train gives him access to a sense of space where the car makes him aware only of distance. After a demure surburban halt at Stevenage it pounds on through Huntingdon, Peterborough and Grantham, through implacably flat counties; Cambridgeshire, Bedfordshire, Lincolnshire, Nottinghamshire, before stopping at the apparently unjustifiable Newark. What is Newark? two rainswept streaks of concrete; why is it there?

At ten fifty-five the train slides on again. He thinks of Adlestrop; no one left and no one came. Why did they stop? He made his first trip to the buffet after Stevenage and bought coffee. Now he returns, walking disconcertingly back down the train toward London, and buys Scotch in three nice little bottles which he will take home for the children; Famous Grouse, deleting his prejudiced guess that it would be some kind of ersatz British Rail blend, faked under licence in Taiwan. Railways are expanding his knowledge. He would not have known that Newark was in Nottinghamshire (he had in fact imagined it to be in Scotland) had he not pored educationally over a map with Chris last night, tracing his route. Now he knows not only this, but that Doncaster, which they are rapidly approaching, is in South Yorkshire. Yorkshire is a miserable chewed-up apology for the big arrogant pink sprawl that once ate a great hole out of northern England, it no longer has Ridings, even. He remembers the economic nipping and tucking of county boundaries, the annexations and amputations, the utter annihilations, remembers it happening, but took little account of it at the time; now he feels an irrational resentment at this erosion of his childhood certainties; England is not as he thought it was. Someone has tiptoed in and changed the known constant while he was not looking. Wasn't Robin Hood alleged to have been Earl of Huntingdon? He should have passed through Huntingdonshire but it has been erased by bloody flat Cambs, the glum featureless fenland. For a moment he can see the mild-mannered, bespectacled Earl of Huntingdon stepping into a telephone booth to emerge in a swirl of green as Robin Hood, much as amenable, well-meaning John McEvoy stepped into Wren Ward and emerged as smirking promiscuous Michael.

He abandons the struggle to be objective; every time he stops thinking of anything specific, he begins to think about *Acid Test*.

'Ladies and Gentlemen, your attention please; we are now approaching Doncaster,' the guard announces over the intercom. 'Change here for Wakefield, Leeds, Harrogate and Hull.' Ah, McEvoy thinks; Doncaster in the rain.

They are halting by one of those red brick barns that serve as railway stations in the north. As the train glides to a standstill he looks out of the window and sees, directly opposite, Ruth Prochak standing on the platform. At first he assumes that he is mistaken, on the grounds of improbability; but she turns slightly – it is. Here are her very eyes, her nose, Prochak in jeans and a navy blue reefer, with a bag on her shoulder. She looks like a rating, home from sea. He waves, but she does not notice; why should she? She can be no more expecting to meet him than he was expecting to meet her and in any case, she is preoccupied, as he can tell. Many people are preparing to leave the train but many more are preparing to board it, and Prochak, like a stoat, is shifting, almost imperceptibly, her weight from one hip to the other, making ready to spring at the nearest door, making certain that she will be nearest to that door when the train stops. She will be level with the next carriage when it does stop, and leanly swaying she slides out of sight.

What an amazing thing, what a coincidence. The woman beside him is trying to leave and he has to rise and make way for her, thereby interrupting the traffic in the gangway. By the time he has extricated himself and sat down again, by the window now, there is no sign of her, but while he is peering the last of the descending passengers leaves the compartment and the oncomers pour in. One of the first, not surprisingly, is Prochak.

'Ruth!'

She is staring, terrifyingly, ahead, looking for a seat; at his call glances down with a puzzled frown, but evidently not one to look a gift horse in the mouth slings her luggage into the rack with one practised movement as she subsides into the seat opposite. Then she smiles.

'Bloody hell,' she says, 'you! I wondered who it was.'

He is momentarily deflated but, after all, they have really met only once and his features are considerably less memorable than hers. No wonder she failed to recognize him immediately.

'I'm sorry,' he says, unable to keep from smiling, perhaps because her own smile is so very emphatic. 'I didn't mean to startle you, I didn't stop to think. I was so surprised to see you.'

Why on earth, he is asking himself, surprised or not, was he so anxious to call her to him? Because, he replies, without any doubts, now he will have someone to talk to and he can stop thinking.

'Surprised?' Prochak says.

'But what a coincidence. I met you for the first time last week and now, here you are, catching the same train.'

'You're more likely to meet me on a train than anywhere else,' Prochak says, reasonably. 'I told you, I live on them. It's a sight less of a coincidence than meeting at Geneva's. I'd never been there before.'

'Yes, but on *this* train. I haven't been on a train in years.'

'OK, OK, it's a turn-up for the book.' Her smile broadens. Jane Stevens is right, she has no cheekbones, no cheekbones and practically no chin; it is the smoothest face he has ever seen, except for the eyes and that avalanching nose. 'I do have this fantasy about meeting people I know on Midland railway stations, but it's never happened before. I spend as much time on Midland railway stations as I do on the tracks.'

'Doing what?'

'Changing trains. I've just come from Hull.'

'And where are you going?'

'Middlesbrough. Would you believe, not fifty miles apart and there's no rail link. Of course, I could have gone to Scarborough but it would have meant a bus to Whitby. Sod that for a game of soldiers, I thought. I can't bear buses – anyhow, this is probably quicker. I'll have to change at Darlington. Where you?'

'Durham.' He glances at the table between them and sees what she has not yet noticed, her book lying face down on the Formica. The blurb asserts that Prochak is widely regarded as one of the foremost young exponents of the English language currently writing. He wonders, a little. 'I'm going to a conference.'

'Sooner you than me, Jack,' she says, then blinks apologetically. 'Sorry, I can't even remember your name.'

'Almost Jack,' he says. 'John. John McEvoy.'

'Do people call you Jack?'

'No.'

'Sorry again, John.'

He folds his arms on the table and leans toward her, smiling still. 'It doesn't matter,' he assures her, seeing by her look that he is pleasing her and realizes, with a sickening jolt to the memory, that he is being charming. She has unexpectedly small teeth. For some reason he has expected huge alabastine choppers.

'Would you like a drink?'

She consults her watch. 'Almost an hour. Yes please. Oh – ' she notices his miniature bottles. 'Don't go specially. I'll have a swig of yours.'

'I've only the one glass.'

'I'll drink out of the other side.'

He pours the two remaining bottles into the plastic beaker and hands it to her. 'Cheers,' he says, as she drinks.

'Good health,' Prochak answers, and passes it back. 'What's this conference, then? You're an English teacher, aren't you?'

'It's a conference of English teachers.'

'How very esoteric. What do you do at it?'

'A lot of listening, mainly – and I'm joining a writing commission.'

Prochak looks suspicious. 'Not poetry?'

'I don't know. I don't write it myself, but I have to teach it. Geneva said I should try it for once.'

'Geneva should have more sense. There's enough idiots trying to write without encouraging the ones who haven't even thought about it.'

'Don't you think I should try it, then, if I have to teach other people to do it?'

'Why teach other people? Anyway, you can't teach it; those who can, will; those who can't, won't. How many kids in a class of thirty-five do you think will end up as writers? yet you give them creative writing lessons. Do you have lessons in creative brain surgery, creative refuse collection?'

'But surely they'll appreciate other people's writing more if they discover how it's done?' he persists, pedantically.

'Leave them to do the discovering then. There's not much connection between reading and writing; more between reading and living day-to-day, I'd have thought. You don't know what's coming next.'

'But you feel curiosity about what's coming next, surely?'

'Uh *huh*. But you don't *know*. I kept a diary once, for a year,' Prochak remarks, pouring Famous Grouse down her throat, 'but I had to leave off in the end, it took up too much time. After a bit I realized how like a novel it was – but not like writing a novel, like reading one. There was a mad scramble to write up the day's events every night before the consequences set in. I had no idea of what would happen over the page, I didn't want to know. And still less did I want to write with hindsight. Memory's a great liar and a great editor.'

'And you wrote down everything that happened?'

'Not everything – '

'*Suppressio veri*?'

'*Omissio veri*, rather; just leaving out what seemed irrelevant.'

'Isn't that *suppressio veri*? The truth, but not the whole truth?'

'I don't think so. I was developing an instinct for what *would* be relevant, not excluding what was inconvenient. Quite the reverse of novel writing, according to Geneva.'

'I know what Geneva says about novel writing. It's all a matter of speculation proceeding from a known constant. Then you back-track and change the known constant. In the diary, I suppose, you had to stick to what was happening – to what you thought was happening. If you were honest, that is.'

'Oh, I was honest all right,' Prochak says. 'I didn't speculate, I wrote it all down straight, the truth. I'm glad I did, because already I remember it differently. It's a surprise to read it now. I wouldn't want anyone who got into that diary to read it,' she says.

'In case they felt themselves to be misrepresented?'

'You should know,' says Prochak, which riposte effectively derails the conversation. They stare at each other, discomforted.

'She *told* you?'

Definitely it is the absence of cheekbones; with nothing to stay them the eyes really do seem about to fall out; she is remorseful, but probably not as remorseful as she looks.

'How much did she tell you?'

'She didn't tell me very much,' Prochak explains; truthfully, he hopes, rather than tactfully. 'In fact, all she did was explain the circumstances – in an academic way.' He can just imagine that, from Geneva. 'After all, she didn't know we'd be meeting again, and she no doubt imagined that I'd have the sense to keep my mouth shut.'

'Definite failure of speculation.' He smiles slightly as he offers his olive branch and she accepts it gratefully.

'Well, you did say it was a coincidence. You know what Geneva thinks of coincidence, don't you? Fatal to convincing fiction.'

'You don't think she'd use us, then?'

'She might, but not as we are. We would be translated. She'd want her known constant, and it wouldn't be coincidence. Geneva belongs to the E. M. Forster school; sudden death; take your reader by surprise.'

'Isn't coincidence a surprise? It surprises me.'

'Not in a book – unless it's rationalized. Long tedious passages where the author reminds you that life's like that.'

'It was Forster who taught me to read properly,' he confesses. 'I used to be a terrible skipper till I read *The Longest Journey*, you know, the man who gets killed during a game of football. There was nothing to lead up to it and I was sure I'd missed something vital, some intimation of mortality, but it just said, "Gerald died that afternoon. He was broken up in the football match." I had to go back and read it all through again.'

'Yes, he does have this tendency to knock people off

suddenly,' Prochak says. 'Mrs May, Leonard Bast, Rickie gets his on a level crossing . . . Geneva does the same – on the grounds that life's like that, I suppose. Have you read *Harold in Islington*?'

Is he blushing? 'She was writing it when I first knew her. They'd just moved from Holloway Road.'

'Well, then, you remember the fight between Harold and the librarian in the booking hall at St Pancras – '

'"One of the great comic set-pieces of post-war fiction,"' McEvoy quotes dourly, from a respected critic. 'Like Jim Dixon setting fire to the bed.'

'Seminal, yeah. Well, it *is* funny, till the librarian falls under a Circle Line train on the way home. You feel a shit for having laughed.'

'You're meant to.'

'Oh yes, it's clever all right, but the whole thing stops being funny after that. Though I guess there is something ludicrous about falling under a train,' she muses. 'Dying under the banner of Huskisson.'

'Who's Huskisson?'

'The original wet blanket. He was Home Secretary in 1830, turned up to the inaugural run on the Manchester–Liverpool Railway and got cut in half by a locomotive coming the other way.' She laughs delightedly, less at the fate of Huskisson, McEvoy guesses, than in the hope that he has forgotten about Geneva's perfidy. She is no doubt congratulating herself on having successfully steered the conversation away from it.

'So how much *did* Geneva tell you?' he asks. The laugh snaps off, as if struck by a power failure.

'Oh, truly,' she says, 'nothing much. What could she tell me? I don't know you and I haven't read the book.'

'I wouldn't bother to,' he says, with some feeling. 'It's very bad. That was about all the comfort Geneva could offer, the fact that it's very badly written.'

'That's her ultimate no–no, isn't it? Bad writing.'

'And coincidence. I still can't get over meeting you like this.'

'Like *Doctor Zhivago*; the length and breadth of Russia to play around in and you've got the same dozen people falling over each other the whole time. You end up feeling the Soviet

Union's about the size of Birmingham. Why did you show it to her?'

'The book? In a sense, because I wanted her to say what she did say; that the character who was meant to be me wasn't me at all, but the way she said it wasn't all that consoling. She said that this character – '

'Is he called John, too?'

'No, Michael. She said that he couldn't be taken as a truthful portrait because there was no attempt made to account for his behaviour; plenty of premisses but no conclusions. Everything was presented as straight fact – like your diary. Perhaps she said that to you?'

'Something like.'

'What she didn't say was that he couldn't possibly be me because I'm not like that.'

'And aren't you like "that"?'

'*I* don't think so. That's why I showed her the thing, for reassurance.'

'You wouldn't get that from Geneva,' Prochak says.

'Ladies and gentlemen, your attention please; we shall shortly be arriving in York.'

At York there are more people waiting to board than there were at Doncaster. 'You'd think the Khmer Rouge were coming,' Prochak observes, looking out at the Gadarene rush alongside the train. 'There's another in twenty minutes.'

'Perhaps it doesn't go where they want to go?'

'Edinburgh; this one only goes to Newcastle. Maybe they all want to go to Durham like you, the next one doesn't stop there – oh, don't make excuses for them. They're just panicking.' She looks impartially with disdain upon the elderly, the infantile, the infirm, the merely confused.

'I'm coming back on Thursday,' McEvoy says. 'D'you think the train'll be this full then?'

'Sure to be. The whole country takes to the tracks before a Bank Holiday. What time are you travelling?'

'Conference ends at one thirty. I was going for the five to two.'

Prochak's face becomes completely blank; her eyes set. 'You'll have to change at Doncaster, pick up the fifteen twenty-two from Leeds which gets you in at seventeen twelve. Or there's the fourteen fifty-three. That's a through train but you won't reach London till eighteen o-two.'

'Do you travel this route often?'

Her expression revives. 'No, but I've got the timetable.'

'In your head?'

She pats a swelling in the pocket of her reefer. 'I'm coming back on Thursday too.'

'From Middlesbrough?'

'Newcastle, but I'm catching the twelve twelve.' Her face glows with anticipatory pleasure. 'The Flying Scotsman. It's non-stop to King's Cross.'

'May I look at your timetable? I've only got a little one.'

She hands it to him. It is a daunting thing, almost fifteen hundred minutely printed pages of India paper, thumbed, grimy, dog-eared and frayed between its mutilated covers.

'Almost time for a new one,' Prochak says, making excuses for it. 'That's as sure a sign of spring as the cuckoo, a new British Rail timetable.'

'You seem to use it a lot.'

'I travel a lot. Anyway, I like reading it.'

Defeated he puts it, as inaccessible as a log table, on the black Formica. A poet, surely, should be nurturing her faculties with Shakespeare and Virgil rather than a railway schedule. As she reaches out to pick it up she notices the other book, beside it.

'Hey, that's mine.'

Her look of pleasure is surely overstated.

'Did you buy it?'

'Yes; for money.'

'Oh, greater love hath no man, than this, that a man buyeth his friends in hardback.'

'It's not available in paperback.'

'Nor it is. Do you like it?'

He admits, 'I haven't read it, yet. I meant to read it on the train – '

'But I got on instead?'

Prochak opens the book and points. *Subsidized by the Arts Council of Great Britain.* 'Reptile are doing me in paperback – without the subsidy.'

'I thought you didn't call them Reptile.'

'Did I say that? A week is a long time in publishing. What *are* we stuck here for? It's only meant to be two minutes at York.'

Obediently, the train moves. 'It's a lovely station,' Prochak says, sentimentally, 'one of my favourites. Carlisle's a beauty, too, but not quite up to Newcastle.'

McEvoy has never considered the possibility of grading railway stations. 'What's your top favourite?'

She spreads her hands as if there could be no argument. 'Paddington; Brunel's own station. They should have given him a nice baroque monument with enormous nymphs – Steam Traction Exhorting the Soul of Commerce, but all he's got is a squat little statue.'

'Wasn't he rather a squat little person?'

'Bleeding cheek.' She looks at her watch again. 'We're losing time.'

'When should we get to Darlington?'

'Seventeen minutes past. I'm going for the twelve thirty, still, I guess they'll hold the connection. Have you been to Durham before?'

'This is the first time.'

'It's the best way to see it first time – from a train. You come in round a curve, over the viaduct.'

'You'd better finish the whisky before you get off,' he says. They take turns at the glass, in silence. 'Would you mind if I asked you something?' he says, diffidently, when it is empty.

'You can ask.'

'Will you sign my book?'

'I had a feeling it would be that. People are always afraid I'll mind, I can't think why. Of course I'll sign it.' She takes out a pen, opens the book at the title page and incises small black characters, adds the date, closes the book and gives it back to him. Contrarily he opens it to see what she has written.

'To John – that's friendly.'

'I wasn't sure how you spell McEvoy.'

'Ladies and Gentlemen, your attention please; we are now approaching Darlington. Change here for . . .'

Prochak rises, lifts down her luggage and prepares to leave.

'Enjoy your conference.'

'I never asked what you were doing in Middlesbrough.' This is terrible; they have not had a chance to wind down the conversation, although peripatetic Prochak shows no signs of expecting to wind down. Bag on shoulder, briefcase in hand, she is poised for departure.

'I'm giving a poetry reading.'

'And in Newcastle too?'

'In Newcastle – two. Yes. Goodbye, John.'

'Goodbye, Ruth.'

'Thanks for the booze.'

Given the chance he would have offered to help her off the train with her luggage, but he can see that any such gesture would be insultingly pointless, like offering to carry a lame man's crutch. She is freighted for maximum ease of motion and almost lopes down the aisle to the door. He leans against the window and watches her move along the platform in pursuit of the Middlesbrough train, manœuvring lithely round the slower and less capable, one who knows where she is going.

Indomitable little figure, he thinks, conveniently forgetting that she is not particularly little, even compared to himself, and built for speed.

6

Geneva, in the public library on Tuesday morning, traps herself in a cul-de-sac with a woman whom she identifies, too late, as Sarah McEvoy.

'Researching?' Sarah asks, brightly, feeling always out of her depth with Geneva.

Geneva, who has come to look for a book on American quilting patterns, grunts noncommittally.

'Haven't seen you in *ages*,' Sarah cries, before Geneva can say the same thing. Geneva bitterly regrets the days when libraries were hung with large admonitory notices demanding silence. 'John keeps me up to date, of course, but I don't think we've met since Christmas.'

'You ought to come round sometime,' Geneva says. Having admitted to research she cannot now go after the quilting book. 'Don't wait for an invitation – ' she has long ago given up issuing invitations to Sarah, ' – just take a chance, or ring, first. I'm usually in.' (And, Sarah, I have nothing to hide – from you. You will not find your husband under the bed.) She begins to move away but Sarah comes too, weaving and tacking from shelf to shelf as if it were simply chance that she should be moving in the same direction.

'But you must be so busy!' Sarah protests. 'John always says how you drive yourself. Anyway,' she continues, meaningly, 'don't you have enough of people dropping in uninvited?'

There is a plummeting contralto voice kept especially for talking to people like Sarah. Geneva tunes in to it. 'You mean the mad academic? Oh, my dear, I was never so glad to see John in all my life. He was rather splendid, you know.'

'Was he?' Sarah says, abstractedly. John would, she supposes, deal summarily with any man who propositioned her but why should it be the dumpy greying Geneva, approaching fifty, who attracts the slavering cad and has to be rescued by someone else's husband? 'Did he hit him?' Here is an unlooked-for opportunity to double-check the story.

'No need for that,' Geneva tells her, briskly, 'he was barely capable of standing as it was. I did feel bad about asking John to drive him home, though.'

'I thought John offered to do it,' Sarah says, as the ratchets of her excellent memory engage with satisfying clicks.

'He did. I accepted.' Geneva is well acquainted with the excellent memory. With the warm lingering memory of Keith Allard still alive between her thighs eighteen hours after she tipped him out from under the patchwork counterpane, she is in no mood to take his name further in vain, but she instantly rejects her plan, should the need arise, to change subtly that name to say Kevin Allardyce or Geoff Collard. If John named him as Keith Allard Sarah will have remembered it. 'Still, I gave him a decent meal when he got back.' She beams, disingenuously. 'Where are the boys?'

'Julian's with a friend. Chris does his own browsing.' They are passing the librarian's desk for the second time; Sarah indicates the door to the children's library. 'He'll be ages yet. I know, let's have coffee.'

Geneva declines in cold cowardice. 'I'd love to, Sarah, but I must get back.' The American quilts will have to wait. 'How's John enjoying his conference?'

'He rang last night,' Sarah says, limp with dejection. 'He says it's fine so far but I do worry so much when he's away. He had to go on his own, you know, by train. His friend was ill, the one who was going to share the driving.'

'Trains are less tiring,' Geneva says, bracingly, as she begins her final acceleration to the door, fuelled as much with pity as with dislike. She knows perfectly well why Sarah, who both dislikes and distrusts her, is proposing a tête-à-tête. How on earth did the wretched woman collar him in the first place? she wonders, fleeing through the biographies to the exit. It would be ludicrous if it weren't so sad; it is certainly too ludicrous to be tragic. But John does take it all rather seriously, indulging poor Sarah's fantods beyond the bounds of good sense. He is afflicted, she considers, with that degree of humourlessness that only the very good-looking can afford.

Sarah, abandoned and balked among the geography books, gazes vacantly at the blind screen of a microfiche. Geneva has something that is rightfully Sarah's and will not even share it. If only she knew what it might be.

McEvoy is missing Simon Headley more than somewhat. There are four hundred delegates at the conference, distributed among enough halls of residence to ensure that if there is anyone here whom he knows, they will not meet until the closing session. Conviviality is encouraged; the bar is good and each day is scheduled to begin with a Fun Run which, given that the college appears to be built on seven hills, must furnish all the fun of a punishment detail. He heard the clammy slapping of this morning's Fun Run pass under his third-floor window at five to eight, as he prepared to go down to breakfast in Hall. After a morning spent trying to write in public he cannot face lunch in Hall; communal living does not suit him. Instead he retires to the attic heights of his residence and makes himself coffee in the squalid cupboard behind a door labelled *Amenities*, these being an ironing board and a kettle, and takes it back to his room.

This is normally occupied by a First Year undergraduate, one Marcus Brooks-Haddon who, to judge by his attempts at interior decoration, is making desperate efforts to hurry on down. The walls are papered with his overdrawn bank statements and progressively unfriendly letters from the manager. Marcus writes memoranda on sheets of lavatory paper, although it does not seem to have occurred to him to recycle it, and painstakingly records his prowess thereon at boaking, wanking, farting and gobbing. No fucking, McEvoy notes, though given his personal predilections he may have trouble finding a collaborator. Over the bed his pin-up pouts, black-lipped, red-haired, corseted in a chainmail basque with a Tory canvasser's rosette gummed by a blob of Blu-Tack to her armoured pubis by way of a merkin. She too probably comes from a nice home, McEvoy thinks, gloomily. He can imagine the residence in termtime, made even more hideous by the belling of young male voices down the concrete stairwells, the boaking, the wanking, the farting and gobbing, as Marcus and his pals strive to shatter their stained-glass images and cut-glass accents. McEvoy balances his cup of coffee on the radiator and fishes out from behind it a fugitive sheet of bog roll. *Rutting*: oh, so he does it after all, but only once; that figures.

On the desk below the window is nothing belonging to Marcus. Compared with the space devoted to Marcus's burgeoning id, the area looks tellingly sterile, occupied only by two books and a block of A4 ruled narrow feint with margin and two malign eyelets for filing purposes. One of the books is *From an Unexposed Film*, the other is *Acid Test*. McEvoy sits down at the desk and draws daisy petals round the eyelets. He has now attended three sessions of the writing commission and is firmly resolved to attend no more. He came to the conference armed with the writing pad and the confidence that he could fill at least some of its two hundred pages; in the event he has filled seven, two of these with some impenetrably erudite *pensées* on the nature of coincidence. He is meant to be writing fiction. His tutor, a cheery and accessible professional, warmly recommended by Geneva, nailed him in the first ten minutes of the first session, nailed him down flat, spread-eagled and emasculated, by telling him, by telling all of them, all fifteen, to write from experience. 'Write an anecdote, if you like,' she said. 'Never mind about planning and plotting, get something down and then we can see what may come of it.'

'Fiction' McEvoy mouthed concurrently, 'is a matter of speculation, conjecture and surmise.' When the group dispersed about the campus to compose in the lukewarm sunshine, as if its creative apparatus were solar-powered, McEvoy laboured hotfoot up the hill, up the stairs to his third-floor drey, to work where he was happiest, at a desk, only to find himself staring at *Acid Test*, the definitive result of writing from experience. Prochak is right; those who can't, won't. He has written five pages from experience and ripped them meticulously into strips, five pages of bland and flaccid maunderings that purported to be his version of the *Acid Test* libel, and when he saw what was taking shape under his pen, he destroyed it. This morning, after coffee, he started again with an anecdote of more recent origin, Ruth Prochak on Doncaster Station, and his astonishment at seeing her, but what astonishes him still is that he called her to him, not that she was there in the first place. Unwilling to pursue this line of inquiry he hounded the coincidence, and coincidence is the death of fiction; such as the meeting between Michael and Gerald outside the library.

But, he thinks, gazing out of the window, coincidence is comfort and joy compared to the alternative. Coincidence obviates explanation, there is no need to wonder why a thing occurred; even if the coincidence is an act of God, God is an arbitrary operator. We have no need to wonder why. Ruth Prochak does not wonder why. A great taker for granted, is Ruth; she does not care for coincidence, but she does not wonder why. He tears his latest essay from the block and shreds it.

The Spinner of the Years said 'Now!' Twenty-two years ago his unsinkable liner holed its buoyant hull on Caroline's iceberg and it has taken this long to go down. He no longer knows what he is wondering about. Watching his face in the shaving mirror, the glass nastily flecked with yellow matter, no doubt pus from Marcus's zits, preserved for posterity (he can imagine the ghastly child sitting here alone, night after night, contemplatively squeezing) he looks and looks at his face, without pleasure or interpretation, until the features lose all meaning, like a word repeated too often. When he was Marcus's age he had no zits, his skin was smooth (it still is), his hair was dark and thick (still dark, still thick), and later, smooth skinned, long haired, he found he could afford to be kind. He was kind, and he did what he could, and because he did no more than he could she tells him it were better he had done nothing.

So? Geneva says, that was long ago, you've changed. Geneva believes fervently in change, her novels chart it; events take place and nothing is ever the same again. He knows he has not changed; he may have improved – he hopes that this is inevitable – but he has not changed. He wonders what Ruth Prochak makes of him.

There are no further writing sessions scheduled for today, to test his resolve; the afternoon is his, if he wants it, his, in which to fret and speculate. Rather than that he decides to go and look at Durham, having seen no more of it after that first sweeping panorama down over slated roofs then up to the cathedral. He puts on a thick sweater, against the flenching northern wind, thick-soled shoes, thick socks, and combs the thick hair.

Outside his door, on the landing, two female delegates are leaning on the banister railings. He nods, amicably, smiling as he passes and they return him stony looks because, he can tell, they think he is making a sexual statement; but he is not, no, he is not. He wished only to be pleasant; perhaps Prochak is not alone in looking more than she means, there's no art to find the mind's construction in the face. Ought he to crop his hair, grow a ragged moustache, cultivate a stoop and guarantee that no one would spare him a second glance? The staircase is a spiral, they can watch him all the way down. 'Not balding, anyroad,' pronounces a voice above his head. Startled, he looks up, and, disoriented by the helical descent, misses his footing, stumbling awkwardly down the last four steps before legging it out into the icy sunshine. He cannot forget the graceless glee with which they witnessed his fall.

Durham, a windy city, is clenched into an elbow of the River Wear. As he crosses the bridge and climbs upward by the steep streets, closed to traffic, he loses sight of the cathedral which he had supposed would remain a towering focus over all. He buys postcards, one for Geneva, one each for Sarah and the boys, which last he punctiliously mails separately; to put all three into one envelope would seem overly thrifty. Then he resumes his climb, coming upon the cathedral unexpectedly and at the same time, as unexpectedly, upon one of his fellow delegates from the writing commission. They exchange greetings.

'How's the writing coming along?'

'It isn't,' McEvoy says, hoping for reciprocal confessions of failure.

'You know, I never wrote a line since I left school,' says the colleague, with unbearable enthusiasm. 'Thought this was doomed from the start, but this morning I had a surgery with Whatsername, Whosit . . . ?'

'Trudy.'

'Trudy. She really took me apart but I haven't stopped since. Really had to tear myself away to come up here. Don't want to risk over-writing.'

He is exactly as McEvoy has always imagined Parsons in *Nineteen Eighty-four*, but unfortunately lacking Parsons's cringing anxiety. He draws himself upright with such an access of self-congratulation that McEvoy seems to hear his shoulder blades clap together under his vigorous sports jacket. 'God! The air, here. Nothing like it in Dudley. Where are you from?'

'Herts,' McEvoy says, vaguely. This is just the kind of eager oaf who would remember an address and look him up, or propose initiating a pen-friend scheme with his First Years.

'Bi⁺ flat isn't it, Herts?'

Flatter than Dudley? 'Not as flat as Cambridgeshire,' McEvoy says, knowledgeably.

'You going up?'

'Up?'

'The tower. Must be a hell of a view from the top – two hundred and eighteen feet.'

'I may do.' McEvoy excuses himself mechanically. 'I think I'll look round inside first. I've not been here before.'

They contrive to lose each other in the nave. McEvoy, oppressed by the massive stonework, the rounded Norman arches, the unexpected twilight, walks the length of the building hunched, drawing his head further and further into his shoulders, so that he is both stunned and uplifted by the airy heights of the Chapel of the Nine Altars at the eastern end of the chancel. He lays a wondering palm on the columns of Frosterley marble, marvelling at the filigree inlay of silver fossils.

'Couldn't fake that, eh?' A slabby hand falls on his shoulder. 'I've seen some bloody good thermoplastic alabaster, but that; that's craftsmanship.'

'It's fossils,' McEvoy says, recognizing the voice of the man who was taken apart, but imperfectly, by Trudy the tutor. 'No one put them there.'

'God's almighty hand, eh? Too true, too true.' How like a fawning publican he looks. (Good evening Squire. What's yours? How's the little woman?) 'Fancy coming up, yet?' I hate him, for he is a Christian.

McEvoy, fearing that if he demurs further he will be carried up, turns from the magic marble, reviewing as he goes his tentative and premature withdrawal from the writing commission. If this cretin can do it, and get away with it . . .

'I fancy a climb on a day like this,' says Excelsior, inexorably, as they reach the foot of the tower.

He teaches English to little children, McEvoy thinks, as they begin the ascent, and no one stops him. Nothing stops him, not even being taken apart stops him. Bloody Christian; a climb of two hundred and eighteen feet fails to shut him up. McEvoy, a step or two ahead so that he cannot get away and with the blood pounding in ears and throat, is effectively deafened, but altitude does not staunch the flow. Such lungs he must have. Now and again a sentence penetrates, evidence of a sustained discourse.

The top of the tower, when they emerge, is spacious and entirely windless, a shock after the cold gale in the streets below. McEvoy reels into an aperture in the stonework and looks down, gulping with exhaustion and vertigo. When he was at school there was a legend, rife before examinations, that by putting blotting paper in your shoes you could make yourself faint. He thinks now that he is going to faint, this must be exactly what blotting paper in the shoes feels like, implacable drainage downward. Only embarrassment keeps him standing. At his ear a voice that would make a serviceable sand-blaster embellishes the view with statistics.

'Nave, two hundred and one feet, total length of church interior, four hundred and sixty-nine feet, six inches. Length of the choir, one hundred and thirty-two feet, six inches. Something missing there. How can you lose a hundred and thirty-six feet?' What bloody man is this?

A posse of Dutch teenagers erupts from the entrance to the tower and engulfs them. McEvoy extricates himself, leaving Excelsior furrowing his brow over a guide book, and sets off, sidling, round the perimeter. Black birds swim below him; ravens? choughs? crows winging to the rooky wood? Smitten with a profound melancholy he wishes he were alone; he would be alone had not the Spinner of the Years floated a maniac into his path. Excelsior wades alongside, intoning feet and inches.

'I think I'll go down,' McEvoy says. 'I don't have much of a head for heights.'

'Saving yourself for tonight?'

'Tonight?' Are they planning a ceilidh? 'Is there something lined up?'

'Haven't *you* got something lined up? *I* saw you on the landing,' rolling a thumb against forefinger. He could be twirling a metaphorical moustache or testing a nipple for freshness. Surely he hasn't got the brains to be a pagan; a venal Christian, then? Simon would have something lined up. McEvoy sees the entrance to the tower gape, and dives.

Geneva grows tired of *Acid Test*'s kinetic green and purple cover screaming among the living-room cushions and picks it up with the pedal bin in mind. Or she could send it to Oxfam; or a jumble sale. Suppose I did, she thinks, and suppose Sarah bought it. But this is stretching fat chance into tenuous coincidence too far for Geneva's liking. In any case, Sarah would never identify the wretched Michael, no grounds for speculation there. Before throwing it away she leafs through it, reading Jane's marginal comments. *Typical!* she jeers, beside one ringed paragraph.

Later that day, in Padders, Katherine told me how they had met. 'I went to this party,' she said, 'and the fellow I'd arranged to meet didn't show. I wasn't too bothered, it was a terrible party, in a fairly notorious flat, and I knew that if he turned up he'd want to stay. I was just fetching my coat from the bedroom when a young man looked round the door. "You're not going already, are you?" he said. I explained that I'd had enough of the party and wanted to leave. "I saw you downstairs," he said, coming into the room, "looking so forlorn. Won't you stay?" I knew that I had not been looking forlorn, being alone doesn't necessarily mean that you are lonely, and I said I was going anyway. "Well, let me walk back with you at any rate," he said. "Back where?" I said. "Anywhere," he said. "I'll walk with you anywhere you like." So you see, Caroline,' said Katherine, 'he only wanted to comfort me to begin with. You can't fault his kindness.'

I explained that in any relationship, Michael had to be the giver, the comforter; he was incapable of accepting anyone on equal terms. 'He insisted on comforting you even then,' I said, 'even though you told him you didn't need it. He wouldn't believe that.'

'But Caroline,' she cried, 'do you mean he only took me to Bath because he thought I needed cheering up?'

'He didn't do it to cheer himself up,' I said.

Jane, who has never known rejection, understands nothing of the awful wounded pride of the rejected. But then, wonders Geneva, how can you trust the judgement of one who senses rejection in everything? Did ever a young man take a girl away for the weekend with any object *other* than that of cheering himself up? Geneva herself wants to know what it is that Katherine, now Margaret, can hope for from Michael, now John, after time has done its best and its worst with them and their perceptions of each other? She discounts entirely Caroline, the recording angel, which sets her off on an interesting line of conjecture; does the Book of Judgement contain cross references, or will the sheep be assumed into Paradise irrespective of the effect that they had on the goats? She has already forgotten *Acid Test*, which lies blaring unregarded on the sofa.

Trudy is not precisely taking him apart but she is holding him up to the light.

'Never mind what actually happened,' she cries, callously stabbing at his writing pad with her ball-point pen, 'the thing that concerns us now is what you can make of it. The incident you've described is interesting on its own, but we're not concerned with recreating the past. This is fiction. What happens next?'

'I don't know what happened next,' he protests, for the second time, as if two negatives will make a positive. For the purposes of this particular fiction, he does not know what happened next.

'I said *happens*, not *happened*. You don't need to know what *did* happen, it's your job to speculate. This is only the starting point.'

'The known constant?'

'You've been listening to Geneva Stevens,' Trudy accuses him. 'There is no theory of fiction, only practice.'

'Tell that to the critics.'

'Critics and writers are involved in two completely different industries. Geneva's one of the few working in both.'

'A kind of a giddy harumphrodite? She's a friend. I haven't been studying her.'

'You mean she talks like that off-duty?'

'Only when we're arguing.'

'You should have said that you knew her.' Trudy beams, delighted with him. 'How is she? I haven't seen her for months.'

'She's very well; correcting proofs and fulminating against Reptile Books. It was Geneva who recommended that I come on this commission, she said you'd be an excellent tutor.'

'And I suppose you'll go back and say that I'm a dead loss?'

'No no, *I'm* the dead loss.'

'If only you'd loosen up a bit,' Trudy sighs. 'It's as if you won't let yourself speculate; as if you're reluctant to face the possible outcome. This guy, what do you call him – ?'

'Stuart.' Caroline called him Gerald, Gerald who was, at first encounter, difficult to place.

'Stuart, twenty-four, draughtsman, mentally unstable, you know him slightly – there's plenty of potential, here. How do you know him?'

'Through friends.'

'You meet him in the street, say hello, pass by on the other side . . .'

'No!'

'Figure of speech,' Trudy says. 'I only meant that you kept walking. He tries to detain you. You talk for a while but refuse to have a drink with him because you have a pressing appointment. You never see him again. Would you have expected to see him again?'

'In the normal course of events, maybe. I didn't really notice that he wasn't around.'

'Did no one mention him to you? these mutual friends?'

'I left the area soon afterwards. Didn't really give him another thought.'

'And yet,' says Trudy, 'you're still wondering what happened as a result of that meeting. How long ago did this happen?'

''64.'

'Residual guilt.'

'I didn't – don't feel guilty. Why should I?'

'You feel something,' Trudy says, 'curiosity if not guilt. There must have been some element in that meeting which makes you remember it after twenty years.'

'I just thought', McEvoy says, 'that it would make a promising start. A minor incident, the outcome of which I didn't know and could therefore speculate about. A known constant.'

'And yet you won't speculate. You know, John, and Geneva agrees with me, the idea of fiction as therapy is anathema to anyone who practises it professionally, but in your case it might be worth considering. I think that you've done your speculating in private and whatever you've come up with is making you very unhappy. If you don't want to talk about it, at least write it down; then you can decide whether or not to let me see it.'

McEvoy takes back his writing block. 'Geneva's tutored courses like these,' he says.

'I know. We've done them together.'

'She says the common factor is the psychologist's couch; people don't come to write, half the time, they come to talk. They use the tutor as an ear, not an eye. She says people fall weeping into her arms, sometimes.'

'Oh, they do,' Trudy says, tolerantly. 'You're not going to fall weeping into my arms, are you?'

'I was just thinking', McEvoy says unpleasantly, as he prepares to leave, 'that you must do a great deal to invite it.'

The commission is housed in a common room, some distance from the residence. McEvoy walks into the wind through courtyards and across lawns, cleaving to walls in the Arctic canyons, his coat blasted open, his hair swiping his eyes. From above Excelsior, sited predictably on a fire escape, hails him fellow-well-met. McEvoy forks two fingers upward and grinds on.

In his room the wind shoulders the door against him, whines at the window hinges and rattles the stay. He tugs the door shut and gazes round in dismay. The place looks as if a fast train has just passed through, errant sheets of lavatory paper twirl under the ceiling and flutter down as the gale subsides, the diaspora of Marcus's cloacal archive. McEvoy drops everything that he is carrying and dips into his inner pocket for his railway timetable. It is six fifteen; the next train will not leave until seven twenty-eight, reaching London at half past ten. He could be home by eleven thirty; and what would Sarah say to that? He is expected home by seven *tomorrow* night. Were he to be late he would be called to account, make no mistake, but how can he satisfactorily account for coming home early, almost a day early? He is known for his devotion to duty; how can he convince Sarah that he has abandoned his post simply because he has had enough and not because of some unconfessable catastrophe; how can one have enough of a NATE conference, have so much, in fact, that one ups stakes and bolts? As far as he can remember, he was supposed to be looking forward to it; even if he had not looked forward to it, he undertook it; he embarks with equanimity upon his undertakings. Putting the timetable back into his pocket he decides he will go home tomorrow but he will not, he will *not* attend the final session of the writing commission – the final session that is reserved for public reading of work produced *in situ* – he will not attend any more talks, he will not face Excelsior again, he will not expose himself to Trudy's penetrating analyses, though God alone knows what she will say to Geneva when next they meet; to which end he had better not go in to dinner, nor to breakfast.

Geneva will ask in all innocence if he enjoyed the conference, how did he get in with his writing, what did he think of Trudy? He will be able to tell her what he tried to write, but can he confess why he failed to write it? He rips what he has failed to write out of the block, crosses to *Amenities* and burns it in the sink. Detachedly assessing this grotesque overreaction he feels that he may as well compound it before embarrassment sets in, returns to the desk for *Acid Test*, stands it in the sink like a tent and sets fire to that, too. It has been lying on the radiator, curling up at the edges as peeled birch bark does; now, tinder-dry, it blazes, flames leap to the ceiling and horrid green and purple blisters squirm on the laminated jacket. One of the great comic set pieces of post-war fiction, he jeers at himself, and pokes it with a fork. When there is nothing left but a devil's breakfast of sodden black flakes he goes back to his own room and drops on to the bed. On the table, on a level with his eyes, *From an Unexposed Film* lies closed and still unexposed, unread.

When he picks it up a fault in the binding causes it to fall open at the middle. On the verso are the five concluding lines of a previous poem:

Children! The very fact that you are alive,
The chance collision of a cruising sperm
And an ambitious egg, that set ticking your blastoderm,
Was an arbitrary thing. So how
Dare you agitate for equity now?

It puzzles him. To be frank, he cannot imagine Ruth Prochak knowing enough words to have written that. Well, Geneva, he says, suppose the known constant *were* coincidence, what then? He turns to the opposite page.

The Long View

Journeys are for gazing; for taking the long view
Where distance makes all diminished and indistinct
And voices dwindle. Details cannot be told,
Disinterest is kind and veils clarity,
How restful to the eye and mind.
One is so small in the long view.

There is more but he returns to the first stanza, reads it again and lies looking at the ceiling, watching Prochak's impetuous progress down Darlington station: 'One is so small in the long view.' He sees her alone at the window of a compartment, mouth drooping, great eyes gazing disconsolately at the passing fields.

On the title page her salutation, more print than script: *To John, with all good wishes. Ruth Prochak*, a controlled and accurate hand, a hand for writing poetry; he had expected a childish eccentric scrawl. He reaches for his jacket, which lies across the foot of the bed, and consults his timetable again; it is unhelpful, giving only the times of the expresses.

McEvoy rolls off the bed with unwonted energy, crosses

the landing to the pay phone at the head of the stairs, and rings Durham station to learn that if he catches the eleven thirty-nine tomorrow he can be in Newcastle twenty minutes later, in time to board the twelve twelve to London, the Flying Scotsman.

7

The final session of the writing commission is timed to run from nine until ten forty-five on Thursday morning. McEvoy lies *perdu* in his room reading the rest of *From an Unexposed Film* which, in spite of his expectations, he finds he is beginning to like. He cannot imagine wide-eyed little Ruth writing anything so carefully phrased and he reads some of the poems twice, three times, drawn against his will to the pervasive air of rootless solitude; rather a lot of them seem to be about trains. One attracts him especially, treating of London streets on early summer mornings, with the low sun flushing the upper storeys of a building while the pedestrian walks in subaqueous shadow; but the street is Pentonville Road and the building is St Pancras Station. Harold Clandon had his celebrated punch-up with the divisional librarian at St Pancras.

Shortly before the session is due to start he makes a final survey of the room, checks that Marcus's memos are more or less back where they came from (though not where they *belong*, he comments, heavily), leaves his keys in the door and sets out for the station by a devious, guilty route that avoids the common room where the readings are taking place. The morning is chill and grey and the wind, however many corners he turns, grizzles always in his right ear until it aches. His baggage is not heavy, he enjoys walking, but this walk gives him no pleasure. He is as hungover with chagrin and embarrassment as if he had indeed been four days drunk and was only now waking up to the realization of all he had done and said meanwhile.

His train, from Leeds, runs only a few minutes overdue, but that is enough to throw him into an agony of anxiety. The Flying Scotsman has a punctual air about its name; a rufous bristly Highlander with a skean-dhu in his stocking; it will not be late; it will not hang about for a straggler approaching perversely from the opposite direction and if he misses it he will be condemned to travel back to London on a slow stopping train, to travel, moreover, alone. Crawling through Gateshead, over the Tyne, impossibly high above the Tyne, he swears and stews and, as he has not done since impatient childhood, urges forward the great articulated slug with will-power alone. It disgorges at Newcastle five minutes late, to an announcement over the public address system that the next train at Platform Nine will be the twelve twelve to London King's Cross; McEvoy fancies that he has never moved so fast in his life. It will be another assault on his mangled pride if, after such calculation and contrivance, he misses the thing. Platform Nine is crowded; travellers, children, dogs, wheelchairs; the incompetent, the halt, the lame. Frith would have loved it: Hieronymus Bosch would have loved it.

He cannot see Ruth; three minutes to go and he cannot see Ruth. He looks in the buffet, the bookstall; Ruth is not there, no way could he miss her if she were. His eye rakes the crowd again as he ploughs through it; it is clustered and tensile, ready to spring in any direction. The public address system keens, in a contentious Geordie accent, that the twelve twelve to London King's Cross is running approximately seven, o-seven, minutes late. The crowd relaxes and swells away from the platform's edge, but still he cannot see Ruth.

Only now, in his disappointment, can he admit that he hoped to, instead of pretending that it would be the merest chance if they did meet. He had no need to fly the conference at ten forty-five; he could have caught an earlier train from Durham itself, if he had not known about the Flying Scots-man, that is what he would have done. Under any other circumstances it would have been no more than a good idea to seize the opportunity of travelling with an acquaintance; downcast and humiliated he sees the bright candle of his idea gutter and burn out. When the train comes he will not board it; he'll go and look at Newcastle instead, that was what he really meant to do all along. Through the murk of this furious sulk he sees Ruth at last, as the crowd parts hurriedly to let her through, her and the briefcase which she swings like an offensive weapon.

Lost for a greeting this time he risks pride and manhood (she might easily mow him down before she saw him) and steps into her path, and just in time she stops. 'Well,' she says, 'this ain't coincidence.'

He cannot tell whether or not she is pleased to see him; twice in four days may be one time too many, which aspect of his planned convergence has not previously struck him.

'I came away early. I remembered you said this was a non-stop train from Newcastle so I came up to get it.'

'Did you make a reservation?'

'Should I have done?'

'You don't travel much by train, do you?' She looks up at him, pityingly.

'You think I won't get a seat?'

'Not if you wait up this end. First Class is always nearer to London. Unless you plan to go First Class?'

'No – but aren't you at the wrong end too?'

'At the moment, but I reserved a seat. Come on.'

In what he takes to be a kind of affectionate irritation but may well be simple irritation, she lays a hand on his arm and propels him back along the platform – no, she has him by the *sleeve*, tugging him along like an impatient child with a slow-moving adult in tow, and he looks down humorously at her fearful scowl.

With the scything pendulum of her briefcase she cleaves a path through the milling passengers and stops: 'Here.'

'How can you tell?'

'My reservation's in coach C. Coach C stops here.'

'But *I* haven't got a reservation.'

'You'll get something if you're first on.'

'If I'm first on.'

'You'll be first on. We ought to be able to manage hailing distance at least.'

The bluntness of her assumption that he engineered their meeting leaves him unable to deny or prevaricate and anyway, there is no opportunity; the yellow locomotive is dragging its train into the station and the unwary crowds are scattering as they discover unanimously that they have been standing at the wrong end of the platform. McEvoy fears failure, but as the train halts the door of coach C is before him; there are some ahead of them and many pressing behind but as the last of the disembarking passengers descends Ruth cries 'Now!'

as if ordering a parachute drop (at least she doesn't yell Geronimo!) and hustles him forward. 'Well, here's luck,' she says, as they storm down the aisle. 'This one's mine and there's nobody opposite. Well done, Jack.'

'Sorry; well done John.'

'Do you always take trains like an armoured division?'

'Not at all; trains are shy elusive creatures – that's why we talk of catching them.'

'I meant you, not the train.'

'Oh, sure. In the footsteps of Sherman.'

Another Home Secretary? A poet? 'Sherman?'

'General Sherman.'

'Really? He was a bit of an animal, wasn't he?'

'He responded to exigency.'

'If it were done when 'tis done, then 'twere well it were done quickly?'

'That's about the size of it.'

The Flying Scotsman, eager to fly, draws out of Newcastle Central before its passengers are fairly seated, except for Ruth and, under her supervision, McEvoy, who had their baggage stowed and filled their places instanter.

'Look out for the Tyne Bridges,' says Ruth.

'I saw them on the way in.'

'I said *look*. There's no finer sight. It's a transpontine museum.'

They gaze at the grid of bridges that span the river. McEvoy shifts his stare and examines Ruth – jaw slightly dropped, eyes wide as they will go – advocate of the Industrial Revolution and the flying column. He can understand her affinity with William Tecumseh Sherman; the urge to get things done.

'You haven't got a paper, have you?' Ruth asks, as the train gathers speed through Gateshead.

'The *Guardian*?'

'Do you mind if I look at it. I forgot to get one.'

'Of course I don't mind.' He passes it over.

'I meant, do you mind if I don't talk to you for a bit?' she explains, with laboured politeness which does not, he imagines, come easily to her.

'Go ahead.'

She handles it with the practised economy of the habitual commuter, elbows tucked in so that the woman at her side, ready to swell indignantly at the first incursion into her air space, can only subside with her tabloid. Ruth reads rapidly, lingering over the inside back page.

'I just want to see if anyone I know's popped off,' she says, catching his eye. 'I feel safer, reading this. They die like flies in the *Telegraph*.'

'Yes, but there's something odd about the way *Guardian* readers die. You can go for days without any deaths at all and then there's a whole bunch, six or ten, like an epidemic.'

'No flowers by request, no flowers by request, family flowers only, no flowers, no flowers; miserable sods. When I go I want lots, not donations to the Poetry Society.'

'You'd better put it in your will. Are you going to write a *Testament*?'

'Oh, definitely. "*Venez a mon enterrement quant vous orrez le carrillon, Vestus rouge com vermillon*."'

It's London French, not exactly Stratford atte Bowe, but certainly not of Paris. Like her English it is delicately ventilated by transposed aspirates.

'I don't know about that,' he says. 'but I'll send you some flowers.'

The couple sitting alongside rise abruptly and move away. Ruth watches them go. 'Do you think we're depressing them?'

'They've probably gone for lunch. Are you going to eat?'

'We can get something from the buffet, later on. There'll be a queue right now. Oh quick!' She points. 'Here comes Durham – but it doesn't look so good going south. Less of a surprise, I guess. You can see it coming. Did you have a good time?'

He would so like to tell her how bad a time he has had, and why, but the question was a formality. She is not, after all, asking if he managed to write anything, and she is returning his *Guardian*.

'Your turn. Go ahead, I've got plenty to read.'

Obediently, since he would not dare to force her unwilling into conversation, he opens it at the book reviews. Geneva is in fine form: . . . *a glum saga of adolescence, punctuated by the monotonous thud of descending testicles . . . a weakness for one-liners which were all very well in a stand-up comedian . . . confessing a debt to Flann O'Brien in the foreword is no substitute for paying it . . .* McEvoy considers briefly O'Brien's theory of molecular exchange by which Ruth should be fully 50 per cent rolling stock. He looks up. She is curled in her corner, head bent devotionally over the British Rail Passenger Timetable, eyes swivelling up, down, across, like a scholar perusing an arcane text. Almost he expects her to sway back and forth in theophiliac ecstasy like a *yeshiva bucher* over his Talmud. In a way, he thinks, it *is* an arcane text, biblical print encoded on wafery paper, impenetrable to laymen such as himself.

'Which one are you reading?'

'65; one of the Greats.'

'The Greats?'

'26, 51 and 65. 135's impressive – I'm never sure whether to include it.'

'Were you', he asks, 'one of those children who used to hang around on the ends of platforms, collecting engine numbers?'

'A gricer. They're mostly adults, you know; nutters. No, I've never been all that interested in locomotives – except for the Deltic.' Her face kindles with the same demented enthusiasm that he observed on Monday, when she mentioned that the Flying Scotsman was non-stop to London. It *must* be the eyes. 'They've got a Deltic at the Science Museum. I go and look at it, sometimes. An inspired name, don't you think?'

'Deltic?' he says, lamely. 'Yes, very powerful.'

'I'm not barmy,' Ruth says, on the defensive for once. 'I go everywhere by rail.'

'You don't drive?'

'Yes, but I don't enjoy it. Anyway, the distances I have to cover, I'd be worn out. At least in a train I can work.'

'And read.'

'Yes.'

'Timetables.'

'Look, I don't read them for fun,' Ruth says. 'Take this one, 65 – '

107

'Oh yes, one of the Greats. What's so great about it?'

'The size, for a start. Look, fifty-two pages, all those trains – '

'Oh, that's it, is it? The timetable encapsulates the experience.'

'Do you always argue when you're flirting?' says Ruth. Slamming shut the timetable she tosses it on to the seat. 'I'm going to Carlisle after Easter', she snarls, 'via Liverpool. I have to work out an *itinerary*, don't I?'

'Whaddya mean, flirting?' He feels his face flush.

'You've got nothing to say but you keep talking in case I forget you're there.'

'Flirting? That's flirting?'

'Well, maybe more than that,' she concedes; 'foreplay.'

'*Foreplay?*'

'While you work yourself up for a proper conversation. You don't have to travel with me.'

In a floundering attempt to rescue the situation he says, lightly, 'Oh, I couldn't bear to think of you all on your own, with no one to take care of you.' This is entirely the wrong answer.

'Come to that, I don't have to travel with you.'

'Ruth – no; I'm sorry. I'm behaving so badly . . . '

'Yes.'

'I've had a dreadful week.'

You don't have to take it out on me, says her unforgiving expression, but, 'I'm sorry for that,' she says. What he wants her to say is 'Tell me about it.' With Geneva he would not have to wait to be invited. He recalls Mary's observation; *She never asks questions*, which he took at the time to be a child's routine complaint at a lack of attention.

'You can't imagine how dreadful. I tried to write; for three days I tried to write. It was like being in a plughole, round and round . . . '

'I know that feeling. It wouldn't be the same for you, though, would it?'

'Wouldn't it?'

'I shouldn't think so. You thought it was going to be easy.'

'The writing was easy – '

'It ought not to have been.'

'Well, it *was*. I'm fluent enough, I don't have any trouble writing; it was what I was trying to write – can I tell you about it?'

'If you want to. Wouldn't you rather tell Geneva?'

'I'm not sure that Geneva would understand.'

'Likely I shan't.'

'I'd like to tell you, anyway. Because you don't know me perhaps you'll be more – impartial.'

'You said tell.' Ruth looks alarmed. 'You don't want me to read anything, do you?'

'No. There's nothing to show, anyway. I burned it.'

'How theatrical.'

'In the sink.'

'Is that what you meant by being in a plughole?'

Overhead the intercom bleats. 'Ladies and Gentlemen, this is your Chief Steward speaking. I should just like to remind you that the buffet car is open for the sale of tea, coffee and light refreshments, soft drinks, alcoholic drinks, hot and cold sandwiches . . .'

'Trains seem to attract people who like lists,' McEvoy remarks, unwisely.

'Lists?'

'Menus, timetables, destination boards . . . I suppose trains themselves are a kind of list.'

'How d'you make that out?'

'Well, one thing after another – almost like a poem. An engine and coaches, a title and stanzas, the light at the end –'

'At the end of the tunnel?'

'At the end of the train.'

Ruth glares at him, exasperated. 'Don't be so bleeding literary.'

McEvoy deflates. 'I'm sorry. I just don't know what to say to you.'

'You should have thought of that before you came haring up to Newcastle.'

'Do you want me to move?'

'Oh Christ, no. You wanted to tell me something, didn't you?'

'I don't think you'll want to hear it, now.'

'Tell you what, let's get something from the buffet before

109

everyone else decides it's a grand idea, and you can tell me while we eat.'

'I'll go.'

'No, *I'll* go. I'm used to it. What'll we have?'

'You won't be able to carry everything.'

'Try me. Do you want booze?'

'Will they have wine? Look, let me pay.'

About to argue she thinks better of it. 'OK. When I come back.'

He watches her down the carriage, surly and competent, and wonders what became of the brave child who hopped off the train at Darlington on Monday, the oddly appealing gamine. She has gone alone to the buffet, he knows, because she can't bear the prospect of him blundering in her wake, no child at all but a cross-grained woman disguised as something younger in her denims; not farouche but irascible. He is wasting her time, time she would have spent happily planning her route to Carlisle via Liverpool, travelling alone. She likes travelling alone, whatever made him think that she would prefer to travel with him? only his own dislike of solitary journeys. Nor does she find him remotely entertaining; Monday's encounter was enough. She may not care for coincidence, but she does not mind chance. Contrivance is too much.

When she returns he admires her passage, loaded, along the aisle, and does not presume to leap up and help. Instead he is content to acknowledge her easy balance, swaying counter to the motion of the train and advancing without recourse to ungainly clutching at the backs of seats for support. He recognizes proper pride; he is a good teacher, Geneva is a good writer, Ruth is a good traveller; he wishes he knew if she were a good poet. How do we know that she is a poet at all?

'Two bottles of wine?'

'They aren't full size. There's a couple of hours to go, yet. I got toasted cheese sandwiches – all right? And apples.'

'How much do I owe you?'

'Call it a tenner, unless you'd like to split?'

'I said I'd pay.'

From a pocket she brings out some more of the little whisky bottles. 'Chasers. These are on me.'

'Are the sandwiches just to soak up the booze?'

'Why – do you get depressed when you drink?'

'Not unless I'm depressed already.'

'And you are, aren't you? Come on, tell me why you're depressed.'

He says, 'That book I lent to Geneva, *Acid Test*, do you know what it's about?'

'You?'

'No, it isn't. I'm in it, but it's not about me. It was written by someone I knew slightly, years ago. It's her own story, I only come into it in an – an – ancillary capacity. You haven't read it?'

'I didn't even know what it was called until you told me.'

'Have you had much experience of mental illness?'

'I meet a lot of very strange people who want to write poetry. Some of them are certifiable.'

'I'm being serious.'

'So am I. I don't care for the idea of writing as therapy but many people do. They regard poetry as a vehicle for the emotions. I'm not saying they shouldn't write – that would be insane in itself – but not for that reason. I try to avoid *them*. Not because they want to write but because they don't write, all they really want to do is talk about writing.'

'Yes, well, I try to avoid the unstable if I can – now. I had a friend once who became severely depressed. You can't avoid a friend, not if you have any real concern for him; anyway, that never occurred to me, *then*. This book, it's about a group of people in a psychiatric hospital in the 1960s, being treated with various new drugs about which very little is known, Librium, Valium, Largactyl . . . in those days they really were new, well, comparatively, I suppose. What I mean is, they were new to us; the general public knew nothing about them. Valium's as common as aspirin now, but it's only recently that people have taken the side-effects into consideration. It's used to keep depressed women out of wards and surgeries, isn't it? Have you ever taken it?'

'Whatever for?'

'One of these people, the girl – woman now – who wrote the book, she wasn't depressed, or suicidal. They didn't really know what was wrong with her; it reads like schizophrenia

– paranoid delusions, hallucinations, voices, but they weren't even sure about that. One of the psychiatrists uses the word mad; that's about as near as they can get. She got the newest miracle of all; LSD.'

'Acid?'

'That's why it's called *Acid Test*.'

'She got it in hospital? I didn't know they used it in hospitals. I grew up with tales of people trying to fly, but it wasn't a medical phenomenon.'

'It was. I wish I knew if they still used it – they couldn't Ruth, could they? I never thought much about it at the time – '

'*You* didn't?'

'I'm in the book too, remember. They used to talk about their treatments all the time, and their transferences and their abreactions. They had this curious jargon and they used it as easily as slang. And odd legends, you know; if you could stay at large for six weeks and a day or something like that, they couldn't force you to go back, even if you'd been committed in the first place. I don't know, it may have been true. I didn't have anything to do with people in the locked wards though I remember once looking out of a window, over a garden wall, and seeing a woman walking round the paths with a baby in her arms. When she turned the corner I could see that there was nothing in her arms, she was holding a space: like a Henry Moore. And the corridors, you'd see people week after week, in the same place, the same corner, the same doorway; it was like the Stations of the Cross, and as far as I was concerned – once I'd got used to it – it was just part of the *ambience*, like the drugs. I didn't think much about the LSD although I didn't care for the sound of it, and I did wonder afterwards why people were taking it for fun – *I'd* heard what it could do under clinical conditions, I mean. One of the hospital jokes concerned Dr Waterman, he was the chief psychiatrist, I think. He tried out the LSD on himself and rumour had it that one of the orderlies shut the hospital cat in with him and he came out screaming about tigers. They all thought that was wonderfully funny – Dr Bedonebyasyou-did. You see, I was aware, but it wasn't something that interested me all that much; I never used drugs myself.'

'You're the straight man, then?'

'How?'

'In the book.'

'Not even that. I got to know these people because the guy I shared a flat with, Andrew Lyle, lay down in the bath one night and slashed his wrists. I came home unexpectedly and found him; at least, it was unexpected to me. He didn't know that I'd intended to be out late. If I had been he'd have died. I could never work out whether he planned to be found in time or not – I was very upset for a long while afterwards because I kept wondering; suppose I hadn't come back . . . Anyway, he went into the local bin – '

He remarks a tremor of distaste in Ruth's attention.

'That was what they called it, the patients; the bin, the Nuthouse, the funny farm. It was us poor idiots outside, trying to be tactful, who called it a mental hospital, mainly because we'd only just learned not to refer to places like that as lunatic asylums. I used to ring Andrew in his ward and often someone would pick up the phone and say, "Hello, this is the Nuthouse." They were all so young, Ruth. Killing themselves was almost like a kind of rather dangerous cult activity. They used to talk about their suicide attempts like bridge players, over and over, *boasting*. I remember Caroline lay down in the drive in front of the hospital bus. I saw her – I was terrified, but she was nearer to death from laughing about it, afterwards. It was only harrowing to begin with, after a bit it got very tedious.

'Anyway, I used to visit Andrew; he was in an ambulant ward, Wren. The wards were named after birds, but the first time I went there I saw Wren and Bullfinch on a signboard – I thought for ages they must be named after architects. He'd made friends there, of course. When he came back to the flat at weekends – he was a voluntary patient, you see – some of them used to come with him..There were three in particular, Robert, Tony and Caroline – the one who wrote the book: and an arsonist, but we only ever met him in the pub. I never knew his name. *He* used to talk about his fires, and how it took him two years to get arrested, standing around at the scene of the blaze with his petrol can, cheering the firemen. I didn't know his name.'

'You said.'

'Sorry. I didn't really know any of them well, except Andy. Tony didn't last long; he nearly killed his brother and ended up in one of the locked wards, Dove or Linnet; and there was another one, on the fringe, whom I hardly knew at all. I think I only spoke to him twice. His name was Stuart. She calls him Gerald in the book.

'That's partly what's so disconcerting. She's still Caroline, but Stuart is Gerald, Andrew's Brian, Robert is David. I'm Michael. When I first read it and began to realize what she'd done, it was like seeing double because the pictures I was getting from her descriptions were not quite like the people I remembered. Especially me. It really made me feel sick, just from confusion.'

'But John,' Ruth says, pouring more wine, 'what *happened*?' She has asked a question.

'I'll tell you what *I* knew, first,' McEvoy says, 'and then I'll tell you what happened, what she says happened. I imagine she's telling the truth. As I said, my part in all this was marginal; I don't think it was worth lying about.'

'It's not fiction and it's not lies and yet it isn't true?'

'Is that what Geneva told you? Look, really, this is all there is. One evening, in early July, I went out to meet someone. That was all. I went out of my front door, walked down the High Street to meet a man in a pub. I left in plenty of time because I wanted to be early; we weren't going to have a booze-up. I'd applied for a vacation job – tutoring in France – but there was no certainty that I'd get it, and this chap, his name was Bailey, thought there might be a chance of my working in the States for a bit; you see, it was important. I needed a job. It was important, wasn't it?'

'It was important.'

'I thought so. I still think so. Outside the library – there's no significance in that, it just happened to be outside the library – I ran into Stuart; Gerald. No, I'll call him Stuart; he *was* Stuart. He seemed perfectly normal, as normal as he ever seemed. Drugged up to the eyeballs, but then they all were, all the time. I'd come to accept that as normal. We stopped and said hello and I asked him how he was, and he said he was fine, I can't remember the details, it was just chat. We had nothing to talk about anyway, as I said, I hardly knew him. I was probably rather surprised that he wanted to talk – to tell you the truth, I'm surprised I remember him at all. If it hadn't been for this particular incident I don't suppose I should have, but I was in a hurry and he was being so irritating, it came to mind as soon as I read it. I used to give him a lift sometimes, with the others, but he wasn't one of their crowd and after a bit I expect I said, "Well, nice to have seen you, must be going," something like that, and he started to come too. He'd been going in the other direction when we met, but he walked along with me. I must have said I had an appointment but he just kept coming. What I remember most is his *being* there, moving alongside me. His face: he was fattish, receding hair . . . I can't remember his feet . . . But I remember being annoyed and wondering how I could get rid of him because I didn't much want him around when I met Dick Bailey. *I* found him normal – not many other people would have done. I think in the end I may have suggested that we meet some other time; anyhow, I did get rid of him and he didn't seem particularly upset. I think he turned off down a side street. I went on to the pub and met Bailey, and that was that.'

'Did you go to the States?'

'No. It all turned out a bit nebulous and then I heard a couple of days later that I'd got the French job. I had to leave within a fortnight, it was a rush to wind up everything. I went up to the hospital to say goodbye, but Caroline was on Largactyl – three weeks' sedation – Robert had been discharged and Andrew wasn't around. He was the one I'd shared the flat with. I still don't know what became of him, the book doesn't say. But I wasn't sorry *then*, to be honest. I went back, told Margaret – she was a girl that I knew, that I was leaving, I think she was the only one I did manage to see, and that was that. I wrote once or twice, but I never got any answers. Frankly, I didn't mind and I didn't think any more about it. I had to readjust pretty quickly to what normality really was.'

'Do stop trying to sound nonchalant,' Ruth says, 'your hands are shaking.'

'I'm trying to convey what I felt, which was nothing very

much; I didn't just wipe them from my mind – I mean, I can't remember now exactly what I thought – but I wouldn't have done. I don't think like that. I suppose I sound callous.'

'No. Exasperated, perhaps.'

'That's it, exactly. They made use of me and I was pleased to be used. There wasn't much I could do *except* make myself useful. Even that wasn't easy; they seemed to think that when I wasn't with them I froze into immobility; in fact I was a teaching student. I wasn't standing around idle, by no means. They made use of me and I made excuses for them, but they were terribly difficult to like. I don't think I'd have liked them even if they had been sane. In a way I was paying them a compliment by disliking them; at least it showed I took them seriously. Still, I forgot them; for twenty years, and then this book arrived. It was sent – no, that doesn't matter at the moment. That's irrelevant. I'll tell you later. The point is, when I read it I discovered what had happened to Gerald.'

'Stuart.'

'That was his real name.'

'Will you call him Stuart or Gerald?'

'Gerald, now, because in what comes next, that's how he's known. You see what I mean about double vision, don't you?'

'Remember, I didn't know any of this at the time; I'm not sure that it would have made any difference if I had done, except that I might have stayed out of Stuart's–Gerald's way on purpose. Gerald was mad about a girl who was singing at the Hothouse; it was a night-club, the first one in the town; people made the same fuss about its opening as they made about coffee bars ten years earlier. This must sound quite unbelievable to you; when were you born?'

'Fifty-one. Go on, Gerald was mad about this girl – '

'I say mad advisedly. He *was* mad. Forget what people say about only the mad being truly sane; that madness is the only sane response to an insane world; believe me, the mad are mad. She was nothing special; she couldn't sing but she made the right kind of noises for the time, and her legs were good – short skirts, you know? We were beginning to discover legs. Up till then only little girls had knees; as they got older their legs got shorter and grown women just had ankles; actually to see legs walking about in the street – it was an experience. A couple of years later we got thighs – and she was pretty, thin and bleached out; etiolated blondes were coming into fashion. Gerald developed a fixation about her – hospital talk again. He never went into the damn place himself, just sat on a bench in the bus station and watched her going in and out. Remember, I didn't know this. I didn't know what Gerald did on his weekends off. She didn't know either, didn't know he existed, till he started writing letters. I imagine they were the usual stage-door-Johnny letters to begin with, declarations of passion from an unknown admirer, but he never asked to see her, never invited her to go out with him; perhaps he knew she wouldn't, just sent these letters, sometimes two a day. This is all in the book, you understand. He said in the letters that he was watching her – which he was – but that she would never see him. I don't know what else he wrote, but in the end she decided they were making her nervous and went to the police, at which point Gerald, quite coincidentally, wrote one final letter saying that as she would never be his she would have to die. They caught him and pulled him in. He was remanded, during the trial he hanged himself in his cell – I didn't know any of this.'

'You said.'

'In the book Caroline describes going to see him with David – Robert, that was – while he was on remand. He told them that the night he wrote that last letter he was desperate, walking round the streets, wanting someone to talk to, and he met me. He said he didn't like Michael much but all he wanted was someone to talk to, and Michael wouldn't talk. He said Michael kept making feeble excuses and trying to get away and in the end he went back to Padders – that was a coffee bar, the Padova – and wrote the letter. He said to Caroline, "Michael could have prevented it. If he'd only let me stay with him I'd have been all right." She says he repeated it over and over again. That was the last time she saw him.'

'I can understand your being upset if you'd found all this out soon afterwards,' Ruth says, 'but surely it's long enough ago for you to see that you weren't responsible?'

'No, I wasn't responsible,' McEvoy says, 'I know I wasn't responsible. If he hadn't written his letter *that* night he'd have done it soon afterwards. He wanted someone to blame – I don't blame him for that. For all their talk of transferences and abreactions, as far as they interpreted it their therapy was all about laying the blame on someone. You never took responsibility for your own actions. Well, even if I had a responsibility for what Gerald did, it was a very slight one; I was twenty-two – I think I'd have forgiven myself by now – no, it's not that. It's just that after Caroline comes away from seeing Gerald she has a long talk with David and Katherine – Margaret, that is – and they try to fit in the Gerald business with everything else that Michael did. They draw the most preposterous conclusions about the things he – I – did and the reasons why.'

'I rather thought Geneva said that there was no attempt to furnish reasons and that was why the portrait was false.'

'No attempt *since*. She writes now what she thought then. She hasn't had second thoughts. I can't believe I was ever like that.'

'Well, you may have been,' Ruth says judiciously, 'but that doesn't mean that you are now.'

'That's very much what Geneva said.'

'Oh, bugger Geneva, she's not the Sibyl of Delphi. Know yourself; you're the only one who can tell. Why elevate the opinions of a group of deranged adolescents above your self-knowledge? It's no good looking at me', she says, 'as if you hope *I* can tell you. I don't know what you're like.'

'I haven't told you everything yet,' he says.

'I'm sorry. Go on.'

'Did Geneva say anything about how I got hold of the book?'

'She said there was a *tertium quid*.'

'The *tertium quid* was Margaret – Katherine – '

'Forget the aliases,' Ruth says, 'we're back in the real world now.'

'A few weeks ago I appeared on television for a few minutes and several old acquaintances got in touch.'

'One of them being Margaret? I had voices from the past when my first book came out – reminding me of things I'd taken care to forget.'

'She sent me a letter, mentioning Caroline and explaining

that she'd written this book. I didn't even know that they knew each other till that moment; they became friendly after I left, that's all in the book. She sent me a copy. If she'd just left it at that I probably wouldn't even have read the thing, but she hinted that I might learn something from it. I might have been annoyed by it – yes, I'm sure I would have been, but no more than that. But it wasn't all she sent. About the same time as all this happened – I mean Stuart and his nightclub singer – I'd been going out with Margaret. I met her at a party, quite by chance. Apparently I drove her to Bath for the weekend.'

'Don't you remember?'

'No. I went to a lot of places, I knew several girls. I had friends in Bath, then, perhaps we went down to stay with them. I've forogtten.'

'But she hasn't?'

'No. In her letter she reminded me about the weekend, and sent me a poem that I wrote for her while we were there. It's a dreadful poem – don't ask to see it.'

'*I* don't want to see it. You don't carry it about with you, do you?'

'I thought we parted amicably, we were never close, but we didn't.'

'You were closer than you thought.'

'Not so close as *she* thought. She could never have forgiven me; she's waited all this time to take her revenge.'

'By letting you think you were responsible for someone else's suicide.'

'Prosecuting counsel said that he was a dangerous psychotic. No, that's not it. I've spent the last three days trying to write my version.'

'And?'

'It always comes out the same; the same as her version, Caroline's, and Margaret's too. They have such a warped idea of him, of Michael, and whatever I do I can't make him, make me, look any different. It's just that *I* see what I did as blameless. For Christ's sake, Ruth, I didn't do anything.'

'Can't you get in touch with Margaret and lay the ghost?'

'I think that's what she hopes I'll do, or maybe not. Ruth, the point is this; the book's written by someone who was out of her mind when all these things happened and yet she, and Margaret, obviously think that her assessments are accurate. I don't come into it much, really, here and there, that's all, but whatever I do or say it's always culpable.'

'The known constant.'

'I'm getting very tired of the known constant,' McEvoy says. Ruth leans across the table and presses his hand.

'What happened to the singer?'

'She drowned in a swimming pool, soon afterwards. Caroline manages to convey that she somehow deserved to. That's the kind of thinking I'm up against; in Caroline's chemistry, even the catalyst must be destroyed.'

8

Sarah itemizes imminent delights. 'Tonight Daddy comes home, tomorrow it's hot cross buns, Saturday is Martin's party and then – ?'

'Easter.'

'Have you written your note for the Easter Bunny?'

'Nearly.' Julian believes wrongly that when he goes to school he will put aside childish things, that this will be his last tryst with the Easter Bunny, to whom he is laboriously copying a begging letter. Christopher could tell him about the canon of Saints and celebrations that await him under the benign regime of Miss Cleeve, high priestess not only of the Easter Bunny but of Father Christmas, Jack Frost and St Valentine; of festivals that the McEvoys never observe; May Day, Mothers' Day, Fathers' Day, Midsummer, Hallowe'en. Their own calendar will prove a meagre shadow of the mainly pagan practices at St George's C. of E. They are not in its catchment area but they were when Chris started school and the headmistress, faced with falling rolls, is happy to slip Julian into the dangerously depleted reception class.

'Will Daddy be home for dinner?'

'Unless his train's late. Clear up now, pet. Chris will be in soon. You don't want him to see his Easter present, do you?'

Julian cannot wait for Chris to see his Easter present; a book made of plasticine with red covers and yellow pages. It even opens, at the risk of falling in half, to reveal a bookmark, but he rolls the surplus coils and pellicles into a ball and drops them back into the box. At Sarah's approach he flings a secretive arm around his creatures.

'Mustn't Mummy see what you've done?'

'This one's for you.' Julian cups his hand over something blue and pink, too late to prevent Sarah from noticing that it represents a tube of toothpaste or a vacuum cleaner, either artifact apposite to her preoccupations. 'But you can look at Chris's. And this is for Daddy.' He exhibits a greyish squid with knobs on. 'It's a lady,' he says. 'I've made a lady for Daddy.'

'Wake up, John,' Ruth says, breaking into his anxiety dream of a bad lesson in which he hits small children with violent blows that never quite strike home. He swinges about the classroom but there is no strength in his arm and the children laugh. The shudder of wheels over points reminds him of where he is before he opens his own eyes to find Ruth's a few inches away as she leans forward alarmingly to press a finger to his throat, below his left ear. It is, he imagines, the way commandos wake each other up.

'We're almost there. Look, the gas holders.' She points to the seven towering crowns, painted black and red, that fill the window.

'Are we at King's Cross? How long have I been asleep?'

'Only since Peterborough. I wanted to show you the brick-works but you were flat out.'

He looks askance at their fellow travellers who are now back in their seats and preparing to leave the train. 'I haven't been snoring, have I?'

'No, I'd have poked you if you had.'

'You should have poked me anyway. I'm sorry. It was terribly rude.'

'No such thing,' Ruth says. 'You make a pleasant after-noon's viewing.'

'When we were children we called them gasometers,' McEvoy says, discomposed. 'Is there any difference?'

'I thought a gasometer was what you have under the stairs. We made up lost time; it's only fifteen ten.'

McEvoy translates this. 'I'm far too early.'

'Aren't you going home?'

'They're not expecting me till after six.'

'Well, no one will mind – will they?'

'I'd have to explain why. Dereliction of duty and all that. It wouldn't sound good,' he explains, as if by neglecting to mention Sarah specifically, her being can be temporarily suspended.

The train has halted. As Ruth reaches above her head to lift down their luggage he sees, looking up unintentionally into the dark tent of her sweater, the firm ogival curve of her ribs and he has to subdue his right hand with his left before it can realize his sudden urge to mould it over her skin.

'Are you hurrying off anywhere?' he asks, as they leave the train, still shaken by the narrowness of his escape; she would have split his head open, and rightly, 'or have you got time for a drink?'

'Well, yes,' she says, 'but wouldn't you rather move on now and miss the rush hour?'

'No, really Ruth, I wouldn't.'

'You could find somewhere to lurk nearer to home.'

'You don't have to stay. I'll lurk alone.'

'Oh, I'll stay, but what time were you meant to get in?'

'If I'd caught the five to two? Twelve minutes past five, *you* said.' An idea strikes him. 'I suppose there isn't a slightly earlier train I might have caught – if I'd missed lunch, say?'

'There's the ten fifty-five from Edinburgh. You'd have picked it up at twelve fifty-three. That would have got you in just after four.'

'The last session ended at twelve. Yes, that'll do splendidly. I *am* glad I met you, Ruth.' She wears nothing at all under her sweater.

'I suppose you'd have managed your own prevarications if you hadn't.'

'I don't prevaricate, I'm just editing.'

Ruth shrugs, declining to be implicated by her disappointing lack of interest in his designs. 'Don't let's have coffee here; they've only got a kind of injection-moulded shebeen on Platform Nine. There's a little place round the corner in York Way.' She starts across the concourse. 'This whole bleeding shop's injection-moulded, like Euston. Specially designed to frighten tourists.'

The concourse is congested with holiday crowds, but Ruth gets through and McEvoy sticks close behind. Her behaviour is, he thinks, appalling even by London standards. Heavily built men skip out of her way, women cringe, loutish teenagers with aggressive haircuts back off and apologize when she shoulder-charges them. He cannot help calling to mind her graceful sonnet about dancing on a lawn; *the gravity of ritual moves* . . .

Where did *that* come from?

Ruth's little place in York Way is very little, but almost empty. McEvoy orders coffee. 'I did enjoy your book,' he says, generalizing from the particular. *Let us be serious in this at least* . . .

'Did you? Good. Thank you.'

'Why did you call it *From an Unexposed Film*?'

'That's a hell of a question for a Thursday afternoon. Didn't you read the one about dancing in the garden?'

Taken aback: 'Yes.'

'Dancing in the dark and imagining someone with a camera taking a flashlit photograph, only there is no one, and the photograph remains untaken, so there is no record of the moment except on the unexposed film, as it were – oh, I hate explaining them. It reminds me of O level.'

'I liked that one especially – I didn't make the connection.'

'But that's the title poem.'

'I didn't notice. Haven't you got another one due out soon?' He knows quite well.

'*Midland City*. The beginning of May, last I heard.'

'I'll get it.'

'I can let you have one.' Ruth searches her briefcase and gives him a paperback. 'Prepublication.'

'Let me pay for it.'

'No, you bought my lunch. It's a complimentary copy.'

He leafs through it. 'Which Midland city? Nottingham? Worcester? Peterborough?'

She smiles patiently. 'It's a railway station.'

'It would be.'

'Just down Pentonville Road; King's Cross Midland City, it's the new one. Good to think that someone still knows how to name a railway station. Midland's a nice word. I like the aural juxtaposition of "d" and "l".'

'I hadn't thought of that.'

'Well, you wouldn't, would you. Tell you what, in return you can lend me *your* book.'

'I haven't written a book.'

'What did you call it? *Acid Test*; let me read it.'

He is put about. 'I don't think you'd like it much.'

'I don't suppose I should, but I'd be interested to read it, all the same.'

'I haven't got it any more.' He cannot quite bring himself to tell her what he did with it. 'I didn't like having it around. All the while I had it I kept reading bits – just to see if it would have the same effect each time. It did, but I couldn't stop.'

'So you threw it away?'

'Yes. No I didn't, Ruth. I burned that, too.'

'In the sink?'

'Yes. Don't laugh. Ruth!'

She hides her face in the crook of her arm and whoops. The girls at the counter and the only other customer glare at McEvoy, implying that if he cannot control his friend he had better take her out. He cuts them dead, with an austere regard of control, but when he turns back and sees Ruth's heaving shoulders he laughs as well, although more quietly, naturally.

'I must say,' she tells him at last, 'you do improve on acquaintance.'

He is glad to hear it. 'Are you beginning to like me?'

Her laugh closes up, her whole face with it. 'Does it matter?'

'No. I'm sorry, I shouldn't have asked.' He is tired of apologizing. 'Yes, of course it matters.'

'It just struck me as an odd question. Most people wouldn't ask.'

'You mean, you wouldn't.'

'Ah, look, John, you don't like it when people make unqualified judgements of your character; no more do I. I suppose Geneva told you that I have no curiosity.'

'Yes, she did,' he admits, 'but I think I'd have reached that conclusion on my own.'

'You'd be wrong. I'm curious about all manner of things, but not about motive, that's all. You may call it a blind spot if you wish, but there you have it. I'm intensely interested in what people do, but setting aside the question of moral values, one motive's as good as another, *qua* motive. I presume you came up to Newcastle this morning because you wanted my company coming back to London; isn't that enough to be going on with?'

'What do you take me for?' he asks, unreasonably in the

light of what she has just said, for clearly the answer is: Only what you seem to be. Are you not what you seem? Her interest, however intense, in what things are is not enough to be going on with. Why can she not, along with Geneva, along with himself, speculate on what they might be, on what they might become? He desires earnestly to make her speculate and, recalling how not long ago she took his hand in sudden sympathy, he reaches out and takes hers.

'Ruth, look, we've only met three – four – times, and that by chance – '

'Today was chance?' She regards the bunch of cold fingers on the table top.

'All right, it was *arranged*. I wouldn't want to arrange to see you again if you didn't want to see me.'

'I expect we'll run into each other at Geneva's.'

'I don't want to run into you; I don't trust chance. All I want to know is, if I rang you, say, and invited you to lunch, would you want to come?' He releases her hand. He can tell that she is not accustomed to having her hand held, poor Ruth, and this thought encourages him wonderfully.

'Yes, I'll come – if you can catch me, I'm not at home very much. You know I travel a lot.'

'So you keep telling me. Why?'

'Why do I travel? I go where the work is, you know, readings, talks . . . I get asked.'

'And that's all you do?'

'*All?*'

'I meant, there aren't many people who make a living out of poetry. Do you really keep yourself on royalties and readings?'

'Not likely. I've a part-time job.'

He tries to envision her in an office, at a check-out, bravely slaving to finance her first love. 'What do you do?'

'Didn't Geneva tell you? I'm a polytechnic lecturer.'

'English?'

'Biochemistry.' At least she can see the joke, too. Heads turn again. 'But I don't like it much.'

This seems even funnier. He cannot recall having laughed so much in months, nor, by the looks of it, can she. What a pity she leans forward when she laughs and not, expansively, backward, allowing him to see the small breasts moving unconfined beneath her sweater.

'How can you "not like" biochemistry?'

'Very easily. But it's the lecturing I don't like.' She controls herself by biting her lip. 'I think we'd better leave. Your train's about due in.'

'My train?'

'The one you caught from Durham.'

'Oh, that train. Yes.'

Back across York Way they go, briefcases swinging harmoniously.

'You want the Northern Line, don't you?' he asks at the head of the subway outside King's Cross Station, attempting to ease the severance by inviting it.

'What about you?'

'I can get all the way back home on the Metropolitan. I may have to change.'

'Won't that be too *fast*?' Sarcastic cow. 'I'll come round with you as far as Baker Street. I can walk home through the park.'

The pedestrian traffic has increased in their absence. Happily he tucks in behind her as they descend the steps to the Underground, trusting himself to Ruth's tactical leadership. Instant reprisal with extreme prejudice is her method; if people do not step aside for her, she steps aside for them and hits them with her briefcase as they go past. A young man moving at speed shoves against her accidentally; too late to reach him she clouts his girlfriend instead, behind the knees, causing her to curtsey. McEvoy is shocked but exhilarated, what a little thug she is. Ruthless. Why does this kind of thing not happen to him more often?

The train is full and they have to stand, by the doors. McEvoy, jostled, although not very much, stands a little closer than he need so that she might, if she wished, nestle under his chin, and is surprised all over again to discover that to get under his chin she would have to stoop considerably. The top of her head is almost level with his eyes. As she is turned slightly from him he sniffs her hair, but it only smells of trains.

'You should have got away earlier,' she says. 'It's the holiday.'

'Do you think I'll have to stand all the way?'

She looks at him. 'Don't be soft. You can trample old ladies and grab a seat when you change at Baker Street; it's only three stations.'

'Is that all?'

'D'you *like* standing?'

He does not have the nerve to tell her that at the moment he is liking it very much indeed and that if Baker Street were six stops on he would be quite content.

'Are you going away for Easter?' he asks.

'Staying at home. That's my treat.'

'I thought you must like travelling.'

'I do like it. Don't you like teaching? You still need a holiday.'

'What will you do?'

'If it's fine I'll go out on the Hill and look at London. It's best seen from a distance. I love the Hill.'

Euston Square: more people get on, but not enough to cause real compression. Great Portland Street; the journey, the time, is rattling away. Just before Baker Street the train gives a great lurch that throws them against each other. Ruth, who has been relying on her own equilibrium to remain upright, staggers and clutches at his shoulder. He steadies her with a gallant arm, but leaves it braced around her and she lets it lie. When the doors open on to Baker Street Station he cannot forbear to hug her, albeit unemphatically, as they step out of the train. On the platform she smiles, ducks her head against his shoulder and so leaves him, to be immediately immersed among commuters. He, following, cannot even watch her go; she does not look back.

Remembering her advice he races for the Watford Line, since there is nothing to keep him standing on the platform. She said he might ring her, but she did not give him the number and he forgot to ask; still, there cannot be all that many Prochaks in the London telephone directory. He can still feel her unexpected softness against his chest.

It is not a bookshop that Ruth would patronize in the usual way although she sometimes buys newspapers there; on her last visit the proprietor was overheard expressing warm enthusiasm for a contemporary poet whom Ruth regards as an over-praised and undertalented little tit. One may purchase slim presentation booklets of platitudes, illustrated in pastel wash, and framed prints of the *Desiderata*. Pensively yodelling 'Kahlil Ghihihihihibrahan' under her breath Ruth begins confidently to search for *Acid Test*.

She recognizes it at once, having seen it lying around in Geneva's living-room without knowing what it was. Hesitating only to suck her teeth over the violent colour scheme on the jacket she picks it up and starts toward the till. Then she stops and looks inside.

Brian's friend threw open the door and paused, as if expecting his adoring public to rise up and applaud. He smiled round at us and swept aside a lock of long brown hair, looking for Brian, but sharing the smile with everyone.

'He must have been practising that for days,' David said to me.

Michael was wearing a green corduroy suit and elastic sided boots. 'Who does he think he is?' David muttered. 'One of the Rolling Stones?'

Brian introduced us. 'This is Michael. If it weren't for him I wouldn't be here.' We all knew what he meant, of course, but Michael took it as a compliment. As David said afterwards, you could see he was thinking, Isn't it nice of me to come?

Ruth, guiltily flushed as if surprised in the act of eavesdropping, closes the book and returns it to the shelf. In those few lines she has detected a grudging resentment that could taint any expectation. This self-satisfied Adonis posing in the doorway is no kin to the bewildered man she has been facing for the best part of five hours, whose *amour propre* has taken such a knock. She has no wish to be caught in the company of those who knocked it, he deserves better than that.

But what does he deserve? For a moment her hand is on the point of travelling back toward the bookshelf, but she desists. To be found endorsing what she knows to be corrupt, by purchasing it, would be unfriendly, underhand. As the assistant is watching her she buys a *Standard* instead and goes out again into the sunshine of Marylebone High Street, and walks quietly in the direction of Regent's Park.

If he were hours late Sarah could not be more perturbed. Christopher and Julian are overjoyed, they swing on him as he walks up the path to where Sarah, mouth elongated with apprehension, stands at the front door.

'What happened?'

He kisses her. 'What do you mean? Nothing happened.'

'But you weren't due back till after six. I wasn't expecting you.'

'Never mind, I'm not that hungry. I can wait for dinner,' he says, wilfully misunderstanding.

'It's salad. Darling, did something go wrong?'

'Nothing went wrong. I just decided to come away early.'

'You didn't miss anything important?'

'I missed lunch.'

'But you must be starving.'

'I ate on the train.'

'But *why* . . .'

'I wanted to come home.'

If only she could believe it.

'Did you bring us anything?' Julian asks, climbing on to his knee as he sits in the armchair. Chris hangs over his shoulder.

'We got your cards.'

'Did you go in that big church? You said you would.'

'Did I?'

'On my card there was a big church. You said you were going to look at it.'

'I went right to the top.'

'All by yourself?' Julian asks, impressed.

Sarah's head twitches but she manages not to look round.

'No, I had a big fat silly man with me. He was very boring.'

'Do you want a drink, darling?' Sarah's voice is not quite steady.

'Lovely. Gin and tonic.'

'Daddy, why did you take a big fat boring man up that church?'

'I didn't. He took me. I was quite happy at the bottom.'

'What was his name?'

'I didn't ask.'

'You didn't ask his *name*?' Sarah holds out a glass that judders and slops over her hand.

'I called him Excelsior.'

Julian says, 'I'm going to Martin's party on Saturday. Is it Saturday tomorrow?'

Chris says, 'Why did you call him Excelsior, Dad?'

McEvoy says, 'Because he kept wanting to go higher.'

Sarah, rigid and trembling, says, 'Oh, for God's sake, John, stop talking such rubbish!'

McEvoy tips Julian from his lap. 'I left my briefcase in the hall. Go fetch. Chris, bring in the bag, will you?' In the minute interval this allows him he gasps, 'Sarah, I didn't ask his name because I didn't give a fourpenny fuck.' Julian is back already, Chris not far behind. 'You must know the Longfellow poem: "The shades of night were falling fast . . . a banner with a strange device . . . '

'No!'

'Then you bloody well ought to,' he mutters to the carpet, as he bends over his luggage.

'We thought you might not bring us anything because of it being nearly Easter,' says tactful Chris, offering him a loophole.

'Yes, well, that's why I didn't bring you anything very *big*,' McEvoy says, sneaking through the loophole with a silent murmur of gratitude. He unzips the holdall and burrows, feeling Sarah's eyes directed at the dark turmoil of socks and shirtsleeves. What does she expect to see: a fugitive garter? rogue knickers? Durex? He brings out two sand clocks, mounted on turned wooden mill bobbins. 'There; you can time your breakfast eggs on Easter Day.' The little boys crow, seize and twirl them. Sarah looks on unbelievingly. 'And there's something else, in my briefcase.'

He opens the briefcase, takes out a bundle of books and papers and unearths the five miniature bottles that once contained Famous Grouse. 'British Rail booze. I'm afraid they won't divide up; maybe you know someone who'd like the odd one.'

'Martin,' Julian says. McEvoy, knowing Martin's mother, privately begs leave to doubt it.

'Put them in your room,' Sarah says. 'Go on. They'll only get lost if you leave them down here.'

When the boys go out she turns on him. 'What are you thinking of? What sort of presents are those for small children? Egg-timers and whisky bottles?'

'But they like them.'

'*Five* whisky bottles?'

'Two going, two coming back and one I found lying around. They don't hold much.' On top of the pile of papers he notices the copy of *Midland City* that Ruth gave him in the café. Sarah sees him see it and picks it up.

'Poetry?'

'Yes. I got it in Durham.'

'Ruth Prochak? Who's she?'

'A poet.'

'Is she any good?'

'I haven't read it yet. I'm trying to put together a collection of contemporary verse to use at school. Geneva recommended this one, so when I saw it I thought I'd get it.'

'Have you met her?'

Christopher and Julian thunder down the stairs and race past the living-room door on their way to the garden. Bright and fair they rollick outside the French windows in the grass that badly needs cutting and he had better do it tomorrow.

'No.' He sweeps up the papers and drops them back into the briefcase, packing them down and buckling the strap over the *other* poetry book which says, on the title page, *To John, with all good wishes. Ruth Prochak. Nr Darlington, 16 April, 1984.*

Pleading fatigue after the journey he will go to bed early, having spent the evening staving off Sarah's interrogation and his own by sorting and filing his conference notes. Darkness drifts in from the garden. He switches on the Anglepoise lamp and sits in its little tent of light that warms and defends him; while he reads and writes and corrects, he need not think. On the wall, at his side, the telephone rings. Afraid that it will rouse the children he quickly grasps the handset but before he can speak the number he hears the sound of the receiver lifted on the telephone in the hall, not with the usual careless clatter, but stealthily.

'Hello?' he says.

'Oh, John, is Sarah there?'

It is his mother-in-law.

'I'll just fetch her.' The room is small. Holding the receiver to his ear he rises, opens the door and calls softly, 'Sarah?' If she were in the living-room or the kitchen she could not possibly have heard him. What he hears is the stutter of the other receiver softly replaced; a moment's pause and then the sound of the living-room door being opened.

'Did you call?'

'Phone. For you. It's Joan.'

'Fine. Thanks.'

He closes the door, replaces his receiver and sits down again to digest the event. 'I cannot bear this,' he says, aloud.

Joan Wood's conversations with her daughter can go on for a very long while. After ten minutes, when the quiet mumble of Sarah's voice below sounds no sign of abating, he decides that now would be a good time to go to bed unhindered. He tidies his papers and drops them into the top drawer of the filing cabinet, then reaches into his briefcase for the copy of *From an Unexposed Film*; he will not be able to get it out of the house before Tuesday, to go down to the garage now would provoke interminable questions; he has not been near the car for five days, he cannot possibly pretend to have left something in it.

Considering subterfuges he looks inside the book again; how unaccountably more attractive the poems seem now than when he last saw them this morning, in Durham. One in particular, which he found peculiarly sullen and left him feeling obscurely insulted, now seems no more than a good-natured comment on the human capacity for self-deception, and a warning to wives rather than a rebuke to husbands. He does wonder now why he ever thought there was anything in it that could harm him, although it offers him little by way of comfort. It is called 'A Common Error'. The error is not his error.

Thinking of savage breasts, she married him,
Music and charm would soothe him down the years.
He did not look so bad, the light was dim.

Bravely she said 'I will,' and quelled her fears,
Seeing the curling tusks, boar's eyes, hog's snout,
Softened by moonlight through her quivering tears.

She clasped his trotter, doused her smouldering doubt,
Looking ahead to years of nuptial bliss,
And turned to follow her swart bridegroom out.

Bestowed upon her sisters each a kiss
And said farewell, forbearing to reproach
Her father, who had got her into this.

Snorting he led his bride toward the coach,
Scattering with snarls and sneers and grimlie scowls
The wedding guests who winced at their approach

And, deaf to father's groans and sisters' howls,
Ardent beside him in her wedding gown
She laid her cheek against his bristly jowls.

The family dried their eyes and drove to town,
Where father rallied and resumed his trade.
The sisters married well and settled down,

And beauty? What became of that poor maid?
A tale of promise dashed and hope betrayed –
This Beast was a real beast, and so he stayed.

The key to his briefcase was lost years ago. He drops the
book into the filing cabinet and for the first time ever, locks
it.

On the landing he leans over the banisters and, as she looks
up from the telephone, hisses, 'It's all right, Sarah, I'm going
to bed.'

It is not all right. Her mouth drops open, free hand begins
to wave and flutter involuntarily in a spasm.

'I'm dead tired. Don't interrupt your chat – I'll see you later.' He blows her a kiss and withdraws from the sight of the upturned palpitating vacuole that is her mouth; like a snail on a window-pane.

In the cooling darkness he lies on his side, facing the edge of the bed away from the door, eyes shielded so that he will not see it open and break the regular breathing that he has rehearsed to mimic sleep. Not quite sleeping, not dreaming, he thinks of a wandering scholar, vagrant poet, covering the country and earning a crust by her art, taking the long view. Indomitable figure, he thinks, having forgotten to scrap that image, restless and endlessly travelling. Then he remembers that she is a biochemist and laughs uncontrollably into the pillow; could anything be more incongruous?

Good God, she might be *Doctor* Prochak. He wildly imagines her the protagonist of a long-running television series which features an itinerant biochemist roving the mighty continent of North America, boldly going where no biochemist has gone before and every week chancing upon adventure wherever, fortuitously, a biochemist happens to be needed . . . he is cackling so hard when Sarah comes in that he has to pretend to choke and wake up.

'John, are you all right?'

'Just coughing.'

'No, but coming to bed so early. It's only half past nine.'

'I didn't want to spoil your talk with Joan. I told you, I feel deathly tired. It's been a hectic week and the train was packed.'

She sits on the bed and turns on a lamp. 'Perhaps you should have caught the other one.'

'I thought that'd be even more packed, that's why I came away early.'

'Which one *did* you catch?'

Bless you, clever Ruth, with your trusty timetable. 'The ten fifty-five from Edinburgh. It got to Durham at twelve fifty-three. We got into King's Cross at three minutes past four, it was dead on time.' It seems never to have struck her that a man with a perfect alibi may be more suspect than a man who cannot account for his whereabouts. 'Sarah, please turn off the light, my head's thumping.'

'Shall I get you some paracetamol – a drink?'

'No, truly, I just need to sleep.'

'I wanted to hear all about the conference.'

'Tomorrow, please.'

'I waited specially till the boys were in bed.'

Of course you did, sweetheart. The inquisition always operates in secret. For once he is adamant. 'Tomorrow.'

Face to the pillow he does not see her extinguish the light but he hears her move out of the room and close the door. Then he rolls over and stares into the darkness, trying to recapture his silly image of the biochemist at large, but it is not funny; no, it is not funny. What he really wants now is to turn again on his side and find her lying by him, silent and willing for him to place his hand on her naked skin, on her little breasts. He knows exactly how well she will fit into his arms, and wraps his arms round the space where she would be, cradling the space, while down the length of him, as he begins to fall asleep, he feels the confident pulse of the speeding train, Newcastle, Durham, Darlington, York, Doncaster, Newark, Peterborough, Huntingdon, Stevenage, King's Cross. The tracks converge ahead of him in sweeping ogival curves as he plunges into the night. The timetable encapsulates the experience.

9

'Now then,' says Geneva, sternly, 'what's all this about your running out on Trudy Petherbridge?'

'She's never rung up to complain?' McEvoy says, appalled.

'Not to complain; she was very worried about you.'

'You mean, she actually got in touch? I only said I knew you –'

'She rang because she said that meeting you had reminded her that she'd been meaning to call me up for ages. Naturally she mentioned what happened, or rather, she said she didn't know what had happened. She was afraid she had upset you.'

'I was afraid I'd upset her. No, it was entirely my own fault; massive loss of self-confidence, you could call it.'

'You might have told her that. She's very understanding.'

'A sight too understanding,' McEvoy complains, ungratefully. 'I told you, it was my fault. I tried to work up one of the episodes from *Acid Test* from my own point of view, but it was a mistake. She *would* have us write from experience and I tried to pass it off as a minor incident that I'd remembered and wanted to use because I had no idea of the outcome. But of course, I knew exactly what the outcome was, only I couldn't tell her that because I hadn't told her about *Acid Test* in the first place.'

'So you bolted. Oh what a tangled web we weave . . . which incident was it?'

'I don't really want to talk about it.'

'That's not like you. Which?'

'Gerald and his nasty letters.'

'Yes, that was a mistake. You're never going to be able to look at that again in the same light now that you know the result. Mind you, it's a pity you had to find out from *Acid Test*, and it was an amazingly foolish choice. Suicide's an emotive subject, it needs skilful handling. I'm very wary of it myself.'

'Of committing it?'

'Don't be frivolous; of writing about it.'

'You don't mind writing about death; I'd have thought dying was quite as emotive.'

'Not in the same way. A casual death – I mean casual in the true sense of accidental, undesigned – is just that; undesigned. It's the writer's problem to disguise the fact that *she* has designed it, but for the characters involved it's unlooked for, unexpected, all they can do afterwards is to repair the wound that's been inflicted on *them*. Now a suicide, that may be unexpected, but afterwards there's the knowledge that a whole life was working toward it; not a wound – a tumour, inexorably growing. Even if it seems sudden to the survivors, they have got to reassess every assumption they ever made about the victim.'

'So do the readers.'

'Of course. It's all done for them, remember. I may not decide to commit suicide until the third draft, perhaps. In that case I have to go back and sow the seeds of that conclusion in the very beginning.'

'At least it can be explained,' McEvoy argues; 'even in real life, to a certain extent. Casual death, as you call it, leaves nothing but outrage.'

'You wouldn't be outraged if you discovered that on leaving you Gerald had accidentally walked in front of a bus, but you know that even while you were talking to him the process of his death was already in action. Even now that hurts, doesn't it?'

'To be frank, no it doesn't. I think it would have hurt me then, if I'd known, but it doesn't hurt me now. What hurts is something quite different.'

'Which is?'

'I said I didn't want to talk about it. It's the whole book, not just the Gerald episode.'

Geneva says, 'I wish I could make you see that it's not the events that hurt you but the handling of them.'

'I do see that.'

'It's bad writing as much as bad thinking. As I've said, any attempt at fictionalization would have come closer to the truth than this apology for factual reporting. It's the potential that interests me, not the raw material.'

'I know: you *are* planning to write a book about a man who finds he's had a book written about him.'

'No I'm not. I said that the idea was appealing, but I wouldn't do it. If I did you'd always be thinking, "Lord, is it I?"'

'I trust you didn't discuss all this with Trudy.'

'Certainly not.' You discussed it with Ruth, he thinks, but cannot say it. He has neglected to mention meeting Ruth and now it is too late. 'In any case,' Geneva says, 'writers very rarely talk to each other about writing; other people's writing, maybe, not their own, not about the way they do it.'

'What do you talk about?'

'Children, mortgages, the cost of petrol; the kinds of thing that anyone else talks about. What do you talk about when you meet other teachers?'

'Teaching.'

'It's people who want to write and can't who talk about writing; the ones who believe they can learn in five days what takes the rest of us a lifetime. Has your Durham débâcle cured you of trying to teach it?'

'I never suffered from trying to teach it; it's something I have to do. You can't teach it, anyway. Those who can, will; those who can't, won't.'

'Spoken like a gentleman. Why don't you try poetry again?'

'Jesus Christ, Geneva, don't you ever give up? I can't write poetry either.'

'Nor can I, much as I love it, but it might settle your *Acid* hash. Fiction dilates an experience, poetry, I'd have thought, would encapsulate it.'

'Poetry encapsulates experience?'

'Wouldn't you say so? I think Ruth Prochak would agree.'

'Why Ruth?'

'It seems to me her poems close over an incident, seal it off, so that there's no further room for enlargement.'

'I've read *From an Unexposed Film*, but I hadn't thought of it like that. It made me wonder . . . perhaps I'd better go through it again.'

'I think *Midland City* will be even better. It should be out next month.'

McEvoy almost says, 'Oh, you can borrow mine,' but after

all he only grunts and Geneva continues, 'The title poem was in the *TLS* last week. I'd assumed it would be about, well, the Midlands, you know, sodden and unkind, Ode to Kettering or something in that vein.'

'It's a railway station,' McEvoy says.

'Fancy your knowing that.'

'Saw a sign to it at King's Cross,' he explains.

'Ruth wants to take care. They'll be sending her up as a cut-price Betjeman if she doesn't lay off trains. Once you develop a style or a preoccupation it's a question of staying one jump ahead of the parodists. She'll end up at the back of the *New Statesman*.'

Mary dances in from the kitchen waving a can of fish in a pantomime of helpless femininity which is more convincing that perhaps she intends. 'Hi, fans! Oh, Mum, be a good chap and open this. Really, British design is the *pits*. No wonder our balance of trade is slumping.'

Geneva takes can and key. 'It certainly stretches the ingenuity . . . but then, of course, the instructions might help. Mary', she says to McEvoy, 'always reads the instructions on everything very carefully before ignoring them. Oh, Mummy, you are rotten!' she shrieks, exactly capturing Mary's siren wail.

'Oh Mummy, you are rotten,' says Mary, but quietly. She turns to McEvoy. 'She's always doing that. When the phone rings she says, "I bet I know who that is – so-and-so," and then she tells you what they'll say and it is and they say it. Too sickening.'

'Take your sordid fish away.' Geneva gives her back the open can. 'How could I write dialogue if I didn't study the way people speak?'

Mary departs, grumbling, 'I know, I know; if you couldn't write dialogue you couldn't write books and if you couldn't write books we'd all starve. Don't tell *me*.'

'You don't hang about in bus shelters with a notebook, do you,' McEvoy asks, 'taking down conversations?'

'Never. It's more a question of listening to the *way* people speak; every voice has an individual signature. That's the main fault in *Acid Test*, everybody sounds exactly the same, which is one of the things that makes me suspect that she never really listened to any of you. Anyway, it's a great social asset; I can usually make a conversation go the way I want it to by conjecturing what the other fellow's likely to say in advance. Once I know people well enough I can write their dialogue for them.'

McEvoy says uneasily, 'Can you write mine?'

'Oh yes,' says Geneva, 'I can write *your* lines.'

'So you knew how this conversation would turn out?'

'Not at all; I said I can, I didn't say I do. What I notice most with you is not so much your lines as the continuo, which in your case is facial. You use your appearance to coax the conversation your way. Ruth's the same though with her, I'd guess, it's largely involuntary and completely misleading.'

Wide-eyed Ruth, McEvoy thinks, and the Homeric epithet irks him. He recalls the progress of his last conversation with Ruth. 'Wait a minute,' he says, 'what do you mean, continuo? What do you mean, I use my appearance?'

'Oh, come now, John, you know perfectly well what I mean; the tilt of an eyebrow, the half smile, the subtle deployment of crow's feet; it's called charm. All poor Ruth can do is gawk, as if she can't believe what she's hearing, which is what I mean by misleading. There's no one less prey to surprise, but I always think of Matilda when I see Ruth.'

'Matilda who?'

'Belloc: "Matilda told such Dreadful Lies, It made one Gasp and Stretch one's Eyes."'

'And you think *I* deliberately dissemble?'

'I didn't say that at all; pretending to be what we are not isn't necessarily practising to deceive, very often one is simply supplying what the observer wants. There's no reason why charm should be inevitably dishonest, but it's certainly manipulative and you do have an air of *bestowing* yourself.'

'Thank you. That's exactly what Caroline Hill wrote, as if I expected my adoring public to rise up and applaud. As if I thought people should be very grateful that I looked at them. As if I felt that I need not *do* anything, just being there was enough.'

'Now I've offended you,' Geneva sighs.

'Yes you have.' He gets up. 'I'd better be going, anyway.'

'John, don't. You're turning this into a quarrel. We never quarrel.'

'We're quarrelling now. You say things like that and expect me to sit there and agree? I thought at least you gave me the credit for being honest.'

'You are honest; that's what makes the charm defensible. If you misused it, that would be indefensible. Oh, I wish a horrible end on that woman. She's poisoned your opinion of yourself.'

'You don't think it needed poisoning, then?'

'You know I don't, but you've become so self-conscious. You never cared before what people thought of you.'

'I never talked about it.'

'Stop working yourself up.'

'I'm sorry; I'm taking umbrage. I'm being silly and I really had better go home – because it's time to go, no other reason. Believe me? I must be hard to live with at the moment.'

'Does Sarah think so?'

'Hard to live with, hard to live without.' He wants to add: She frightens me, I'm frightened for her; but that would be too blunt.

'Sit down again, John, and I'll kiss you goodbye.'

'Why not standing up?'

'I'm too short for you. I don't like kissing on tiptoe.' Geneva omits to explain that kissing on tiptoe has lately become such an intoxicating delight that she cannot bear to dilute it, even with poor old John. Then she remembers something and says, 'I met Sarah in the library while you were away. It was odd, she invited me to come and have coffee.'

'Did you accept?'

'I made my excuses and left; I hadn't the nerve. She was angling for information about the amorous academic.'

'Who?'

'The lecher you drove back to St Albans for me. I wasn't in the mood to extemporize; but John, do you think she'd like it if I dropped in for coffee one day?'

'Would you want to expose yourself to that?'

'I felt rather sorry for her; and guilty for making excuses. I really had no business to spin her that yarn.'

McEvoy sits down again. 'Kiss me goodbye then, Ginny,' he says, but he scarcely feels it when she does.

The old Esso map of London has endured such usage in the past that McEvoy has to open it face down and apply librarian's tape to the folds before he can risk turning it over to read the streets.

How green London is. Regent's Park lies near the top and on the northernmost margin is Primrose Hill. King Henry's Road passes narrowly between the edge of the park and the edge of the map.

'What are you looking at that for?' Sarah asks over his shoulder as he crouches on the living-room carpet.

'Ebury Teachers' Centre. I'm going to a meeting there in June.' This is true. It is written in his diary. He has the papers to prove it.

'Ebury? Won't that be round near Victoria?'

'It is. Sutherland Street.'

'You're kneeling on Victoria,' Sarah says.

'That sounds painful.' Sarah does not smile. 'I've already found it. I was just having a look round; I like maps.'

'What are you looking for?'

'I told you, not for anything, just looking. There's so much possibility in a map.'

Perhaps Sarah thinks there is too much possibility in a map. 'Lean back,' she commands, and when he does she tugs it away and folds it up.

'What did you do that for? I was *looking* at it.' He is shocked to confess himself author of this childish howl, protesting at injustice.

'You said you'd found what you were looking for;' she chides him for his outburst. 'I want to Hoover.' The Hoover is in the bedroom. If her brisk sleight of hand were successful he might pursue the argument, but the map will not fall into the right folds, she has bent it back awry; the adhesive tape beings to peel away, the sheet mysteriously slits itself and Sarah stands red-faced and sweating, helplessly rending the thing that drops to pieces from her fingers. McEvoy is beyond intervening, afraid to look at what he has wrought. He subsides crosslegged on the hearth rug, head bent and hands locked together while Sarah, whimpering now, frantically destroys the remainder of the map and severed rectangles fall into his lap.

Even Sarah has to go shopping. For half an hour he might have the house to himself but at the last moment he looks down from his study window at Christopher and Julian playing at the end of the garden, and fears for them. He cannot yet ask himself for how much longer he dare leave Sarah to claw at her own vitals but already he wonders if she ought to be alone with the children, longs for and dreads the beginning of term when they will be at school and she will be alone, alone.

He goes out on to the landing and calls over the banisters, 'Sarah, leave the children to play. I can keep an eye on them.'

She stands in the doorway of the kitchen to reply; he can see her feet, restlessly assuming ballet positions.

'But don't you want to work?'

'They look pretty engrossed. I can get on; don't worry.'

'I'll be able to go round faster without them.' He hears a note of glad relief inform her voice; after all, he can hardly be planning anything if he wants the children left behind; or can he? Is this deviousness beyond ordinary human comprehension?

'But I thought you'd want to be quiet for a bit.'

'No, really, I'm fine.' The feet twitter; fourth, first, fifth. Then they go away. The door closes. The back door closes. After a few moments the side gate closes, the car door slams. The car starts; it drives away. He times five minutes by the bug-eyed clock, upon which balances his lady, Julian's Easter gift, then he dials.

On Primrose Hill the telephone rings four times only before the receiver is lifted.

Brusquely: 'Prochak!'

'Ruth?'

'Ruth Prochak, yes.'

'Ruth, it's John.'

'Which one?'

'John McEvoy.'

144

Does he fancy that her voice softens, minimally? 'Hello, John.'

'Will you still come to lunch with me?'

'When?'

'Unless you could make it tomorrow or Friday it would have to be a weekend. School starts again on Monday.'

'I go to Liverpool on Friday. Weekdays are out, you say?'

He could go sick – no, Christ, not that. That way madness lies. Suppose someone rang from school. 'I'm afraid so. Next weekend?'

'Uh huh . . . Southampton. Still, that's not till the afternoon. What about Saturday next? The fifth?'

'Yes, that's marvellous.'

'Is it?' She sounds honestly doubtful.

'Shall I come to Primrose Hill?'

'You don't know the address.'

'I looked you up in the phone book.'

The suspicion of a chuckle: 'I suppose you must have done. All right, take the Tube to Chalk Farm, come out into Adelaide Road and cross over. There's a little slip road called Bridge Approach and then the bridge itself, over the Euston line, you can't miss it. Someone's painted "Nuclear waste passes under this bridge. How safe do you feel?" on the pavement. Turn right and you're in King Henry's Road. I'm on the right, opposite the junction with Ainger.'

'About twelve?'

'That's fine. I'll see you, then.'

'Enjoy Liverpool – and Carlisle. Oh, Ruth?'

'Yes?'

'Have you got your new timetable, yet?'

'Yesterday, why?'

'I saw them on sale and thought of you. Spring's begun. Goodbye, Ruth.'

'Goodbye, John.'

Now, what reason can he concoct for going to London, Saturday week? Starting today he has nine days in which to do it. Unmarked essays left over from last term and approaching their deadline lie neglected under his hand as he sits and thinks, while guilty sweat trickles between his shoulder blades.

2 a). Macbeth is a very odd play, for a start you have just got Macbeth and lady MacBeth and except for the porter they have not got any servants or anything, it is just them. The porter is drunk all the time, this is meant to be funny. Lady mcBeth says she knows what it is like to have a baby but there is not any baby she has not got any children, this may be why she does not mind killing other peoples. I think later on she mind's when she is asleep but not when she is doing it although she doesn't do it he does. When his wife goes mad and dies MacBeth does not mind very much. She should have done it some other time, he says . . .

Rhodri Davies. McEvoy writes automatically *Punctuation!* and wonders what question he could possibly have set to have elicited such an answer. Squid Woman falls from her perch on to the essay, with a soft plop.

He is still staring at it when he hears the car turn into the drive, the engine cut, the door slam; then the side gate, the shouts of the children as he sees them, from the window, run up the garden to greet their mother. He goes down.

'Coffee? Have a good shop?'

'I got everything, I think.' She checks her list, worriedly, unable to believe that she has *not* forgotten something. 'Did anyone call?'

'No one.'

'Daddy called,' Julian says.

'That was out of the window, when you threw the trowel,' Chris explains. 'Mum meant on the phone.'

'Daddy used the phone,' Julian insists. 'I heard the one in the hall go ping.' Sarah looks at Daddy.

McEvoy says, 'I rang Simon Headley – to see if he'd be fit for Friday's staff meeting.'

'And will he?'

'He was out. I'll try later.'

'I met him in town,' Sarah says.

'And how was he?'

'He seemed all right. He said he'd call you this evening.'

McEvoy, to fill the coffee pot, turns his back and feels the trap clash shut behind him. Missed! but only just; how close, how close; how careful he must be. Blameless for so long, whatever he does now she will be there before him and the trap will always be waiting, jaws ajar.

Not until the end of the staff meeting does it occur to him to wonder what he would have done if Ruth had agreed to lunch with him today. When he stammered out his ill-prepared invitation over the telephone he had given no thought to prior commitments, he wanted only to hear her say yes. He decides to waste no time now in pointless conjecture; the matter does not bear thinking about and since disaster was averted, does not need thinking about. Averting future disasters is all his care now, avoiding the snares and the night lines.

'Scotch?' Simon Headley asks, skittering up to him crabwise after the meeting. 'I've got a flask.'

'You'd have been in trouble in Durham,' McEvoy tells him. 'Ask for a Scotch up there and you get a pint of bitter. Yes I will. Let's go to The Shed.'

It is unusually hot for the end of April. The Shed smells already of creosote and LEA disinfectant, empty, swept and garnished against the first day of term. Some kind of utility polish has been applied to the scuffed tiles under his desk. At McEvoy's first post the cleaners put down tea leaves on bare boards before they swept.

'You had a good time?' Simon asks, pouring trebles into plastic cups from which he has rinsed the coffee.

'Not very,' McEvoy says. 'I made a complete cock-up of the writing commission but the rest wasn't too bad. You can read up the notes.'

'No deathless prose?'

'No. You'll have to carry on with the creative writing, I'll stick to critical appreciations and creative brain surgery.'

'*What?*'

'Oh . . . nothing. What's creative about the writing our mob turns out?'

'Nah then, boys; write an essay. What I done in the holidays.'

'I sometimes wonder if they don't prefer that to being played "The Ride of the Valkyries" and then having to describe the end of civilization as we know it in four hundred words, finish it for homework.'

'A Faber paperback broke up in my hands this morning,'

Simon says. 'A *Faber* paperback. That's the end of civilization as I know it.'

Paperbacks remind McEvoy of *Midland City* and *Midland City* reminds him of *From an Unexposed Film*, cased, and signed near Darlington. He takes it out of his briefcase and lays it on the desk where no one will give it a second look. People do not come into the English Department office in search of books; old books go there to die, *vide* the Warwick Shakespeares.

'Well, cheers.'

'Good health, and may your sperm count never grow less. Do you think Thomson will go in the summer?'

McEvoy bangs his head on the desk. 'Don't. Don't. I could hear it coming; I can write his lines for him. "Let's face it. We all know that basically teaching is a matter of classroom control." He's been talking of going for six years but as he's got classroom control it doesn't make any difference to him whether he goes or stays. He just sits there.'

'He doesn't like working for a younger head of department.'

'He could hardly hope for an older head of department.'

'What say we mount a campaign; subvert his Third Years.'

'They're beyond subversion, they're jelly in his hands; dissolving with boredom. I'll tell you what, if he does go, we'll get a woman.'

'What for?'

'To replace him. There aren't nearly enough women on the staff and only one in the department. When Marian retires we shan't have any.'

'"We got sunlight on the sand, we got moonlight on the sea . . ." Why do you want women, John?'

'I like women,' McEvoy says.

'So do I,' says Simon, crunch crunch. 'So do I.'

Mother wants them all to go down again next weekend, John too, this time. She was very disappointed that he couldn't get away for that last visit. She was even more disappointed that they could not go down to Sevenoaks for Easter, although Sarah did explain that with John away at the conference everything was so rushed this year. If they all go they will take the car, no more trains. Even if John did not come she could have the car; he wouldn't mind, but he must come. The conference wrung her out, she cannot face another separation so soon, all those unaccountable hours and minutes. He gets on well enough with her mother; if he has work he can bring it with him. It will make a nice break for Julian after his first week at school, of course they must go. She will ring at once and then tell John when he comes home tonight. He will be pleased with her decisiveness.

Sarah is alone. Half an hour ago she watched Julian turn his back on her to investigate the sand tray, the modelling clay, the Wendy house; the minuscule seductions of Miss Cleeve's scaled-down domain. How does the girl stand it, day after day; all that activity at knee-level, the little investigative hands?

As she is already upstairs Sarah goes along to John's study to make her telephone call, but in the doorway she shudders and pauses. Her hands begin to sweat. Between the door and the desk, where the telephone hangs, stands the filing cabinet. On Friday morning, before John went to his staff meeting, she stood here, she stood here speaking to him as he worked at the desk, speaking about the visit to Mother, and she touched the filing cabinet, just touched it, he didn't notice, slid her fingers under the handle of the top drawer and eased it, eased it. The cabinet was locked. When he had driven away to the meeting she ran at the stairs, staggered, ended the ascent on hands and knees, almost falling into the study and without stealth this time launched herself at the filing cabinet. The drawer slid out so far that she slammed it shut in a panic before she could see what was inside and become the spy that he suspects she is. For if he did not suspect her, he would not lock the cabinet. If she did not suspect him she would not need to look because if there were no need for suspicion it would not be locked, but now she knows it has been locked and she must look. On how many other occasions was it locked when she cried to herself Avaunt and would not even test the handle?

Friday, Saturday, Sunday she has come, and stood, and faltered, fingers under the handle, easing, easing. The drawer, unlocked, slides out; the hanging files creak and swing and shunt together as it reaches its extremity. This is the domestic drawer; details of insurance policies, bills, birth certificates, bank statements, the medical cards, the mortgage. There should be nothing else here, but what might not be hiding in the folds of that innocent concertina? Nothing else.

The second drawer is Work. The files, unlike the slim pocket above, are stuffed with notes, forms, Xeroxed memoranda, *letters*. It could take hours to go through it all, but hours she has, hours, days, weeks uninterrupted; the knowledge breaks upon her slowly. There is no need for indecent humiliating haste, she can take her time and search at leisure, systematically, check and recheck. No one has responded to her advertisements.

The bottom drawer houses debris; old desk diaries, outdated documents that methodical John can never bring himself to throw away in case they may turn out to be useful. They may indeed turn out to be useful. The cabinet was locked and now it is unlocked. The bird has flown but there will be other birds and she will trap them. Trap, trap, trap, her knuckles rap the desk. A pallid, repellent insect drops on to the wooden surface. Sarah jumps and gasps and swats it reflexly with a book under which it flattens, but does not crackle. She can scarcely bring herself to look at the corpse which is grey and the size of a cockchafer. There is no blood. It takes her a moment or two to identify it as Julian's lady. Guiltily she remoulds the bent and horrid thing.

When John comes home she tells him, a thought defiantly, that she has phoned Mother and they will all go down to Sevenoaks on Saturday morning. John looks very pleased. 'Lovely,' he says, 'but I can't manage Saturday morning. I promised some of the boys extra tuition for their A levels.'

'Rhodri Davies?'

'He's a Second Year. These are Sixth Formers, you wouldn't know them. You take Chris and Julian down by car and I'll follow on the train after lunch.'

'It's all right,' she says, 'I'll phone Mother and we can all go down in the afternoon.'

'Why spoil the day for everyone?' he says. 'I don't mind coming by train. You can drop me off at the school when you go in the morning. At least I shan't have any luggage to bother about.'

Why does he look so *pleased*?

10

It has been a horrible morning; the children recalcitrant, the Sixth Formers preternaturally gaumless, the traffic uncooperative; Sarah, stricken with a last-minute crisis of confidence, almost refused to go and harassed him with her estimated time of his arrival. Trapped in the subterranean junction at Camden Town he tells himself that he has earned his lunch and prays that it will be worth the earning, since the memory of it will have to succour him over the rest of the weekend as the prospect has sustained him through the morning.

He always forgets how much hotter London is than anywhere else. Adelaide Road quivers with greasy mirages, dwarfish shadows crawl behind their owners through the litter. McEvoy finds the railway without any trouble; *Nuclear waste passes under this bridge. How safe do you feel?* When did I last feel safe? he asks himself and hurries across. Already made late by the long wait at Camden Town he compounds the delay by missing the turn out of Regent's Park Road; reluctant to lose more time by retracing his steps he digresses farther; a slip of shining green tantalizes at the end of a left-hand turn; Primrose Hill. At last he finds himself in Ainger Road and comes out, as promised, opposite the row of high grey brick houses where Ruth has her flat, unapproachable as a sheer cliff on a hot day at the beach.

The sign by her bell is characteristically abrupt: *Prochak.* He rings; a seedy face hovers in the dark bay window at his side as he hears footsteps descending. Groundlessly he has assumed that she lives in the basement, coming up like a fugitive Persephone among the dustbins.

He says, 'I'm sorry I'm late. The train . . . '

'Uh huh; Camden Town. Come in.'

He follows her up the stairs, feeling better already. It is a good, solid wooden staircase and the house smells neither of cats nor of cabbage – why did he think it would be a flea-pit? – and Ruth is wearing a skirt, no, he was not expecting the skirt, either. No reason at all why he should have visualized any skirt of hers hanging at different lengths above down-at-heel shoes and laddered tights; it is a well-cut, well-fitted skirt, quite long, and as he follows her up, eyes level with the hem, he notices that her large feet make her ankles look very slender.

'Are you right at the top?'

'Second floor, here we are. Someone's got a couple of rooms in the attic, I think.'

'Don't you know?'

'We haven't met, I hear him walking up and down; John Gabriel Borkman.'

'Does he play *Danse macabre*?'

'Clog dances, by the sound of it.'

McEvoy is mainly taken aback by the bareness of Ruth's flat. Standing in her narrow hall he can see across the living-room, into the kitchen and along a passage past a closed door to an open door which must lead into a bedroom; this is all. When she ushers him into the living-room he counts, at one glance, five pieces of furniture excluding the crowded bookshelves; an armchair, a couch which does not match the armchair, a kitchen chair drawn up to a desk, and a coffee table. For the rest, something in the region of four hundred square feet of mouse-brown carpet tiles and grey curtains at the windows, three narrow sashes in the opposite wall. In spite of the golden heat beyond them a cool gale seems to sweep the room.

'Coffee?' Ruth asks.

'Please.' What is it about him that immediately makes people offer him coffee? As he said to Mary, it is exactly his image. He does not at once follow Ruth into the kitchen, where he may well find her crouched over a candle with a billy can, but sits on the couch. As his eye level drops the room expands, an airy vastness; the furnishing is not modishly minimalist, nor impoverished, but of a Spartan functionalism like a temporary office, a bivouac, confirming his earlier impression of rootlessness. Here one sits to work, here one sits at ease, here is where one places one's coffee and here is where one places one's guest; all necessities are accounted for. Geneva's flat, with its herbaceous riot of patterns, colours, textures, to nourish her novelist's eye for detail, looks garish in retrospect. His picture of Ruth nesting in warm frowsy squalor bleaches out; it is all so clean.

Crockery chimes in the kitchen. McEvoy rises to join his hostess but as he does so his attention is drawn to a welcome element of disarray; along the wall adjacent to the desk is a row of carrier bags, stuffed and propped against the skirting board, as bright as Geneva's cushions; perhaps she does use them as cushions; Sainsbury's, Marks & Spencer, Camel cigarettes, Selfridge, Fenwick, Jarrold of Norwich; who he?

'I was admiring the decor,' he explains, when she comes in with the coffee and discovers him hunkering in front of them.

'My filing system,' Ruth says, and opens the Marks & Spencer bag. It is packed with folders and papers, a squab of stationery. 'I like carrier bags, they keep things flat.'

'So would a filing cabinet.'

'But these are free.'

He does not take in the implications of this, saying as they sit down he on the couch, she on the chair, 'But then you don't care for furniture, do you?'

'I haven't got much money.'

'Oh Ruth – I'm sorry – I didn't think – ' He's off again, everlastingly wrong-footed.

'This place is comparatively cheap because I got it through the friend of a friend, but it's not *very* cheap. Living in London's expensive – especially living alone.'

'Had you ever thought of sharing?'

She lets out an unseemly laugh. 'Can you see me sharing with anyone?'

Well, no, he cannot; she would be a disconcerting flat mate, bed mate . . . At least there is a shade on the light, which hangs economically from a boss in the centre of the ceiling and, like him, she has an Anglepoise lamp on the desk.

'Where shall we eat?'

'Have you anywhere in mind? It would be nice if I could feed you here, but I'm a rotten cook. I heard Jane Stevens telling someone that I can burn water.'

This is more in line with his image of the louche *trouvère*. 'Can you suggest somewhere local?'

'No,' Ruth says, frankly. 'Well, most places would do well enough, but not for an occasion.'

'Not a meal to *ask* a man to?' Who's asking whom? Still, it is an occasion . . .

Before he can work this one out the telephone rings in the hall. Ruth, an inveterate sprawler, is already draped across her chair in an attitude that suggests, when she leaps up to answer it, that she may leave a third leg dangling negligently over the arm. 'I bet that's for Nigel.'

Nigel? The door closes behind her and although incisive her voice is pitched too low to penetrate the woodwork. He cannot hear. Nigel? Has she lied already?

'It was,' she says, returning; grinning.

'Was what?'

'For Nigel. He lives downstairs in some opulence but with no phone. He lends me his second-string telly, sometimes, and in return I let him use my phone number.'

'Why doesn't he get a phone of his own?'

Ruth sinks into the chair again; her skirt settling in quite elegant folds over her long thighs; she is always so much taller than he remembers.

'Oh, much too complicated. He keeps three girls in total ignorance of one another's existence. In fact he does have a phone, a sort of ormolu candlestick nonsense, but he had it disconnected. There was always the danger that if one of the girls rang, one of the *other* girls would answer it; too wearisome. He doesn't do terribly well out of the deal, though; I'm away such a lot – no, that's not quite it; the girls don't do terribly well. They can go for days during which he's unreachable.'

'Don't you disapprove?'

'I just think he's untouchable; reaching wouldn't enter my head – you know? The bargepole principle. They used to come to the house on spec, but now he sees people only by appointment. There were scenes on the doorstep and weeping concubines dripping away down the road.'

'That was one of the concubines on the phone?'

'Eithne. Eithne, Lucy and Jilly, they live in a treacle well. I'll tell you what, we could walk over the hill down into Marylebone and eat in town somewhere, unless you'd like to chance your arm in Chalk Farm and take the Tube – where are you going afterwards?'

'Sevenoaks. We're visiting my mother-in-law.'

She feels no urge to inquire about his family. 'Waterloo, then, same as me.'

He is foolhardy enough to argue. 'Charing Cross.'

'If you must, but you can pick it up at Waterloo East. Shall we go, if you've finished your coffee? Loo's down the hall, on the right.'

She thrusts herself out of the chair and scoots into the kitchen.

McEvoy, in the little windowless bathroom, sees himself looming in the mirror-tiled wall above the bath and wonders why he is there; no, no; that's not quite it. Why doesn't *she* wonder why he is there? She greets and entertains him like an old and not very close friend. While her eyes cry: This cannot be! everything else about her demeanour says: But this is how things are. What does she expect from him? Come to that, what does he expect from her? The telephone rings again and as swift as Sarah he is at the door, leaving the anonymous little bathroom in darkness. It is as impersonal as a well-kept cloakroom, except for the unexpectedly vernal scent of her soap which now clings to his hands, too.

'Oh no, don't do that!' Ruth is protesting into the receiver, as he comes out of the bathroom. She is shocked; something has disturbed her even tenor. He listens shamelessly, walking back to the living-room. 'Don't go through *Ely*; you wouldn't be in Carlisle till fifteen forty-five. Wait, I'll tell you the trains from Euston – '

He closes the door. What else but a timetable could rouse her to such impassioned pleading? While her voice rises and falls as she recites her favourite lines, he passes the time by looking into the carrier bags. Some of the contents are evidently connected to her regular employment, a memo addressed to Dr Prochak – so he was right – pokes out of Woolworth's, but through the weed-green of Laura Ashley he can see rows of the black even characters that knit up her handwriting; perhaps she must keep it small and neat so that she can see the shape of her work before it gets near the typewriter. Her machine stands uncovered on the desk, an ancient manual model. McEvoy recalls his first sight of her in Geneva's kitchen, pecking like a hen at Geneva's portable.

How strange, he thinks, she was nothing to me then, and is the further confounded because if she is anything to him now he does not know what it may be.

'Ready?' She stands in the doorway dressed and equipped for travel, bag on shoulder, briefcase in hand and a light leather jacket over her skirt and sweater.

'Must you take that lot with you?'

'I'm sure as hell not coming back for it.'

'Then may I carry something?' Seemingly surprised by the offer she hands him the bag.

'Isn't the briefcase heavier?'

'Probably, but I'm used to schlepping it. I must drop in on Nigel and give him his message.'

Nigel's front door has a bronze knocker which Ruth slams once as if she would send it straight through the woodwork. Nigel, about McEvoy's age, suave and Wildely overweight, peeps out.

'Oh, Ruthie! A wee message?'

'I've brought the result of your Wassermann test,' Ruth says, raising her voice slightly as a pallid girl with a tried expression droops jealously into view. McEvoy recognizes that expression.

'Ruthie, for God's sake, have you no shame?'

'All the shame that's going round here, by the looks of it,' Ruth says, but mutters discreetly, 'a phone call: Eithne Stretton desires that you ring her at this number, before six; you can't borrow mine, I'm going out.'

'I can't possibly ring her today,' Nigel says, pettishly, weary with surfeit. His eyes narrow, slyly. 'Unless you could lend me your key for a tiny moment?'

'I'm going *out*.'

'A nano-second?' Ruth hands him the key, wordlessly. 'Fabulous of you. Why don't you pop in and watch the box while I'm gone?'

'Telly? At this hour?' Ruth seems genuinely disgusted.

'I videoed *Arcade* for the Erté feature. Do take a look.'

'Five minutes,' Ruth says sternly, 'or I'll be up to unplug it. Come on, John.'

Nigel has been studiedly ignoring him; McEvoy follows Ruth the more eagerly into his living-room which, being directly below Ruth's, enjoys the same dimensions. However, Nigel's decision to furnish it as an hotel foyer effectively reduces the impression of space. Gilt mirrors and console tables hide the brocade wallpaper, the windows frown darkly beneath crimson plush pelmets. Nigel, McEvoy suspects, finds all this kind of thing frightfully amusing. Perhaps he thinks it resembles a brothel. An aspidistra in a heavy earthenware pot stands on top of the Biedermeier television set and below its fronds Geneva's face beams with rosy animation at Ruth and McEvoy as they stand together at the far end of the room. McEvoy starts guiltily and half raises his hand to his face.

'That's never Erté,' Ruth growls. Geneva is delivering aphorisms.

'Remember, one has to do one's characters' thinking for them. It would have been more accurate to ask if I can keep myself out of my books, rather than if I put myself in them.'

'Why does she get herself up like that?' Ruth demands. Geneva is wearing a pewter velvet frock with a large hand-tatted collar of the style once known as a Bertha, looking fully ten years older than she is, like someone's sensible granny.

'Creating characters is a kind of parthenogenesis.'

'Shall we run it back?' Ruth says.

'Do you really want to look at Erté? I'd quite like to see this.'

'So how would you define the difference between genius and talent?' the interviewer is asking. Geneva appears to give this question serious consideration. Ruth makes derisive noises.

'I suppose that you might say that genius is a vital organ,' Geneva pronounces, 'the body which depends upon it cannot survive without it; however you abuse genius it still functions – although of course it can destroy you. Talent is a muscle; it needs exercise or it atrophies.'

'And which do you have?' asks the interviewer.

'Talent,' says Geneva.

'If Geneva isn't careful she'll end up in Pseud's Corner,' Ruth says.

'But she's right, isn't she?'

'Yeah – but fancy *saying* it.'

'What's that woman doing here?' a plaintive voice demands, outside the door.

'She's a very dear friend, that's all. You spoke to her on the telephone, yesterday.' Unctuous Nigel has returned already; Eithne is on short commons.

'Who's *he*?'

'One of her very dear friends, I expect, Tootsie-Woo. They'll be going in a minute.'

'Who were you ringing?'

'A client,' Nigel explains, obscurely.

'Oh, Niggy, the soufflé . . .'

'Don't let's spoil their fucking soufflé,' Ruth snarls, turning her heel. If I called Sarah Tootsie-Woo could I run three simultaneous women? McEvoy wonders. 'And don't ask to garage your extraneous tarts on me next time you have a backlog,' she hisses, as they sweep past Nigel and out on to the landing.

'Oh Ruthie, not a tantrum – '

'Nor presume on my discretion. I'll write your next message in lipstick on the wall.'

'What's that about extraneous tarts?' McEvoy asks, following her down the stairs.

'A couple of weeks ago he got me to field one when she arrived early. She cried in the kitchen for twenty minutes, I was trying to *work*. Then she locked herself in the bathroom and screamed. John Gabriel Borkman was banging on the floor and a small crowd collected on the pavement.'

'Do you object on moral grounds?'

'Aesthetic, mostly; greasy little muff-diver. Too bleeding idle to tell his own lies.'

They spill down the steps on to the pavement and Ruth strikes out vigorously to the left, in the direction of the Underground Station. McEvoy thinks longingly of the green hill at the end of the road, but is too cowed to argue. Ruth's vile temper is brought on, he discovers, less by the reprehensible Nigel, whose mere existence should be enough to incense any woman of discernment, than by the sight of Geneva dictating literary theory.

'It was a shock, seeing her like that,' he says. 'I felt as if I'd been discovered *in flagrante* by an old friend.'

'Just being in Nigel's knocking shop is enough to make me feel as if I'd been caught *in flagrante*.' Ruth does not smile. 'Do people on telly know what kind of an audience they're preaching to?'

'I don't know,' he says. 'I did my preaching to the rest of the panel; I never gave a thought to anyone watching. Which was short-sighted,' he adds, thoughtfully.

'How she has the brass neck – she *deserves* to be watched by people like Nigel.'

'It was an interview,' he says, in mitigation. 'People ask you the most ridiculous questions.'

'That's no excuse for giving ridiculous answers. You think it's right to come out with things like that in public?'

'But she does it all the time.'

'Don't tell me. Half the things she says to people like us are milk runs for the lectures and interviews.'

'We get them free.'

'I don't see why we should get them at all. I'll swear I heard half of that malarky when I stayed with her. All that about organs and muscles.'

'She is physiological, isn't she? The other day she was telling me that sudden death is a wound and suicide's a tumour.'

'And the answer's a lemon.'

'I've known Geneva a very long time,' McEvoy says, declaring his loyalties.

Ruth looks almost contrite, she slackens speed. 'I shouldn't criticize your friend but John, really, you must notice how she uses us as sounding boards. She has a fund of things she would like to say and when the moment presents itself she says them. They're not necessarily true or apposite, they simply guide the conversation along the lines she wants to pursue.'

'She said something of the kind to me quite recently,' McEvoy says. 'It's her method of propagating fictional dialogue. She doesn't cultivate candour as you do.'

'I'm not candid,' Ruth says.

'You say what you think.'

'I say what I want to say but no, you're right, I don't lie for the exercise. I prefer to do it by omission.'

'Like John Gabriel Borkman?'

'My *opstairsiker*?'

'No, in the play. Mrs Borkman says that her husband lied to her. Ella Rentheim says, "He may have concealed the truth from you. But he didn't lie."'

'Uh; nothing but the truth but not the whole truth.'

They are back on the bridge.

'We still haven't decided where we'll eat.' He sees Chalk Farm on the far side of the tracks and wishes that they had gone the other way.

'There's a Greek dive up the road. You wanted to go through the park, didn't you?'

'You still could.'

'You should have said. We could take the Tube into town and look around.'

'I'd rather walk through the park.'

'It's a bit late now – I've got a train, remember.'

'When haven't you got a train?'

'Why didn't you say something sooner?'

'I didn't like to,' he says, pointedly.

'If we don't make up our minds we'll be here till the nuclear waste comes through at four a.m.'

'The park, then.'

'Oh, decisive at last. What about my train?'

'You and your bloody trains!' He is infuriated to see how little she cares what he thinks of her – how can she take such risks with his opinion? – then instantly chides himself for so belittling her. He would not, after all, want her to ingratiate.

'We'll go through the park,' Ruth says, either acknowledging his apology before he makes it, or suddenly comprehending the risk she is taking. She begins to walk back the way they have come, head bent. McEvoy, turning to follow her, is smitten with remorse; poor little Ruth.

The silence lasts them along the length of Ainger Road. McEvoy wishes he could work up enough speed to draw ahead, so that she would be hurrying behind him, but she maintains her lead. They are at the gate of the park before he can formulate a pleasantry that is sufficiently anodyne to avert an irritable backlash. Ruth, he realizes, has no small talk.

'Do you know,' he says, truthfully, 'I've never been up here before.'

'Let's walk over the top, then. There's a splendid view.'

'Won't that make you even later?'

'It doesn't matter.' Her eyes swell with the effort of being amenable. He is very touched and a little dismayed; ought she to capitulate so easily?

The top of the hill commands a hazy sunlit view of London, a pale and peaceable city too distant to reveal the grievous bodily harm that it inflicts on itself. Close at hand a magpie flies into a May tree. McEvoy, at this moment, thinks that he loves London.

Stirred by the same impulse, for once, they begin to move downward, on the path that leads to Albert Road and the Zoo, beneath plane trees whose young leaves are almost blond against the intensely blue sky, the catkins golden and spherical.

'Oh look,' says Ruth, 'aren't they like the balls on tom kittens?'

The sweetness of the simile so overcomes him that without any forethought he wraps his free arm about her shoulders and draws her to him. Apparently Ruth does not mind. She smiles sideways and upwards, looking, through no fault of her own, startlingly coquettish.

'What's the matter?'

'Nothing's the matter. It was such a nice thing to say.' It would be presumptuous and premature to leave his arm where it lies so he withdraws it, but they walk more closely and the silence between them softens. McEvoy at least stops trying to think of conversational openings. He remembers a madrigal that he sang once:

She was pleased, she was pleased, she was pleased and she my pleasure.

They eat at last in a restaurant somewhere in the vicinity of Madame Tussaud's; McEvoy, on foreign territory here, is content to let Ruth direct him; this is her manor. The room where they eat is dark and the waiter lurks among foliage with a priapic pepper mill, fully three feet long.

'A wistful satyr,' Ruth says, as the pepper mill grinds

suggestively over a plate of fettucine behind the grape ivy. They have got as far as coffee and the talk up till now has been pleasingly general; a civilized debate on the teaching of poetry at O level, a scabrous rehearsal of the fortunes of Nigel and his nymphs.

'Do you find his behaviour reprehensible because he's a man?' McEvoy asks.

'What a peculiar question. I'd find it reprehensible in anyone. It stems from unadulterated conceit, but you may be right. Only really beautiful women can risk that attitude but the most repulsive men take it as read.'

'What attitude?'

'That one's mere physical existence justifies one's behaviour. "Don't look a gift horse in the mouth," is what our Nigel is really saying. "I have bestowed myself upon you, what more do you want?"'

McEvoy inhales coffee and chokes.

'I don't think it was *that* funny,' Ruth says, wonderingly.

'It wasn't. No, no, it wasn't funny. Someone said that about me not very long ago.'

'That you're conceited?'

'That I bestow myself; that very word.'

'At least you've got something to bestow,' Ruth says, consoling him kindly. He cannot take it as a compliment, since she is contrasting him only with Nigel. 'Not that bleeding book again?'

'Not directly. It came out of a conversation on something that was in the book.'

'If I were you,' Ruth says, 'I should stop talking about it. Leave it alone. You're like a kid who keeps picking at a scab to see if it's healed. Every time you lift it the wound begins to bleed again.'

'It won't heal. I find I'm analysing everything I do to see if I really am what I thought I was, or really am what I seem to be.'

'You'd have to be unnaturally objective to admit it if you were. Surely the things that other people notice about you aren't the things that you'd notice about yourself? A man who truly acknowledged what a shit he was would be insufferable.'

'I hope that doesn't mean what it sounds as if it means.'

'I'm not calling you a shit,' Ruth says. 'What have you ever done to me?'

'I didn't think I'd ever done anything to anyone, till *Acid Test* turned up. That woman, Margaret, waited twenty years to pay me back for a wrong she thinks I did her.'

'That says more about her than it does about you. Can't you forget her – or has she been in touch?'

'No. I thought she might have been. I don't know if she's waiting for me to dig her out or whether she's content with thinking that sending it must have done the damage she intended it to.'

'If you really were as appalling as she seems to believe, I'd have thought you'd be impervious to remorse. She doesn't know how you've reacted, does she? I'd guess she's entertaining herself by imagining your reactions, she doesn't need to *know*. You're the villain in her story and you've got your comeuppance. You don't have to have her in your story at all.'

'People aren't as easily disposed of as that even in soap operas. I can't just write her out.'

'Write yourself out,' Ruth advises. 'I think it's time we left. I've missed one train already, I won't lose the sixteen thirty-five.'

'You don't know the times of the trains to Sevenoaks, do you?' McEvoy asks, hoping to imply: Of course you do.

'Not the precise times,' she says, disappointingly, 'but there are three or four every hour. You'll be all right.'

The unseasonable heat of this May Saturday has brought out an early crop of citizens and tourists; where better to spend a balmy spring afternoon than in Madame Tussaud's or the Planetarium? Ruth and McEvoy bore through the crowds in Marylebone Road, a barge and its butty, and descend into Baker Street Station.

'Take your choice,' Ruth says, 'you can get your train at Charing Cross or come on with me to Waterloo. You won't have to change.'

Is this an invitation? McEvoy buys his ticket and follows her down to the platform as the train draws in, a traditional Tube train, red outside and green within, rackety and redolent of post-war transport. It seems very small inside and they squeeze in together, clutching Ruth's luggage, on a double seat.

'How long to Waterloo?'

'Fifteen, twenty minutes.'

He has fifteen, twenty minutes.

'Ruth, shall we do this again; have lunch, talk, walk in the park?'

'Walking in a park's best for autumn. Can you wait that long?'

'No,' he says, 'I can't. I don't have very much free time, may I ring you?'

'I don't have much free time either,' Ruth says. 'Our term started when yours did.'

'But aren't you part-time?'

'When I'm not teaching I'm travelling. I'm giving a reading at Oxford in three weeks, why don't you come to that? I'll ring you.'

Oxford? Why should he not go to Oxford? 'No; no don't, Ruth. I'll call you and perhaps, if you're free, we could lunch again.'

'Well, all right,' she says. He may not ask if she will look forward to that, if she wants to see him again. She has invited him to Oxford; if he wants to divine the strength of her inclinations he will be thrown back on his own powers of conjecture. Waterloo.

Walking along the curving concourse toward her platform he says, 'I'll ring you soon, then?'

'Uh huh. You go through here,' she says, indicating a left turn. 'Waterloo East.' He has been working things out. Does she agree to their meeting through inertia, or indifference, or because, as she once said, he makes a pleasant afternoon's viewing? It cannot be for the harmonious conversations; every time we meet we have to start over from the beginning and talk ourselves back into amity; no, she doesn't, I do. After all this, I still don't know what to say to her. We need a password, a sign, that will admit us immediately.

Ruth has already regained possession of her travelling bag, is thanking him for her lunch. Now she raises her hand and starts to turn away toward the gate of Platform Nine. McEvoy, very quick for him, swings round, clasping the hand, and kisses her on the mouth. It has to be brief for he has no idea what she will do; bite perhaps, but no, as far as he can tell she kisses him back. Next time they meet they can kiss and be friends at once, and the talking can serve its turn.

He rings Joan's house from Sevenoaks Station. Sarah's voice, when she answers, is high and constricted as if she clutched at her own throat in terror. When he sees her searching for him through the windscreen, ten minutes later, he knows what he is going to get; the face is white, muscles twitching round the mouth.

'Where have you *been*?'

What kind of a front has she put up for her mother all afternoon, or are there no pretences here; has she told all? (Told what?) He thinks not; to confide in her mother would be an admission of failure. (Failure to do what? To have netted a perfect husband?)

'John, it's nearly half past *five*.'

'Well, you knew I'd be late.'

'Not this late. I thought you'd had an accident.'

No you didn't. You thought I was with a woman. Well, all the other times you thought I was and I wasn't can pay for this one time when you were right. You should have trusted me while you had reason. However, you saw me wallowing in a wicked double bed; I was quarrelling on a railway bridge. I am developing this taste for trains, Sarah . . .

'I stayed in London for a bit, to look round Foyle's and Hatchards.'

'What did you buy?'

'Nothing. I only wanted to look – for school. It was such a nice day I went for a walk in the park.'

'What park?'

'St James's,' McEvoy says. 'I travelled from Charing Cross.'

11

The main area of the staffroom is laid out with the rigid informality of a departure lounge; banks of low orange armchairs face each other across veneered coffee tables stacked with file paper, exercise books, folders, newspapers and those turd-brown ashtrays peculiar to school staffrooms which evidence the existence of a pottery department. With forty teachers in it, it is only less noisy than the Sixth Form common room; a blue fume of cigarette smoke hangs over one corner where the card school sits. People who wish to work uninterrupted retire pointedly to the Quiet Room, which is furnished with two deal kitchen tables and hard Windsor chairs, slamming the door as they go. Years of slamming have loosened both the door in its frame and the frame in the wall, so that at peak periods the Quiet Room is only less noisy than the staffroom.

McEvoy, wishing to work uninterrupted or at least to get through the poetry reviews in the *Times Literary Supplement* before the bell rings, sits hunched over the table below the window, his paper open in front of him. At the other table Simon Headley, who is conscientious when not fornicating, works his way through a pile of books.

'It was like a school concert,' says a voice, unseen, on the far side of the partition, 'I mean, the audience were like kids, you know, restless; talking all the time, not even talking quietly, some of them; getting up and wandering about and then, every now and again, a great yell of laughter. That's what really gave it away, the laughter. Grace Peel.'

McEvoy looks up and catches Simon's eye, mouthing, 'Who?'

'Thatcher.' Thatcher is young and fairly new, with a reputation as a raconteur that cannot quite be called undeserved.

'Every now and again' says Thatcher, 'the performance was interrupted as some maniac went streaking through pursued by a nurse. Nobody stopped. They just went on as normal – well, I suppose it was, to them. The best moment was when the same maniac came streaking back in the opposite direction, pursued by the same nurse. *Charley's Aunt* wasn't in it. Nobody laughed at that though. That was the really unsettling thing, the laughter had nothing to do with the concert at all. It just broke out sporadically, with Grace Peel doing the solos.'

A burst of appreciation, not unlike that which Thatcher has been describing, erupts on the far side of the partition. Simon thumps the wall, approximately where he hopes Thatcher's head may be. 'Do you suppose he means Grace Poole?'

'Who?'

'The woman in *Jane Eyre* with the demonic laugh, only it turns out to be Mr Rochester's mad wife, locked in the attic.'

You examine me, Miss Eyre, do you think me handsome? Are you beginning to like me, Dr Prochak? 'What on earth is he talking about?' McEvoy says, perturbed. The review of *Midland City* is a good one, excepting an uncalled-for gibe about gricers which would have passed over McEvoy's head a month ago. He wishes he could finish it.

The door opens; Atkinson, Physics and PE, comes in with books and football socks. He looks industrious and slightly shame-faced.

'You shouldn't laugh,' he says.

'We aren't laughing,' McEvoy says.

Simon says, 'Could a bit of consciousness-raising be in order out there?'

'I don't imagine Thatch finds it all that funny really,' Atkinson says, 'but it's the way he tells it. It's all very well trying to make people Concerned, capital C; when you get down to it, that kind of thing makes you laugh.'

'What kind of thing?' Simon says.

'His wife's brother's a charge nurse at Haselfield. They had a concert last night and Thatch went along. He told us yesterday he was going, dead serious; you could see he thought he was doing the right thing but when it came down to it . . . '

'And then came the *pièce de résistance*.' Thatcher, unfortunately, has not finished. He pronounces it piece de resistance. 'Just as we were leaving this girl comes up and says, "I've been watching you." This is to *me*, mind. "I've been watching you and I've realized you're a believer. You're the one I have to tell." "What's that, love?" I said. "It can't be written down," she said, "I have to tell you." She had my arm in a grip – you hear about them having supernatural strength. Pauline was looking daggers but I had to go with her. We got round behind a sort of buttress by the front door and she whispers, "We have to tell everyone we can. There isn't much time." And I said, "Come on then, dear, you tell me," and she says, "It's this. Glorious God desired children, and he put something into nothing, which was Time, and the Devil said, You have offended us." I said, "Well, what do you want me to do, dear?" and she said, "You'll have to pass it on. That man with the microphone is the prophet Isinglass, but no one can switch him on!"'

'He's making this up,' Simon says, mouth turned down in disapproval. Simon has his standards.

'I don't think he is,' McEvoy says. He folds away the copy of the *TLS*, brushes past Atkinson and goes out into the staffroom. Thatcher's audience, which probably began as two or three intimates, has swelled to comprise half of the staff. Even if half of that half disapproves of what they are hearing, the rest are having an uncommonly good time. The little group round Thatcher's chair is backed by a semi-circle of wheezing adults on their hind legs like basking meerkats, with their forepaws dangling.

'She was still yelling "Isinglass! Isinglass!" when I made a break for it.'

If we caught the boys behaving like that, McEvoy thinks, we'd read them a stiff lecture on others less fortunate than themselves. We'd say to them: Don't you know that it's wrong to mock the afflicted? How can you be sure the afflicted's husband isn't listening? He seems to fly down the corridors, winged with rage and the Erinyes at his back. Nervous little boys and some quite large ones scatter as he bears down on them. When he gains The Shed he slams the door, as he had not the nerve to do in the staffroom, as he had not the nerve to do, for instance, when he came home yesterday lunchtime, having left his briefcase accidentally in the study, and ran upstairs to find the filing cabinet violated, two drawers yanked out by someone who had forgotten the safety device and jammed them and could not push them back. Would that have required supernatural strength? No, he could have done it himself, the cabinet is old, weakened; but the strength of fear and fury, yes. And did not his nerve fail him again when he looked out the window and saw Sarah standing – or hiding? – behind the apple tree. No doubt it was failure of nerve the night before when he rang, from the study, Bob Lake, the Deputy Head. Bob was out but his wife answered. The low womanly voice engaged him in conversation for several minutes (it is some months since they met) and when Delia Lake hung up, McEvoy did not. He pressed the receiver rest and listened, hearing the receiver in the hall softly replaced, but his nerve failed and he said nothing, yesterday he said nothing. While he says nothing, nothing can happen. Until he is told, he knows nothing, and he cannot act upon what he does not know.

The Shed, this public room in a state institution, is safer than his study. He dials Mrs Mitchell in the secretary's office. 'May I have an outside line, please?'

Ruth, never late for trains, objects to being late for anything. Her life, so far from meandering in the manner that McEvoy finds so appealing, is straitened by schedules of her own devising, as unyielding as any metrical form. She allows an exact length of time for her favourite walk to work across the hill (although McEvoy would perversely assume that she preferred the Underground), an exact length of time for shopping, for eating, working, sleeping, to allow herself as long as possible in which to write, so it is as much impatience as anything that makes her snap 'Prochak!' when the telephone rings as she is about to leave the flat.

'It's John McEvoy.'

'Again already?'

'I'm sorry. Are you busy?'

'About to be.'

'When can I see you?'

'I don't know; next weekend? That's the Oxford gig, are you coming?'

'Can you make it sooner, Ruth, please? I want to talk to you. Are you doing anything on Monday afternoon?'

My, he is impatient. Ruth jams the receiver under her jaw, juggling books and briefcase while she searches for her diary. 'No, I'm not, as it happens; but aren't you teaching?'

'Free periods – three straight off. I can get away – shall I come to the flat?'

'Are you going to be pressed for time?' Ruth says, acutely. 'I have a seminar in the morning. You could meet me from work.'

'I don't think I could get there before two.'

'I eat in the canteen. Look, I'll meet you outside the main entrance – you know? I showed you last time. Marylebone Road.'

'Yes. Two o'clock. Ruth – '

'Better make it two fifteen,' says sensible Ruth. 'Don't kill yourself.'

'No. Monday then. Thank you.'

'That's all right,' Ruth says, hanging up, because as far as she is concerned, it is all right. She shoves the books into her case and leaves the flat at an urgent canter, baring her teeth at Nigel on the way down, as he comes up.

'Oh Ruthie – '

'Hop off.' She has decided, over the last couple of weeks, that she has been too tolerant of Nigel for too long, but being Ruth, it does not occur to her to wonder why she should have arrived so relatively suddenly at this decision. Nigel's monstrous conceit is something she has always taken for granted, since Nigel's entire being feeds off it. Only very recently has it struck her that Nigel might be otherwise, that it might cause her active pleasure to see him put out, but she will not be going far on this particular train of thought. By and large and paradoxically Ruth avoids trains of thought. She believes that they lead to loss of spontaneity.

Another fine day, though not so hot as it was a fortnight ago, when John was with her on this same path. The grass on the hill flickers under a sprightly breeze and Ruth hurtles across the park, jacket flying open.

Whatever can he want? surely not to talk about his book again? He must know by now that even if she read the wretched thing she would still make up her own mind. He really ought to be able to see that she likes him; he must be used to being liked, he seems generally likeable. She would like him even more were he a thought less patronizing, humouring what he takes to be her foibles – doesn't he know bloody-mindedness when he sees it? – figuratively patting her on the head and at the same time begging her to assure him that he has the right to do it. No doubt it will all be resolved on Monday. Surmise is not her strong point.

If he knows what she is doing he does not say. When he came home yesterday at lunchtime, rushing through the hall calling, 'Sarah! Sarah! I forgot my briefcase,' she had just time to slip into the bathroom before he came round the bend in the stairs and then, while he stood surprised before the filing cabinet, to slip out again, silently down and out into the garden. She saw him as she went by, his back was turned, but she knows how he must have looked. She was in the garden, behind the apple tree where he could not see her when she heard, through the open window, the drawers crash shut. He did not see her, must have thought she was out, for he left again at once and he must have thought he left the drawers like that himself, easily done, because he has said nothing; yes, that's what he must think, or he would have mentioned it. This morning the cabinet was not locked, but it no longer matters if he does lock it, if he has ceased to trust her it no longer matters because she need no longer trust him. He ceased to merit her trust the moment he turned the key on the day he came home from Durham. Ten years' rigor of apprehension is relaxing; she need no longer surmise; she knows. Quite soon she will discover exactly what it is that she knows.

She has another hour before she must go and fetch Chris and Julian from school, an hour to make a serious start on the contents of the middle drawer, having satisfied herself that top and bottom are innocent – for the time being. She will have to update her checks, regularly. Yesterday she was too frightened, after John had left the house, to go back. It was in sheer panic that she had in the first place tried to open the middle drawer before the top was fully closed, jamming them both. Today she can be as methodical as she promised herself she would be, and *conduct* the search; that's the word she wants.

Sarah opens the drawer and slides forward the hanging files, so that she can begin with the hindmost and work through to the front; in any case, clandestine correspondence is more likely to be at the back.

Dear Mr McEvoy, Dear Mr McEvoy, Dear Sir, Dear John . . .

Dear John? It's from Simon Headley, about set books: 18 August 1979 – this is history – *Dear Sir, Dear Sir, Dear Mr McEvoy* . . .

Yours faithfully, yours sincerely, yours sincerely, yours sincerely, yours truly, love from Alison . . .

His sister.

Everything is here except the truth!

'We had to watch you on video this afternoon,' Jane complains. 'That arts programme thing you did. Oh Mum, the things you say.'

'It's all good publicity,' Geneva says. 'Look what I got from the library today; *North American Quilts!*'

'Don't try and change the subject,' Mary says, 'it's not good publicity for us. Half the fellas come groping round at break; "How's *your* vital organ?" they say. You should think of the effect these things have in mixed schools.'

'Did you have to watch it too?' Jane says. 'Poor baby.'

'I reckon the teachers have a catalogue of people with embarrassing parents. Old Brocklehurst, the one you think's so dishy, Mum, well, he came up to me in English and said, "And how's our little authoress today?"'

'Bite him in the leg,' Geneva advises. 'He won't do it again.'

'Let's kill her,' says Jane, 'and claim the insurance.'

'People ask you such ridiculous questions,' Geneva defends herself.

'I think Ruth Prochak would make a good mother,' Mary says. 'Ask her an embarrassing question and she'd just blink. She certainly wouldn't answer it.'

'"One doesn't write about people one knows, one writes what one knows about people." Is that a quotation or did you make it up?'

'I made it up. It could become a quotation.'

'Ruth could never have children, her hips are too narrow, don't you think, Mum?'

'It doesn't signify,' Geneva says, 'especially these days. The thinnest woman I ever knew gave birth to twins.'

'Yeah, but Ruth's so straight up and down.'

'And great big feet. I always expect them to spread, you know, like a camel's, when she walks. Oh Mum, look at this pattern you got in Debenham's. I do think peplums are the most hideous sort of frill ever invented. Do you think she'll come here again?'

'If she could hear this conversation she certainly wouldn't. We can make it without the peplum, you know.'

'Let's invite her,' Jane says. 'I like Ruth.'

'Why?' Geneva asks, frankly curious.

'Why do I like her? Dunno. Why not?'

'She reminds me a little of Maud; splendidly null.'

'But not icily regular, not with that conk. I thought you liked her, Mum.'

'Oh, I do, but we have work in common, to a certain extent, and mutual friends. What do you have?'

'Nothing really; I just like the way she takes everything as read.'

'Don't you think that might be a complete abdication of moral judgement?'

'*Can* we invite her?' Mary says, abruptly, out of her depth. 'We haven't had anyone round for ages. When's John coming again?'

'How should I know? He comes when he can; you know how busy he is.'

'Why don't you go and see him? Oh, *let's* have Ruth. Ring her up.'

'You ring her up. I don't suppose she'll be home, though, she travels a lot.'

Mary sweeps from her lap the shawl she is crocheting and crawls to the telephone. They sit round expectantly while the bell trills on Primrose Hill. 'She's not in,' Jane predicts. Mary nods and hands the receiver to her mother. 'She's in.'

'Ruth?' Geneva smiles and bridles as though Ruth were in the room. 'The girls and I were just talking about you. We

174

are wondering when you could come and see us again.'

'I'd like that.'

'When are you free?'

There is a pause and the flutter of diary leaves. 'The First of June? A Friday; I could stay till Saturday evening.'

'That would be lovely. You can be here for dinner on Friday?'

'Yes, thanks. I saw you on telly t'other week.'

'*Don't*. That woman and her stupid questions. The girls have had to watch it on video at school, they've been threatening reprisals all evening – oh, Ruth; what's a gricer?'

'You been reading the *TLS*?'

'It's a good review. Congratulations.'

'By him it's good,' Ruth says, grudgingly. 'Gricers are those loonies who stand around on the ends of railway platforms collecting locomotive numbers.'

'I'd have thought that'd be right up your street. Well, we'll see you today fortnight. Goodbye, Ruth.'

'I wonder if she's got a fella,' Mary says.

'What put that idea into your tiny mind?'

'Oh, I don't know . . . I just imagined her necking when the phone went and swearing a blue streak while she answered it but having to be fearfully polite.'

'She's never that,' Jane says.

'Can't imagine her in bed with anyone, though,' Mary says, 'she's got such hellish sharp elbows.'

Ruth and her student part company on the steps down to the pavement. Assuming optimistically that they are bound in opposite directions the girl begins to move away before they have reached the pavement; but Ruth pauses and stares, with customary effect.

'I'll be handing in my assignment late.' The girl's own eyes are transparently mendacious. 'It's not quite finished.'

'It's not quite begun,' Ruth suggests, heavily amiable.

'It's drafted.'

'I don't think so.' Ruth knows all about drafting. A completed draft furnishes an armature of confidence absent from this spiel. 'Make sure I get it by Friday or I shan't read it.'

'Oh, right. *Thank* you, Dr Prochak.' The child takes the

remaining steps at a skip, skirts swinging. She is strangely flounced and frilled, with a knot of pink ribbons streaming from among her blonde curls, reminding Ruth of a musical comedy nursemaid; almost she expects her to clasp the handrail and twirl skittishly, exposing an ankle and rolling a roguish eye over one shoulder to the rude old gentlemen sitting in the stalls.

Ruth always feels sage and sere after being addressed as Dr Prochak. It ages her with the same painless surprise that she felt when she first noticed the premature grey threads on her temples, although her hair is so colourless that it will be some years before the grey becomes noticeable to anyone else except, maybe, to an observant lover. She was even more surprised, and mildly fascinated, to discover that her pubic hair also shows traces of grey. Till then she had never thought that one might go grey *all over*.

Along the street little Pink Ribbons has o'erskipped herself and dropped her folder, which bursts open. The passers-by, disclaiming their boorishness by considering themselves streetwise, London fashion, make no effort to help her. Undismayed, in a surf of lace and netting, the girl stoops to gather her scattered papers, splashing about on the sunlit pavement with the grace of a maiden scooping lilies from a limpid pool. She seems charmed by her own foolishness and Ruth, leaning on the balustrade, openly staring, could almost envy her the facility; she is not herself a foolish woman. A youth, cycling along the pavement, tips the corner of the folder and sends the contents flying. 'Oh!' cries Pink Ribbons and bends beautifully earthward to begin all over again the task of recovering them. Her skirts spread and her fingers flutter like wounded butterflies.

Into this pastoral walks John McEvoy; chivalrous John, of course, stops to help. Ruth folds her arms on the concrete coping and gives herself up to the pleasure of watching the comedy played out. John stoops, his shadow falls across the folder; Pink Ribbons glances up, prettily startled, to see a tall dark handsome stranger leaning over her and 'Oh!' she says again. Ruth can scarcely refrain from applauding.

He helps her to her feet, brushes dust from the lacy petticoats, tactfully directs the dainty sandals away from the pile of dog shit on the kerb stone and sweeps up the file papers in strong masterful fingers; even puts them back into the folder, closes it with a manly flick of the wrist and hands it to the palpitating owner. Wow! was that ever a curtsey she dropped?

He smiles down at her, he really can smile down at this one, she barely reaches his shoulder, and walks on.

'That was nicely done,' says Ruth, descending the last few steps to meet him. 'That was really nice.' They kiss. Over his shoulder Ruth can see Pink Ribbons, gazing open-mouthed and thinking, probably, What a waste.

'What did you expect me to do?' John asks. 'Tread on her fingers?'

'That's the form round here, I'm afraid. You've done more than you know. Now she'll slave to get her assignment in by Friday so she can ask me who you are with a clear conscience. Do you want to come in for a coffee or shall we walk?'

'Perhaps we should walk, I haven't got all that long.'

'In that case walk me home. We can go through the park; you'd like that?'

'You're not going to make me wait for autumn, then?'

'No,' Ruth says, sensing with a shock his radiant unhappiness. 'I won't make you wait for autumn.' They turn in step and pace gravely down the street.

'Shall I carry your briefcase or would you rather – schlep?'

'I'll schlep.'

'Did you wonder why I wanted to see you?'

'I suppose you'll tell me, otherwise you'd just have gone on wanting, like the poor cat i' the adage, letting I dare not wait upon I would.'

'How does a biochemist come to be so well read?'

'English specialists always think that scientists must be illiterate, which given the incidence of scientific knowledge among English specialists is not surprising. I've read widely, but not too well; it isn't all timetables. I did Macbeth at O level.'

'I'm teaching it. You must confess, you're unusual, though.'

'If you want me to be. Isn't that what you prefer to think?'

'I'm attracted by the unusual. I don't find much to enjoy in the prosaic.'

'Oh, glory be to God for *normal* things,' Ruth says, 'what price the rise of the mediocracy? You're one of those people who insist that their friends are unusual because it makes them feel singular without having to do anything.'

'I should like to be singular for you,' John says, humbly.

This guy is treading water, Ruth thinks.

He says, 'All my life I have thought of myself as entirely ordinary, that I had never done anything untoward or influential.'

'Oh-oh-oh, *Acid Test* again. Has Margaret come out of the woodwork?'

'Whatever's coming out of the woodwork, it isn't Margaret. I've been thinking, I'm beginning to believe you were right; she's quite content to imagine what I'm suffering now though, God knows, she can have no idea what's happening.'

'Suffering?'

'Have you any family, Ruth?'

'You have a grasshopper mind. Of course I have a family, I was begotten, not created. Did you think I sprang fully armed from the brow of my publisher?'

'You never mention them.'

'I've no particular cause to mention them. Should you care about my brother the ad-man, staked out in Manhattan, or my widowed father, living in very cheerful sin in Bournemouth?'

'Go on.'

'There's nothing more to tell. That's all there is; you must admit it was a very comprehensive summary.'

'I only mentioned it because you never ask about mine.'

'I'd consider it an impertinence to ask; anyway, when I make a friend I don't feel the need to take his wife and kids on board.'

'Doesn't that make your social life rather circumscribed?'

'Ah, come on, John; have you ever tried to make friends with a whole family? It's hard enough to like any two people equally; if you always see them together it's impossible. I'd sooner not try. Why d'you ask, anyway; you're not thinking of inviting me to your house, are you?'

No, clearly that was very far from his mind.

'I won't drop in on you, then. Geneva's asked me over next week; I could have done. Shall I see you there?'

'I don't think so. Oh Ruth . . . '

'Uh?'

'Ruth . . . '

'Don't stand there saying oh Ruth; they'll nick you for loitering round here if they see you with both feet on the ground at once. John, move.' She takes his arm and tugs. They walk on, closely, toward the park.

'I've never told Geneva that I know you.'

'But she knows. We first met at her flat.'

'She doesn't know that we've met since – unless you've told her.'

'I haven't seen her. I was quite surprised when she rang up on Friday and asked me over. It wasn't the moment to say, oh, by the way, I've been seeing your friend John on the quiet.'

'Don't say that. It's not on the quiet.'

'It seems bleeding quiet to me, Jack. You pretend to Geneva that we haven't met, you tell me not to ring you at home, you're wagging it this afternoon – '

'I told you, I don't have to be in school – '

'Oh, now I've hurt your professional pride; what a sensitive plant you are.'

'For Christ's sake Ruth, can't you for once set aside five minutes to try and feel what someone else is thinking?'

'I know what you're thinking. I've put your nose out of joint because I don't want to talk about *you* all the time.'

'*I* don't want to talk about me all the time, but Ruth, it's so hard to talk to you about anything. It's such hard work – nothing moves you.'

'That's the attraction, is it? You plan to dance in with a sunbeam and melt my splinter of ice?'

'I want to know you, I want you to know me; you don't want to know anything. I can't talk to you like this, side by side. Isn't there somewhere we can sit down?'

'Over there, under the trees? The grass is dry.' Still holding his arm she guides him across the turf to the shade of a rural grove, where he sits abjectly among the daisies. Ruth drops the briefcase and stretches out beside him in a streak of sunlight.

'Now John, what a state you're in. Why go on seeing me when I always turn out such a disappointment?'

Poor wretch, he gnaws his lip and grinds his knuckles together and frowns. Ruth, actively curious for once, thinks: Why me, when he could have all the pink ribbons he wants?

'I find you very stimulating to talk to.' Oh, there's stately; Ruth is on the point of a jeering rejoinder but gnaws her own lip and keeps quiet. 'That's all. That's all there was, to begin with. To begin with, there wasn't even that. When I saw you at Doncaster I was feeling very miserable, I just wanted someone to talk to. And I was so amazed at seeing you.'

'The coincidence, yes. Go on.'

'Then after the conference, I wanted someone to talk to even more. Going up to Newcastle was a gamble – it gave me something to think about.'

'And you like chancing your luck with strange women.'

'That's not fair; I don't think like that. I told you what I'd been doing at Durham, didn't I; trying to prove the portrait false.'

'Or trying to find some truth in it.'

'No, I don't believe there is any truth in it, but I don't know how to prove it. It was just that, with you, I seemed to have a chance of starting from scratch with someone who didn't know me at all, had no notion of what I was like, so that I could tell if I was what I thought I was.'

'And you still don't know? Oh, I see.' Ruth props herself on one elbow and wills a comprehending expression.

'I doubt if you do. I don't even know how to proceed. You give nothing away, I'm afraid to ask. You've made asking seem an impertinence to me, too.'

'I have a nasty feeling I've made you feel even worse than you thought you were.'

'You've made me more confused. I think the reason I've never mentioned you to Geneva is because I don't know how to.'

'I know that feeling. Give her an idea and she'll be off speculating.'

'She's not the only one. Ruth, nobody I know has any idea that you exist, except as a name on a book.'

'Well,' she says, 'that's how most people know me.'

'I'd like to be able to boast about knowing you, wave your books around and say: This is my friend. I can't. You told me to write Margaret out – I haven't even written you in. You know I'm married, don't you?'

'I think you must have mentioned it.'

'I have two children – Ruth, why don't you *ask* me if I have children? I have two little sons, Chris is ten, Julian's almost five. We live in a three-bedroomed house with a fairly small garden. I use one room as a study. I have a filing cabinet.'

'Don't stop,' Ruth says. 'You have a filing cabinet; many much better men have not – or were you confessing to it? I thought you were boasting.'

'Please stop making it difficult for me.'

'You're making it difficult for yourself. If you didn't keep stopping I wouldn't get the chance to interject.' She rolls on to her back and waves an arm in his direction. 'Here, catch hold.'

'What?'

'It's my hand. I thought you might like to hold it.' He catches hold gratefully, kneading the ball of her thumb with his thumb. 'Keep talking.'

'Shall I tell you what I *would* like to do?'

'Keep talking.'

'I've got to go back to the station in a little while. I can't walk you home now, we've spent too long sitting here. You must think I'm mad, coming all the way to London just to go back again, but I only have an hour. I must get home about the same time as I would get home from school. Nobody knows I'm here, like everything else about you it's been left out of the records. That's not an insult, Ruth, believe me, it isn't.'

'Keep talking.'

'What I'd like to do is, walk home with you, very slowly, perhaps stopping for coffee somewhere out of doors, then back, over your hill to the flat and sit for half the evening talking in your empty living-room, with the windows open, sitting by the windows, till it got dark. Then I'd go, when I was ready, not before, I'd go home and not mind.'

'That sounds reasonable.'

'I can't stay with you, Ruth. I can't stay with you this evening, I can't stay with you for more than another ten minutes under this tree. I have to go back, Ruth; my wife is insanely jealous.'

Into Ruth's mind, maliciously, comes an unbidden figment of a woman in a dressing gown waiting behind the front door with a rolling pin. She bites on her involuntary smile. 'Has she cause?'

'I mean it,' John says, looking down at her with bright bleak eyes, while the grip on her hand becomes painful, 'she's going out of her mind.'

'And this time you can't get away?'

'Get away?'

'The last time you had to deal with the insane you went away when it became too much for you. Now you can't.'

'It's been coming on for so long; at first I didn't notice. She's always been possessive, that seemed reasonable – '

'I'm sure it did.'

'I didn't mean it like that. You can't really believe I'm so conceited. But people are possessive of each other, especially in early marriage. It seemed normal. I saw it happen to other people and in the end they grew out of it.

'Sarah hasn't grown out of it. It used to annoy me when she kept asking when I'd be home, but I never thought much about it until she started counting the minutes I was late. She wanted to know when I'd be home to the nearest second. I always told her the truth, but the truth was never enough. She started inventing excuses, little ways of checking up. When we were first married we had a flat in the same house as Geneva and Eddy – I told you. Sarah never liked her much but we've always been good friends. I've gone on seeing her regularly, *I* like her very much, but Sarah's convinced it's more than friendship. She hates my going on residential courses and conferences and I know a lot of people take advantage of being out of bounds, I never have – don't make some clever comment, Ruth, I'm not congratulating myself, I just never have, but she doesn't believe me. She pretends to believe me but she doesn't. I don't know if I shall ever be able to go away again. I could never tell her I'd met you on that train, even the first time, by accident. She'd have persuaded herself that there was more to it than that.

'But now it's all much worse. I have this filing cabinet and

I never lock it. If I locked it she'd think I was hiding something. That book you gave me, you signed it, you wrote *To John* because you couldn't spell McEvoy; when I realized I had that in the house I had to hide it. I put it in the filing cabinet and locked it – just that once, the first time ever, and Sarah found it locked. Now she's searching it, Ruth. While I'm at school she goes through it, looking for evidence. For all I know she's searched it regularly for ten years, but there was nothing to find, before. There's nothing now. And I wish, I wish she had asked me directly, while there was still time, "Is there anyone else?" when I could have said no, and meant it.'

'Would she have believed you?'

'No. No she wouldn't, but it would have been true. Now –'

'"He who denies belies denying . . ."'

'You think I protest too much?'

'Evidently *she* does. I don't see what you can do, except thole it. Anything you say will be used against you.'

'I daren't say anything. What could anyone say? If I stayed with you this evening I wouldn't want to go home, do you realize that? I'd delay and delay it and in the end I'd say: Must I go? Would you make me go?'

'Probably not.'

'Not because I'm afraid to go home – I'm always afraid to go home; because I couldn't bear to leave you. I hardly know you, we've not met half a dozen times and this is the closest we've been, but I can't let anyone know. Even Geneva doesn't understand what's happening, she still thinks it's a sad joke, nothing more. I've seen to that.'

'Is that why you wanted to tell me – because you can't tell Geneva?'

'In a sense, but not really. I thought I owed it to you – to let you know why I can't go beyond this. I don't know what's going to happen. The worse she gets, the faster she gets worse. When I rang you on Friday I'd just heard one of our staff talking about a visit he'd made to a psychiatric hospital. He was talking about a concert, but it reminded me of the dances they used to have where I went to visit Andrew. Can nothing have changed in twenty years? I've got to go, Ruth, I dare not be late. She might ring the school.'

Ruth stands and pulls him to his feet. 'I'll walk back to the gate with you.'

'I didn't think the afternoon would work out like this,' he says. 'I thought I could tell it better than that.'

'It's not a short story,' Ruth says, to comfort him, 'where you have to know how it's going to end before it starts. It's only uncertainty that gets us from day to day. Tell me something, John; you were hurt by that book because it held you responsible for things which you felt were none of your doing. Do you feel responsible for Sarah?'

'I feel a responsibility for her, of course I do – or do you mean that what's happened may be my fault?'

'I wouldn't put it as crudely as that. I'm just trying to understand why the book has upset you so. I know it arrived at absolutely the wrong time, but is there more than that?'

'What do you mean, the wrong time?'

'I dunno – perhaps I mean the right time. Here's the gate. I shan't see you again, then?'

'I want to see you again very much.'

'There's always Geneva's. We can run into each other, Friday week.'

'No.'

'Well, you won't be coming to Oxford.'

He takes a while to consider this. She walks in silence and allows him to consider.

'When are you going?'

'Saturday. It's an evening engagement.'

'Will you be staying the night?'

'With friends, off Banbury Road. The last train leaves at twenty three o–five. That's too early for me.'

'Suppose I missed it? Would I be able to . . . ?'

'They're old friends, very accommodating. Shall I tell them I may have somebody with me?'

'You understand what I'm asking, don't you? You're not offended?'

'Offended? Being a sexual objective isn't at all the same thing as being a sex object. I'm catching the seventeen o–five from Paddington, shall I meet you there?'

'Yes. Please.'

'I don't like a last-minute rush. Make it a quarter to, by

Brunel's statue. It's a frightful thing, you can't miss it. Are you sure about this?'

'I don't know what's going to happen. I don't know what to do. At least I shall have this.'

'No need to ring me if you can't make it,' Ruth says. 'If you aren't at Paddington I'll know you're not coming.'

'I'll be there. Goodbye, dear Ruth.' He presses his cheek against hers, does not kiss her, and walks away.

12

Craven, he waits till they are at table, the meal is served and the dialogue has become comfortably commonplace.

'Martin has his tea round the television. They all sit round with a coffee table.'

'Well, I think people should eat meals at a proper table,' Sarah says, 'where they can see each other and talk.'

'They talk while the telly's on,' Julian says. 'It's nice round a little table.'

'It's because his feet don't touch the ground,' explains his understanding brother.

'Don't be silly, darling. Neither do yours.'

'I can reach the rung, though.'

'What did you do at school today?' Sarah asks. Julian, who once broadcast a commentary on all his activities, clams up. School is another country, he has taken out citizenship and his allegiances are declared. Careless talk costs lives.

'Nothing.'

'Nothing at all?'

'Pictures.'

'Just pictures?'

'Numbers. A bit.'

'What sort of numbers?'

'Shapes.'

'Have you planned anything for the weekend?' McEvoy asks, dissecting a sausage with scientific precision, as if to divert attention from his question.

'No. Have you had an idea, then? Hush!' Sarah holds up an admonitory butter knife and by demanding the children's silence instantly involves them.

'I'd like to go to Oxford.'

'Oxford? Whatever for? I haven't been there for years. That might be rather nice.'

'I didn't mean all of us. *I* want to go to Oxford; on my own.'

He did not intend to state it so baldly. Sarah's face begins to collapse as though the flesh under her skin were melting; the contours sag, her lower lip flops loosely. Oh my God, how can I do this to her in front of the boys, McEvoy thinks, simply because I am too afraid to say it when we are alone?

'On your own? What do you want to go on your own for, what are you going to do in Oxford – ?'

'Do you remember', he says firmly, pleasantly, normally, passing salt and sauce to Christopher, 'I told you I was trying to put together a collection of contemporary poetry for school? There is to be a series of readings on Friday and Saturday. I'd like to go on the Saturday.'

With an heroic effort Sarah wrenches her degenerating features into some semblance of an intelligent face. 'But we'll all go! We can drive over in the morning, and have lunch somewhere – I suppose the Mitre's still there, and then I can take the boys round the sights and you can go to your readings – '

'It's an evening performance.' Sweet Christ, why did he have to tell her it was Oxford? Why could his habit of telling the truth not fail him for once? Why didn't he say it was in Grimsby or Macclesfield or Newington Butts? 'I don't have to be there till six. I won't take the car, there are plenty of trains.'

'Suppose you miss them?'

'All of them? Don't be silly, Sarah. The reading won't go on past nine thirty. There are at least two after that.'

'Don't be seeeleee, Sa-a-a-arah,' Julian croons to his sausages. 'Sahaharahaaaha, Sahahahahahahahahah, Saaahaaa-hahaaah . . . '

'Julian! Stop it at once! I won't have silly noises at table.'

Oh, that was superb, McEvoy thinks. From nought to mother in two seconds; how long can she keep this up? Not for long; Julian, enchanted by the idiotic sound he has produced, is loath to silence it.

'Seeely noiyoiyoises. Saaaarrrrrahahahah seeely sahahah-aha – '

'Stop it!'

'Saaaaahrrrrrreeeeeeyaaaaaheeeeyoiyoiyoihaaahaaahahaha - ha . . . ' He cannot stop.

'*Julian!*'

Startled and hysterical, Julian chokes on his sausage, panics, gropes for his glass of water and upsets it. Sarah slams down the Dartington Daisy butter platter, hits the vinegar flask and smashes both. Chris ducks below the table, a swift dive that strikes his frightened father as sinisterly practised; Julian, purple now and terrified, thrashes the air with his hands as Sarah rushes out of the room, leaving McEvoy to rescue his younger son while the elder surfaces and begins to mop up the mess on the table.

Too breathless to cry Julian recovers rapidly and innocent, untouched like all catalysts, falls to his sausages again. He assumes that the bust-up was caused by his misbehaviour and that, since he is now being demonstratively good again, everything will return to normal. McEvoy looks at Chris; too much to hope that Chris will be similarly unmoved. He grins weakly at his father.

'Will you pick up the glass? Mum says not to touch broken glass.'

'I don't think Mum's feeling very well. Keep an eye on Julian, will you? I'll be back in a moment.'

Sarah sits on the bed in the big front room, sniffing and retching. McEvoy sits down beside her and moves smoothly into a routine of reconciliation.

'Sarah, what happened? Why are you so upset?' As he puts his arms round her Sarah contracts and makes herself heavy like a recalcitrant child. 'Julian was being very silly but, he's so little. He went over the top, that's all. Children do.'

Keep talking.

'You broke your lovely plate and all for nothing, you frightened Chris. You mustn't get so worked up.'

Keep talking.

'Surely it's not because I want to go to Oxford? I don't often go anywhere on my own. It's only this once.'

There follows a miserable slobbering and gulping, in the course of which he can make out the word Durham.

'I only went to Durham alone because Simon was ill, you know that, and I had a rotten time, I told you. It would have been more fun *with* Simon.' (That's another alibi lost to future use; Simon was always his guarantor of good behaviour. What future?) 'I just want to go and listen to some poetry.

It'll be a wonderful chance to hear poets read their own work.'

'Which poets?'

She's recovering, getting back to normal, normal, glory be to God for normal things.

'I don't know. I haven't checked.'

'Anyone famous?'

'It depends what you mean by famous; I think they're all quite minor poets.'

'What about that woman?'

'What woman?'

'I can't remember her name. You had her book.'

'Oh, that one.'

'What was her name?'

'Prochak.'

'Will she be there?'

'I doubt it; it's just for one evening, Sarah. Say you don't mind.'

She says it.

Ruth has set aside Wednesday evening to work on two new poems that she would like to have ready for Saturday. The chance that more than a few of her audience will have had time and opportunity to read *Midland City* is remote, but it is always a pleasure to produce something entirely new that *no one* can possibly have heard before. On the way home she drops in at the bookshop in Marylebone High Street to buy a paper, and also to see if they still have a copy of *Acid Test*.

They do: she sees it glowering poisonously from its corner as soon as she opens the door of the shop. Outside in the sunshine the green and magenta sing in exquisite discord and she has to slip the thing into her briefcase to mute it. There is not much in the case today. She jerks it and feels the book thump hollowly as she walks across the grass of Regent's Park. Untroubled by sentimental considerations she does not even glance at the clump of trees where they two sat on Monday afternoon; moreover, she is feeling guilty. Having refrained so far from reading *Acid Test* on grounds of delicacy, she now berates herself for a breaker of confidences although her purpose in buying the book has been the wholly laudable one of wishing to make some sense out of John's incoherent ramblings on the subject of truth and fiction. Since he is never going to be able to tell her exactly what the book has done to him, she will have to find out for herself: After all, she says, giving the case another jolt, he does want me to know.

Mrs Oliver, as usual, invigilates from her dirty ground-floor window as Ruth ascends the front steps. From behind Nigel's door come sounds of unsuppressed weeping, John Gabriel Borkman paces his attic. Ruth opens her windows, makes coffee and settles down on the living-room couch to relax with a book before she starts work on the poems, the book being *Acid Test*.

The temptation is to flip through it until she comes to a relevant bit, but Ruth considers skipping a reprehensible habit. Being committed to a literary form which demands that every word should earn its place she can do no less than she would expect her own readers to do, and give each word its due. Almost she could regret this punctiliousness; *Acid Test* is a very dull book and far from earning their places many of the words seem to be swinging idly upside down from branches. The impulse that keeps her reading is the gradual discovery that it is not about what she thought it would be about. The dullness is in the writing, emphasized by the unvarying voice of its author, a monotonous drone, and she can understand John's exasperation with a narrator who as a mature woman can give as much credence now to her perceptions of half a lifetime ago as she could have done at the time; but surely, Ruth thinks, this is what the story is about. It is entirely out of the hands of its unreliable narrator, the telling is part of the tale. Geneva should have noticed this, but Geneva's brief is fiction. Writing first-person narrative is not the same as being the narrator. No wonder that Hill's bid for omniscience has failed.

Ruth preens herself a little for being the first to recognize this, to understand that whatever began to happen to Caroline Hill in 1964 is happening still. Possibly Caroline herself does not understand it; if she did she would never have so exposed herself, but what about Margaret, the *tertium quid*? unscrupulous Margaret who seized upon this sad flawed self-portrait as a means to her own ends? Margaret, Ruth thinks, understands very well.

Margaret will be Katherine when she finally makes her appearance; the rest will do well enough under their aliases, but John will be Michael. When is *he* going to turn up? She breaks her rule and looks ahead to the passage she encountered by chance in the bookshop on the day she came home from Newcastle. Almost there; virtuously she returns to the page she is reading and proceeds with what she regards as exemplary persistence.

Michael arrives; he opens the door; *and paused, as if expecting his adoring public to rise up and applaud.*

No, that isn't fair. There is too much anxiety in John's approach to allow the truth of that description, although the anxiety may be a very recent acquisition; but then, look at him with Pink Ribbons (silly cow; brought in her assignment two days before the deadline. 'Who's your bloke, Dr Prochak?' Jesus wept!), bestowing himself. Maybe; maybe . . .

As David said afterwards, you could see he was thinking, Isn't it nice of me to come?

Unfair, unfair: and yet . . . she wishes she had read the book sooner. She is very much afraid that she is too near him now to make an objective assessment. Here he is again, at a dance. Didn't he mention a dance?

There was a dance held every fortnight in the recreation hall. We went to it because it was somewhere to go, not because it would be fun. The older male patients came in carpet slippers but the women put on their best dresses and inexpertly applied make-up. It was possible to date the time of their admission to the hospital by the style of the dresses. Dropped waists, bias-cut skirts, padded shoulders from the Forties, the New Look. In my short skirt and white stockings I began to see myself at forty, fifty, still here and still wearing the clothes that had looked so pretty on a girl of twenty.

Oh yes, says Ruth, now I see why you are so afraid for your Sarah.

The dances were played on a record player, waltzes, fox-trots, the Lancers. Sometimes we would try to Twist to a fox-trot but it upset some of the older patients, although even that amused us. Anyone could come to the dances if they were ambulant, although patients from some wards had to be accompanied by a nurse. Some-

times a patient grew excited and ran screaming among the dancers
followed by a nurse. No one took any notice. The occasional peal
of laughter that rang out was usually due to someone's private
delusion, not to anything that was happening. Trendy Michael
looked very out of place . . .

I bet you did, says Ruth.

Michael pursues his heedless path; he visits the Nuthouse, he acts as errand boy, chauffeur, messenger, confidant, he fetches, he carries, he listens. In point of fact he does not turn up all that often, but when he does he is doing a favour. When he fails in what has clearly become his duty the recriminations are merciless, as on the famous trip to Bath. He has found a new girlfriend Katherine, hello Margaret; in the excitement of taking her off for what at the time was looked on as a dirty weekend, he forgets the birthday of another girl whom he scarcely knows; there is no concrete evidence to suggest that he ever knew it was her birthday, (definitely this is not a work of fiction; Caroline has no notion of how to load dice or cook books) but she, poor overwrought creature, can measure his dereliction only by the pain it inflicts on her. Ruth goes back a page and rereads.

'Michael can't do anyone a favour,' Brian explained to me, 'unless
he feels that people will suffer if he doesn't do it. He's so tremendously
insecure, and we all have to overreact to compensate for his in-
adequacy. Haven't you noticed how he waits to be thanked if he
gives you something?'

I had no idea whether he would give me a birthday present but I
knew that if he did I must make an effort to seem extra grateful,
even if it meant running the risk of making David jealous.

No no, she cannot have that; but something sours their friendship; always she leaves him feeling that she has failed his expectations, but what does he expect from her; gratitude? Gratitude for what?

Katherine returns to pay a visit on her own account; Caroline finds her *simpatica*, they talk. They talk about Michael. Gerald meets Michael in the street, Michael rebuffs Gerald (again no suggestion that Michael was being deliberately cruel), Gerald writes his dastardly letter and is very properly nicked.

Michael vanishes. He is not written out, he simply ceases

to function, but his name crops up one last time, after Gerald tops himself. Caroline and Katherine hold a kind of wake in the Three Horseshoes, which turns out less of a wake for Gerald than a celebration of themselves. They plan to share a flat, a nest which Katherine will feather against Caroline's discharge from hospital, Katherine will eschew men and find her true self as an independent human being. It will be hard but together they will achieve self-fulfilment in sisterhood and the name of Jesus.

Hindsight, Ruth comments, her tolerance fraying, an anachronism at any rate. Where was sisterhood in the Sixties? They hadn't invented it yet.

'Look, I'll be straight with you,' said Katherine. 'I can't pretend that I'm not hurt. I'm hell's hurt, and it's going to take a long while to get over it, but one thing about Michael I won't miss; that sense of being pitied all the time. It's probably something you've never noticed, I mean, this must sound terrible, Caroline, but you must be fairly used to people being sorry for you. I'm not. Right from the first time we met at the party he used to look down on me as if to say "Poor little Katherine". Oh, Caro, that awful pitying look, I shan't miss that!'

Ruth stops reading. She skims through the remaining pages but as Michael's name does not appear again she closes the book and gnaws it thoughtfully. She has the word she was searching for, she has the key, but it is almost midnight and the poems lie untouched.

'Sod you, Jack,' Ruth says. Not only has she done no work, she has had nothing to eat. She spins the book across the room where it pitches, fluttering, into the typewriter, and uncoils from the couch to find sustenance in the kitchen. For one who expects to be well fed in restaurants Ruth is a free spirit when it comes to feeding herself. There is nothing in the refrigerator except for a jar of cockles, another of mayonnaise and half of a honeydew melon with the seeds scooped out. Caroline and her friends wore melonseed neck-laces. Ruth drains the jar of cockles on to a matzo, cements a second matzo to it with mayonnaise and conveys the leaking tile to the living-room window. With the lights switched off she leans out, crunching and thinking as nacreous drops of brine and mayonnaise fall past the glow of Nigel's uncurtained window below, and fancies, pleasingly, Nigel looking up in a post-coital daze to witness this miraculous drizzle of celestial semen.

She has allowed John, in the interests of comedy, to believe that her involvement with Nigel's shenanigans is frequent, and now regrets her light-mindedness. What can he, who professes to admire her candour, think of her casual dishonesty in this matter or does he dismiss it – as she feels uncomfortably he might – as evidence of a disarming amorality? What would you do? she asks him, in his absence. Tell them the truth? Like hell you would. In any case, Nigel's overspill is becoming a nuisance, but no more so than Nigel himself. Ruth's attitude to Nigel is hardening into active disapproval. His duplicity, which once she regarded as a mildly diverting exercise in social engineering, has become abhorrent, and the nymphs, no longer a risible trinity, wring her heart with their jealous ignorance. How pathetic, she thinks now, to be not only besotted *and* stupid, but duped as well. Each must know that he is triple-timing her, but all three strive to retain his worthless attentions by eagerly participating in their own betrayal. Perhaps the truly successful liar is the one who induces his victims to connive at the deception, who coaxes them to meet him halfway across that suspension bridge of disbelief, customarily the preserve of a fiction writer and his readers.

So where does that leave John's Sarah, desperately believing lies that have never been told. Now that John has stopped telling her the truth as well, what depthless chasm does she find yawning at her feet, or is the fabric of John's falsehood like Geneva's drawn threadwork, the unwanted strands removed, leaving decorative holes?

Ruth, coming to the end of her dinner, sits back from the window and considers going to bed; going to bed tonight and going to bed on Saturday. Does she yet have the measure of the man who will probably sleep with her three nights hence; does she need it? A lewd pun occurs to her and she grins round the last mouthful of cockles and matzos. In a way she is sorry that he expressed his hope so clearly; she would like to have been surprised with joy.

At last Sarah has found something, tucked between a letter from a conference convenor and a circular from the Regional Arts Association, something poked there recently and hurriedly, no doubt, since it is out of sequence with the adjacent dates. It is a Dear John letter, although Sarah has taken to reading the Dear Sir letters, too, in case they should be *billets-doux* disguised as business. This is not disguised, it is boldly forthright, almost shockingly: *Dear John, you won't remember me I'm sure, but perhaps you will remember the enclosed.*

The paper bears the mark of a clip in the top left-hand corner, but of the enclosure there is no sign. Sarah plunges back into the files, between the NATE convenor and the Literature Officer; nothing. It must be somewhere, later she will look. Could it have been a photograph?

Dear John, you won't remember me I'm sure, but perhaps you will remember the enclosed. To tell you the truth, I had almost forgotten you, until I saw the television debate the other night. I was on the edge of my seat wondering where I'd seen you before, until I heard your name mentioned, and then it all came back, and of course, I couldn't really ever forget that weekend in Bath. Does it come back to you now? You wrote a poem for me in the restaurant. I thought it was sweet at the time. At any rate, I kept it.

It really did seem then that there might be something between us, until you met me that day and said, 'I shan't be seeing you again, but it's been a lot of fun, hasn't it?' I was so hurt at the time, but John, it's a long while ago. It's strange how things turn out, isn't it?

Someone you must remember though is Caroline Hill and what an effect she had on us all at the time. I don't think any of us realized how frightfully she was suffering, or what tremendous inner strength she must have had – I'm sure you didn't, at any rate. Well, anyway, now she has written a book. Clockhouse brought it out in January, so I'm sending you a copy. Do read it. I'm sure you'll find what she says a revelation in more ways than one, and do feel free to get in touch if you need anything explained.

I'm posting this to your school as I don't know your home address. With warmest regards, Margaret Anderson (née Hardwicke)

From the roiling soup of Sarah's imagination one item surfaces; poetry. John wrote a poem. Could it be the poem that was attached to the letter? John is going to Oxford in pursuit of poetry, he had a book of poems by a woman called

Prochak. Sarah was not telling the truth when she said that she could not remember the name; Sarah never forgets anything.

John is the one who forgets things, who keeps letters and documents long after the dates they refer to have passed in case he needs to jog his memory, who leaves things lying about. Where is the poem? When did he write it? When did he go to Bath he went to Durham he is going to Oxford.

The letter was written nearly two months ago, 27 March (today is Thursday, 24 May). How much longer ago was the time to which it refers; months, years, ten years, twelve years? She has known John for twelve years, they have been married for eleven, was he taking women to Bath before they were married? After? But – and a smile, almost a triumphant smile, flirts at the corner of Sarah's mouth – this Margaret failed where Sarah succeeded. Margaret allowed him to say goodbye and he went; Sarah crept to him by dusk, weeping silently, pleading with mouth and hands and eyes; Sarah languished and declined until clasped and comforted and promised a whole lifetime in exchange for her forgiveness. Evidently Margaret did not understand how to handle him, which is why she is now Mrs Anderson and not Mrs McEvoy.

'I've come to apologize,' McEvoy says, hangdog in Geneva's living-room. 'I was in a foul mood last time.'

Geneva tats and nods. 'You should apologize for staying away so long. It's more than a month.'

'I was ashamed to come back – and it's been a little difficult recently.'

Geneva nods again, understandingly; he wonders that she does not call him a silly boy. 'Are you staying?'

'Just for a little.'

'Sit down, do. You look so meek and enormous looming over me.' She raises her voice. 'Daughter! Coffee!'

What on earth is she making this time? With the loops and skeins of cotton, the darting hook, she might be gutting fish over a lap full of entrails.

'How's school?'

'All the thrills of your average institution; we're in the middle of Os and As.'

'Don't mention them,' Geneva sighs. 'Jane's locked in her

room from the minute she gets home, moaning faintly. Mary's been exiled, poor love, she mopes in the kitchen and forecasts a gloomy future for both of them. I don't remember suffering this much.'

'I doubt if the pressures were as strong, then. I've got boys of eighteen almost in tears at the thought of losing their University places if they don't get the required grades. It's a diabolical lottery; I keep wondering if I ought to associate myself with it.'

'Go teach in a prep school; you'll only have Common Entrance to worry about.'

Mary, apparently untouched by educational stresses, sashays through the door, the complete ingénue, with the coffee tray.

'Hi chaps!' She switches her curls and streamers of pink satin shimmy between her shoulder blades.

'I met someone who looked just like you, the other day,' McEvoy says.

'*Where?*' Mary demands, jealously. 'No one looks just like me,' which gives him pause for thought so that he can say, 'Oh, in the street. Don't worry, it was a superficial resemblance. You are undoubtedly unique.'

'Don't be so condescending,' Mary says, 'or I'll sit on your knee and make goo-goo eyes and you'll sing "Thank Heaven for Little Girls".'

'Oh, go away,' Geneva says, 'or pipe down.'

'I know when I'm not wanted.'

'Chance would be a fine thing.'

The door slams.

'You see,' Geneva says, 'it's infectious. Have you ever known Mary slam a door?'

'Practising an exit. She can't always be flying into the sunset on a rosy cloud. Actually, I'm glad she's gone, I wanted to ask you a favour.'

'Anything, John, of course.'

'Well, it was something you offered to do, but I'm not sure if you'll want to stick by it.'

'Money?'

'Nothing like that. It's – you've never offered to lend me money, have you?'

'I might have done, in your salad days. You never took it.'

'You offered to drop in on Sarah one day. I take it you haven't. She's not said anything.'

'Of course I will.'

'Tomorrow?'

'If you like, but why tomorrow?'

'I'm going to a poetry reading in Oxford. I'll be home late. Could you make it during the evening?'

'I don't see why not. Any particular reason?'

'She's rather depressed at the moment,' McEvoy says. 'When I said I wanted to go to Oxford she thought I meant we should all go. I couldn't make her see that there wasn't any point. She's not a bit interested in poetry, anyway.'

'I didn't think you were.'

'I do teach it.'

'Dear John, that's got nothing to do with it, as well you know. You don't have the slightest interest in half the books you teach; why this sudden urge for poesy?'

'Guilt, mainly. We've been taking a long hard look at the school collections; two or three of us have been trying to put together some contemporary stuff – it's impossible not to get hooked. Anyway, I like Oxford. I want to go.'

'You don't have to prove anything,' Geneva says. 'I don't see that it's so very heinous, going to Oxford. You go; I'll drop in on Sarah.'

'I do appreciate it,' McEvoy says.

'Who's reading?'

'Uh?'

'At Oxford – who's reading?'

Oh what a tangled web we weave. 'I'm not sure. A chap at school mentioned it – he did tell me; no one very prestigious.'

'Do you know what prestigious used to mean? Deceptive. Strange how words evolve. I wonder if that's the one Ruth was talking about.'

'One what?'

'Reading. She said ages ago that she was giving a reading in Oxford; I don't know if it was tomorrow, though. She's coming over next week, on Friday. Why don't you look in?'

'I might,' McEvoy says. Geneva knows too much, a sight

too much about too many things. How is he going to get out
of this one?

'I'm sure', Geneva says, 'that Ruth is prestigious.'

13

McEvoy's image of Isambard Kingdom Brunel is the popular one; broad-gauge genius in a stove-pipe hat posing with transcendental confidence against his mighty chains; it does not prepare him for the anonymous chair-bound bronze bureaucrat that he finds on the Paddington concourse. No wonder Ruth thinks so little of it; she would like something more dynamic, no doubt, in cast iron.

He arrives early on purpose, buys his ticket and takes up his post by the sedentary engineer; the purpose was to get there before Ruth, in case she were to become impatient; and to leave home as soon as possible, to leave Sarah's incredulous gaze. Encountering that gaze he realized that until the very last minute she could not bring herself to believe that he would go. No question this time of insisting that he must be driven to London; she has been dismissed, relegated, fit only to stay at home and look after the children; oh Christ, the children. No; he will never be able to come away again; tonight will be his last opportunity to warm himself before the long winter closes down.

He sees Ruth before she sees him, heading for the booking hall at twenty-seven minutes to five. At eighteen minutes to five (what timing!) she comes out again, briefcase in hand, head carried at a poke – that curious up-hill walk. At sixteen forty-five she is at his side; in deference he switches to the twenty-four hour clock.

Ruth puts down the briefcase and looks up at him sidelong, speculatively, there is an uncertainty about her that he has not expected; a hesitancy. In fact, not to put too fine a point on it, she looks downright cagey, but when he nods to kiss her she kisses him back and catches his lower lip between her teeth, a blunt but unarguable nip, as if to ascertain that he is flesh and blood.

'You little vampire,' he says.

'I'm not little,' Ruth says, and not lightly but as if it is something he *must* understand; the wary look is back again.

Oh well, he thinks, it's all in the eyes, and longs for darkness.

Ruth scans the destination boards. 'It'll go from Platform One or Two. Shall we move? If you want coffee we can get some at the kiosk.'

'Let's do that.' As always, she leads, he follows.

The public address system announces with glum defiance, 'British Rail apologizes to passengers for the late arrival of the sixteen thirteen train from Slough. This was caused by an incident at Westbourne Park. We are sorry for any inconvenience caused.'

'He sounds sorry, doesn't he? You can almost hear him salivating.'

Ruth frowns. 'Two white coffees, please. It wouldn't matter if he did sound sorry. No one would believe him.'

'Incident sounds exciting. Could it be an ambush?'

'Body on the line,' says Ruth. 'Look, it's in; Platform One.'

He follows her swerve. 'Body on the line? How horrible, how do you know?'

'It's a British Rail euphemism. What they call staffing difficulties means the guards are on strike; a mishap is a crash. Derailed freight wagon or two expresses meeting head on, cow on the line, that's a mishap. Loss of air pressure means the brakes have failed – come on, this one will do. They used to call it brake failure but people panicked and thought it meant the train wouldn't be able to stop. Actually it means that the train won't start, but people don't notice things like that in a crisis. An incident is a death on the line.'

'A suicide?'

'Not necessarily, but you're probably right. Serious suicides are drawn to trains.'

'What a ghoul you are. Have you made a study of all this?'

'Throwing yourself under a train confirms intensity of purpose. No one's going to come along afterwards and diminish it by saying it was a cry for help that went tragically wrong. If you dive in front of a 125 you don't need much margin of error, it's not like mucking about with paracetamol or slashing your wrists – sorry. I don't suppose you find that a subject for levity.'

'It's all right – but are you sure? Someone died out there and that's why the train was late?'

'I'm afraid so, though it may not have been a suicide. I don't think I'd choose Westbourne Park.'

'Oh, really? Where would you do it?'

'I'd go down to Surbiton for the Portsmouth train. They come through at a hell of a lick.'

'Dying under the banner of Huskisson?'

'Fancy your remembering that; well, it would be appropriate, wouldn't it? Churchward was struck by one of his own locomotives.'

'Yes,' says McEvoy. Who was Churchward?

Ruth stretches and yawns in the seat opposite and flips the lid from her coffee. 'What sorts of methods did your friends use?'

'Oh, God, Ruth! Andrew slashed his wrists the first time, and his elbows the second. Robert overdosed; Caroline wasn't suicidal but she used to bang her head on sharp objects – and she lay down in front of that bus in the hospital drive. I told you. Fortunately the driver was used to that kind of thing.'

'Dilettantes. None of them took the permanent way?'

'Succeeded, you mean?'

'It would have been successful, I should think.' Ruth smiles privately. McEvoy thinks he must have missed the joke.

'Stuart hanged himself, I told you.'

'Gerald. Yes, now that did surprise me. He was the last person I'd have expected.' He looks at her, puzzled. 'I think I should tell you, I've read it.'

'Read it?'

'*Acid Test*. In a way, I'm sorry; I'd more or less made up my mind not to, out of a sense of, well, delicacy, I suppose. I didn't think you'd want me to, at first, but you kept talking about it. I thought I ought to look for myself.'

'When did you read it?'

'Does it matter? Wednesday, I think.'

'You're certain?'

'Wednesday or Thursday, why?'

'Definitely since I last saw you?'

'Oh, definitely. What difference does it make? John – I've upset you – why do you mind so much?'

'I'd hate to think', he says, 'that you had read it, then listened to me talking about it, and pretended not to have done. I don't mind your having read it, not a bit; it's a book, you're entitled. But to think that you'd been measuring me against what you'd read, saying nothing . . . '

'I haven't done that.' As before she leans across the table and takes his hand. Paddington Station slips away unnoticed. 'That's why I told you just now, before it could come up in the conversation.'

'You just about drove it into the conversation.'

'Don't pretend it wouldn't have arrived in its own good time. I'm not all that different from Geneva – I know how to make dialogue go the way I want.'

'Doesn't that involve a degree of speculation?' he asks, sourly.

'No; certainty. As I said, it was bound to intrude sooner or later. I think I'd like to talk about it now, and then never mention it again.'

'It's quite possible – do you realize this – that I may not even see you again.'

'You said that on Monday, and here we are.'

'I also said that I didn't know what would happen afterwards. I thought I'd made you understand. Sarah has driven herself out of her mind convincing herself that I've been unfaithful to her, not once but continually. It's a horrible coincidence that the first time I really want to be it should turn out so very important that I'm not. You might think it makes no difference now – you know, as well for mutton as for lamb, as well for lamb as for nothing would be nearer the mark, but it does. I'm afraid for her, I'm even more afraid for my children. I want tonight because it may be the last thing I have.'

'I wonder what made me think it was me that you wanted.'

'It is you. If I just wanted a therapeutic screw I could have noted down a couple of numbers from a phone box at Paddington; don't take offence where there's no need.'

'That's a point,' Ruth concedes. She wraps her other hand round his and props her chin on the triple fist. 'So tell me, because this is a very pertinent question and you know I don't often ask questions; why?'

'Why what?'

'Why me?'

'Oh, Ruth, for Christ's sake, do you want an anatomy of attraction? How can I tell you why?'

'Hm, I didn't think you could,' Ruth says, 'drink your coffee.'

'May I have my hand back?'

'No.'

The train is non-stop; a flier; it skims through Acton, Ealing, Southall. Finally McEvoy says, 'What did you think of it?'

'The coffee?'

'*Acid Test*.'

'It's very sad.'

'Sad?'

'Don't you think it's sad? Or were you so incensed by what she'd said about you that you didn't notice the rest? It's sad that what happened to her has wrecked her for life: no?'

'Has it wrecked her?'

'I rather thought you'd pointed out the evidence already. Her illness may not be cured but at least it's controlled now. It's written by an ostensibly sane woman of forty who still perceives the world as a schizophrenic teenager. I think that's sad. It's sad that her trusted friend Katherine – Margaret – takes her book and uses it for a purpose for which it was never intended, namely, to damage someone else. The unreliable narrator is a very sophisticated device in fiction, Margaret must have seen the similarity at once, and also seen that since this isn't fiction, no one would question the reliability. It would never attract the attention of a really trenchant reviewer.'

'Geneva read it.'

'As your friend, not as a critic. She *thought* she was reading it as a critic, but she was only trying to see what you'd seen. When you said that you wanted to talk to me on the train because I didn't know you, you were being braver than you knew. Geneva thought the portrait was false because of the *way* it was drawn. I don't agree. The real trick of using an unreliable narrator is just that; the unreliability; the narrator need not *always* be wrong, or untruthful. I can see why you're so hurt by Michael; a young man who gets his kicks from being kind to those less fortunate than himself.'

'Is that so culpable?'

'I didn't say he enjoyed a virtuous glow; perhaps kicks is the wrong term. Michael judged himself against people he believed to be inferior. Finding a bin full of loonies must have been like opening the box of delights.'

McEvoy, queasy and apprehensive, tries to withdraw his hand but she holds it fast. Iver passes.

'My sister-in-law, the one in New York, is an average intelligent woman, but she can evaluate herself only by believing everyone else to be a fool or a failure. She's very attractive, well heeled, thanks to George – my brother – older than I am, two charming children who have been officially designated Gifted, and she used to patronize me something chronic. I was at Cambridge when he married her; doing well but not spectacularly, and they were still living in England. I saw them often. She condescended to me; interrupted my remarks, laughed at my clothes, snubbed my friends, pitied my looks; she did it to everyone but she had a field day with me. "George, darling, we must do something for poor little Ruth." Yes, it *was* sadistic, you can imagine the effect it had on a nineteen-year-old who'd already begun to think that any man who wanted to bed her was just making do till the queue shortened elsewhere or worse, out of kindness – no, I'll come to that. I got my BSc but she wasn't impressed by first degrees; she had one herself although it wasn't as good as mine. But I didn't stop there, I got a research fellowship, another degree, she began to back off. When I got my doctorate she shut up entirely. It didn't matter any more that I had funny eyes and dressed at Oxfam; I wasn't only clever, I had the papers to prove it, and what she thought was a stunningly handsome lover into the bargain. No doubt he was handsome, I mean she thought he was my lover and I let her. That was cheating, wasn't it? In fact he was just a friend, but I was as proud of his friendship as I would have been of a lover. I'm sure she's glad we've got the Atlantic between us now; she must die a little every time I publish a new collection.'

'What was that other thing you were going to come back to later?'

'Was I? Oh yes, fucking as a favour; I used to be grateful for favours in those days. There are plenty of men who think women should be grateful for their attentions. I met one quite recently, when I was in Southampton, as it happens; you remember, the day we had lunch? I don't know whether he'd have got as far as rape, I clocked him one before he had the chance to try, but he was so taken aback when I did, and he called me some shocking names as I was seeing him off. He really believed that I'd welcome anything he forced on me out of gratitude that he should think me worth forcing.'

'Is that how you see Michael? As a rapist *manqué*? As someone who assumes that people will be grateful for his attentions?'

'Nothing so crude.'

'Patronizing? Condescending? Feeding his own ego at the expense of other people's?'

'I don't think he did it on purpose; he really thought he was doing the Right Thing, and up to a point he was. It was a disinterested kindness, in a way, but that wouldn't have made it any easier to bear. I only found the clue towards the end.'

'What clue? Clue to what?'

'Remember Katherine and Caroline in the Three Horse-shoes, drinking to Gerald's memory and planning the future? Katherine says that she will miss Michael, what she won't miss is his pitying look. She says something wonderfully tactless to Caroline: "You must be used to people feeling sorry for you, but I'm not." Michael had no reason to be sorry for Katherine, but all the same, he made her feel pitiable. She was obviously in love with him and she was left looking pathetic, perhaps Michael was one of those people who regard love as a sign of weakness, I don't know, but no wonder when Margaret saw what had been written she grabbed it and sent it to you.'

'After twenty years?'

'Maybe she never gave you a thought until she recognized you on telly and saw that you were still as pleased with yourself as ever.'

'Is that how you see me? Pleased with myself? *Me?*'

'Not now. I don't know what you were like two months

ago – before she sent you the book. Do you understand what I'm getting at?'

'You think *Acid Test* got it right.'

'Not precisely that, but you've persuaded yourself, and Geneva *and* me, near as dammit, that you are hurt by the portrait because it is false, because it suppresses the truth. Aren't you the more afraid that it may be accurate?'

'You think it is.' Her great grey eyes are sorrowful; she thinks it is true.

'I hope not – John, I hardly know you, how can I be sure? That's why I asked, why me? You could pick and choose, you know you could; I think you've made a good choice, naturally, but not an obvious one. Are you doing what my sister-in-law did, persuading yourself that I'm in some way an object of pity? John, listen, you're always making me out to be a strange little creature, small, young, gauche, whimsical; a kind of innocent elemental; don't think I can't tell. You see me as a wayward child, not a short-tempered adult. I'm none of those things; young, yes, but not *that* young. I'm five foot eight – that's not *little*. I know grown men shorter than that. I'm clever, well-organized, quite as successful as you are if not more so. Can't you accept competition from equals?'

He never expected her to frighten him. He presses his free hand against his mouth and feels the fingers trembling. 'How can you say that? I don't pity . . . Geneva, for instance. How could I pity Geneva?'

'Exactly. Geneva was already a roaring success when you first knew her; she's gone from strength to strength. Her books get better and better, her kids are lovely, she's a very merry widow, is Geneva – and right out of your league. Why else have you stayed friends for ten years, or whatever? She's all right; by your standards she's sublime; but what about your wife?'

'Ruth, if you could see her – '

'I don't mean now, I mean when you married her. Was she like Geneva, pretty, bold, independent?'

'No, nothing like that.'

'Clinging? Weakminded?'

'Ruth, please, I didn't expect this – '

'I know you didn't. If you had done we'd have got no-where. Let's finish. Tell me about her.'

'I met her in '72. I was teaching in Tonbridge, she was a secretarial assistant at the same school. We lived quite close to each other and sometimes I gave her a lift home. We began to meet outside school, it wasn't serious – '

'Nor was Margaret.'

'She was a nice little thing – '

'*Little?*'

'Yes, she is little; shorter than you are, very petite.'

'Is that all you can say about the woman you married; she was a nice little thing? Didn't she have any personal characteristics, a voice, a mind; no bad points? Nothing? Just a nice little thing? What sort of a thing – a corkscrew? A soap dish?'

'We weren't close – '

'God blind O'Reilly, John, do you never learn? You mean, *again*, that you thought you weren't close – '

'We *weren't*. I've got closer to you in two months than I've been to Sarah in twelve years. I was getting tired of the niceness. We didn't quarrel, she was afraid of quarrels, she'd never go for me the way you do. And the voice, yes, she did have a voice, she's still got it, when she's worried or upset which is nearly always, a sort of keening. She can make four syllables out of my name. I hadn't found anyone else, I just wished I could; someone who could talk, and think, and argue. It's funny, I'm the one who avoids arguments, now. I wanted someone who had something in common with me. I wasn't plotting or making any plans – '

'You were just fed to the back teeth with her?'

'If you want to be coarse, yes.'

'So you ditched her.'

'I never ditched anyone.'

'Margaret?'

'It wasn't *ditching* – and I certainly didn't ditch Sarah, I just tried to ease us apart. I said, "Look, Sarah, you don't enjoy concerts; why don't you go out with your friends and I'll go alone. Sarah, darling, poetry sends you to sleep. Why not go to the pub with your sister and I'll join you after the lecture." She wouldn't have it. She preferred to be bored out of her skull *with* me than moderately entertained without. One weekend I said I wanted to visit some friends – '

'Bath?'

'No, Oxford. Oh Christ, oh no, Oh Jesus Christ . . . '

'Stop it John. You didn't mean it – accidental symmetry. What happened?'

'She said, "Lovely, I've never been to Oxford." Ruth, I think she must have remembered; I hadn't. I think she has. I said, "No, I'd like to go alone," and I went. She was devastated; she couldn't believe I'd go. She saw me off at the station, I swear she thought that at the last minute I'd lean from the window and sweep her into the carriage as the train pulled out. When I came back on the Sunday night she turned up at my flat, she must have been watching it all evening, and begged me never to leave her again, not to abandon her. She pleaded and wept and said she couldn't live without me . . . '

'*She* didn't try to do herself in, did she?'

'No, she had the sense to stop short of that. Next morning she was at work, of course. She was in the school, every day. Over the next fortnight I watched her go into a sort of decline; the kind of thing you read about in Victorian novels. I couldn't believe I could have done that to anyone, but I had to believe it, and then I couldn't go on doing it.'

'"They that have power to hurt and will do none . . . ?"'

'I gave in. Have you ever watered a very flabby cactus, one that's so dehydrated you can see the veins in it? It was like that. She seemed to fill out, grow, flourish.'

'And when you saw that you had the power to do that, you couldn't resist it?'

'We got engaged, we got married, awful trendy white wedding with a cartwheel hat instead of a veil. She's been in agony ever since; because she knows what she did and she knows what I did. She wakes up in terror every morning in case I've reached the end of my tether; in case I go out and don't come back. She goes to sleep wondering if I'll still be there in the morning, or will the covers be thrown back and the suitcase gone from the top of the wardrobe? I don't know what she's going through now. She thinks I'm coming home tonight; I'm going to ring up and tell her I've missed the last train, just for once I'm going to do what she's been accusing me of for years. I don't know what I'll find when I get back. I don't know what to do.'

'At the risk of sounding prosaic,' Ruth says, 'I'd suggest that you get her to see a doctor.'

'And then what will happen? Therapy? Valium? Hospital? Is she going to end up in a Nuthouse? What will they do?'

'Is that what you're frightened of? You think that what happened to Caroline will happen to Sarah?'

'I don't *know*.'

'But Sarah isn't like Caroline, you must know that. She's too old for a start. Schizophrenia wasn't called *dementia praecox* for nothing; it starts young. And Caroline was never definitely diagnosed as schizophrenic; she wasn't given the LSD as a treatment, was she? It was exploratory; they wouldn't use it now. Sarah doesn't hear voices, does she; believe everyone's against her?'

'She believes I am; and all my hypothetical women, I suppose.'

'Didn't you wonder about Caroline at the time, what was happening to her? Didn't you wonder what was wrong with Brian and David and Gerald? Weren't *you* curious?'

'No,' he says, too ashamed to look up, 'I was sorry for them, that's all. Do you know, when I first started reading *Acid Test* I was bored. I was bored because all they did in it was talk, about themselves. That's all I seem to have done since I finished it. You know how children talk, very hard, very fast, to distract attention from something they don't want you to see? That's what I've done. I wanted to talk to you because you knew nothing about me, I thought I might persuade you into giving me back my self-esteem, and you've taken away even what little I had left. You must think I'm a disgusting creature.'

'Why no,' Ruth says, 'I don't think that. I'd guess that most people your age must carry a similar can of worms; you've opened yours, that's all. You are extraordinary, John; do you think I have no secrets? You and Geneva call *me* incurious, but you don't know a thing about me. And you still haven't answered my question; why me?'

'If I'd told you before, it wouldn't have been the same

answer; it's because in spite of everything you know now, you're still holding my hand; you haven't told me to turn around at Oxford and catch the next train back to London.'

'No more I shall,' says Ruth, 'and I hope we please each other tonight so we can still be friends tomorrow.'

The train is passing through Reading.

'Has it struck you', Ruth says, 'that a lot of that book may simply be misremembered? Memory is the biggest liar of all.'

'I've heard that before – going to Darlington.'

'*My* memory was jogged; Reading Gaol – Oscar Wilde. He said that memory is the diary we all carry with us. Geneva said that it is the biggest liar of all.'

'I thought you said that.'

'I was quoting. What I said was that memory is a great editor.'

Under Hythe Bridge brown industrial mallards bob like flotsam among the junk.

'Oxford is never as I remember it,' McEvoy says. 'I had friends who were up in the early Sixties, I thought it was beautiful then. Each time I come back I look for what I saw in 1961. It changes while I'm not looking.'

'It's an awful dump,' Ruth agrees, cheerfully, 'but that's part of its attraction. The English love eyesores.'

'Oh, come now, that's not true. We're wedded to the myth of a green and pleasant land.'

'Because we know it's a myth, this happy breed of men, this little world, this lump of rock stuck in a septic tank. What we really enjoy are sidings and slag heaps, winding gear, gas holders. Battersea Power Station has a stronger grip on the nation's affections than Westminster Abbey.'

'Not on mine.'

'You're Scottish . . . aren't you?'

'About as Scottish as you're Polish.'

They walk on to the junction with Worcester Street, slowly, with their arms about each other, openly committed to the liaison.

'Where are we going, exactly?'

'The Arts Centre; just up here, in George Street, but look, we're early. Let's go to a boozer.'

'Do you know a good boozer?'

'Oxford's full of good boozers; it's what the boozers are full of that's the problem. Still, it's only a quarter past six, say we've got an hour. Let's try the Red Lion, it's only round the corner.'

She asks for draught Guinness (as being good for the throat) and McEvoy leaves her sitting at a table on a kind of mezzanine, guarding their briefcases while he goes to the bar. When he comes back she is leaning on the table, jaw cradled in hand, gazing abstractedly across the room; taking the long view. How she must have made her sister-in-law suffer. Geneva said she was a killer. He aches all over as if he had been beaten to his knees, allowed to stagger to his feet and then been knocked flat again, over and over; she will not allow him even the consolation of feeling wronged.

'What have you got in that briefcase?' Ruth asks when he returns with the drinks.

'It's my overnight bag, pro tem. I'm not supposed to be staying overnight, am I? The briefcase aroused no suspicions.'

'Uh huh.' She smiles. Now will she allow him the dubious luxury of feeling guilty.

'Though I wouldn't put it past Sarah to be in the airing cupboard right now, counting my underpants.'

The hazy well-being that has gathered round him since they stepped off the train into the mild Oxford evening evaporates. He feels his face fall.

'I asked Geneva to go round there this evening. She doesn't know why.'

'You mean she thinks you'll be there?'

'No, she knows I'll be here, but she doesn't know I'm staying away. I couldn't make Geneva a party to it. I shouldn't have told either of them where I was going. Apparently the last time you saw Geneva you said you were reading here, though she couldn't remember if it was this weekend or not.'

'It must be. I'm not doing any more Oxford gigs till the Poetry Festival, and that's in October.'

'You'll be seeing her on Friday. Will you tell her?'

'Tell her what? That you came too? That we slept together?'

'Whatever you tell her, I'll tell her. I wouldn't want to be like your neighbour Nigel, too bloody idle to tell my own lies.'

'I'll say I saw you in the audience, which will be true, unless you'd rather stay here and meet me afterwards.'

'I want to hear you read.'

'Good.'

'Who else is on? Sarah and Geneva both wanted to know and of course, I couldn't tell them.'

'David Rhys Owen is on with me. Alex Kirk and Tom Bellfounder were doing a stint for a schools audience this afternoon; I'm hoping they'll come along this evening.'

'Bellfounder: what a wonderful name for a poet.'

'It would be a pretty wonderful name for a bus conductor. He wears three-piece suits and carries an umbrella. Terrible to think that someone who sounds so resonant should be so stolid.'

'What's wrong with three-piece suits?' McEvoy demands. 'I've got one.'

'I'm sure you look splendid in it,' Ruth pacifies him, 'some men do. Tom looks like a VAT inspector at a funeral.'

'What are his poems like; clerkly?'

'Oh, not at all what you'd expect; long and lovely and lush.'

'What about the other two? I think I've read Kirk.'

'You should have done. He's a goody; good poet, nice guy and comfortable company. I always expect to see a stout tabby tail curled round his feet; I think you'll like Alex. Rhys Owen is your fleshly poet, writes in sixty-nine positions and for an encore will whistle "Land of My Fathers" through his sphincter, but a close examination of the text suggests a voyeur rather than a practitioner. When you meet him you'll see why. To be perfectly frank, I don't think he's written a poem in two years, he's dried up and started writing letters to the *Guardian* instead; that's always a bad sign, letters to the *Guardian*. It's a pity he doesn't dry *out*, too. He carries cassettes of his poems and when he gets too drunk to talk he hands out the tapes – well I'm buggered.'

The door of the bar has opened and three men walk in.

'Here's a turn up, we've got them all at once; the mesomorph, the pyknic and the leptosomatic.'

'Is that them?'

'Yes, shall we call them over or would you rather not? We can always converge on the way out.'

'If you don't mind, I'd rather not,' McEvoy says, 'I'm quite happy like this.'

'All right,' Ruth says, equably. Their fingers are entwined on the table top, which is where McEvoy would like to leave them, but the poets have seen Ruth. They wave, pick up their drinks and approach.

'Kirk's the normal one,' Ruth whispers. McEvoy tries tactfully to disengage his fingers but Ruth will not have it. She greets her colleagues and conducts introductions, single handed.

'John; Tom Bellfounder, Alex Kirk, Rhys Owen. This is John, lads.'

Kirk and Bellfounder nod and beam approvingly as if they think that it is entirely proper for Ruth to have brought along someone to hold her hand. Owen settles into folds.

'Have you checked into the Arts Centre yet, Rhys?' Ruth asks, 'because I haven't. The organizers will be shitting bricks if they don't know we've arrived.'

'I have,' Owen says.

'But of course, they don't know that *you're* here,' says Bellfounder, adding, with robotic logic, 'the fact that he is doesn't mean that you are.' McEvoy sees what Ruth means about the VAT man at a funeral.

'Then we'll wander round in a minute. How did your session go, lads?'

'Mostly nobs and a few of the *hoi polloi*. We played to the gallery and had a ball,' Kirk says. Without being fat he is firmly built but with a suggestion of furriness about his outline; he might well have a sleek tail down his trouser leg.

'Are you stopping for a drink, after?'

'Certainly; we aren't missing the boozy bit.'

'Prochak'll drink us under the table,' Owen announces, tapping a forefinger against his fleshy nose. 'It's worth coming just to see that. Hollow legs, eh, Ruth darling?'

The calculated offensiveness of Owen's delivery stirs in McEvoy an urge to protect. Ruth, divining this, clenches her fingers hard over his knuckles – *Don't be a bloody fool.*

'Where are you staying, Ruth?' Bellfounder asks. 'We're at the Welsh Pony, but we didn't see your name down.'

'I think Ruth's made her own arrangements,' Owen says. Kirk and Bellfounder look at him with distaste. 'Ruth'll be all right tonight.'

Very well, McEvoy says, I will not smash Owen's fat snout into his baboon's arse of a face, even on my own behalf.

'We're staying with friends in Park Town,' Ruth says, keeping a tight hold on McEvoy's hand. 'You're right, Tom, I ought to let the organizers know I'm here. We'll see you later.' She stands, hauling McEvoy with her, and heads for the door.

'*Did you ever hear about the strange case of the Midwife Toad?*' Owen bawls after them.

Outside on the pavement Ruth leans lightly against McEvoy's shoulder and he strokes her hair, because it is the first chance that he has had.

'Is he re*volt*ing?' Ruth says.

'What was that about the Midwife Toad?'

'I can't imagine; some arcane insult of his own devising. The Midwife Toad was suspected of being an evolutionary fake – done with ink. I think he's trying to make a statement about my poetry.'

'Why is he so rude to you? Why you?'

'Not just me, any woman, especially any woman with no visible means of support, by which I mean a husband. Usually I'm on my own, which he cannot bear to see; apparently he can't bear to see me with a man either. You wanted to beat him to pulp for me, didn't you? There's no need, I can pulp him quite well myself. The other two are OK though, aren't they?'

'The mesomorph and the leptosomatic?'

'I think Tom's still growing; his sleeves get shorter and shorter.'

At the Arts Centre Ruth is greeted fervently by a twitching young man with an illegible lapel button. They are shown to a room where the reading will take place and there are joined shortly after by Kirk, Bellfounder and Owen.

'Where are you going to sit?' Owen asks McEvoy. 'Front

row's usually a good bet with poet*esses*, but of course this one doesn't wear a skirt.'

'I was going to the back,' McEvoy says to Ruth, over Owen's head.

'Leaving the front row empty; just like bleeding school kids. Stay up front – no, not that end. Come my side.'

Owen hawks. She leaves him and steps on to the dais, where a table is set out with glasses and a carafe. Owen has brought a glass with him. It is full, and not with water. McEvoy takes a chair to the extreme right of the front row. Owen disappoints him chiefly in that he would have expected a poet to produce a rather more lyrical line of invective.

This is terrible, Geneva thinks; like an amateur theatrical production where no one is sure of the words.

'Perhaps you'd like a real drink?' Sarah suggests, archly.

Geneva, awash with coffee, nods eagerly.

'And does Mary . . . drink?'

Sarah sways to the sideboard and flings open the doors to reveal a row of bottles. Geneva, who is wishing sincerely that she had not brought Mary along for moral support, was not expecting anything like this. Sarah exhibits no signs of depression within Geneva's definition of the word. Were Geneva asked to describe her she would say, rather, that Sarah seemed high. She covers the carpet with a disconcertingly floaty gait, as if she had been inhaling something volatile and lighter than air.

'What would you like?'

'Scotch?'

'Mary; and you?'

Mary, experiencing genuine embarrassment for possibly the first time in her life, peers into the sideboard with the anxious half-witted expression that children assume when they wish to be seeming to understand.

'A fairly weedy Martini with plenty of tonic for Mary, I think,' Geneva says.

'Fetch lemons, Chris. Ice!'

'He's having to be man of the house this evening,' Sarah

explains, as Christopher slinks out of the doorway. Julian, thank God, is in bed. What was John thinking of to leave her alone like this, or has he become so used to it that he no longer sees anything *outré* in Sarah's demeanour? His accounts of her jealousy have been threadbare; he has left things out.

It is half past eight. Geneva and Mary have been at the house for an hour, have had two large cups of coffee each and have listened to Sarah talking. Geneva has no very clear idea of what Sarah has been talking about, a lot of it seems to concern the thirty-foot garden, the living-room carpet, Julian's new teacher; John has not been mentioned once, except just now, obliquely: Christopher is having to be man of the house, this evening.

Chris returns from his errand and Sarah sets about preparing the drinks as if approaching the climax of a complex conjuring trick. Geneva hopes that Sarah is not planning to have a drink herself, especially when she discovers that there is ice and lemon in her Scotch, which turns out to be brandy. Sarah hands Mary a tumbler with a kind of grotesque Bunny dip to avoid spilling it. The butt end of a lemon teeters on the brim.

'Well, don't let's talk about me,' Sarah declaims, perching with painful gentility on the arm of the settee, a claret glass of dark sherry in her hand. 'How's your latest novel coming along?'

Geneva is not working on a novel at the moment, but senses that Sarah will take it as a slight if she says as much; moreover, her projected work is currently too fluid to be pinned down by description. 'Oh, I'm writing a book about a man who's writing a book, but the more he writes the further he gets from finishing it. It's an autobiography,' Geneva says. 'Of the man, not of me.'

'What man?'

'The man who's writing the book. He's writing an autobiography, but he doesn't get born till halfway through.'

'What's it called?'

Geneva, who hoped to stop this conversational train dead in its tracks, tries again. '*Zeno Was Here*.'

'Fascinating,' Sarah says, vacantly. 'Oh, is that the time?' She has been looking at the clock at two- and three-minute intervals ever since they arrived. 'I think you should go to bed, Chris.'

Christopher seems unnaturally eager, for a ten-year-old, to go to bed. Sarah calls after him, 'Perhaps Mary will read you a bedtime story if you ask her nicely.'

Chris calls inaudibly from the landing; Sarah goes to the door to answer. Mary turns a face piquant with appeal toward her mother; whispers.

'She's barmy.'

'No, no. If Chris wants you to, go and read to him.'

'What for?'

'I'll tell you later. Please, darling.'

'Chris would love that,' Sarah says, returning, with the over-bright emphasis of mothers whose children have to be told what to love. 'Mary, there are simply heaps of books by the bed. You can imagine,' she adds. Mary goes out, mouthing at Geneva.

'I'll get you for this.'

'More Scotch?'

'I'm fine, thanks,' Geneva says, a defensive hand over her glass.

'I'm glad she's gone up,' Sarah says, leaning forward, confidingly; 'I wanted to ask your advice. Have you heard of anyone called Margaret?'

'I know two or three people called Margaret.'

'Margaret Anderson; does the name mean anything to you?'

It does, but Geneva cannot think why it should. 'Who is she?'

'Well, that's it. We don't know.'

'We?'

'We've had a very funny letter. Look.' Sarah takes from her handbag a folded sheet of paper and holds it out. 'Really rather mysterious.'

Geneva reads the first line, *Dear John, you won't remember me* . . . and takes a mighty swig at her brandy. 'Doesn't he know who she is?'

'He says not. He says he can't remember anyone called that.'

'But Sarah, how could I know?'

Sarah's façade disintegrates. 'He tells you things . . . '

218

'Sarah, he doesn't. Not very much.' Which is certainly true on this evening's showing. 'Why should he tell me about this woman? If he doesn't know who she is I certainly wouldn't.' What on earth possessed him to show Sarah? The very last thing –

'Look what she's written. He took her to Bath; for the weekend – '

Geneva re-reads the letter, to gain time. 'He threw her over, Sarah, she says so.'

'He doesn't know I've seen it. It was hidden in his filing cabinet. He hid it. This woman's writing to him and sending him things and he's hiding them. What's this book she's talking about?'

Geneva takes Sarah's shaking arm and holds it. 'I think, Sarah, that if he says he doesn't know, he doesn't know, and that he hid it, if he did hide it, because he guessed you'd be upset if you found it.' As to the book, let John talk his own way out of that. How dare he drop her into this mess? 'This is probably someone he knew years ago. He did say that a lot of odd people had got in touch after the television debate.' Why didn't he *destroy* it?

'He wouldn't let me go to Oxford with him.'

'But hasn't he gone to a poetry lecture or something like that? I didn't think you were interested in poetry.'

'He doesn't know what I'm interested in. He doesn't care. You're the one he cares about.'

'No,' says Geneva, 'no, no, no, no. It isn't me.'

'Who is it, then?'

'I didn't mean that. There's no one. Sarah, you must know that, there's no one else. Where would he find the time?'

Sarah flings aside the letter (thank God the poem has gone), falls to her knees and buries her head in Geneva's lap. 'He'll be back late. I don't know what he's doing. I don't know who he's with. Stay with me, Geneva. Stay with me till he comes back.'

'All right,' Geneva says, thinking of Christopher and Julian, patting Sarah's shoulder, absently. 'I'll stay.' She wishes she had brought her patchwork.

14

Ruth stands and moves to the centre of the dais. Lean and poised in her jeans and denim jacket she looks as if she might be about to demonstrate techniques of unarmed combat. On the far side of the table the unspeakable Owen subsides like a wrecked dirigible and adjusts his dress, but to no avail. All eyes are where they should be, on Ruth.

McEvoy, after forty-five minutes of fleshly poetry, would give himself up to the precisely detailed pleasure of imagining what he would do to David Rhys Owen given a chainsaw, a Black and Decker or a blow torch; shred him, perforate him, reduce him to a heap of fuming tallow but after all, he came to Oxford to hear Ruth Prochak read her poems and he will hear them.

Ruth does not say anything. She jams her hands into her hip pockets and takes a step backward. McEvoy is terrified for her; this public Ruth is an unknown quantity; has she dried up, forgotten to bring her poems, been poleaxed with shyness? As a lock of hair drops over her forehead she looks at her audience from under it, at them all, and then at him. McEvoy recognizes a performance and relaxes. How slight, how well-formed she looks after the gross Owen with his loins and pricks and wombs, his sonnet to his mistress's cunt, his pubic odes. They are not so much erotic as gynaecological; he seems to have clambered around inside every woman he has ever met, peering testily into orifices; even his envoy was addressed to a discarded condom, sentimentally – *Well, little grouch bag*: a circus metaphor, as he explained.

'I had intended to begin with four poems from *Midland City*,' Ruth says, 'but then I thought I'd rather kick off with something you couldn't possibly have heard before because I only finished it last night. "Lines for Garbutt".'

McEvoy is disappointed. He finds it very difficult to take in a poem at first hearing, especially as now, when his whole attention is focused on the voice and not the words, to which end he has been reading *Midland City* assiduously, the better o appreciate it. The audience, though, small but more than average for a poetry reading, seems to like it, a neat, punning, affectionate encomium to Paul E. Garbutt who, it turns out, designed the original map of the London Underground. They applaud; on the dais, in full view, Owen belches, a pontifical, Johnsonian belch which the applause is not quite loud enough to drown.

'Virgin's piss,' he pronounces. The audience murmurs, dismayed.

McEvoy has heard from Simon Headley about drunken poets who rant and break up the furniture, poets who have thrown up over the front row, who have to be conveyed paralytic from bar to bed or worse, from bar to platform. Owen has not reached that stage, he is only sniping drunk, but this shocks McEvoy profoundly; that he should publicly attempt to undermine someone else's performance.

Ruth shows him her shoulder and proceeds with the four *Midland City* poems, prefacing them with a self-deprecating quotation from the *TLS* review, which kindles a sympathetic laugh from the audience. Owen takes exception to the first line of the first poem, 'A Railway Fantasy: Knebworth'. He finds the metre displeasing.

'The lock on the door of the salt store's broken – ' Ruth begins.

'"This is the night mail crossing the border,"' Owen chimes in, *sotto voce* but not *sottissimo*. 'Fucking railways; they all choose dactyls. "Faster than fairies, faster than witches, Bringing the cheque and the postal order . . ."'

Ruth begins again, and McEvoy holds the sides of his chair, to anchor himself.

> The lock on the door of the salt store's broken.
> Salt Store it says, in sans serif on the sign.
> Frost is sprinkled in crystals along the platform,
> Here's where the gangers come, to garnish the line,
> But the lock is snapped on the door
> And the padlock dangles.
> Did the cold snap crack it or
> Did felons break in, taking
> British Railway salt?

The man with a can in the rimy moonlight,
A lonely ganger abroad in the white
With a permanent-ink black shadow,
Is out there salting the track:
A man with a can from the vinegar vat,
Tripping the sleepers from station to station,
To pickle the joints, to brine the line goes the man
In charge of sodium distribution,
Furnishing a saline solution
To the problem of frozen points.

Alone he treads the tracks,
With salt from the store in a sack on his shoulder,
A can in his hand. He makes permanent the way.

Owen interjects at intervals; Ruth ignores him; everyone else is hotly embarrassed, leaning forward with expressions of such rapt interest – to assure Ruth of their undivided attention – that they look like a group of devoted acolytes watching the guru levitate. When she finishes they applaud her a shade more enthusiastically than the poems perhaps warrant, in sympathy. But if this goes on, McEvoy fears, the sympathy will turn to pity (Poor girl, but what can she do?) and Ruth will get very nasty afterwards. The organizer is at the far end of the row in worried conference with Alex Kirk, who is sadly shaking his head, possibly advising against violent intervention. But Ruth, it seems, has no intention of having her evening spoilt. The cutting edge of her voice slices through Owen's soggy burbling and when Owen rises unsteadily and shambles toward the door, urgently investigating his flies, in search of the lavatory, one must assume, she only shrugs and explains, in mitigation, 'He comes from Sidcup.' The announcement draws livelier applause than the poetry.

When it is over people drift forward with books to be signed, to ask questions, to express condolences. Kirk and Bellfounder press round with earnests of solidarity.

'Has he been like that all day?' McEvoy asks. Kirk shrugs, gloomily.

'He's like that all the time. He was well tanked-up when

we met him going the wrong way down Turl, we should have let him keep going. Unfortunately there's a sizeable section of the public who expect poets to be like that; they think it's the Life Force, poetic licence. I saw a room full of teachers watch in rapture once while he smashed up a book display. You could see them thinking: Ah, a Wild Man. Loving it. He's not the only one.'

'Getting the rest of us a bad name,' Bellfounder complains, spinsterishly.

A woman with an aged parent in tow taps Ruth on the shoulder. 'Will you be coming straight away or shall I give you a key?'

'Key please,' Ruth says. 'I think we'll be here a little while, yet, if you don't mind, Cynthia.'

'Of course not; which is your friend?' This must be his hostess, McEvoy thinks, if he stays; of course he will stay, but he has yet to ring Sarah to say that he has missed the train. Will he have the nerve to stay after that?

'This is John.' Ruth takes his hand and holds it out to the woman in an oddly proprietorial gesture. 'John, this is Cynthia Black and her father.' Cynthia smiles cordially but McEvoy can see that she was expecting a woman.

Father has attracted a little circle of adherents to himself, although he appears to have forgotten who they are. They address him as Professor, and he nods and smiles, vaguely. Emeritus, McEvoy hopes.

The groups begin to trickle out of the room; Kirk and Bellfounder head for the bar to buy in a supply for Ruth; Cynthia is helping Professor Black into a heavy overcoat. His gloves dangle out of the sleeves on strings.

'Father gets cold,' Cynthia explains, seeing McEvoy's curious eye upon the gloves. 'And he does leave so many things lying around. We'll see you both later; don't hurry.' She takes the old man by a glove-string and he toddles after her.

'One of your genuine loopy academics,' Ruth explains fondly. 'I've been visiting them for ten years, nearly, and he still doesn't know my name. He can't remember who Cynthia is either, half the time, but he knows she's where the food comes from so he does what she tells him. They've got a big house.'

'What about the Frau Professor?'

'She dresses to match the carpet and gives no trouble. Right, that's that last of the Fancy; let's go where the booze is.' Wonderful, McEvoy thinks; he hasn't had a cup of coffee since five o'clock. These people don't drink coffee.

The bar is on the next floor, dimly lit and crowded, but neither so dim nor so crowded that McEvoy does not immediately intercept a grave and warning look from Alex Kirk. He is sitting against the wall. By the adjacent wall is Bellfounder; in the corner, between them, sits David Rhys Owen.

'Ruth, are you sure you want to go in?'

'Well, yes – there are quite a lot of people I want to see.'

'Owen's over there, in the corner, minded by Kirk and Bellfounder, but he doesn't look very containable. Would you rather go somewhere else?'

'The Nose with a luminous dong; you have a protective look; if you can't save me from anything else you'd like to save me from myself. I think I can bear it if you promise not to hit him.'

'I refuse to promise. How can you stand him?'

'With difficulty, but one must. He was highly regarded while he was writing and he does more harm to himself than to anyone else. I'm sorry for him – isn't that sufficient insult? Come on in; Alex has set them up for us.'

She takes his arm, a move that does not escape Owen.

'Here's Prochak with her fancy man.'

'Do shut up, Rhys,' Kirk pleads, without much conviction.

'Heroine of the half rhyme.'

'That's rich,' Ruth mutters, sitting down and rolling up her sleeves truculently, 'that's rich coming from a man who likens a vagina to a volcano so that he can consonate magma with smegma.'

Mary Stevens pays off the cab, lets herself into the dark hall and runs up the stairs. 'Jane!'

Jane is sulking in the living-room with cocoa and Goldsmith. When she sees that her sister is crying she pulls her down on to the sofa and puts an arm around her.

'Where's Mum?'

'Still at the McEvoys'. Jane, John's wife's mad.'

'Barking mad? Throwing wobblies? Climbing the walls?'

'It's not funny. He's never said anything.'

'Well, he wouldn't, would he? Not to us.'

'Mum would have let something slip if she'd known. It was awful. She put lemon in the brandy and wouldn't stop talking. She was shaking all the time and making funny noises. And John hasn't come back from Oxford; she thinks he's run away.'

'She's all right when we see her in the street. I know she doesn't like us but she's never spat in our eye, or anything. She's quite normal.'

'She isn't normal; she's weird. Do you think he has run away?'

'Don't be soft,' Jane says, but her active mind runs ahead. She recalls John in the kitchen a few weeks ago, reluctant to go home, she realizes now. Suppose he has bolted; what seismic revolutions they will have to make in their assessment of him. It could be quite interesting.

The room has emptied in direct proportion to the rise in Owen's volume. Kirk and McEvoy have taken the coward's part and slunk away to the bar, leaving Tom Bellfounder trapped between Ruth and Owen. Owen's one-liners have corroded into an unintelligible slur which Ruth seems able to interpret for she responds at intervals, meanwhile making notes on the reverse of the yellow Xerox that is the evening's programme. McEvoy discards the suspicion that she is taking down everything he says for future reference. 'I didn't think poets talked to each other like that.'

'What a quaint picture you must have of us,' Kirk says, tolerantly. 'Rhys is not at his prettiest, tonight; it was not always thus, but he's been getting steadily worse since his wife left him. He likes his women at home, warming the bed, and he's insanely jealous of Ruth.'

'Literally?' McEvoy asks, with a tremor of recognition.

'Near enough. Drink will get him if envy doesn't. You can see a myriad of brain cells destroyed in a single evening and nobody likes to be the warm-up.'

'Is that what it was? I didn't realize Ruth was the star turn. I thought she was a minor poet.'

'We're all minor poets,' Kirk says, heavily. 'Where did you meet her?'

'At a mutual friend's.' McEvoy thinks it might be safer to leave the celebrated Geneva out of the conversation. 'I haven't known her long. I like her work very much.'

'I admired the sestina,' Kirk says. 'I'd like to have written that.' McEvoy is touched by his generosity. 'Rhys, of course, doesn't wish he'd written it, he just can't stand the thought that she did. I don't know what we're going to do with him when they throw us out of here.'

'Have you far to go?'

'Personally, no; it's two minutes' walk. Somehow we've got to get that idiot out to Kidlington. You don't have a car with you, by any chance?'

'I'm sorry. I came by train.'

'I suppose you would have, if you came with Ruth.' He smiles. 'But we'll have to break up the party somehow; can't you take her away?'

'*Take* her?'

'I see your point. Could you persuade her that it will ease the pain for me and Tom if she'd make a tactical withdrawal. Rhys will call her a quitter but no one will believe it.'

'I could try.' McEvoy is doubtful. He looks across the room, through the smoke. Ruth does not quite have her fangs into Owen's jugular but her upper lip is caught drily on a front tooth, exposing a wolfish grin. She is alert, bellicose and still articulate. Owen is incoherent, sweating; his empurpled bald patch glistens like mange under the threads of hair. 'She's enjoying herself.'

'No she isn't.' Kirk looks apologetic. 'Sorry, you don't want a stranger telling you things about your woman, but I've known her a long while. She's not enjoying it.'

'She doesn't mind laying into me,' McEvoy says, deeply melancholy.

'Then be sure it's for the sake of your soul. She was good this evening, she ought to be high on that, not dissipating it in a slogging match with that deliquescent oaf. Try and break it up, there's a good person. I must go soon; I've got to get to Cardiff in the morning and I can't leave Tom to sort it out. He has the strategic instincts of Jubilation T Cornpone.'

'What time is it, then?'

'Quarter past eleven. They're officially closed here, now.'

'Oh, sweet Christ! Is there a phone?'

'On the landing. Were you meant to make a call?'

'My wife,' McEvoy says, without thinking. Kirk's expression in the half light is sad.

'All is not sweet, all is not sound?'

McEvoy goes over to Ruth, who looks up, red-eyed, several shots in her locker, yet. 'I must phone. I promised Sarah; can you meet me downstairs?' He leaves her to finish her fight as best she can and runs for the stairhead, not that a few minutes will make much difference now; the matter is out of his hands. He really has missed the last train to London, and by accident. That was God-given, surely; now he will have to stay and his lie will become truth, though not the whole truth.

The telephone rings only once before the receiver is ripped from its rest. No preliminaries: 'John?' It is Geneva.

'For Christ's sake, John, where are you?'

'In Oxford. I missed the train.'

'All of them?'

'The last one. I'll have to stay here. Geneva, what are you doing there? Where's Sarah?'

'Asleep in the living-room, I didn't like to leave her. I sent Mary home in a taxi – '

'Mary?'

'I took Mary with me. I didn't know what – *John*: how could you do this?'

'I didn't mean to. There's a bar here; some of us got talking. I didn't notice the time.'

'You mean you were too drunk to care.'

'Do I sound drunk?'

'No, you don't,' Geneva says, tiredly. 'I'm sorry; anyone would think you made a habit of this – but Sarah's taken your defection rather badly. You should have warned me, John. It wasn't fair.'

'I'd have been much later than this if I *had* caught the train.'

'I didn't mean that I – '

The pips intervene. 'I've no more change. I'll be back by lunchtime.' The telephone goes dead. He replaces the handset.

Indefensible; he should get some more tenpenny pieces, ring again and ask what, exactly, is wrong with Sarah, ask to speak to her; find out if Geneva means to stay all night. In despair and remorse he turns and finds Ruth behind him, setting down their briefcases. Ruth will have change. As she looks up at him he sees slate-coloured crescents beneath her swollen eyes; her mouth droops with fatigue.

Oh Ruth, poor tired Ruth, beleaguered Ruth. He gathers her into his arms and kisses her, gnaws at her, tongue and teeth drawing as much of her into him as he can contain. It is the first time that he has properly kissed his woman.

At the top of the stairs Owen lurches into view flanked by Kirk and Bellfounder. He raises an apocalyptic arm and points.

'Whore! Bitch on heat! *Midwife!*'

Ruth has had enough; she slumps against McEvoy although swearing foully rather than pleading for succour. McEvoy takes her by the shoulders, sets her gently to one side and bounds up the stairs to where the three poets stand unsteadily, there to land the basest blow of his career and then to dance away down again before Owen's ill-considered intake can disgorge.

'Sorry,' he says, to Owen's armorial supporters. Kirk waves an understanding hand.

'Sorry,' he says to Ruth. 'That was for all poetry as much as for you. Come home now, darling. Come home.'

Home, in the quiet peninsula of Park Town, is a fifteen-minute walk away, along the empty pavements of St Giles and the Banbury Road. They are in a hurry, now, oh yes, they are in a hurry to reach it, but they cannot walk quickly. They have to keep stopping, ridiculously putting down the briefcases, to lean against each other, face to face, in shadows; to gaze, below street lights. The fifteen minutes becomes twenty, thirty; midnight has struck somewhere before they reach Park Town. The windows of Professor Black's tall house are dark, but a light glows far down a passage and when Ruth turns the key in the lock Cynthia Black, wearing a loden coat over cotton pyjamas, wades out of the darkness to meet them.

'Do you want anything to eat?' she whispers, furtively. 'Cocoa?'

'No no,' Ruth says, muffled against McEvoy's shoulder, 'only bed.'

'I could bring some cocoa up when you're in bed. You're in the same room,' she says, sportingly.

'Oh goody,' Ruth mutters. McEvoy fears high words if they are delayed any longer. Over her head he sees Professor Black's overcoat hanging from a hook, with dead hands depending.

'We're terribly tired,' he says.

'Second floor. Ruth knows the way. Tippy-toe; Mummy's got neuralgia.' Chaste and plain she stands at the foot of the stairs, an incarnate newel post, clutching the loden across her breasts. 'Bacon and egg for breakfast?'

Ruth shudders against his heart. 'Thank you very much,' McEvoy whispers. 'I think just coffee and toast.'

They ascend, tippy-toe. Cynthia leaves a decent interval before creaking up behind them; poor love, she is trying so hard. He can feel her eyes on their backs as they gain the second landing.

'In here,' Ruth says, palpating a distressingly soft wall in search of the light switch. The room is at least as large as her living-room at Primrose Hill, illuminated villainously by a yellow forty-watt bulb. The bed lies high and long with a shot silk eiderdown quilted into the pattern of the rising sun.

'Where's the bathroom?'

'On the first floor, opposite the stairs.'

'Oh shit. Mummy's neuralgia.'

'Mummy and Daddy are under us. You can go first.'

He takes the briefcase and sneaks down again, alarmed less by the thought of Mummy's neuralgia than by the prospect of running into the maiden Cynthia coming out of the lavatory.

The bathroom predictably clanks and gurgles; much steam and little water. The lavatory looks like the Portland Vase, the bath has feet. This is the setting for low comedy, he thinks, washing hurriedly and imagining the dark floors and staircases alive with scurrying figures in nightshirts, whiskery shins a-twinkle, and cushiony matrons wearing curlers, in outraged pursuit as doors open and close, faces peer round corners, gartered housemaids twirl with trays and clergymen lose their trousers. What is he *doing* here? If he has given any thought to whom Ruth's friends might be he's pictured them young, living in sparsely furnished flats with sofa beds and duvets.

Returning to the upper floor he finds Ruth sitting patiently on the bed in a white, lace-trimmed lawn nightdress, pin-tucked and frilled, and what appear to be black stockings. She looks like a naughty Victorian child, or a Victorian harlot pretending to be a child.

'Why are you wearing that?'

'Because it's bleeding chilly, Jack. Anyway, I like pretty nighties.'

'But the black stockings – ?'

'I haven't taken my *socks* off.' She peels her feet, rolls one sock into the other, housewifely, and picks up her sponge bag. 'I won't be long.' She strides, fabulously silent over the threadbare carpet, the extraordinary night-rail frothing in the draught as she passes on to the landing, where she hitches it up to her knees and runs.

McEvoy undresses and climbs into the bed which Ruth has thoughtfully turned down. For all that this is late May the sheets cling, unseasonably clammy, the feathers in the pillows are flocked moistly together. He hugs his shoulders, cringing, and feels the hairs on his legs spring up in protest as they touch the sheets. No wonder Ruth is wearing her nightie; a pretty nightie; how out of character, or is it? As she said on the train, what does he know of her character? It is an expensive looking thing. (Paying herself back for all those years spent dressing at Oxfam.) If only there were a fire in the grate, that cast-iron pouch in the wall surrounded by lichen-green tiles and stuffed with computer print-outs. If only the bed were warm and aired, if candles could replace that ghastly light bulb under its grainy parchment shade, and if there were a great fur rug in front of the fire they needn't sleep in the bed at all, they could nest and tumble in front of the blazing logs . . . the blazing faggot . . . the flames die, the embers fade; was it for this he risked Sarah's peace of mind and Geneva's good opinion? His eyes snap open as the door closes and he finds Ruth standing by the bed.

'Is it all right?'

'Terrible. Like lying in blotting paper. I didn't know people used flannel sheets any more.'

'Flannel sheets never wear out, unfortunately. Think of *me*. I usually have to sleep in here alone. I did think the silly mare would air them.'

'Do you usually sleep alone?' He takes her hand and draws her down toward him.

'More often alone than not, but always alone here. I met Cynthia on the landing – '

'Are you making an exception for me?'

'She said, "Oh Ruth, I do hope you're making the right decision," and clasped my hands – at waist level. Very odd. I don't think people ought to be allowed to live in North Oxford after the age of twenty-five, she's in the wrong novel. Yes, I'm making an exception for you. Let go, John, I want to switch off the light.'

'Must we make love in the dark?'

'Tonight, yes. That bulb looks like something in the outside loo.'

In the darkness he hears her approaching again and opens his arms to receive her. 'Won't you take that thing off?'

'When the bed warms up.'

'I'll warm you. Take it off.' He unfastens strings and tugs. As she slides out of its tenting folds she wraps herself round him, long legs, long arms, long and desirous, shivering. He winds his fingers into her hair and fits her mouth against his and she is ready there before him; oh, the fitness of things. He wants to say – Ruth, your hair, your hair, I'm lost in your lovely hair – but it is too short to be lost in – it's like corn silk – but it hasn't the greenish-yellow lustre of corn silk, it isn't silk or floss or fur; just hair, ur-hair; perfect original hair. All hair must be judged against this. 'Oh Ruth, your hair. Your hair.

'Ruth, let me kiss your eyes, I've always wanted to kiss your eyes, your beautiful eyes, and your breasts, your lovely titties, they're so small my hand can cover them. Oh Ruth, Ruth.'

'Come on,' says Ruth, underneath. 'Come in. I want you now. Come in.'

When he wakes she is still in his arms, they have not stirred all night; he looks at his watch on the wrist that lies across her shoulder; half past five, they have not stirred for an hour. He feels light-headed, acutely wakeful; he will not sleep again, he thinks, but there is no need to move yet. In four hours perhaps they will be back on the train to London, he cannot think past that, cannot think toward what he will find on his return. *Carpe diem*; he may lie here for a while in this warm unwholesome bed whose cavernous mattress has so engulfed them that their entwined legs raise no more than a shallow barrow beneath the blanket. The eiderdown has slithered to the floor where its cretonne underside eclipses the rising sun. Outside the window the true sun, swimming up through early cloud above the brick garden walls of North Oxford, flushes the pear tree on the Blacks' back lawn. Below them Mummy and the Professor lie embalmed like Tudors on a tomb, each on a marble bed, toes turned up, hands pointed in prayer. Somewhere on that lower level Cynthia may turn and twist in restless envious slumber or, after a sleepless night of febrile imaginings, weep drily for the deflowering of her protégé. Ruth, Ruth, how can you shield her so, how could you let her think that you too were as arid and sapless, knowing all the while that you are a lovely fuck.

He wants her again at once, and then does not because to see her still and sleeping for once, to see her aching eyes at rest and her bruised mouth, bruised as much by her ardour as his, a little open, is as tender as rousing her would be. She turns away from him, to his sorrow, but turning wakes and comes back, stretching and spreading herself along the length of him at which he is certain, where just now he only feared, that this cannot be for the nonce, whatever he may have intended. It cannot be the last time.

'Now we can do it by daylight,' she says, smiling. The smile splits her swollen lip which issues blood, which he licks away. 'Are we still friends?'

He says, 'I love you, Ruth.'

'But are we still friends?'

'We are still friends, does it matter? I love you, I love looking at you, oh, Sweetheart you are so lovely to hold, you have such a bloom on your skin.'

'I think it's quite likely mildew.'

'Don't spoil it for me. You're not a bit romantic, are you?'

'Ah no,' she says, regretfully, 'women aren't.'

He kicks away the swampy encroaching mat of bedclothes and leans over her where she lies revealed at his side. Can a woman show her trust more completely than when she lies on her back with her breasts uncovered, her arms at ease?

'Do you trust me?' he asks.

'Why, what are you going to do?'

'Nothing you wouldn't want.' He begins again the exquisite exploration, throat, armpits, belly and breasts, bending to gloss the areolas with his tongue. 'Your breasts are like fruit, Ruth, did you know? Fruit and sepals and stems.' His hand moves downward.

'And what does that remind you of?' Ruth inquires, amiably. 'A hamster?'

She *will* not be serious. Her kneels above her, and takes the little stems between fingers and thumbs, until she gasps and gazes as he holds her half-suffocating until her hips arch to meet him, he plunges to meet her.

Afterward he stacks the pillows against the foot of the bed and reclines against them while she lies aslant him, face up, her head against his shoulder. With one hand he cups her breast, with the other he comforts her between her legs, very tenderly; they have been so rough with each other, but his thumb brushes slightly against her clitoris, he cannot help it, drawing from her a thin but not displeased wail of exhaustion. The bed is so high, higher than the sill of the open sash window, they seem to float becalmed above the pear tree, the brick walls, the greening gardens.

'Out of doors, next time,' he says. 'I'm glad we began in bed, that was proper, but next time we'll go somewhere else. Shall I tell you?'

'Tell me.'

'In the country, a field, a meadow, in long grass – no; in an orchard under the trees. The grass is very green, it hasn't been cut for weeks. We can look up at the sun through the leaves. Shall we lie down there in the orchard?'

'Yes, please.' Her eyes are closed. The level sun gilds the fair lashes that do not show in ordinary lights.

'At night, by the sea, in dunes among the marram grass; the sand is so soft; shall we do that? Shall we have each other there?'

'Where else?'

'We'll stay on the beach, go down and lie on the sand. It'll still be warm from the sun and we'll lie there and let the tide come in round us.

'And somewhere cold, in the snow, let's go out while it's snowing; it'll be so cold, but we won't notice. I'll fill your mouth with snow and kiss you until it melts. Darling, will all this do for you? I'll have to be romantic for both of us. I suppose you'd want to do it on a railway track. It wouldn't matter. It wouldn't matter where we were, it would be right. You'll always be with me now, wherever I am, wherever you are.' He strokes the little red node, but this time she does not stir or moan. She has fallen asleep innocently supine in his arms, so that a lascivious watcher in the pear tree, say, could see the whole wonderful truth of her. How worn out she must be after travelling, the reading, the unspeakable Owen and then, the strenuous night. Of course she must sleep and he will lie awake and make the moment last for both of them, and so he does for a little while, but his fingers involuntarily dabble in the warmth between her thighs; he wants her again, now, very urgently. How can he wake her and ask her to open to him?

But, he thinks, it would be very sweet to enter while she sleeps, unknowing, and surprise her with joy on waking. With infinite care he eases himself from under her until she lies on the blankets, his hand beneath her head, and spreads her thighs to kiss the soft fronded cleft and alert it to his intentions; even while she sleeps it seems eager to admit him. She is ready, agreeable, even though unconscious. Down he comes, over her, like a quilt.

'Oh Ruth.'

He grows into her and his heart lurches with fear. Now he realizes the enormity of his presumption. It is too late to withdraw, what will she do when she wakes to find herself transfixed, outraged by his unwarranted intrusion, his burglarious entry? He must confess.

'Ruth . . .'

'Aaah?' Her mouth opens, only a little but enough to allow his tongue. He pleads for admission, insinuating between lips and teeth, not daring to take his eyes from her eyes. This is how the Sleeping Beauty was saved, not with a chaste peck on the forehead. She wakes and attempts to move and the eyes widen with astonishment. Her throat quivers; he retracts.

'Don't talk with your mouth full.'

'How did you get in?'

'I was invited. You were out when I called, but you left a message. Didn't you want me to come in and wait?'

She nods and wraps her arms round him. She was pleased and she my pleasure.

Afterward, and this time they cannot delay for too long, she slides out of bed, extinguishes herself in the rococo nightdress and goes silently down to the bathroom, leaving him alone in his amazement. When she returns he must go down, and having no dressing gown makes a sarong of a towel and prays that Cynthia is still abed. It is after seven, but the house is silent except for strange honks and garglings farther along the landing; the Professor or the water pipes? He washes, shaves and sternly makes himself dress right down to his shoes against the excesses of temptation; presciently, for when he returns she is sitting on the bed, having progressed no further than taking off her nightdress; staring out of the window, at the long view.

'Oh, Ruth! I thought you'd be dressed by now, I thought . . . no, no, don't.'

'Not get dressed?'

'No, not yet. Let me look at you again, all of you. Lie down.'

She does as he asks, rolling on to her back, her arms loosely flexed above her head. 'Like this?'

'Like that.'

'What are you going to do?'

'Only look at you. See, I'm standing by the door, I'm not coming any closer, I only want to look. I daren't come any closer. Oh Ruth, I can't bear it. I don't know how long I shall have to make this last.'

'Come here, then.' Her fingers curl; her hips lift.

'No!' He puts his hands over his eyes and turns his back. 'I'm going to count to a hundred. Get dressed quickly.'

But he cannot help counting very fast and when he looks, through cheating fingers, he sees her with her back to him, stepping into a pair of little white cotton knickers and – how has he missed it, before? She has a mole on her right buttock, perfectly placed in the centre of the hemisphere. He must look at it properly.

'Wait.'

He kneels behind her and rolls down the fabric into a twisted cincture according to the legend on the label; *tour des hanches*. It is a lovely mole, a little dark blister of velour which must be kissed and consoled for having been missed. Ruth stands, arms hanging, looking at him over one shoulder; by her raised eyebrow he can see her smile. His hands fold flat across her belly as he presses the small blemish to his mouth. He turns her to him, investigates her navel with his tongue, exploring the minute corrugations.

'It's perfect. You should wear a jewel in it.'

'I should wear something somewhere, I hear Cynthia prowling. There's no lock on the door.'

The threat of discovery arouses him all over again. He rises to his feet and holds her firmly against him. Naked in his arms against his clothed body she really does feel small, her head is level with his mouth as she stands in bare feet, bare backed – he can see her reflection in the freckled mirror behind her – utterly bare except for the negligible white figure of eight looped about her thighs.

'Supposing Cynthia found us like this?'

'I don't want Cynthia to find *me* like this,' she whispers, against his neck.

Stricken to think that she might feel he is enjoying her disadvantage he kneels again and remorsefully untangles the garment, rolling it up over her crotch, her hips, kissing farewell to the pink bud as he shrouds it.

'Stand quite still,' he says, 'and I'll dress you and comb your hair.' He pulls the black cotton sweater over her head and then cannot take his hands from the two hard studs that emboss it.

'It won't always be like this,' she says.

'Won't it?' He is dismayed. 'Why not?'

'I only meant, me lolling about while you do everything. Truly, I'm not usually like this. But I was so tired, and I *do* enjoy it.'

He pushes the sweater up, under her arms, and begins to bid her goodbye, all over again.

15

The train is halted by engineering work somewhere outside Didcot. Nearby six cooling towers, like grey titanic corsets, steam lazily above the power station. The English love eyesores.

'What will happen when you get home?'

'I rang before we left. It was hard – I could see Cynthia in the shadows.'

'What was she doing?'

'I asked if I might use the phone and she was very tactful about closing the door to the kitchen, but then I saw it open, an inch or two, and there was something blocking the light. Geneva had gone home.'

'*Geneva?*'

'I didn't tell you last night; when I rang from the Arts Centre Geneva was still there. Sarah was frightened because I hadn't come home, though God knows, if I'd left as soon as the reading finished I wouldn't have been home by then, and Geneva stayed with her. The money ran out before I could ask if she was staying all night.'

'I had some change. You should have said.'

'I didn't want to know. I was past caring. I knew I could do nothing until today. When I rang just now Sarah answered, very rational. Geneva stayed till two, saw her to bed and let herself out. Geneva's a heroine. Sarah wanted to know who I'd stayed with and where, but it was no worse than usual. I wish I hadn't used Geneva. I should have told her. She was very angry last night, rightly. She thought I'd deceived her.'

'How deceived her?'

'I hadn't told her the whole truth. Ruth, how could I? If she'd invented Sarah as one of her characters she'd have understood, but she had to rely on what I told her and I told her so little. She thought it was everything, she thought she was my confidante – she *is* – but it would have been so disloyal to Sarah to tell her everything – whoever did tell anyone everything? It's past concealing now, but I had to let

238

her find out for herself, only she doesn't see it like that. She thinks I deliberately misled her. She misled herself.'

'You mean that for once she failed to speculate?'

'I suppose she wasn't interested in Sarah enough to speculate.'

'What did you tell her?'

'Nothing about us – Ruth, what are we going to do?'

'We?'

'I know I said that last night must be the first time and the last, but it can't be. You must know that. Or is it different for you?'

'Of course it's different for me.' She sees by his face that he has made the obvious interpretation of her misinterpretation and instantly regrets the swift return. This is all very new for you, she thinks; finding yourself in the suppliant's seat.

'It's different because it's easy. I go on as usual, working, writing, travelling. You are the one who must contrive and conceal. I can take a lover openly; nobody notices one above another.'

She has never aroused such anguish in anyone before. He grasps her wrists across the table. 'This is just an episode?'

'You *are* tender,' she says, not meaning it as he would mean it. 'My fault – my bad habit of being succinct. You said: What shall we do? All I meant was, it's going to be much, much worse for you, much harder, much sadder. Of course this can't be the last time. How could you think it?'

'However easy it's going to be for you, I'm involving you in a deception; and you know how I've done it, by leaving you out. I've omitted you, suppressed you, like an unfinished painting, there's a gap where you should be. You're a non-person. If this goes on, you'll have to do it too, like when you go to Geneva's, for instance, or is that asking too much? I'm ashamed to ask you at all.'

'I used to think that concealing the truth was a simpler way of lying than constructing a falsehood, but not any more. There's no excitement in it, no challenge; just a constant fear of letting something show. You remember what Bacon said, "A mixture of a lie doth ever add pleasure." Putting together a good lie is artistic, there's skill in it, exhilaration at keeping the whole thing airborne and functioning, but not in this.

This is just keeping a lid on, always fearful of stains and traces, of something escaping.'

'I can't ask you to do it. You seem to me very honest.'

'Yes, I am honest, but I shall do it whether you ask me to or not.' She can see that what he is longing to ask her is, 'Do you love me enough for that?' but not daring, remembering how once she castigated him for asking if she liked him. 'Why are we sitting on opposite sides of the table?'

'I wanted to look at you.'

'Now you've seen me. Come here.'

Folding her to him, feeling her body mould against his, he gets his question out, after a fashion. 'Am I making you happy?'

'What happened to Daddy last night?'

'He missed his train home, but he'll be back by lunchtime. He rang earlier; didn't you hear the phone?'

'Sort of.' Julian mashes his shredded wheat and shovels wet hay into his face. Martin's father never comes home at all, a detail that has only recently commended itself to Julian's attention.

'Did he have to sleep in the station?' Chris asks. He recalls television reports about down-and-outs, dossing in railway stations, seeing his father sitting awkwardly upright among them, in collar and tie.

'No. He found some people to stay with.'

'That girl was funny,' Julian remarks.

'Which girl?'

'That girl what read to Chris last night. She looked sticky.'

'You should have been asleep. That was Mary Stevens, Mrs Stevens's daughter. We sometimes meet them out shopping.' Sarah looks conspiratorial. 'I really asked her to read to you because I wanted a word with her mummy.'

Christopher shrugs. He guessed as much.

Julian says, 'A word?'

'A grown-up word.'

Julian knows about grown-up words, the ones that he is not allowed to say. A surreal image skims through his mind, of Mummy and Mrs Stevens sitting in the living-room swearing at each other, and fades. Why not?

'What did she read to you, Chris?'

'*Cathy and Claire.*'

'I don't know that one. Which book is that? Who wrote it? Who gave it to you? Where is it?' Sarah gulps and clenches her hands, stop, stop. She might be talking to John. 'Was it her own book, darling?'

'It was a magazine. Letters, you know; Dear Cathy and Claire. It was all about fellas.'

'Fellas?'

'These girls, they had fellas that all went off with other girls. And they all thought they had something wrong with them, and so they wrote to these people, and Cathy and Claire wrote back and said, no, you haven't got anything wrong with you but go and see your doctor. They kept saying they ought to go to the doctor even though they hadn't got anything wrong with them. It was dead funny,' Chris says, 'but it wasn't really a story.'

Reading? What happened to Didcot? Slough: Langley: Iver: 'Keep talking, Ruth, keep talking.'

'Talking hurts my lip.'

'Good. While it hurts you'll remember.'

'I suppose you'll hurt it some more, to make sure. I don't need scars for battle honours, John. I'll remember.'

'Talk. I may not hold you again for a long while. At least let me know what you think; I'll have that.'

'I'll write to you.'

'Write to the school. Tell me about "Unexposed Film".'

'Tell you? The whole bleeding book?'

'Just that poem; so I can read it again and know you.'

'You won't know me from that, Jack. Sorry, habit dies hard. I don't mean to back-answer. I was at a party, in a garden, not a garden party; it was quite a small garden – no, wait. Do you have falling dreams?'

'Once or twice, as I'm about to go to sleep. I wake up with a terrible jolt.'

'I do too, but there's something else, instead of the falling, just on the edge of sleep, when everything is going dark – I see a white light, like a magnesium flash; brilliant and very sudden. That wakes me. At this party, in the dark, I was dancing with someone I knew quite well, and liked very much, but hadn't expected to be . . . stirred by. We were hardly dancing at all, just swaying, I was nearly asleep, rather drunk, and then I saw one of these flashes and I woke up. It seemed to come from over his shoulder, as if someone had taken a photograph of us – only no one had. The picture of us dancing would exist only on the unexposed film; no one else would ever see it; no one would ever know. That's all; very mundane, really.'

'Was it important to you, that moment?'

'No it wasn't – except as material, later. Don't be jealous, John.'

'I'm not. How can I be jealous of what I don't have? I'm envious. I want your past. Your friend Kirk made that mistake last night, confusing one for the other. Shocking bad form for poets. Last night is an unexposed film.'

'Nine-tenths of our lives are unexposed. How little we know of each other.'

'You said that yesterday. When you write you can tell me your story.'

'All my secrets? Why – so that you can watch me write you in? What if it comes out like *Acid Test*?'

'It couldn't; sweet, sane Ruth, clear-sighted Ruth, it couldn't. *Acid Test*'s done with.'

'Is it?'

'Don't say that. You frighten me.'

'*Acid Test* will never be done with, you don't need me to tell you that. We'll live with it.'

'Cool, temperate, oceanic Ruth.'

'Oceanic?'

'Your eyes. Grey Atlantic eyes.'

Westbourne Park. 'We're nearly there, Ruth. When you were a child, did you believe that if you tried hard enough, things would never be over, things that you'd looked forward to? That you could stop time and make them last?'

'I still do.'

'I was doing it this morning, before you woke up. I thought, this is the perfect moment; I can hold it; it will never be over. It's over now.' The train is drawing into Paddington, a languorous curve. 'How will you get home? I can't come with you, that would be taking such a fistful I couldn't get my hand out of the jar. I have to go back. Will you walk through the park?'

'Not this time; I'll take the Underground to King's Cross and change on to the Northern Line. Home over the bridge and the nuclear waste.'

'I'll come with you as far as Baker Street – or King's Cross. I can back-track easily enough.'

'That way madness lies. You wouldn't back-track, you know you wouldn't. I'd rather we said goodbye here.'

'Why here?' They stall on the platform to let other passengers disperse.

'Because it's Paddington. It may be so long before I see you again; it will hurt less to remember you here.'

'Will that hurt too?'

'Don't look so hopeful. Of course it will hurt. How you do want me to suffer.'

'Don't you want me to suffer for you?'

'I don't have to want. I can see. Can't you see?'

'With you I'm never sure of what I see.'

'Be sure,' she says, 'be very sure.'

They dawdle through the barrier, under the destination board, past Isambard Kingdom Brunel. 'Here,' Ruth says. 'You take the Bakerloo Line and I'll go by the Circle. Say goodbye to me here.'

He closes his arms round her and kisses her very gently.

'Now, get down your bolt hole and I'll down mine. Remember, I'll be at Geneva's on Friday – should you be passing . . .'

'I dare not, Ruth. How could we hide what we – it would expose the film.'

'So it would. Well, write to me soon John, dear John. Goodbye.'

The place is full of people saying goodbye. He kisses her once more, releases her and watches her walk toward the Circle Line platforms. At the top of the steps, for which he did not hope, from that absolute figure, she turns, searching, sees him and waves; hesitates as if to come back, but shrugs and shakes her head; must not; and hurries down the steps. However long he knows her she will always be hurrying from

243

him in railway stations; Darlington, Baker Street, Waterloo, Paddington. Next time he must be resolute and hurry away from her.

Chris is watchful, Julian absorbed as he plays with his toy cars, using the cat as a crash pad.

'Geneva will tell you,' Sarah says. 'I'm afraid I was very silly last night. I panicked.'

'I should have phoned earlier. I'm sorry, really, but you know, I wouldn't have been home till after eleven in any case.' It is alarming, this calm acceptance, as if now that he has at last appeared to have done what she always expected him to do, she can rest, recuperate and plan the next assault. For an instant he sees a wildly hopeful future in which he dares to do what is expected of him, and then she says:

'What were they like, the people you stayed with?'

'Extremely strange. Professor Brown was senile. I was introduced to him by one of his ex-students, but I don't think he recognized him and I'm sure he didn't even know I was there. His family prop him up and point him in the right direction.'

'Where did you say they lived?'

'North Oxford.'

'I thought it was Kidlington.'

'Much the same thing.' Is he going to get away with this? *Did* he say Kidlington when he rang this morning? 'Do you know, Julian, he has his gloves on strings, just like yours, because he keeps losing them.'

'Is he in the infants?' Julian asks, fazed.

'What sort of a family? It's usually the daughters who get landed with responsibilities like that.'

Oh Christ, here we go again. 'Wife and daughter. He's over eighty; I should think she must be pushing sixty.'

'The wife?'

'The daughter.' Sorry, Cynthia, for those extra twenty years. It is ungrateful, but if you knew me better you would realize that I have to do this all the time, to worthy and blameless women. The only alternative is to excise them. Could you bear to be excised, Dr Black? You have to be young and very wonderful to survive that kind of surgery.

'Where's Kidlington?'

'Somewhere out past the Ring Road. I didn't notice the address. I don't think I'll be going back there, do you? The bed was unbelievable. It was soft and damp, Chris, like sleeping in a swamp. There was this clump of toadstools growing out of the mattress and the pillows were mossy. And they had this great big loo that played "Land of My Fathers" when you pulled the chain.'

Chris and Julian fall about laughing. Even Sarah smiles. Is it that the small bits of honest fabrication mitigate the yawning vacuum of his untruth and lend him confidence, for certainly the tension is released. He expected mayhem and yet temperance has defeated chaos. How careful he must be to conceal his happiness, oh no no no no no . . .

'That bed was a punishment.'

'For what?'

'For missing the train.'

But Sarah is looking very oddly at him; very smug; *I know what I know*. What can she know? Somehow he has to discover what passed between her and Geneva last night and he will, as soon as he can get to a telephone. But tomorrow is the Spring Bank Holiday, next week is half term. He cannot call even his telephone his own. He is so tired. Sarah will have to go out at some point; failing that he can go to Geneva's in person, if he can find an excuse to get away. He is *so* tired.

'What have you done to your lip?' says Sarah.

Darling Ruth, I said goodbye to you only yesterday, this time last week we were together in the park. I'm at home writing this on Bank Holiday. It's been raining all day, everyone's been at home but I've been so patient, marking books and assignments, setting exam questions. Now Sarah has taken the boys to the park for a little while so I am spending this half hour with you although in a sense I have spent all day with you, you are never out of my mind for a second, I find I am saying your name under my breath and I am so afraid I will say it out loud by mistake.

Darling, don't think that I meant what I said yesterday, I didn't mean I was glad I had hurt you. I would never willingly hurt you and I am so afraid that I may, but my darling you came at me so boldly it was a collision, it was two express trains meeting head on, it was a mishap Oh Ruth, such a mishap. Darling you will wreck me. This is a terrible letter, it is illiterate, my hand shakes. I always go back and reread letters and make corrections and rewrite but I shall not reread this one because like this it is as if I am talking to you and cannot unsay what I have said, and I think if I could see what I am saying I should not have the nerve to post it. Darling write to me soon, write a beautiful clear letter like one of your poems, how can you be so rational and passionate? Things are strange at home. Someone said to me, all is not sweet all is not sound. This is right. I do not know what will happen Ruth but if I have you if I have the knowledge of you I will make some good of it. Darling, on Friday I shall not be able to bear knowing that you are so close. I dare not come while you are there. Something would shine between us darling perhaps I shall find a way to pass the house and know that I am only a few yards from you. Oh my love I am only a few miles from you and I cannot reach you. Write me a letter Ruth and hold it to yourself secretly so that when I get it I can taste and touch you and kiss it with your poor broken lip, your beautiful bleeding mouth so that I shall have something of you until I see you again. Is it possible to make dreams happen? I went to sleep thinking of you last night but all I dreamed of was buying a wardrobe in Tottenham Court Road, it was so unfair. Have you ever read Peter Ibbotson? *He is in prison and meets the woman he loves in his dreams; I am not shut in I am shut out, and I dream of wardrobes. There is no justice, but should I not pay for my happiness by day with disappointment by night? This is becoming quite sensible now, at least I think it is, but there is no time to write more, darling, goodbye. Darling goodbye. I love you.*

There is no postal collection on Bank Holidays. On Tuesday morning he is confined at home, under surveillance, but after lunch he escapes to the library, returning by a circuitous route. He posts the letter in the pillar box at the corner of Geneva's road, before crossing over to ring her door bell. Waiting on the step he is exalted and disturbed. Snatches of the letter return unbidden, he was hard when he wrote it; it is lying there a few yards away, smouldering. The scarlet column should become a pillar of flame. Now, purged and sad again he must face Geneva.

The door opens behind him. He turns his head from the

mail box and finds himself facing not Geneva but Jane, a strangely muted Jane. 'Hello,' she says.

'Hello Jane.' What's this? 'Is Geneva in?'

'No.'

'I saw the car – '

'Someone gave her a lift. She's gone to an RAA meeting. Won't you come in?'

'Well, she won't be back for ages, will she? I'd better – '

'Oh no. Please come in.'

She holds the door open for him and closes it behind him and escorts him up the stairs. Well, he usually does come in, whether Geneva is there or not, but usually he is left to close the door himself and make his own way up the staircase, while Jane or Mary skips ahead to put the kettle on.

Mary is in the kitchen. She puts the kettle on.

'Hello John.'

'Hello, Mary. There's really no need to make coffee, I can't stay long.'

'But you always have coffee,' Jane says, ushering him into the living-room. Doesn't he just? 'Did you enjoy Oxford?'

'Yes, thank you. For most of the time, only I missed the train – I suppose you know that?'

'Sarah was very upset,' Jane says.

'Were *you* there?'

'Mary told me.' Does he imagine the accusing stare, or is it really there?

'Sarah's not very well at the moment,' he says.

'You shouldn't have left her,' Jane says. He is so astounded by attack from this quarter that he can find no immediate reply. 'Not just to go to a poetry reading.'

'I didn't know she was unwell when I went.'

'Mary said it wasn't that kind of being unwell.' Jane grows more and more confused until she looks at the carpet, unable to meet his eye.

'I don't often go to poetry readings. I don't often go anywhere. Jane, aren't you being rather unreasonable – and interfering?'

'I'm sorry.' She is, he can see, but none the less convinced of the justice of her objections. She will suffer hideously in later life on picket lines and demonstrations, weeping while

247

she belabours fascists and vivisectors and scabs. 'Mary was upset. So was Mum. She said you should have warned her.'

Oh Christ, this is not fair, this is not what he was expecting; trial by child. With dreadful presentiment he sees the Stevens women, all three of them, Graces, Furies, moving in to rescue his marriage. 'I didn't realize quite how bad – look, Jane, when you live with something, someone, very closely, for a long while, you can't always see exactly what's happening. It takes an outsider to notice. I'm sorry it had to be Geneva and Mary.'

'Mary's too young for that sort of thing.'

He does not argue with the big sister. It is on Mary's behalf that she has raised her standard, not Sarah's. 'I know. I came round to apologize – to both of them,' he adds, as Mary brings in the coffee. 'Chris says thank you very much for reading to him on Saturday night.'

'Oh that.' Mary wells up with giggles but they are not very nice, not very mirthful giggles. 'I thought it would make a change.'

'What was it, exactly?'

Mary sniggers behind her sleeve and holds out a tattered magazine that has clearly passed through several hands. 'It's a bit old for him, but I thought it would make a change.'

He comprehends, drearily, that she thinks she has corrupted his son with this pimply adolescent *Angst* and so avenged his wife's abandonment.

'It makes a change, dunnit?' she persists, in her horrible *ersatz* Cockney accent, which is currently the fashionable argot. The giggles bubble in her throat and he predicts a manic outburst similar to Julian's.

'Stop it!' Jane says severely, and with rather more success than Sarah had. 'Give John his coffee.'

Mary subsides but continues to shoot sidelong glances at her sister. He knows the signs; he has taught fourteen-year-old girls before; they giggle and dote in season.

'Did you hear Ruth read?' Jane asks formally. 'You remember Ruth, don't you?'

'The bug-eyed poet,' Mary chortles. Jane ignores her superbly.

'We thought she might be there. Was she good?'

248

He fears a trap, naturally enough, but this line of questioning is innocent at least. 'She was very good. Far better than the other chap.'

'What was he like?'

'Drunk, for a start,' McEvoy says. 'That didn't help. I can't say I cared much for his poetry, either.'

'Did you talk to her?'

'Only to say hello and thank you. There was quite a crowd, for a poetry reading.'

'She's coming to see us on Friday,' Mary says. 'I love watching her blink.'

Oh Mary, so do I. I love to watch so many things you could not even guess at; no one could, who knew only cantankerous Dr Prochak. He will invite her to the school, under the RAA scheme, to talk to the boys. In the staffroom he will introduce her to Simon and Marian, Thomson, Thatcher, Atkinson, Pamela Richards and Bob Lake, and they will think, as he thought once, what a strange-looking woman. And then they will arrange seats in the library, a semicircle, Sixth Form boys and some staff who will sit attentively, impressed by the erudition, the lean authoritative figure, while he dreams of the round pale fruit, the sepals, the stems, the bud, the mole; hides his desire and waits.

Afterward, back to The Shed, coffee in the office. Simon stays awhile, then leaves. They sit on, in the upright chairs beside his desk. In the corridor the cleaning machines whirr; boys from late classes linger in the playground; the caretaker inspects doors and windows; the headmaster strolls and chats with a prefect on the other side of the wooden wall. As he passes the window he smiles in and nods, to see them earnestly in conference. What he cannot see is that below the level of the desk she is already shoeless, shucked of her skirt. The piles of books on the desk top conceal from his glance the sight of his Head of English reaching out his hands to roll her sweater up beneath her armpits, freeing her breasts which seem to swell eagerly forward at his touch, suffusing the delicate pink tips that he has not seen for so long. The headmaster and the prefect pass out of sight, still perilously in earshot. Then he places his hands under her thighs and lifts her toward him, astride his lap, and dipping between her legs he engages his finger with the elastic at the back, drawing it down and forward, questing for the furled and sheathed bud which he will coax into leaf, into flower, while only yards away the boys shout, the headmaster drones, the Hoovers hum. His lips are busy at her breast; he finds he can take the little gourd entire into his mouth.

'I'll tell her you liked her poems,' Jane says, 'when she comes.'

He drinks the rest of his coffee and leaves as soon as he decently can. 'I'll see myself out,' he says, as always, and this time they let him, two censorious Vestals in the ruins of an idyll. On the corner of the street stands a red van, and the postman is emptying the pillar box. McEvoy would like to run across the road and intercept, but instead he walks very slowly back to the car so that he has time to see his letter driven away. Then he wishes that he could write another one, at once, and put into words for her his brief arousing vision.

God rot his wretched memory; when he told her to write to him at the school he forgot that this week was half term. Should she answer his letter quickly hers will lie in the entrance hall of the empty building until Monday next, unless he can contrive an excuse for going there. That is not un-reasonable – he normally looks in once during half-term holidays – but only once. Which day should it be? If she receives the letter on Wednesday she may reply by return and then perhaps he will get it on Thursday – no, that would be too much to hope for; passionate, ardent she may be, but not impetuous, not where the written word is concerned. Friday, then – no. Friday is possible but what depths of disappoint-ment might it not hold? say Saturday. Saturday is feasible, but if he had a letter by Friday afternoon he would be the better able to get through Friday evening when he will know where she is, down to the very bed she will sleep in. He will not begin to hope until Friday and on Friday he will go to school, let himself in via The Shed and make his way through silent corridors to his pigeonhole in the staffroom, in case Mrs Mitchell has been there before him; and if balked there, to the doormat in the hall to root like a truffle hound through the humus of letters until he finds what he seeks. To confirm his intention, and to obviate the risk of premature investigation, he rings Simon Headley and arranges to meet him then, to discuss examinations.

'Friday, Simon?'

'Friday's fine.'

'Friday then.'

The receiver on the extension gently clicks.

The torments begin on Thursday. She may be away from home, she may be repelled by his own letter, she may be ill. He sits in the study at lunchtime and looks at the telephone. In the evening he is restive and distracted, and Sarah taut with fear again, continuously on the verge, so it seems to him, of making a declaration. Something is wrong; she took his defection too calmly; she has not asked enough questions, as if there were no longer any need for questions, as if she already knew the answers, answers that she cannot know. Ruth Prochak is a name on a book.

This was not what he promised himself, this is not the ease and consolation which he foresaw. *You will wreck me.* On Friday he goes to his pigeonhole in the staffroom, sick and unsteady, guts knotted, bile in the throat. It was not for this, oh, it was not for this. There is a letter in the pigeonhole, with her little words on it. He bears it away to The Shed where he finds he cannot open it. He gazes, as he would read the letter without opening the envelope, terrified to acquaint himself with the contents. How disgusted, how *deterred* she must have been by that sticky emission that has come back to haunt him, line by line, until he has the whole thing complete. Will she chastise him, administer a cool rebuke, return his own words torn to shreds? He seems to hear her speak, over his shoulder.

Open it, you silly bugger.

He does open it, very carefully, prising the flaps apart and then licking the gum where last her tongue rested. He unfolds the letter, a single sheet, and at first can focus only on the densely worded column, exquisitely written, never in hot haste, with justified margins on left and right. It's not a *poem* is it . . . ?

Dearest John, I don't know how this will turn out. I very rarely write letters – I didn't think of that when I promised to write. I live by the telephone. Don't be disappointed if you can't recognize me in this.

Recognize her? She isn't there. The sentences unfold, elegant and controlled, as measured as stanzas. Where is the juice? Where has she gone, his lovely fuck? Has the habit of precision become so ingrained that she cannot be fluent any longer on paper; has she drafted this, as she drafts everything else? Only toward the foot of the page, where a certain relaxation sets in, does it occur to him that it is informed by shyness, that the painful caution is a brake reluctantly applied, that the formality screens any feeling. Then the writing deteriorates dramatically as if she cannot bring herself to linger for shame over what she is telling him.

You will think I'm mad – no, no madder than you, perhaps – but when I got home on Sunday I did not drink all day because I could not bring myself to wash your last kiss away. I lay on my bed all day pretending that any moment you would walk in and lie down on me because, dear John, I could still feel you everywhere, round me and in me, and it was only in the evening when my mouth was so dry I couldn't swallow I knew you had gone. And I have had my period now, so you have gone from there too. I am alone again. I keep seeing you in the street and it isn't you. I start to wave, I start to run, and it isn't you. Dear John, come to me soon.

'Love letter?' Simon Headley asks, coming in quietly.

McEvoy jumps, horribly startled. 'Do us a favour. An absence note.'

'Dearest John? Whose mother are you screwing?'

McEvoy rises mightily and his hand balls into a fist. For Ruth he dealt the loathly Owen a blow below the belt (and for all poetry); for Ruth he will now crush Spiderman. Simon, extremely alarmed, backs up against the Warwick Shakespeares, spines incarnadine, and raises his arm to deflect the coming blow.

'John. *John*, lay off. It was a joke. *A joke!*'

'Will you share it in the staffroom on Monday?'

'What do you take me for? That's better.' McEvoy sits down again. 'I'm sorry. I didn't mean to offend you.'

'You do offend me.'

'Look, mate, no way are you going to convince me that

it's an absence note, not after that performance, but what the hell? Should I care?'

'Mind your own fucking business,' McEvoy mutters, head down, his elbow defending his letter; aghast at his self-exposure. Simon, his good friend Simon who has a perfect right to be in the English Department Office, who is there at his request, who has only said the kind of thing he normally says, with impunity, backs out.

'This will not *do*,' McEvoy says, laying his face against Ruth's letter. 'This will not *do*.'

Simon had a wife; where is she now? What became of Mrs Headley and little Georgina when Simon walked away? Atkinson left a wife and two children; Philippa Richards who teaches French was married a year and called it a day. John McEvoy is going home to his family tonight, tomorrow, and tomorrow, and tomorrow.

'I suppose you can't stay till Sunday?' Jane says. 'I'm in purdah till the exams are over. I could cook dinner and you and Mum could put your feet up.'

'I'd like to,' Ruth says, 'but better not. I've got to go to Worthing Sunday night. I'm visiting a school on Monday and then on to Brighton Poly on Tuesday morning; back in the evening. It means travelling from Victoria; it's not my favourite station.'

'What's wrong with Victoria?'

'There's nothing worth calling a station south of the Central Line, except Waterloo. Charing Cross is beyond redemption. Have you ever been to Fenchurch Street?'

'But you could still stay till Sunday morning, couldn't you?'

'I was away most of last weekend, too. I ought to see to a few things at home.'

'Of course, you were at Oxford, weren't you?' Geneva says. 'John told the girls he saw you there. How did it go?'

'Which one?'

'Which what?'

'Which John?'

'John McEvoy. He came round here once while I was out and you gave him coffee.'

'That's right, he was there. It's always heartening to see someone you know in the audience. Sometimes it's heartening to see *anyone* in the audience. I thought we might get the chance for a word but there was such a crush in the bar I ended up going to a pub. It went off quite well, except for the guy who was reading with me.'

'John said he was drunk,' Jane remarks. Are they testing her?

'He was as pissed as a bleeding newt. It was a disgusting exhibition – David Rhys Owen, of course. Tom and Alex were there to prop him up, but that's half the trouble. People have got so used to Tom and Alex propping him up that they've forgotten that even a poet should be able to stand on his own two feet. Those lads ought to ask a fee for wheeling him round. Alex sends his love.'

'Did he come to the pub with you?'

'Rhys? If he had've I'd have left. No, he stayed in the bar. A lot of people actually believe that poets should be like that; I dare say your John formed part of the fascinated throng.'

'He said he thought you were very good,' Jane says.

Mary looks malicious. 'He's in very bad odour, is John. He missed the last train home and his wife – '

'Mary!' Geneva looks really angry. 'Go and wash up. You too, Jane.' They barge out, sullen and loutish, knocking against furniture and overturning an occasional table. Ruth, who remembers two coruscating damsel flies, raises her eyebrows.

'Exams?'

'How they've got the brass neck, after what they said to John. We had the most appalling weekend. I dropped in on Sarah McEvoy with Mary, because John had said she was feeling depressed, last Saturday evening. She was very odd indeed, on the edge of hysterics most of the time. I had to send Mary home in a taxi and then bloody John rang up in the middle of the night to say he'd missed his train. I was so angry with him, poor devil, but really, that woman is in no fit state to be left. I've always known she was jealous but this was beyond all reason. To make matters worse she'd found a silly letter some woman had written him – '

'This was *last* weekend?'

Geneva looks mildly irritated by the interruption. 'Yes, I said, while he was in Oxford. Actually it was the same woman who sent him that book – I dare say you don't recall, anyway, he came round here on Tuesday to apologize to me but I wasn't here, and the girls took it into their heads to haul him over the coals for abandoning his wife. Can you imagine? Mary was quite vindictive by her own account and now they're laughing about it. I despair. They've known him since they were babies.'

'Didn't he say he was a teacher?' Ruth asks, short-winded but composed. 'I expect he's used to teenagers.'

'Well, I hope so, but he hasn't been back since – in fact, I haven't seen much of him at all, lately. I want to warn him about that letter, because I think Sarah will brood and not say anything to him, and it's all so harmless, when you get down to it; but I don't like to phone him in case Sarah answers. Aren't I a coward, Ruth? Coffee?'

'Won't the girls bring it?'

'I think not.' Geneva rises wearily, puts aside a muddle of knitting and goes out.

Ruth leans back against a cushion, sighing, and touches her breasts, each smaller than a man's hand, or her own, come to that, feeling the nipples hard and urgent. Even to think of him is not safe, to read his letter is disastrous, a dreadful pleasure to be saved for night and solitude. What a prim little snippet she sent him by return, although she sweated and trembled an hour over the one sheet. The next will be different; if only she could see him again before she writes, before he writes. Next time won't be in an orchard, she decides, nor in Oxford, it will be in her flat, on her home ground, where she can lead and he can follow.

Not the bedroom – enough of beds – in the living-room, her brown desert; kneeling in front of him, on the carpet tiles, and she will have to be wearing a skirt so that he can lift it and fold it back and take her knickers down again – oh, the feeling of defencelessness, of helpless exposure as he did that – slowly rolling them out of his way, and then he can slide into her from behind, as smoothly and simply as when he took her sleeping, for she will be ready, she will have left a message. He kneels and draws her on to his lap and as she settles on to him, round him, he lifts the skirt – no, dress; she must get a dress, loose and simple that he can slip over her head, and as her arms drop she will fall back against him as he imprisons her arms and clasps her breasts, so that her breath leaves her, she cannot move, she is suffocating, paralysed, impaled, and if he should come in now, because he should happen to be passing, if he should at this moment be stepping out of his car, crossing the pavement and ascending the steps to ring Geneva's doorbell, if he should, if he should

The following afternoon, after driving Ruth to the station, Geneva, searching for a truant ball of yarn that has rolled out of sight, fishes under the sofa and discovers a blue carrier bag, stuffed with papers.

'Whose is this?'

Mary looks up, sulkily. 'Ruth's I expect. Yes, she had it when she got here. She said it was her filing cabinet, or summing.' Mary yawns, crudely indicating her contempt for both the filing system and its owner.

'Oh damn, I hope it's nothing important. I'd better ring.'

'She won't be home yet, will she? She'll still be on the train. And then she'll get on another trayayain.'

'Stop whining. It's a pity you couldn't have been more pleasant to her while she was here. It was your idea to invite her.'

'Oh, I dunno. She's so *blank*.'

'Got any blue ink, Mum?' Jane looks round the door. 'Who's blank?'

'Ink's on the dresser.'

'Ruth. Don't you think she looked blank, this time? Not all there?'

'I thought she might help me with my biology, but all she seems to know about is cells. She looked half-canned to me. Is she on something, Mum?'

'No she is not. Go and get your ink.'

'You can't always tell at first. Maybe she's in love.'

'Who with? Hey, maybe it's one of us and she hasn't the nerve to say. You know, the love that dares not speak its name. I wonder what it's like?'

'What, with a woman? You don't even know what it's like with a man.'

'You can get things for it, can't you?'

'To cure it?'

'Nah, cretin; to do it with. Dildos.'

'Llandildo!'

They slam out of the room in the nearest approach to gaiety they have reached all week.

16

Her interest in clothes is not great. So long as she can have exactly what she wants (the leather coat, the denim jacket, the pretty nightdress) she does not want very much. She has not worn the nightdress since Oxford and from where she lies, in the narrow room at the back of the flat above the Euston line, she can see its snowy flounces thawing over the arm of the single chair. Now she sleeps naked, the sheet turned down to her waist, arms folded behind her head, waiting. On summer mornings, as on this, the sun strikes the wall opposite, waking her early, and then she lies, remembering. She can reduce herself to a gasping exhausted stupor, just by remembering: his hands, his mouth, his tongue: remembering with sharp revivified pains how she crept between those dank sheets an affectionate compassionate friend and stumbled out again, only hours later, in love with him. Now back and back she goes, trying to discover the exact astounding moment of her fall, and again, again he takes her. It is exhausting to drag herself from the bed and stand upright; her body, that always seemed to her so meagre, feels enlarged, breasts heavy and tender, belly rounded, the composed folds between her legs engorged, occupied, and the bud, as he called it, swollen to a bulb. She feels a pulse there now, always.

Searching the wardrobe for clean jeans she recalls that she is lunching with a colleague before she travels and goes instead to the drawer for stockings. Without covering herself she proceeds to the kitchen, absently fingering the mole grown surely as large as an oak gall on her buttock, puts the kettle on and retires to the bathroom to shower and dress. The black stockings are the kind that hold themselves up, without suspenders which she hates, and on her slender legs they express no unsightly dints and bulges. Smoothing them pleasurably over her thighs she sees in the dark mirror tiles, suddenly, startlingly, the image of one of Lautrec's foxy whores and feeling it suitable to her mood goes to make her coffee without putting on any more clothes.

There is no milk. Coming home late last night from Geneva's she saw her pint standing on the hall table, thoughtfully brought in from the heat of the doorstep by Mrs Oliver, or Nigel. Does she want to dress before she has her coffee? No. She puts the front door on the catch and, swaggering pardonably, descends the two flights, in her black stockings, to collect the milk. Sounds behind doors on the way down cause her nipples to prick with alarm, but she will not hurry, almost dawdles, coming up again, swinging the bottle, until the click of the lock on the attic door alerts her to danger; but she will not take the last half flight in an ignominious scramble and wills herself to continue slowly upward, gaining her own door not quite soon enough to escape the fleeting but gratified attention of John Gabriel Borkman leaving his lair, for early Mass, as it happens.

In the kitchen she presses the cap off the bottle, but cannot recall where she left the coffee. She dips a forefinger into the cream which, after standing a day and a night in the warm hall, clings thickly, a coating consistency; abstractedly she anoints each erect nipple and then, dipping again, paints the cupolas that support them; a soothing bleb on her poor hot small node.

Her mouth is so dry. In the almost empty refrigerator lies the half melon, too ripe and soft to slice. She claws out a whole handful of chilled pulp, crushing it into her mouth with the flat of her palm (I will fill your mouth with snow and kiss you till it melts) and dazed, dribbling, leans over the table, with impeccable, idiot precision, to dip each milky breast into the sugar bowl then, bearing her candied fruit gravely before her, one in either hand, she walks to the living-room, where she left the coffee.

It is cooler here; the windows were open all night. Ruth drops a round hard cushion on the carpet, beside the coffee mug, and sits down, knees drawn up, feeling the sugar crystals stiffen and prickle as the thin breeze dries her glazing. Deliberately she leans back on her elbows, the cushion beneath her hips, gazing through the fork of her curving black thighs, over the blonde crest that spans them, toward the blue morning sky in the window, and then melts to the floor, arms loosely extended above her head. As her knees fall akimbo she knows why the Little Mermaid wanted to be human, to exchange her scaly tail for legs; not for the legs at all, but for the fiery insatiable gullet between them. She stretches and trembles and grows rigid, alone; all alone.

When she wakes the sun is skimming the front of the house. The milkless coffee is cold. She lies inelegantly folded, face down, knees drawn up, arms trailing, and sitting stiffly, turns her eyes in shamed dismay from the crusted sugar, the slack and twisted stockings, crying silently in her bewilderment: Why am I doing this? What is being *done* to me? She crawls to her feet, blushing all over, and slouches to the bathroom with the flat-footed lassitude of a wide-hipped Aphrodite.

'Ebury Street; do you remember? We looked it up on the map.'

'But you said you wouldn't be going away again.'

'I'm *not* going away again. It's a meeting, this evening, it ends at nine. I shan't be home all that late.'

'You said that last time and look – '

'That was fucking Oxford, for Christ's sake.' Sarah reels and sits down. 'I'm sorry, but Sarah, please, I think that was the first time since we've been married that I've ever failed to come home. I'm damn sure it's the first time. You'd never have let me forget it if I'd done it before.'

'I get so worried – '

'In case I'm raped in the Underground? See, here's the programme. Ebury Teachers' Centre, seven thirty till nine, Tuesday, fifth of June. Can't you ask a friend round to keep you company if you think you'll be worried?'

'I haven't got any friends.'

He would think she were regressing, were there anywhere to regress. For eleven years she has excluded everyone but him: Look, John, all this is for you; what do you mean, you don't want it?

'Look, Sarah, I swear I will be home before ten thirty, even if it means leaving early. I will run. I will fly. I'll jump over ten buses laid end to end.'

She will not laugh. 'Suppose the trains are delayed?'

'I'll check before the meeting starts. I'll ring you. Goodbye, Sarah.'

On the bus he curses himself for a fool all over again. He had forgotten the Ebury meeting until he looked in his diary yesterday afternoon. If he quits school at four sharp he can be in London by five, which will leave at least two hours clear; Primrose Hill and back, and she might have been waiting for him. If only he had remembered sooner.

In front of him the hitherto respectable Rhodri Davies with two friends is merrily effing and blinding his way to school. They have not seen Mr McEvoy because they do not expect to see him. Mr McEvoy rarely takes the bus; they cannot know that he is going to the station after school and will not need his car tonight. With unholy glee he leans forward and taps Rhodri on the shoulder.

'Gerroff, shitface!' Rhodri bawls as he jerks round, expecting to confront a close friend, no doubt. His expression, when he sees whom he is addressing, renders further reproof unnecessary, except that McEvoy cannot allow the incident to pass. It is not a school bus; the passengers are fare-paying members of the public who have to listen to Rhodri and his chums every morning. The three little boys, one ash-white, the other two carmine, stare at him in pitiable terror. They cannot even stammer an apology; this is awful. This is worse than what they wrote on the wall of the bog about Mr Thomson, which was true. Mr McEvoy is nice. They called him shitface.

'Break,' McEvoy says, 'in The Shed.' That is all, it is enough.

The bus gets him to school only just in time for assembly, then he teaches for two periods. He cannot reach a telephone until break, and break is now occupied with Rhodri and the twain. Furious with himself for this oversight McEvoy delivers a savage sermon, at length, awesome in his rage; he is Authority, he is Nemesis, he is the Destroying Angel. The three Mohocks depart in tears and an innocent Fifth Former, Dermot Crane, who knows a poem when he sees one, slinks away deciding that discretion is the better part of valour. The bell rings and two more periods intervene between Mr McEvoy and his telephone call.

At lunchtime he caroms from the staffroom, where he notes his empty pigeonhole, to The Shed, where he asks for an outside line.

'It's before one o'clock,' Mrs Mitchell tells him, sternly.

'It's urgent. Please try.'

'It's Mr McEvoy, isn't it? Well, just for you . . . ' She connects him. The telephone rings on Primrose Hill but no one answers. He must try again at afternoon break, and at the end of school, and then if he cannot raise her he can chance a visit to the flat. She might be there. She might be travelling. Come to me soon, she wrote, and he wrote back, I will try – and forgot tonight's opportunity. His letter should have reached her by now, unless she has not been to the flat this morning, in which case it will be among the miscellaneous envelopes on the table by the front door, with Nigel's *billets-doux* and sundry milk bottles. It was a better one, his second letter; continent, loving and coaxing, with some pretensions to punctuation. It is over a week since he has seen her. Possibly he can leave early.

When it comes to four o'clock he is not able even to leave on time. Bob Lake, the Deputy Head, waylays him in the corridor.

'John, a word.'

They go through the staffroom into the Quiet Room. Philippa Richards, who is crouching over a pile of papers, looks at them nervously and scuttles out.

'What's the matter?'

'Perhaps you can tell me. Philippa came to me at lunchtime saying that three of her class – yes, *those* three – were in tears after break because of certain things you'd been saying to them.'

'Good.'

'What the hell did you say? They're Second Years. They're the hard men.'

'I can't remember what I said. I was very angry.'

'Because they'd been fooling about on the bus?'

'They were not fooling about.' Dear God, what futile interjection is this? He and Bob pass the time of day once a month, and this is not the day. They spoke yesterday. Oh, down, down, he mutters to his rising temper. 'They were using the most filthy language.'

'But everyone swears on the bus.'

'This was a service bus. I imagine, from their ease of

262

manner, that they behave like that every morning. It's a one-man-operated double-decker and crowded. The driver can't hear what's going on. I was on it by chance and caught the full flavour. I don't see why our villains should be allowed to inflict themselves on the rate-payers. This is a school estate agents recommend, God knows why. You're not suggesting I should have let them get on with it?'

'Filthy language? What do you call filthy?'

'Davies called *me* shitface,' McEvoy says. 'Do you mind if I go now, Bob? I've got a meeting in London.'

'Not on purpose, surely?'

'The meeting?'

'No no, Davies.'

'Christ, no. I'm not complaining of *lèse majesté*. I don't think he ought to call *anyone* shitface – do you?'

'Wouldn't it have been better to tell the form tutor?'

'Philippa?'

'It's properly her province.'

'Are you telling me I should have said nothing?'

'John, don't lose your temper. I can see you're in a hurry – '

'Then for God's sake let me go!'

'When's the meeting?'

'Seven thirty.'

'You won't be late. Seriously, John, this kind of thing can undermine the credibility – '

'Oh, I see.' McEvoy does see. 'It's Philippa you're concerned about. Afraid she's having her rightful status usurped?'

'If you'd just administered a rebuke on the spot and then informed her – '

'What the hell for?'

'It's hard enough for a young woman to assert herself in a mainly male institution.'

'For that particular kind of young woman, I dare say you're right. You haven't got the hots for her, have you?' he asks.

'John!' Now he has overstepped the mark, but his frustration and anxiety propel him headlong into foolhardiness.

'You don't give a fuck for those foul-mouthed little sods, do you? It's bloody Philippa – '

'I suggest', Lake says, icing over, 'that before you rebuke

263

the boys for their language you might choose your own with more care.'

He stalks out: stalks. Appointed in the days when Thomas Paine was a grammar school he still wears a gown, even a hood on high days; M. A. Lond. Only a man in a gown can risk a gait like that. McEvoy, badly in the wrong, and knowing it, listens to his footfalls in the corridor, watches his own knuckles whiten over the back of a chair.

What is a traitor? Why, one that swears and lies.

So he is late getting to London and although he catches a fast train into Euston the evening dwindles; but if he can find her he will miss the meeting. Is not that wha he intended all along? He rings from the concourse but no one answers. Oh Ruth, taking the long view again?

He descends to the Underground for the train to Victoria, only to discover that it is a fifteen-minute walk, up Buckingham Palace Road and over Ebury Bridge, to the Teachers' Centre. The meeting is wordy, acrimonious and political. He does not listen; it is astoundingly easy not to listen when there is nothing you want to hear. No wonder the boys are so good at it. He almost regrets the four decades of earnest attention which he has visited upon his preceptors and superiors; how much of it did he actually need? Does anyone listen to him?

So, she has bled him away and he is gone from her; suppose he had stayed? He sees her standing, as she stood in Cynthia Black's spare bedroom, stark as she was then, startled out of what he suspects to be an instinctive modesty (for when did she ever flaunt?) staring down perplexed but proud at the first signs of ripening below the ribs, a little tump patted smooth between the pelvic bones, that within weeks consolidates to an unconcealable paunch, not that she tries to conceal it. By five months, to his mind the most delightful stage, Sarah considered her body misshapen and covered herself, even in private, in spite of his longing to look and honour her. Ruth will gallantly display her brave contours, the pale globe beneath her breasts that are waxing gradually, wantonly fat, the madder-pink tips shading to umber. Sarah carried her babies trimly. For Ruth he conceives a prodigious gestation, together they will marvel as she sits with her lap full of her helplessly swelling self, navel forced outward into an endearing irrepressible knop, while he strokes the taut sensitive skin and eases her until at last she reclines heavy-eyed, mute, languid, imprisoned beneath the great defenceless dome of her belly and he, denied access from before or behind must devise new subtle ways of pleasing her. She will lie upon him as they lay on the bed at Oxford, their four arms clasping the shared burden that only she can carry.

But oh, then, the violence; the voiding, gushing, bleeding, rending. Could he do that to her, stuff her, shackle her, blunt and muffle her and then rip the very core out of her? Think not on that till tomorrow; let her for now be eternally *enceinte*. She would be beautiful; she would be so beautiful.

And so deep is his inattention he does not notice that the meeting has overrun by ten minutes. What price his promise to leave early if need be? He springs up, considerably disrupting those around him who have assumed that he was asleep, and hares for the exit, down clammy flights of concrete stairs and out into the drab light of a rainy evening. He runs mindlessly over Ebury Bridge, round into Buckingham Palace Road and past the coach station; a heart-wrenching skid on the oily tarmac of Elizabeth Bridge as a bus lunges at him. In a moment, he promises himself, he will stop running, he must have made up for lost time by now, but he keeps going, fuelled largely by the pleased discovery that he *can* run so far and so fast. With his briefcase he cleaves the crowds, jumps the lights at Eccleston Bridge and on down past Victoria Station. Behind him brakes squeal. Hoping he is not responsible he glances over his shoulder to see the traffic congealing, bounces off a huge youth with a backpack who falls against the wall, and reaches the steps of the Underground Station at exactly nine twenty, as calculated. He should make it on schedule, oh God forbid that he should not. Standing in the train he can think again, but suspends conjecture; reaches Euston in good time. In his spare five minutes he calls Primrose Hill, but the telephone rings unanswered.

There is no one he can ask. Kirk could tell him, but where can he look for Kirk? On Primrose Hill the telephone rings and rings, no letter comes, he begins to realize how casual they have been: he never thought to ask about her plans, she never thought to tell him. All the sensible, precautionary things that should have been said at Paddington, might have been asked in letters, occur to him now. He does not know where she is and he does not know how to find out. She could be anywhere.

No, that's not true; for three days of the week she will be teaching, he must ring her college. He finds a likely number and dials. 'May I speak to Dr Prochak?' He is afraid that they will ask, 'Dr Who?' but the switchboard operator simply says, 'I'll put you through.' This telephone makes an odd whirring sound, but to no avail. It rings unanswered.

Daunted rather than encouraged by the reality of Dr Prochak at the Poly, with her own office and telephone, he waits and tortures himself. There is so much of her about which he knows nothing. He may not be one of many lovers, but he is not the first. How many does she run at once? No, not Ruth. Anyway, he is overreacting; it's not quite a week since he heard from her. Where have you gone? Why don't you answer my letter?

'Have you lost something?' Sarah demands on Thursday evening.

'No.'

'Are you sure?'

'No!' He stifles the impulse to snap. 'I mean yes, I'm sure.'

'A letter?'

He is so mindful of letters that his sudden attentiveness must be obvious. 'No, I haven't lost a letter.'

'Not this letter?'

There are sheets of paper in her hand. 'I don't know.' (*Her* letter? Is that why – ?) 'Let me see.' He reads it. *Dear John, you won't remember me I'm sure, but perhaps you will remember the enclosed.*

How could he have forgotten this, forgotten where it was? Easily, oh easily; there has been so much else to conceal. This is what Ruth feared, the stains and traces.

'Who is she?'

'Sarah, this is very ancient history.'

'27 March 1984? Ancient history?'

'Someone I knew a long while ago, twenty years ago. A friend of ours wrote a book. She sent me a copy.'

'And what's this?'

It is the Bath poem, which he last recalls seeing at Geneva's. She must have given it back, how could he not have noticed. Easily . . .

'Something *I* wrote twenty years ago, look at the date. Sarah, what's the matter with you? Twenty years ago, I didn't know you then, you were a schoolgirl.'

'And this?' She slams a book down on the coffee table, a paperback with a green and purple cover. Against all expectations, his own and Sarah's, he begins to laugh.

Sarah clenches her hands and rises on her toes. 'You think it's funny?'

No, by God, it isn't funny. McEvoy slumps back in his chair. 'Where did you get this?'

'Menzies.'

'No – how? Why did you buy it?'

'It's the book in the letter, isn't it? The book that woman told you about.'

Something has been happening in his absence, in his absence of mind. 'Yes, it is. How did you find out?'

'I rang up and asked.'

'Rang who up?'

'Her, this woman, this Margaret Anderson.'

'*You rang her up?*'

'Her phone number's on the letter. I rang her this morning. She told me everything.'

'I doubt very much if there was anything she *could* tell you.'

'About you and her and all those other girls.'

'What other girls?'

'A different girl every week, she said – '

'I don't believe that.' He doesn't believe it. Margaret is too subtle to tell her own lies, she lets others do it for her. Sarah has been editing.

'I do.'

'Believe it, then.'

'You mean there were other girls?'

'Of course there were other girls, did you think I was a

virgin when we met? But it certainly wasn't one a week. Haven't you read the book?'

'Not yet.'

'I'm surprised you haven't finished it. You seem to think it's the fifth Gospel.'

'I can't make out what it's about. Why did you keep it a secret – two months – that letter, hiding it, locking the cabinet, staying out late, sneaking off for the weekend, hiding behind Geneva, lying to me, lying to me, lying to me – '

'I kept it a secret because I couldn't face what you'd make of it. I can't face it now. I can't take any more tonight.'

'What do you mean, you can't take any more? You haven't taken anything yet. We're going to have this out.'

'We're not going to have anything out. There's nothing to have out.'

'Where are you going?'

He does not answer, striding for the stairs. Sarah follows him into the hall, watches him climb, but when he opens the door of the study he feels her behind him, at the very moment he sees the filing cabinet with its middle drawer pulled out.

'See,' Sarah says, 'I know everything.'

'You know fuck all!' he shouts, and slams the door in her face, shooting home the bolt. It was put on to keep wandering Julian out while he was working, but it is a long while since he has used it. Sarah smashes her hand against the door, once, and no doubt would again, but she has woken Chris. He cries out.

McEvoy, petrified, stands in the middle of his study, mouth open, hands raised, but Sarah has performed one of her lightning transformations into a caring parent. The boys' door opens; he hears her reassure Chris with soothing falsehoods and allows himself to relax, to sink down at the desk.

What rich ingredients for farce: Sarah rabidly sleuthing after a cold scent, digging up long-dead relics, soliciting hostile witnesses to substantiate the charge of which he has already been found guilty; himself madly burying evidence which inexorably resurfaces; the letter, the poem, the book; how many more times is that vile cover going to rise to confront him? Such manœuvrings and sidesteppings, while the real drama is played out *in camera*.

What on earth did they say to each other? His powers of surmise are unequal to this grotesquerie; he cannot imagine the conversation, nor does he wish to, it no longer exists having been recorded, as it were, on a blank tape. Ruth could write a poem about that.

Outside on the landing silence obtains. For all he knows Sarah may be leaning against the door with her ear to the empty keyhole, but does that really matter? reality she does not need. He lifts the telephone receiver and dials. Be there, darling; be there, be there.

He listens to the insistent hooting until he realizes that he is hearing the engaged tone and hangs up, hot with relief. At last, she is there. After five minutes he tries again, and this time the telephone rings. No one answers it. She must have gone out, but the barometer clock tells him that it is ten forty. Not gone out now, surely? in bed. But only just – why doesn't she answer, she must know who it is? Numbed, defeated, he replaces the receiver, picks it up and tries again; again engaged. What is she thinking of? Slowly it dawns on him that someone else is trying to do exactly what he is trying to do, at ten to eleven at night, someone else as urgent and alarmed.

After the third attempt he hears a strangled wailing from beyond the door. On the landing Sarah sits, leaning against the banisters, rocking backward and forward over folded arms, hair sleeked black against her red swollen face, spittle and tears mingling round her mouth. Beyond speech she looks up at him, gaping, and his stomach contracts in a spasm of nauseous pity. Kneeling beside her on the landing carpet he lets her fall against his shoulder, lets her wilt there in the shelter of an unfeeling arm. Later they creep to bed where he consoles her with what he can only regard as an act of necrophilia, balked of his hope that she will spurn his advances with a proud cry of disgust, turn disdainfully from him, deny him both her bed and her body. She will never learn pride now, she would rather share him than lose him, a leech clinging to his heart. Later still, when she is asleep, snoring tearfully, he goes to the lavatory and is terribly sick.

And still he has not seen Geneva. Over and over again he regrets that he did not drop in last Saturday night, curses his caution; if he had done he would not be so suffering now. Then it strikes him that Geneva herself may well know where Ruth has gone. He cannot ask her straight but he has learnt a thing or two about directing conversations. He hopes the girls will be out.

In order to arrive before they do he takes advantage of his last free period on Friday and leaves school early. Geneva's street is quiet, the gardens gently cheerful with flowering trees and shrubs; it is a gracious zone. You may still see yellow privet in Avenue Road, and rising suns on the gates. He rings the bell and composes himself. Footsteps come down, Geneva opens the door.

'John, how lovely to see you. Come in.'

'Am I forgiven?'

'For what?'

'For Oxford.' He follows her upstairs, into the living-room.

'You haven't been hiding away because of that? Jane told me what she said to you, it was unpardonable. I suppose she thinks she's reached the age of indiscretion. You ought not to have frightened poor Sarah like that, even if she does ask for it. I was very cross at the time, but really, John, have you ever known me to sulk?'

'I was going to ring you, and then I thought you might ring me – I don't know, we don't seem to have met much, recently. Anyway, it's been a bad week; how was yours?'

'I was going to ring you,' Geneva says slowly, 'but it went out of my head. It *has* been a bad week. Oh John'; she turns to him, hands clasped, and with prescience he sees her as she will be, a little old lady with thick ankles. Perhaps, conversely, this is why he always thinks of Ruth as very young; because he cannot imagine what she will look like when she grows old.

'Oh John,' says Geneva, 'something rather dreadful's happened.' Her mouth twitches and she tries to control it, like a nervous child who cannot help smiling at moments of sad occasion. 'You remember Ruth Prochak – of course you do, you saw her in Oxford. She's dead. I only heard, yesterday. She was here last weekend. It's been such a shock.'

He is looking at a blue cushion on the sofa, no, not a

cushion, a carrier bag. On top if it lies a ball of white wool with two steel needles thrust through it and on one needle a frill of knitting. Geneva is saying, 'It happened on Tuesday, but they took so long to identify her. She never carried a handbag, you see, and she doesn't seem to have had any credit cards or a cheque book on her and I suppose she had her briefcase, she never went anywhere without that, but no one could find it. I'm afraid it may have been stolen. It's unbelievable, isn't it? People steal things from the scene of accidents. Do you remember all the rescue equipment that went missing after the Moorgate Tube disaster?'

McEvoy says, 'She didn't fall under a train, did she?' Oh no, Ruth, no, not under the banner of Huskisson.

Geneva looks at him angrily, glazed with tears. 'Is that meant to be a joke? She was killed in the street. She ran in front of a taxi.'

'On purpose?' He can barely open his mouth – is this how tetanus feels? 'But she would have gone to Surbiton.' Fortunately Geneva does not hear this last part, she is already off again. 'I don't know whether it was suicide or not; there'll be an inquest – they may have had it. I can't imagine her committing suicide, she was so – well, Mary called it blank. Calm? Collected? She seemed to me happy and successful; she had no reason to kill herself, or do I mean happy? I'm not sure that I ever thought of her as *happy* . . .'

He has his back to the light. When Geneva moves and sees his expression concealment will be at an end. He can feel the blood leaving his face, the flesh blanching, the skin deadening; he can feel his pallor, it anaesthetizes. His hands are quite without sensation already, he too is dying, by inches.

'But how can one tell – we none of us know each other. I didn't know Ruth at all well really, but it's the outrage one feels. No one was expecting it. If she'd been ill or depressed . . . but just to die like that. No one was ready for it.'

'People should die suddenly only in novels, is that it? Otherwise we are entitled to plenty of warning?'

He was once told that after a serious accident the victims are often able to run away on broken legs because the muscles can hold a fractured limb together for as much as twelve seconds; or was it twenty-two? It is only his muscles that are holding him upright. He has a very erect posture, like Harold Clandon, head up, eyes down; he might at least unbend a little and put a consoling arm round the bereaved Geneva in her distress; she will be wondering why he doesn't.

'All she had was an address book, in her pocket. I suppose the police went through it looking for someone who was able to give them some idea of who she was – I mean,' Geneva looks shamed by the thought, 'she was awfully easy to describe.'

'I should think they took photographs,' McEvoy enunciates, with difficulty. 'If there was anything left to photograph.'

'She was killed outright. The first one who could help was Tom Bellfounder. Poor Tom, he had to go to Town to make a formal identification. He said she'd been dreadfully injured but – as I said – you couldn't mistake Ruth.'

The name beats like a clapper in McEvoy's skull. He says, 'Do you know Tom Bellfounder?'

'Do *you*?' Geneva looks surprised. 'Oh, of course, he was at Oxford. I hardly know him at all, but we both know Alex Kirk and naturally Tom told Alex and Alex rang me. He's terribly upset, he's known her much longer than I have. That's where I first met her, at Alex's place.'

McEvoy thinks: Why don't I faint? I should not have to endure this. He says, 'You all seem to know each other.'

'Writers account for a fairly small percentage of the population; we do tend to move in overlapping circles. Alex was with Ruth at that Oxford reading. He said she had some man with her – no, that sounds dreadful. Alex said that she turned up with this man who was obviously her lover, he was quite crazy about her, he said, you could see. He's afraid he won't know. They were introduced, but Alex can't remember his name. They'll put an announcement in the papers, there might even be an obituary, but what a way for him to find out. I don't suppose you noticed who she was with?'

There was a legend at school that you could make yourself faint by putting blotting paper in your shoes, to draw the blood from the head, presumably. This is just how it feels – blotting paper in the shoes, vertigo, Durham Cathedral, Excelsior! He crashes on to the sofa.

Geneva has just finished saying, 'And if they'd quarrelled, and she *has* committed suicide, what will he be feeling?' Her face is beginning to register what has happened; she thought he was going to sit down. The walls, the windows, the curtains are streaming away from him, pinheaded Geneva elongates like an El Greco as he goes on falling, but gradually the fugitive shapes and merging shadows separate and redefine themselves as consciousness invades, for all he wishes to exclude it. You cannot make yourself faint with blotting paper, nor by wishing. When he looks up Geneva is stooping over him and there is no evading the pity in her eyes.

'It was you, wasn't it?'

'Oh John, oh John,' Geneva mourns, chafing his cold hands, 'why did you let me go on like that? Why didn't you stop me? How could I know?'

'I think', he says, 'much coincidence must go unremarked because things are left unsaid.'

She cannot make head nor tail of this. 'Don't try to talk; you've had a frightful shock. I'll get you a drink.'

She fetches brandy from a tray in the corner, one for each of them. She too has had a frightful shock.

'I don't want a drink.'

'I don't know what to say; I've said too much. Why didn't you stop me – why didn't you *tell* me? Did you think I'd condemn you, don't you know me better than that?'

He is shaking so violently that she dare not give him the glass. His clenched teeth rattle as he says, 'The film has been exposed.'

'John, you're rambling. Oh God, what am I to do with you? Does Sarah know you're here?'

'No one knows I'm here. No one knows anything, except Kirk. Kirk exposed the film. We didn't exist without Kirk.'

'Of course you did. I'm sure that whatever you had was wonderful; oh John, I don't know how you are going to get through the next few days, but at least you know you were happy together. Alex said that. He said you held her as though she were the egg that contained your life.'

'Yes, Kirk confirms it. Kirk shapes it. We needed a poet to seal it off.'

'Please stop talking for a minute and have your drink. You don't know what you're saying.'

He takes the glass and drinks the brandy in one go. 'I know what I'm saying. The incident is finished, it's sealed. It is not to be prised open. It goes no further.'

'But it would have done. How could you hope to keep it a secret? We have so many mutual friends, it seems. People would have begun to talk . . . wonder . . . '

'Not now, it goes no further. It's not a matter for fiction.'

Geneva would dearly like to cry: Do you think I am not as upset as you are? but that would be patently untrue. Geneva is upset; John looks destroyed. He shudders and stammers so that she can scarcely make out the words, portentous and meaningless. The poor fool, why didn't he speak sooner. Why can't he weep? 'Why couldn't you tell me?' she pleads. 'You could have told me. You could have told *me*.'

'No,' he says, 'you would have made something of it it never was. I forbid you to speculate.'

'You think I would have used you? Used your love – ?'

'You wouldn't have been able to help it,' he says, lucidly. 'It's the way you think. Kirk will tell you how we looked, but you will never know what we were and I forbid you to wonder what we would have become.'

'Oh, very good, John, very elegant.' Geneva regrets the brandy, if this is to be the result. 'Do you want to lie down?' He does not hear.

'I promised to send her some flowers. She wanted flowers. You can see to that, she wanted lots of flowers. Do you know, Ginny, I never gave her anything, not once. I never gave her *anything*.'

Feeling seems to be returning. She strokes his hair. 'You gave her yourself. Alex said – '

'Hooray for Alex. I can't send her flowers. I can't even mourn her, I have no right. I can't go home and lock my door and cry for her because I have no right. I have no right even to send her flowers. I always wanted to give her presents and I never knew what to choose, but she would have liked flowers, wouldn't she? I could have given her flowers. I can't even do that, now.'

'Of course you can; all the flowers you want.'

'No donations, she said, but lots of flowers. She didn't think much of people who wanted donations in lieu.'

Geneva's progressive unease manifests itself.

'Do you mean you discussed this?'

'On a train. We talked a lot on trains. She said she would go to Surbiton for a train. She said Westbourne Park would be no good.'

'No good for what?'

'For dying at.'

'Westbourne Park? It happened at Victoria.'

'You said it was a taxi.'

'In the *street*. There are some friends in Chester Square, she might have been going there. She was crossing the road, well, no one knows if she was *just* crossing the road. It was wet. One of the witnesses said, apparently, that she was halfway across to a traffic island when she suddenly threw up her hand and ran back. He said she looked as if she was hailing a taxi. Someone else – you don't want to hear this – '

'I do.' Yes, he does. The witless look has gone, he has begun to think again. 'Tell me.'

'Someone else said she dived in front of the cab, but she may have slipped, the roads were greasy. It was sudden, the light was bad, you know how hard it is to remember even things you've watched on purpose, and these people were upset. It will be settled at the inquest.'

'Will it? How nice. When I know she committed suicide I can rest easy?'

The import of this exchange strikes Geneva cruelly as she foresees the effect on him of a suicide verdict. 'It wasn't suicide, I'm sure it wasn't. I thought it was unlikely anyway, didn't I, I said so. Now it seems impossible. Perhaps she saw someone she knew.'

He seems to be breathing with difficulty; should she call a doctor? *Shock is a condition of prostration of the body arising from the sudden exhaustion of vital activities*; she learned that once at a first aid class. But where has she been for forty-nine years that this should be the first time that she has ever seen someone in shock? For all her conjectures and surmises, she does not know what sudden death can do to the living. Eddy took two years.

He is whispering, 'When did it happen?'

'Tuesday, I told you.'

'No, *when*? What time?'

'I don't know. In the evening, it was getting late.'

'You don't know exactly?'

'No, I don't. Does it matter so much?'

'It does to me, I have to think about it.' This is just what she is afraid of. 'I'm going now, Geneva.'

She jumps up before he can move. 'Don't be ridiculous, you can't go anywhere like this. You certainly can't drive.'

He levers himself from the sofa and towers over her, swaying. 'I'm going.'

How can she stop him, short of a right hook? He has always listened to her before, which compliance she has attributed more to her air of command than to his amenability. 'John! Sit down at once. You are not to try to drive.'

'I'm not drunk,' he says.

This is worse than drunk. 'I'll ring Sarah.'

'Oh no you won't,' he says, 'not this time. That's what you're good at, isn't it? I'll tell my own lies. *Suggestio falsi* is easy. We did it the hard way.'

And my God you are paying for it, Geneva thinks. I don't know what you are talking about but this is Hell nor are you out of it. 'Please don't go, John.'

From the sofa he picks up the blue carrier bag.

'John – no. *Please*. It's Ruth's. We've no right to go through her things.'

'I've no rights at all,' he says.

'There'll be next of kin.'

'Now her sister-in-law may feed in quiet,' he remarks, pleasantly. His mind has gone. She cannot let him go home like this.

'Look, I'll come with you, I'll drive you. Put that bag down.'

'There's a good boy.'

'You mustn't take it. I don't know what's inside.' She blocks his path, a tiny risible figure. She can see herself.

'Why should you keep it and not me?'

Below the front door opens and subdued voices ascend. Mary and Jane have come home. They are not only sorry about Ruth's death but remorseful, because they were not very nice to her when she came last week, and they made fun of her looks behind her back. When they enter the living-room and see John they stop, alarmed. No wonder, Geneva thinks, looking at him anew, at his grey collapsed face, cyanosed mouth, sunken eyes: This is how he will look when he is old; and instantly amends the thought. This is how he will look when he is dead. John says nothing. He brushes past the girls and walks out of the room, along the hall and down the stairs, still clasping the carrier bag.

'That's Ruth's,' Mary calls after him. 'That's Ruth's bag. You can't – '

'Shut up!' Geneva screams, as the front door slams.

'Mum, what's the matter?' Jane clings to her mother. 'Did you tell him about Ruth? Why's he got her bag? He didn't know her, hardly.'

'Actually,' Geneva says, 'he did. He knew her very well.' The tears of two days' restraint break out at last. She puts her free arm round Mary's shoulder and the three Stevens women draw together, grieving Graces. 'Yes,' she says, 'cry for her. Let's cry for her. He can't.'

Mary's head jerks up. Very sharp, Mary has become. 'Do you mean', she snaps, 'that he's been playing about with Ruth while his wife's going round the twist?'

'Mary, no,' Geneva protests, but that is about the size of it.

He stops the car in one of the many straight, tree-lined streets that lie on his route home, and leans forward over the steering wheel, his hands at ten to two but crossed at the wrists for comfort and piety. In the dark of his mind he sees her lying on wet tarmac, on her back as on the Oxford bed, arms loosely flexed above her head, fingers curling, light hair darkening at the ends. Blood? No blood yet, eyes still open, wide, wider as the world contracts, swelling in final enormity to catch the dwindling light, seeing nothing now but street signs and pale faces, myopic bubbles that ring her dying.

Dying in public who so loved decent privacy, who kept her secrets. Oh Ruth, better to have died in the dark, I would have held your hand, I would have cradled your poor head,

I would have pulled you back, halted your trajectory. The stove-in chest whines, blood surges from the slackening mouth, the eyes fix.

He cannot retain this picture, it fades, although he knows it will be back, that it is the image that will haunt him by night, in vacant moments, the test card on his eyelids. Now she faces him across a table, as in cafés, restaurants, trains; leaning forward, eyes and mouth combining in her smile of intelligent sympathy.

Never on purpose, Ruth, you would have gone to Surbiton for the Portsmouth train. Never by accident, you are too careful, you do not make mistakes. Why did you write yourself into my story – solely to write yourself out again? to leave me with a wound? How can you be dead, there is no purpose in it; nothing is improved by your dying, nothing is served. I don't have enough of you to sustain me, we had such little time. All I've been thinking about is what we *shall* do, now all I have is what we *did* do and we did so little. Already it may be inaccurate, my diary, my memory, the great liar. Are you beginning to change already? Can I be sure that this is how you looked now that I can never look again? Where are you, Ruth? What will they do with you, bury your poor cold bones in the ground, burn you? He cannot entertain either thought, especially the second. We are all mortal, being subject to change. We shall all be changed, in a moment, in the twinkling of an eye, changed, yes; but not *gone*. Where have you gone? Where are you waiting for your final change? How like a filing cabinet a mortuary is, all those long sliding drawers. He has seen them on television, in comedy sketches, corpses in filing cabinets. Does black comedy amuse because these days we are so insulated from the realities it mocks? Corpse abuse is funny because we know that in this England our relics are safe, hurriedly disposed of and not hung in chains, swung from public gibbets, dragged behind chariots. You'll be left in peace in your chilly filing cabinet, darling, until they cut you up to see what killed you, although they still won't know why you died.

A furtive, discreet tapping on the glass by his head. Looking up and sideways, over his sleeve, he sees the earnest spectacles of Rhodri Davies peering in, oh God help us, what horrible arm of coincidence.

No, not even that, the boy must live round here, has recognized the car. His expression compounds childish curiosity and the incipient social conscience of a future Good Samaritan. McEvoy winds down the window and the hovering face lapses into relief.

'I thought you'd had a stroke, Sir. You read about people having strokes in cars – and heart attacks.' Given any encouragement the child would ask him to explain the difference between a stroke and a heart attack. ('And, Sir, what is a myocardial infarction? I read this article . . . ')

'No, I haven't had a stroke,' McEvoy says. Not a stroke, Rhodri, a blow. 'It was very kind of you to stop.' (Especially after what I called you on Tuesday.)

'You don't look very well, Sir.'

'I've had a shock.' He cannot stop himself elaborating. He must tell *someone*. 'I've just heard that a friend of mine has died.'

Rhodri's self-esteem is restored; he is Sir's confidant; he must be extra understanding. 'Is that why you blew up on Tuesday, Sir? You were worried? Were they dying then?'

Untimely to explain that he blew up mainly because he objected to being called shitface. 'Yes, Rhodri, in a way they were dying. They'd been dying for a long while.' We are all dying, I am, you are, some of us do it faster than others. We call it change. 'May I ask you a favour?'

'Of course, Sir.' Now he can hardly keep from grinning, the unsinkable brat.

'Would you mind not mentioning this to anyone – anyone at all. People would be kind and sympathetic and tiptoe round me. I couldn't bear that.'

'I understand, Sir.' He doesn't, of course. He is still young enough to air his grief in front of his kind lady form teacher; he wants it acknowledged. God knows if he will be able to contain this information.

'Goodnight, Rhodri. I'll see you on Monday.'

'Goodnight, Sir.'

There again, I might not see you on Monday. In the midst of life I might be struck down tomorrow, I might finish my changing tonight. I might go down to Surbiton for the

Portsmouth train. Oh Christ, how can I live with this?

On the passenger seat lies the blue carrier bag, the last of her, is there anything in it for him? She must have left it at Geneva's by accident; or was it by design, not her design but some kind of authorial predestination left especially for him to assuage his carefully plotted grief? He up-ends it on his lap; grey envelope files slide out, a spirally bound notebook, loose sheets of lined paper, a couple of paperbacks. Rhodri diminishes in the near-side mirror and turns the corner, pausing only once to look back. He need not drive on, he can stay here under the lime trees, and search these slim effects as thoroughly as Sarah combs his filing cabinet. My darling, let there be something here for me. I shall never see you again, never hold you never have you again, there will be no more letters. I shall never hear your voice, ever again. Please, my love, may you have left something for me.

One of the paperbacks is a Penguin book of verse; the other, larger, heavier, has a green and purple jacket. For the second time in twenty-four hours he finds himself looking at *Acid Test*, by Caroline Hill, the holy fool, author of everything, and the completeness of Margaret's revenge comes home to him. Setting out only to remind him of a woman he slighted, she has ended by killing the woman he loves. The broken body that lies tonight in a West London morgue would be an unknown poet, were it not for Margaret's intervention, a careless poet who lost her footing in heavy traffic. Had it not been for *Acid Test* she would have remained the pathetic spinster he first thought her, who looked like a chicken; he could have comforted Geneva, as she expected, for the loss of her friend. Although it is not his to destroy he rips *Acid Test* in two, along the spine, feeling the futility of his rage. He burns it, he breaks it and still it comes again.

Next looks into the book of verse to see if there is an inscription from the author, until he notices that the author is François Villon. The file house work sheets, the biochemistry connection; essays that have been annotated in her handwriting, how strange it looks in red; course notes, examination papers of previous years. He opens finally the spiral-bound notebook.

Does someone as young as Ruth have a literary executor?

He cannot imagine that she ever made a will (even were there a Testament) but it is to a literary executor that this must go. It is a record of her work, her drafting pad; page after page of the small confident writing; scored, scratched out, underlined, overwritten; this is where poems grow. One or two of them he recognizes from *Midland City*; others are incomplete, no more than a couple of reworked stanzas, two or three lines, notions.

> One of these days I shall make my statement plain,
> If I can refrain from modifying,
>
> The lock on the door of the salt store's broken,
> SALT STORE it says in neat white words on the sign.
> The padlock dangles
>
> All things counted, derivative, square, straight,
> Slow, slow, slow, slow, andante, dim.

One line:

> This Beast was a real beast, and so he stayed.

Was that the first thought; she began with the end and worked toward it?

But now he is moving into his own period. From the back of the book slides a folded yellow sheet, with typeface on one side and writing on the other; it is the programme of the Oxford reading. She scribbled upon it at intervals throughout the evening, while battling with Rhys Owen. I would have killed him for you Ruth, had you not pitied him. That is a kind of murder. Is self-pity suicide? He opens the paper out fully and reads the lines, not in her working hand but scrawled heatedly, in haste. This could be your last poem. Oh Ruth.

> This poet's a tit-and-bum man,
> He hymns of crotch and fly.
> His fingers stipple
> A well-turned nipple,
> And probe the nether eye.

This poet's a bed-and-bawd man,
He's at it all the time.
But the randy old codger
Can only roger
In consonantal rhyme.

This poet's a cock-and-ball man,
As he's told us, all and some.
This verbal stunt-man,
This prick-and-cunt man,
Can come in rhyme
(Does it all the time)
Though he can't find a rhyme for come.

This poet's a ram, he's a rutter,
He's a stallion, a goat, he's a *man*.
At the metrical fuck
He's a bull, he's a buck,
But he's too busy screwing to scan.

Oh Ruth, how could you? Have you no shame?

All the shame that's going round here, by the looks of it. You do realize, don't you, she goes on, that if it weren't for you I'd still be alive. You can't blame Margaret for that.

No, he cannot blame Margaret for that; as well blame Simon and his chest infection for directing him to Doncaster Station. And where can he lay the blame for his headlong flight down Buckingham Palace Road, through the traffic at Eccleston Bridge? He can see it so clearly: coming one way, himself, running, dodging, jumping the lights; in the middle of the road, Ruth, also jumping the lights, turning, seeing him, raising her hand and running back. Behind him brakes scream. He glances over his shoulder, hoping he is not responsible. Ruth, Ruth, am I responsible or am I not?

Who can I ask? Who can I tell? I am not responsible, and yet you are dead because of me. I thought that coincidence was comfort and joy compared to the alternative, but it will be everlasting torment. I wanted your last thought to be of me, and it was.

Or did you not see me? Perhaps you were there before me, or after. Did you turn to hail a taxi; and slip?

Or did you decide that I was too much for you and dive? No, you would have gone to Surbiton for the Portsmouth train.

But it wasn't that, Ruth, was it? You saw me because you were looking for me. Can I live with that or shall I deny the coincidence, the convergence; The Spinner of the Years said 'Now!'

Yes, he says, I will live with it; I have a lifetime left in which to speculate, conjecture and surmise. Coincidence is my known constant. Geneva would never touch it, but this is where it begins, my story of infinite regress.

He turns the key and the car starts, moving away from the curb, over the stripes of shadow that lie across the sunlit road like sleepers. He is crying now, the street diffuses and sparkles; ahead of him the rails are shining; Oxford, Didcot, Reading, Maidenhead, Slough Iver Langley Westbourne Park Paddington, Paddington, Paddington. The timetable encapsulates the experience.

Ann Beattie
Where You'll Find Me £3.99

The supreme chronicler of the Me Generation, Ann Beattie's unerring eye for aimless, ex-urban, middle-class drones and silences matches her sympathetic ear for the dramas and disasters that stem from life's absurdities.

By turns satirical and poignant, the stories in *Where You'll Find Me* chronicle an estate agent's fascination with a beautiful bowl in *Janus*, an elderly woman's vision of the stairway to paradise in *Heaven on a Summer's Night*, a couple coming to terms with the loss of a daughter in *In the White Night*, and a dozen more tales of our time.

Here are private sorrows that haunt benumbed social selves and polite silences that speak of the voids of loss and age, grief and frustration.

'*Where You'll Find Me* surprises us again and again . . . lyrical and compact, heartbreaking and wise, this is the music of our spheres, etched on microchips' JAY McINERNEY

Christine Bell
Saint £3.50

'We have suspended time to prevent the Señora from dying. Each day is an eternity. Each second of that eternity is as dense as the heat. I married into this family fifteen years ago, when my husband was a foreign exchange student in New York. I have been here ever since.'

On an isolated hacienda near Santa del Rio in the South American interior, a Yankee called Rubia ('Blondie') and her dying mother-in-law join forces in a comedy about love, power and faith.

'*Saint* is both beautifully written and very, very funny. I haven't read any other version of this book anywhere; it's a true original' ANNE TYLER

Joan Didion
Democracy £2.95

Inex Christian is without doubt Didion's most memorable creation – the wife of Harry Victor, who wants to be president of the United States, and the lover of Jack Lovett, a shadowy fixer on the grandest of international scales . . . Didion moves confidently from the daydreams of Inez's childhood on Hawaii to the nightmare of her daughter's evacuation from Vietnam, and from thence back and forth among the smoke-filled rooms of Washington and New York . . . *Democracy* is funny, and moving, and effective' GUARDIAN

'By far the wittiest of Didion . . . she has a perfect ear for her character's edgy, brittle repartee and a gift for bringing her scenes to a crisp curtain line' NEWSWEEK

Maggie Hemingway
The Bridge £2.95

'Very assured . . . *The Bridge* is set in Victoria's first Jubilee year, 1887. At its centre is Philip Wilson Steer, the painter, a young man just beginning to make his way. He's a regular summer visitor to Walberswick on the Suffolk coast. This particular summer he comes across a young mother on holiday with her three daughters. Without an explicit word spoken or gesture made, Philip and Isobel know that they feel an immense attraction for each other – and know that nothing can be done.

'With exactness and delicacy, Ms Hemingway follows this "quiet, sad sliding of all aspiration, all longing and no hope down some dark chasm," furnishing the slender plot with surrounding detail which is authentic and minute' OBSERVER

Ira Wood
The Kitchen Man £2.95

Gabriel Rose, a young Jewish playwright frustrated in love and hustling for his big break in the theatre, grasps a golden opportunity the night famous director Cynthia Kagan dines at the select Boston restaurant where he makes ends meet as a waiter. Gabe ends up spilling the port all over Cynthia's silk dress. But she does leave her phone number. Cynthia, thirteen years his senior, is a strong, capable and very loving woman, and Gabe soon finds himself drawn into an unusual and lively relationship . . .

'Gabriel Rose, the "kitchen man" of Ira Wood's engaging first novel, is that all too rare creature in American fiction – neither a ladies' man nor a man's man; Gabe is a *mensch* who not only loves women, but can also like them as friends and equals' NEW YORK TIMES

Joseph Olshan
A Warmer Season £3.99

By the award-winning author of *Clara's Heart*.

Seventeen-year-old Daniel Fell was raised in Italy, and has difficulty readjusting to suburban American life and facing adolescence in a town divided between its Jewish and Italian community. On top of this his parents are going through a divorce.

Joseph Olshan astutely captures the plight of the innocent casualties of marital breakdown. He portrays the teenage years when life decisions were taken while driving round in a buddy's Triumph; when the more you found out about the frailty of love and life, the more you just wanted to remain on the brink of maturity.

The coming of a warmer season could crack the ice beneath you.

'Coming of age in the suburbs is a subject many writers have a hard time doing straight . . . Joseph Olshan brilliantly captures that curious mixture of material comfort and spiritual melancholy that is peculiar to middle-class America. The low-grade tensions between ethnic groups; the shared assumption that these are places where families stop off on their way to something better; the erosion of traditional values in favour of self-fulfilment; the sexual preoccupations of late adolescence – he covers them all. But, as in his previous novel *Clara's Heart*, he is best of all at finding great souls where no one else would think to look for them' THE OBSERVER

Lisa St Aubin de Terán
The Bay of Silence £2.95

Rosalind and William have all the appearance of success: a couple of beautiful people in their thirties, she an actress and he a graphic designer, revisiting Sestri Levante on the Italian Riviera where they once spent their honeymoon. But they have been driven there by paranoia – by a slow dread of what will happen to the two of them if anyone finds out about their baby Amadeo, whose identity, and even whose existence, is at the heart of the schizophrenia from which Rosalind has long suffered . . .

'It draws, inevitably, parallels with *Tender is the Night* and, beside it, stands up as equal. It is a quiet yet astonishingly powerful and absorbing novel at the forefront of contemporary British fiction' BRITISH BOOK NEWS

'Compulsively readable and written with grace and a new authority which adds to the appeal of this most interesting author' COSMOPOLITAN

Geoffrey Wolff
Providence £2.95

Providence, Rhode Island, is a mean city with a festering colonial past, a corrupt no-hope present, and the biggest organized crime racket on the Eastern seaboard . . .

From the moment that Lieutenant Corcoran of the city's Police Department fishes the slashed, bullet-ridden body of a minor hitman from the river, events conspire to change the lives of five of Providence's citizens forever.

Skippy, a would-be mobster, his good-time girlfriend Lisa, Adam Dwyer, an honourable lawyer who has six months to live, his beautiful wife Clara, coping with her own private terrors, and the Lieutenant, who is about to sacrifice everything for the coked-out Lisa, discover that Providence is just murder.

'The atmosphere is entertainingly breezy and sleazy, with a wise-cracking, side-of-the-mouth narrator and some of the tightest meanest dialogue this side of Elmore Leonard' TIME

'Stylishly and scatologically written, with pace and wit' LITERARY REVIEW

'Absolutely dazzling' NEW YORK TIMES

All these books are available at your local bookshop or newsagent, or can be ordered direct from the publisher. Indicate the number of copies required and fill in the form below.

Send to: **CS Department, Pan Books Ltd., P.O. Box 40, Basingstoke, Hants.   RG21 2YT.**

or phone: 0256 469551 (Ansaphone), quoting title, author and Credit Card number.

Please enclose a remittance* to the value of the cover price plus: 60p for the first book plus 30p per copy for each additional book ordered to a maximum charge of £2.40 to cover postage and packing.

*Payment may be made in sterling by UK personal cheque, postal order, sterling draft or international money order, made payable to Pan Books Ltd.

Alternatively by Barclaycard/Access:

Card No.

Signature:

Applicable only in the UK and Republic of Ireland.

While every effort is made to keep prices low, it is sometimes necessary to increase prices at short notice. Pan Books reserve the right to show on covers and charge new retail prices which may differ from those advertised in the text or elsewhere.

NAME AND ADDRESS IN BLOCK LETTERS PLEASE:

....

Name————————————————————————

Address————————————————————————

————————————————————————

————————————————————————

————————————————————————

3/87